The LOST FRAGRANCE of INFINITY

The LOST FRAGRANCE of INFINITY

MOIN MIR

IndiaInk
ROLI
BOOKS

IndiaInk

All characters and events in this book are fictitious and any resemblance to real characters, living or dead is purely coincidental.

First published in 2021

IndiaInk
An imprint of
Roli Books Pvt. Ltd
M-75, Greater Kailash II Market
New Delhi 110 048
Phone: ++91 (011) 4068 2000
E-mail: info@rolibooks.com; Website: www.rolibooks.com
Also at
Bengaluru, Chennai, & Mumbai

Cover Design: Akankshya Padhi
Layout design: Bhagirath Kumar
Production: Lavinia Rao

ISBN: 978-81-86939-88-8

Typeset in Minion Pro by Roli Books Pvt. Ltd.
and printed at Sai Printo Pack Pvt Ltd, New Delhi.

FOR LEONIE

CONTENTS

ACKNOWLEDGEMENTS

I am grateful to Frederick Starr for having written *Lost Enlightenment*. The lectures of physicist Peter J. Lu on geometric Islamic tilework and the article by Sebastian R. Prange that termed the interlocking geometric girih tiles as 'tiles of infinity' were immensely enlightening. Dr Saiyid Athar Abbas Rizvi's two volumes titled *A History of Sufism in India* were profoundly educational. Ernst Bloch's *Avicenna and the Aristotelian Left* compelled me to think deeper about the philosophy of Ibn Sina and its relevance today. Mir Khwaja Kutbuddin's *The Path of Peace* that brilliantly captured the very essence of Ibn Arabi's philosophy was greatly insightful. William Dalrymple's fabulous documentary on Sufi music, *The Mystic Music of Islam* was inspiring.

I am thankful to the khadims at the shrines of Hazrat Salim Chishti, Hazrat Qutub Sahib and Hazrat Nizamuddin Auliya. Ever cheerful and merry in their ways, their warm hospitality was greatly touching as it spanned across sugary chai to simple caps and even biryani. In Bursa-Turkey, at the Green Mosque where in the morning silence as the sun's rays streamed in and I admired the tilework, I had a chance encounter with a Sufi who sat head lowered, turning his prayer beads. He didn't say a word. Just smiled. I am grateful for that smile that came my way. At the shrine of Hazrat Jalaluddin Rumi in Konya, Turkey, I am grateful to the caretakers of his tomb. For my stay in Istanbul, I thank Asli Tunca and Bolka Basaran for their hospitality.

I got to observe the art of paper marbling in great detail at the Galata Mevlevi Museum, Istanbul and had the most uplifting evening in the sama khana witnessing the whirling dervishes. I thank them for their open hearts that radiated with nothing but pure love and compassion. In Andalusia, Spain, I thank Kamran and Negar Diba for their hospitality during my visits to Gaucin, Zahara de la Sierra, Cordoba and Granada. As I spent time admiring the geometric patterns on the wooden roofs of the Alhambra and on the tilework, the cool breeze blowing down the lofty Sierra Nevada mountains reminded me of the fragility of empires and the immortality of the creative spirit. In Greece, I thank Zou Zou Delerue who provided me a wonderful environment for writing. As it was impossible to travel to Herat, I am immensely grateful to SOAS, London for organizing 'The Night of Herat: Celebrating the Pearl of Khorasan' a series of lectures on Kamaleddin Behzad, the fifteenth-century miniature painter and the history of the city.

My heartfelt thanks to Roli Books, my publishers, and in particular to Priya Kapoor for her seemingly never-ending faith in me. I thank Carenza Parker, my editor. Above all I thank my wife Leonie for her love. Simply put, without her, this book would not have been possible.

DRAMATIS PERSONAE AND HISTORICAL REFERENCES

MAIN HISTORICAL CHARACTERS

Muhammad Shah Rangeela: Mughal Emperor of Hindustan (r.1719–1748). A connoisseur and patron of the arts, he ruled a weakening empire, but one which had the wealthiest treasury in the world.

Nadir Shah: King of Persia (r.1736–1747). A ruthless military genius who waged war with the Mughals and the Ottomans. He had a chilling reputation for enjoying cruelty.

Sauda: (1713–1781). One of the most dazzling Urdu poets in eighteenth-century Hindustan.

Dard: (1721–1785). Considered a poet given to Sufi mysticism, Dard, which means pain, wrote verses steeped in spirituality.

Mir Taqi Mir: (1722–1810). Arguably the greatest Urdu poet ever.

Grand Vazier Nizam Asaf Jah: (1671–1748). The 'Prime Minister' to Emperor Muhammad Shah Rangeela.

Saadat Khan: (1680–1739). The Subedar of Awadh who fought on the side of the Mughals and against Nadir Shah at the battle of Karnal.

Khan Dowran: (d.1739). Mughal statesman and General who fought against Nadir Shah at the battle of Karnal.

Sayyid Niaz Khan: (d.1739). Mughal aristocrat who led the resistance in Delhi against Nadir Shah's Afsharid soldiers.

Khan of Bokhara: A ruler in Central Asia who was eventually subjugated by Nadir Shah.

Khan of Khiva: Like the Khan of Bokhara, this Khan – after brief resistance – was defeated by Nadir Shah at the end of 1740.
Mahmud I: Sultan of the Ottoman Empire (r.1730–1754). He felt deep sorrow for the Ottoman losses of Vienna, Buda and Belgrade.
Ferdinand VI: King of Spain (r.1746–1759). Also known as 'The Learned' and 'The Just'.

MAIN FICTIONAL CHARACTERS

Qaraar Ali: The craftsman from Delhi with a cherished lineage of being among the chosen artisans at the Mughal Court for generations. Inclined towards Sufism, Qaraar Ali is not a practising Sufi.
Faiz Ali: Qaraar's father.
Zainab Begum: Mother to Qaraar.
Abeerah Khan: A Mughal beauty and Qaraar's lover.
Shahbaz Khan: Abeerah's father and a general in the Mughal army.
Askari Begum: Shahbaz Khan's sister and Abeerah's aunt.
Natiya: Abeerah's personal maid.
Janbaz Bakht: A leading figure in the Mughal army and the one who wants to possess Abeerah.
Hari Das: Qaraar's dearest friend.
Shah Rezaan: The Sufi from Isfahan.
Aalf Olsson: The slave trader of Viking descent.
Hova: An Armenian woman who becomes one of Qaraar's closest friends.
Izzet: The acrobat.
Hikmet: Izzet's brother, who is also an acrobat.
Gul Khatun: The fiery Ottoman princess.
Saad: The drummer.
Juan: The simple village farmer of Andalusia, Spain.
Catalina: The village beauty and Juan's daughter.
Almudena: Juan's wife and Catalina's mother.

MAIN HISTORICAL EVENTS

1492: Fall of Granada, the last stronghold of the Moors in Andalusia, Southern Spain, to Isabella and Ferdinand of Castile and Aragon.

1492: Christopher Columbus's expedition headed towards India and China ends up with the discovery of the New World.

1609–1614: Expulsion of the Moors from Spain.

1659: Assassination of Dara Shikoh, the Sufi Crown Prince of Hindustan.

1666: Death of Shah Abbas II, Safavid King of Persia.

1683: Ottoman defeat at the walls of Vienna.

1728: Last recorded persecution of a Moor in Spain.

1739: Battle of Karnal, 110 miles from Delhi; the Mughals against the invading Nadir Shah.

1739: Local resistance in Delhi against Nadir's Afsharid soldiers.

1739: Massacre of Delhi's inhabitants by Nadir's Afsharid soldiers.

1740: Nadir Shah's attack on the Khans of Central Asia.

1746: Treaty of Kerden, signed between the Ottomans and Nadir Shah.

1746: King Ferdinand VI of Spain ascends the Spanish throne.

FICTIONAL BUILDINGS

Hunar-Abaad: Qaraar's ancestral house in Ballimaran, Shahjahanabad, Delhi.

Basalat-Gah: Abeerah's ancestral house next to the Red Fort, Shahjahanabad, Delhi.

Husn-e-Jahaan: 'The beauty of the world' – the Pavilion in the mango orchard.

Gazebo: The wooden refuge near Zahara de la Sierra, Andalusia, Spain.

INTRODUCTION

In the latter half of the seventeenth century, a lost battle and two deaths would be the three events that signalled the beginning of the end of three great empires that spanned from Budapest in Europe to Bengal in India. Over time, not only would their territories shrink, but the radiance of their cultural realms would diminish in lustre. The Ottoman defeat at the gates of Vienna in 1683, the death of Shah Abbas II, the Safavid king of Persia, in 1666 and the assassination of Dara Shikoh, the crown prince of Mughal India, in 1659 would sow the seeds for declining Sufi influence in the intellectual theatres of these empires. Sufism represented the inward, esoteric and mystical side of Islam.[1] The philosophy of self-examination, compassion and immersion in 'Divine Love' made the Sufi, curious, scientifically innovative and spiritually magnetic. The khanqaahs of the Sufis were bastions of knowledge where the study of philosophy, mathematics, mysticism, art, craft and science flourished. In these khanqaahs young Sufis were guided by their murshids about their role in this world, worship of the Divine and the concept of Khidmat-e-Khalq – The selfless service to mankind.

For years, I strived to find a way of demonstrating the importance of Sufism and its voice that stands lost today. An entirely academic body of work would not reach out to the vast audiences that have an interest in Sufism. How does one communicate the spiritual love that Zulekha had for Yusuf that was so brilliantly captured by the fifteenth-century artist Kamaleddin Behzad in his miniature painting? Or the philosophy of Ibn Sina and Rumi's compassion for mankind? Or for that matter, how does one write about Omar Khayyam's mind in which mathematics and mysticism mingled seamlessly? Questions like these kept me awake at night. In order to show the effulgence of the Sufi mind, I came to the conclusion that the most effective way of doing this would be the building of a fictional character and telling his story against the backdrop of thoroughly researched philosophy and historical events. Occupying centre stage of my work would have to be a character that would be relatable. As a result, the character Qaraar Ali was born. Against the dust clouds of declining empires and a violent carnage led by Nadir Shah, Qaraar Ali, who is not a practising Sufi but a craftsman with an inclination towards Sufism would be forced to undertake a journey. Qaraar would become a travelling prism through which a fading cultural realm could be witnessed. His own story of passionate love, violent losses, wandering, creative pursuits and spiritual quest would be synonymous with the turbulent times in which he lived. Through the progression and evolution of Qaraar's human story and through his extractions and interpretations of Sufi philosophies, I have strived to show the reader the magnificence of Sufism. From the bustling bazaars of Delhi into the deathly solitude of a lost desert city in Central Asia, through Ottoman lands and across the blue Mediterranean, Qaraar's would be a life glazed in the rich colours of Sufism. But before the reader engages with the story of Qaraar Ali, I believe it is vital to gain a historical understanding of the three events that occurred in the second half of the seventeenth century which led to the alienation of the Sufi.

OTTOMANS ARE DEFEATED AT THE GATES OF VIENNA – A PRICE FOR OVERAMBITION

On 12 September 1683, the defeated army of the Ottoman sultan, Mehmed IV, began its slow retreat from the outskirts of Vienna. Kara Mustafa, the grand vazier of the Ottoman Empire, on his mount cast a despondent look at the remains of his tent. The sumptuous designs of cypress trees on Turkish carpets that had once kissed his feet in obeisance were in shreds. Torn maps of Vienna that he had pored over, strategizing the city's siege, now flew aimlessly in the wind as if the tent itself, dismayed at the turn of events, had dismissed them from its ravaged environs. Kara Mustafa's tent was now in the hands of the princes of Baden-Baden, Habsburg and Bavarian troops and the Polish king who had united to shatter his plans of taking Vienna for Sultan Mehmed IV.[2]

For hours, Kara Mustafa dejectedly relived the moments with the sultan and the sultan's initial reluctance to acquiesce to the Vienna campaign. The majestic Topkapi Palace in Istanbul is where it had all brewed, particularly within the confines of the Baghdad Pavilion. The Europeans were not united, and the fall of Vienna would annihilate the Habsburg Empire. It would open the floodgates for the Ottoman armies all the way to Andalusia, Spain – the lost jewel. For Kara Mustafa, Andalusia, which the Muslim Moors had lost when Granada had fallen in 1492 to the Spanish armies driven by the fervour of the Reconquista, was now within the grasp of his sultan. But only if he first took Vienna. The scent from the olive groves and orange orchards in Andalusia still blew across the Aegean Sea and into Turkey; almost beckoning the sultan. It was a passionate argument that Kara Mustafa made. At times, bored and unconvinced, the sultan would dismiss Kara Mustafa. Then opening a window of the Baghdad Pavilion, the sultan would peer into the vistas. The glorious Bosporus with its deep blue waters seemed an extension of the tiled mosaic surroundings of the Pavilion. Seagulls glided over its waters and then flew over the Baghdad Pavilion as the sultan's eyes followed their skyward ascent.

Finding himself alone, Sultan Mehmed IV inhaled deeply and took in the spectacular sights of his Istanbul. He admired his city and its cosmopolitan fabric. The multicultural Galata area caught his eye. Its narrow lanes were home to the Jewish quarter housing merchants and traders. A large number of Jews had chosen to migrate to Ottoman lands fearing persecution in Europe. Advised by the Sufis, the sultans had welcomed them and under the Ottomans the Jews thrived economically.

Not far from the Jewish quarter were the seventy churches of Istanbul, some restored recently on the insistence of the Sufis they represented Ottoman tolerance. Lying next to the sultan was a spyglass. Focusing south he saw the mosaic of girih tiles glistening in the sun on the Mosque of Bursa.[3] Varying shapes of stars, hexagons and polygons were repeated to form a seemingly never-ending pattern of infinity symbolizing the Sufi's constant mystical quest.

Through the spyglass, the soft light blue hues of a mosque's dome dedicated to Hazrat Jalauddin Rumi caressed the sultan's eyes. He reflected on how he had sought out their counsel regarding the Vienna campaign. Knowing well that Mevlavi Sufis did not visit court, the sultan had gone to see them in their music rooms.

Here a sultan was not the ruler. He left his titles at the door. That evening, Mehmed sat on the floor with his legs folded under him. As the lights were dimmed and only a few candles flickered, five dervishes entered the sama khana. A sweet sound of a flute then slowly filled the faintly lit music room. Besides the flute and the waves of the Bosporus as they rushed to embrace Istanbul's shores, nothing else was heard. After a few moments an elderly Sufi recited Rumi's verse:

Hearken to this reed forlorn
Breathing ever since was torn
From its rushy bed a strain
Of impassioned love and pain
...The reed flute is fire.[4]

Rumi's restless and passionate desire for union with the parted lover, like a rising wave, engulfed everyone. Gently drawn into a trance by the sound of the flute, the dervishes began a slow whirl. As rhythm, whirl and melody merged seamlessly, the dervishes languidly lowered their arms from their chests. One arm lifted and its open palm faced skywards. The other arm was lowered and its palm faced towards the earth. The head tilted slightly. In their white flowing robes, the whirling dervishes resembled doves taking flight. But there was more to admiring beauty that evening. The sultan wanted to know about his prospects if he undertook the Vienna campaign. And so he put the question to the Sufi masters. The sultan was asked to continue watching the whirling. 'Life was all about balance,' a Sufi explained. The open palm of the whirling dervish that faced heavenwards received and the open palm facing downwards gave. The Ottoman Empire was well balanced. The Sufis advised against empire expansion. They warned the sultan not to succumb to greed. Instead, they advised him to invest in scientific innovation and wider ocean exploration.

After listening to them the sultan left their sama khana and proceeded to the khanqaahs of two other Sufi orders. They were the Bektashi order and the Seh Bedreddin order. The Bektashi order with its eclectic nature made it exceptionally liberal. This order looked acceptably on all religions, attaching importance to the esoteric and not the strict rules and rituals. It did not compel the observance of Islamic rites such as ritual prayer and fasting, allowing women to go unveiled in public and to mix socially with men.[5] Their influence had spread all across Bulgaria and the Balkans. When they heard about the Vienna campaign, like Rumi's Mevlavi order, they advised the sultan against it. The last and final stop of that spiritual evening was at the khanqaah of the Seh Bedreddin order. Seh Bedreddin's disciple, the fifteenth-century Börklüce Mustafa had ignored differences between Muslims and Christians and had encouraged his disciples to treat Christians as 'though they were angels'.[6] Here too, at the Seh Bedreddin khanqaah, the sultan was advised against wild ambition.

Having reflected on that mystical evening, the sultan saw the dogged Kara Mustafa return yet again with an even more determined plan to conquer Vienna. It worked. The sultan succumbed to over ambition and gave his approval for the conquest. But disaster awaited. After months of desperate fighting at the walls of Vienna, Kara Mustafa tasted bitter defeat. The balance that the Sufis had spoken about to the sultan had been lost and the defeat at the walls of Vienna triggered the long and steady decline of the Ottoman Empire and Sufi influence.

PERSIA'S LAST INTELLECTUAL GASP

In October 1666, seventeen years before the defeat of the Ottomans at the walls of Vienna, Shah Abbas II of Persia died. Shah Abbas II had come to see himself as the custodian of the Great Persian Cultural Realm which had a magnetic quality unlike any other. The Seljuks, a Turkic tribe; the Mongols; and even the Arabs at some time in history entered Persia as conquerors. But Persia with its language, music, poetry, philosophy, art and architecture would galvanize itself into Venus and transform the sword-in-hand invader into its wine-cup-bearing lover. While they would conquer Persian land, Persia conquered their hearts. The 'foreigners' would eventually adopt the Persian way of life, speak the language, understand the land's ancient history and become custodians of it rather than try and expunge it. The Great Persian Cultural Realm would sparkle in Central Asia under a branch of the Seljuks. Cities like Merv, Samarkand and Bokhara would become epicentres of learning. Merv in particular would glitter with libraries, observatories and universities, attracting thousands of students from all over the world. The Persianised Turks, became for many years the most enlightened champions of the Great Persian Cultural Realm. In

India, the Persian Cultural Realm would sparkle through the twelfth-century Delhi Sultanate right until the end of the Mughals in the mid-nineteenth century. In Anatolia it would flourish under the Seljuks of Rum. Such was the influence of the Persian language that Rumi, the thirteenth-century mystic born in Vaksh-Balkh (near the modern Afghan-Tajik borderlands, earlier also known as Khorasan), would eventually make Konya in Anatolia his home under the Seljuks but would write only in Persian. Poetry would be Persia's most glittering gift to world literature.

The first visible colours of a Persian autumn in 1666 emerged in the garden of the Chehel Souten Palace, Isfahan. Shah Abbas II was just thirty-five. He lay down on the porch slowly, resting his head on a cushion which had the Persian mythical bird, a simurgh, embroidered on it. Surrounded by forty pillars and overlooking a cobalt pool the shah witnessed how the autumn breeze's gentle nudge broke a yellow leaf from its branch and sent it into a descent to its end. He saw himself in that leaf. Shah Abbas II was ailing. Rumours had it that he had developed an incurable lump in his throat. But he craved a last dash of colour in his fast-fading life and a festival of literature and philosophy is what he had organized. For centuries the illuminated Persian Sufi mind had broken the barriers of conventional thought and had became an explorer of philosophy and science.

To the Persian intellectuals, it did not matter if the works of non-Muslims became catalysts to new discoveries. In fact, they embraced them. Inspired by Indian and Greek forays into mathematics and literature, they became innovators. Here the Persian champions were the ninth-century Al-Khwarizmi who forged pathways with logarithms and algebra and the twelfth-century Omar Khayyam. Khwarizmi's respect for the Indian mathematician Brahmagupta (598–688) was immense and he acknowledged his debt unequivocally.[7] Omar Khayyam scaled new heights writing mystical poems in his *Rubaiyyat*, simultaneously writing his landmark work *Treatise on Demonstration of*

Problems of Algebra, which was the greatest work in that field before modern times, creating new theories for modern cubic equations, computing the solar year to the eleventh decimal point: 365.24219858156 and while in Merv he set down an algebraic method of using known weight of silver and gold to determine their ratio in alloys.[8] Besides his *Rubaiyyat,* Khayyam's strong Sufi leanings were evident when consumed by mathematics he forayed deeper within himself asking questions of 'how and where did the orderly phenomena of mathematics and geometry come from and how it corresponded with the natural world. As a result, he went onto further acknowledge the role of prophesy in one's search for certainty and the possibility of direct knowledge of God's world that Sufis seek to attain. In an astonishing summary that would shock his peers in mathematics, he urged his readers to 'tell the reasoners that for lovers of God, intuition is the guide, not discursive thought'. He made it clear that he accepted revelation and sympathized with the basic quest of the Sufi'.[9] It was this mind that Khayyam possessed that attracted other Sufis like Ayn-al Qudat-al Hamdani to study mathematics and spirituality at Merv.[10]

To exhibit the achievements of the Persian Sufi mind, Shah Abbas II had chosen his court poet, Saib Tabrizi to be the master of ceremonies at the festival. The first of the week-long evenings began. Saib Tabrizi stood in front of his audience that consisted of Russian dignitaries, European diplomats and Persian aristocracy holding aloft *Diwan-e-Hafez.* From the book Saib Tabrizi read one of Hafez's most intense verse:

> Of this fierce glow which Love and you within my breast inspire
> The Sun is but a spark that flew and set the heavens afire![11]

The audience sighed. The power of Hafez's words seemed to set the evening ablaze. For Hafez, love's flames could inspire man to great heights; such that even the sun could be a mere spark. As Saib Tabrezi read, rubaab and santoor players gently struck their chords to the composition 'Flight of the Lark' which illustrated the flight of the Sufi mind. The musical notes were soothing, like a flowing freshwater mountain spring which mingled with Hafez's verses filled the hearts of the listeners with a serenity never experienced before. Then Saib Tabrizi held aloft two other books. *The Book of the Map of the World*, a *magnum opus* compilation by Al-Khwarizmi, it had accurately mapped out 2,402 localities and places. The second book was the works on astronomy of Omar Khayyam and his solar calendar, also known as the *Jalali* calendar.[12] After a few moments, on Saib Tabrizi's signal, two silk screens dropped down on either side of the palace, each approximately 30 metres (100 feet) long. The screens were covered with graphic illustrations of the mathematical achievements of Al-Khwarizmi and Omar Khayyam, particularly those made for algebra and cubic equations. As a hundred candles flickered under the screens, the audience roared in appreciation.

Distributing minitaures of the *Shahnameh* in which Ferdowsi the tenth-century scholar had praised pre-Islamic Persian Kings, Saib Tabrizi recited a message for mankind. A message of unity and for nurturing the heart by Sanai, another Persian Sufi of the past.

> Once one is one, no more, no less: error begins with duality; unity knows no error. The road yourself must journey on lies in polishing the mirror of your heart... The body is dark – the heart is shining bright; the body mere compost – the heart a blooming garden.[13]

Amidst huge applause, the first of the festival evenings ended on this note.

The following five evenings were each a spectacle in their own right. On the last day the shah decided to give his guests a short tour of Isfahan. Foreign dignitaries gasped at the honeycomb muqarnas at the Shah Abbas Mosque. At the Darb-e-Imam Shrine, where Sufi artists lay buried, the shah and the delegates inspected the façade in detail. Girih in Persian meant 'knot' and girih tile patterns with repeating geometric shapes demonstrated symphonic beauty in complexity as each tile shimmered in the mellow orange light of a Persian sunset.

At Chehel Souten, Saib Tabrizi was dressed in a black robe as if in mourning for the future. Both he and the shah knew that Sufism was under threat from the orthodox clergy. Saib Tabrizi looked at a flag that fluttered in the distance. It had 'Iqra' written on it. The first revelation of the Quran, it meant 'Read'. The Sufis had taken a deeper dive into its interpretation believing it meant 'read' not just the Quran, but seek knowledge. Saib Tabrizi clutched two books close to his heart. They were masterpieces by Ibn Sina who had lived and taught in Isfahan in the tenth century.[14] Holding aloft with both hands Ibn Sina's groundbreaking *Kitab-al-Shifa* (*The Book of Healing*), Saib Tabrizi lowered his head and explained.

Ibn Sina developed new theories on existence. He unflinchingly believed in One God and was driven to understand Islam as a philosophy. His stupendous philosophical achievement was the painstakingly articulated distinction between essence and existence.[15] Essence could be present but not necessarily bring about existence. He created the concept of 'the necessary existent' that did not need a cause. This necessary existent had to exist.[16] In his analysis of the body and soul, he innovated a new theory: according to Ibn Sina, the soul in all animals was full of desire and closely bound to the body. In the human soul though, there was the extra powerful dimension of understanding and knowledge. The knowledgeable and understanding part of the human soul was the intellect and it was indestructible even after death.[17]

This living dimension did not feel anything. It was pure existence. Ibn Sina's elevation of the soul to an intellectual existence was superbly innovative. The theory took away the main weapon the clergy had to create fear in the minds of followers of faith.[18] They could not threaten with the fear of tormented souls as a price for their sins. Ibn Sina had lifted the bar of philosophy so high that small-minded clerics could not understand his thinking. He faced immense ridicule and was targeted by the orthodoxy for heresy and his drinking habits.[19] In order to demonstrate how completely adequate rationale thought is, Ibn Sina invented a character who lived in complete isolation but nevertheless came to full intellectual cognition through an 'awakened mind'.[20] Such was the glow in the ink that dropped from Ibn Sina's pen in Persia that in faraway Andalusia, Ibn Tufayl, a century after Ibn Sina, would write *Hayy ibn Yaqzan* (*Alive, Son of Awake*), one of the first philosophical novels.[21] It was inspired by the concept of Ibn Sina's 'The Awake' as a general intellect that fills and connects all people. Centuries later Ibn Tufayl's novel served as a model for Robinson Crusoe and all Robinson-esque tales.[22] Ibn Tufayl praised Ibn Sina alongside the Sufis as a master of mystic ecstasy and cited Ibn Sina:[23] Some had doubted if Ibn Sina had been a Sufi, but when he came out with words like these explaining enlightenment and mystic experiences in quest of the Divine, all doubts were laid to rest.

> Then, when his training and will power reach a certain point, glimmerings of the light of Truth will flicker before him, thrilling him like lightening... If he is diligent in his ascetic practise, these spells grow frequent... Thus he begins to see the Truth in everything... He has gained an understanding as unshakable as that of an old friendship,... his inmost being becomes a polished mirror facing towards the Truth... at this point communion is achieved.[24]

Such was the flight of Ibn Sina's genius that he could navigate it in any direction, nest on the branches of an undiscovered science and after being nourished by its fruit could fly back and give the world the base for modern medicine, *The Canon of Medicine*. This book served in the East and West alike for many centuries as the standard work of medical practice.[25] When

Saib Tabrizi held it aloft and began an explanation, a sigh which seemed like a deafening roar left the breasts of each one seated in the audience. Then the bass-laden slow beats of a daf drum resounded signalling the end of the festival. A few days after the festival Shah Abbas II died in bed. Saib Tabrizi too died a few years later. From the chaos that followed, one man rose to seize power in Persia – Nadir Shah, a man who would plunge it into savage warfare with its neighbours – the Ottomans and the Mughals. Nadir Shah was not given to Sufism but instead his obsession with Sunni jurisprudence would widen the Sunni-Shia schism in an already deeply Shia Persia.[26] Driven by this obsession Persia would become a myopic place with study being focused on micro-religious jurisprudence rather than innovation, science, art and philosophy.

ASSASSINATION OF INDIA'S SUFI CROWN PRINCE

Dara Shikoh was the crown prince of Mughal India. He had been chosen by his father, Emperor Shah Jahan, to lead India into the future. Shah Jahan's reign had been long and generally peaceful. India was fabulously rich and stable. It was multicultural, vibrant and an economic giant. The Mughal Empire stretched from Kabul in the west bordering Safavid Persia to Bengal in the east. And from Kashmir in the north to the Deccan. The wealth of this empire was astounding – an envy of the West. The Taj Mahal was the epitome of architectural splendour. The Peacock Throne, the pinnacle of opulence. The red sandstone city of Fatehpur Sikri that was built for the love of the Sufi mystic Hazrat Salim Chishti enveloped his pearl white marble mausoleum and was the empire's symbol of spirituality. The imperial Red Fort in Delhi personified sheer might. Right opposite the Red Fort, the Jama Masjid was the largest mosque in India. The courts in Kabul, Delhi, Agra and Lahore attracted Persian poets such as Saib Tabrizi, and the imperial patronage of arts ensured that a gifted musician such as Tansen could rise with his skills to unprecedented heights.

But on 30 August 1659, seven years before the death of Shah Abbas II of Persia, Dara Shikoh the crown prince of the Mughal Empire lay on the damp floor of a dark dungeon. Dara rose, held the iron bars of a small window and looked outside. It was a thunderous monsoon night. A few drops splashed on his face. The wind whistled, sharp. There was a sense of impending danger. From the crevice in the door he saw an approaching candlelight. The light was soon eclipsed by shadows. The door flung open. Men hustled in – the henchmen sent by his brother Aurangzeb.

Dara's life flashed before him. The vast and diverse landscape of India was the ideal pasture grounds for this deep-thinking crown prince. Dara thought of the days he sat legs folded under him listening attentively to Mian Mir, his Sufi master in his khanqaah retreat at Lahore. Surrounded by wild deer that bounded around the khanqaah the Sufi spoke to the prince. The master's words moulded the prince's character. He thought of how Mian Mir's teachings of universal love for all faiths had made him interested in the great religion of Hinduism. Dara developed a thirst to know more about the Upanishads. On the banks of the shimmering waters of the Ganges in 1640, Dara assembled the greatest Hindu intellectuals and sanyasi ascetics to translate the Upanishads into Persian.[27] He did not want the Upanishads concealed from the Muslims of India, which was another reason for him undertaking the translation.[28] He titled the translation of Upanishads, Sirri-e-Akbar (The Greatest Secret). Furthermore, he boldly went on to state that the work referred to in the Quran as the Kitab al-Maknun (The Hidden Book) is none other than the Upanishads itself.[29] Not satisfied, Dara would go on to translate *The Yoga Vashisht* and the Bhagwad Gita into Persian.[30]

Dara read and re-read the works of Sufis like Miyan Mir and Hazrat Bari both urging him to look after the cultivators whose taxes had swelled the Mughal treasury.[31] This made the Sufi crown prince of India an even more compassionate man. What Dara had worked on for years shone back at him. His book *Majma-ul-Bahrain (The Mingling of the Two Oceans)* was a comparative study of Islam and Hinduism. Dara had flung himself into deep study while writing it. He wrote about the similarity of the concept of the soul in Hinduism and in Sufism. In Hinduism it was atma (individual soul) and parmatma (soul of souls). In Sufism it was ruh and abul arwah (also known as ru-e-azam) respectively.[32] Dara emphasised the concept was the same in both faiths. Such was the desire of Dara's enlightened and cross-pollinated mind to learn from varied influences that many days had been spent with a wandering Armenian poet – Sarmad and a Hindu mystic – Baba Lal Das Bairagi. Dara reflected on those days. Sarmad was a dervish poet of Jewish and Armenian descent who had made India his home. He embraced Sufi philosophy and the teachings of Hindu Yogis. Originally a merchant, he gave up business to write. Wandering from court to court reciting poetry, he was scathing of the Christian, Jewish and Islamic clergy. Dara found him interesting and a friendship developed. Dara also received an education on yoga and meditation from Baba Lal Das Bairagi.

Dara thought of how the illness of his father Shah Jahan opened up a succession war for the Mughal throne of India as the Islamic clergy aligned with his rival brother Aurangzeb. In a final showdown between the two brothers, Dara was beaten in battle and taken prisoner. Now in the damp dungeon, Aurangzeb's men homed in on Dara. Looking at his assassins in the eye he recited a verse he had once written:

> The true mystic will enlighten your heart and your soul
> Make a garden from thorns pulled from your foot's sole
> One burning candle will a thousand light… make whole.[33]

A studded Mughal dagger entered his abdomen. Another punctured his liver as the two assassins twisted their blades within the prince's body. With Dara's death, Aurangzeb was the undisputed emperor of India. Under his reign the empire expanded territorially, while at the same time his court shrunk in intellect. Meanwhile in 1671, twelve years after Dara's death, Francis Bernier, a French traveller took the slain Sufi prince's translation of the Upanishads to France awakening an interest in Indian Philosophy in the West.[34] On Aurangzeb's death in 1707, the Mughal Empire cracked wide open and hurtled towards its end.

These three events set into motion the irreversible process of the collapse of three empires inextricably entwined with the diminishing influence of the Sufis. By the 1730s, intellectuals from Istanbul to Delhi were filled with an ominous feeling of impending anarchy. A flame of cultural renaissance though was flickering in Delhi under Mughal Emperor Muhammad Shah. An effervescence of philosophers and artists were coming together to create new expressions. A desire to discover new shores was on the rise. But in 1739 it would be extinguished by a barbaric massacre of Delhi's populace by Nadir Shah, the invading Persian king driven by greed and an obsession to plunder.[51]

Qaraar Ali would witness this. His skill fired in kilns would fuel a passion for a lost craft and his intellect would take him into the depths of Sufi thought where mathematics, mysticism and art merged. Traversing the lands where the Sufi call still had a faint echo, his journey would completely change his life and the lives he touched.

PART 1

CHAPTER 1

THEIR ORCHARD, THEIR TIMES

DELHI, SPRING 1738

Abeerah's father didn't approve of her love for the twenty-two-year-old Qaraar Ali. They were the same age. She didn't love him only for his almond-shaped eyes or his tall lithe frame. Not for his slender upper lip that she had only gently kissed a handful of times. She loved him for his mind. It was a mind that would take her places within herself that she didn't know existed. When his mind would wander, it would return with words that made her feel as if she lay under the winter sun. When she saw him, she would feel as if her heart had turned into a sparkling diamond.

Her father didn't approve of Qaraar's wandering ways and the impact he had on his daughter. It wasn't as if Qaraar didn't have means. He did. For centuries, his ancestors had been the chief artisans attached to the supreme architects of the Mughal court. Red sandstone chiselling, marble cutting and brick making happened at his ancestral workshops and kilns. Some of the finest monuments across Delhi and Agra bore the stamp of their brilliant craftsmanship. The red sandstone walls and the three marble domes with inverted lotus designs of the Jama Masjid had been chiselled and given shape at the Ali workshops. So had the ones at the Red Fort in Delhi and at the Fatehpur Sikri Palace. As a result of these pursuits the family was considerably wealthy. Qaraar's father, Faiz Ali had inherited these workshops and kilns from his father and Qaraar, being his parents' only child, stood to inherit them in time. But Qaraar hardly showed any interest in the financial aspect of the workshops. He was driven by the creative spirit. Avoiding laborious accounting and supplier interactions, he would escape and spend time with the craftsmen in the kilns or in the workshops, chiselling marble.

But Qaraar was also known to wander away from his workshops. He would be found at Sufi shrines and in the company of poets who sat at the steps of the Jama Masjid reciting their new verses. More recently a strong friendship had grown between him and three young poets who were finding their mark in the twilight of the Mughal empire. Qaraar, like most in north India spoke Persian, Hindi, Urdu and Arabic. His ancestral heritage of being close to the Mughal court gave him access to the finest libraries in Delhi and there he would be seen immersing himself in the works of Hafez, Bedil, Rumi and Ibn Arabi. All this led people to believe that he was more mystical than grounded in running the workshops and kilns. Abeerah's father, a general in the Mughal army, had learned of Qaraar's wandering ways and this was the main reason for his opposition to the romance.

Known as Basant, it was the first day of spring in Delhi. There was colour in the trees. The mustard fields around the city had burst into a bright yellow. Faiz Ali's workshops were in that part of Delhi known as Shahjahanabad. This was the pulse of Delhi, bustling with activity. Its landmark was the Jama Masjid. Doves flew around the minarets and also dotted the quadrangle. Around the Jama Masjid were a myriad of winding narrow lanes where one could find everything. Persian carpet-weavers sat on the floor of their shops sipping qahwah. In the morning the fresh smell of their hot beverage effortlessly mingled with the slight chill in the spring air. It brought a sense of uplifting anticipation to the day. The Persian carpet-weavers took great pride in their profession and maintained a refined decorum in selling their carpets.

In contrast to the dignified selling skills of the Persians were the Bokhari boot traders. Ahmad Bokhari was the lead seller. The knee-length leather and wool boots had sold brilliantly in winter, but now with the advent of spring, the demand was dropping. Ahmad Bokhari waved a pair, explaining the troubles he had undertaken in getting them to Delhi from Bokhara. The treacherous mountain passes of Central Asia and Afghanistan, the innumerable river torrents – he had crossed them all. And now these magnificent specimens stood discounted. Covering his face with his turban tail, he pretended to wail at the sad affair of conducting a sale. His dramatics attracted a massive crowd. All were clamouring for the boots. Some fell with their faces in the boots, but the odour convinced them they were being duped into buying second hand and off went Ahmad Bokhari again, this time weeping aloud at the accusation. The haggling would continue for hours.

Afghan dry fruit sellers, turbaned and shawled sat beside their jute sacks bursting with fruit. Next to the dry fruit sellers was the Shekhawati merchant Hari Das's shop. The Shekhawatis were originally from Rajasthan and had the reputation of being the most adventurous of traders. They were master travellers and their camel caravans would reach as far as Istanbul. Hari Das took spices, mangoes and silk with him. He would return with fur coats and large fluffy woollen caps known as chugirmas from Uzbekistan, blue lapis lazuli stones from Badakshan and turquoise from Nishapur. To Hari Das, spring meant the melting of snow in the Central Asian mountains and the preparation of caravans for their summer journeys. Rich but modest, Hari Das was efficient and meticulous. Every morning he would come down to the ground floor beginning his day with the worship of Laxmi, the Hindu goddess of wealth.

Hari Das's father and Faiz Ali were known to each other but Hari Das and Qaraar's friendship was deeper despite both of them having utterly different personalities. Hari and Qaraar had grown up together in Shahjahanabad and had come to understand each other well as they strode into their youth. It wasn't surprising to find Faiz Ali citing Hari Das's example to Qaraar. Yet their friendship remained unaffected.

Approaching the steps of the Jama Masjid were open-air shops of the two Kaleem brothers who made halwa. In winter and spring their halwas were a favourite of the *Dilliwallas.* Sitting almost entirely on the streets behind their large iron pans they cooked gajar ka halwa and suji ka halwa. As customers devoured them clustered around street-side pans, they would find it hard to resist watching the animal trainer Holar Pasha next door. Holar Pasha was of Turkish origin and had somehow made it to Delhi. Rumour had it that he was a descendent of one of the generals in Kara Mustafa's army that had lost at the gates of Vienna. It was further rumoured that Holar Pasha's ancestor had fled the battle. Hounded in Istanbul for his ancestor's alleged cowardice, Holar Pasha had found it impossible to live in that city. In order to avoid further humiliation of the family in Istanbul, people said that Holar Pasha had left the city. Here in the bazaar of Shahjahanabad's Jama Masjid, besides claiming aristocratic descent he entertained the crowds with his animals – the somersaulting sloth bear, an inquisitive rabbit and the talking parrot who called out in Persian to pedestrians to stop and watch the entertainment: 'Yaar! Nigah kun, Nigah kun!' ('Oh Friend! Look here! Look here!'), squawked the bird.

To the right of the grand steps of the Jama Masjid was the kebab shop of Hatim Khan. Every afternoon Hatim Khan and his crippled sidekick, Munna Mia, served customers kebabs, onions and green chillies with freshly made naans. Hatim Khan's vigorous fanning of the coal on which his kebab skewers lay created a warm smoky enclosure that attracted crowds wrapped in their shawls both for the kebabs and the warmth. Huddled together, men ate their kebabs and chatted about the state of the empire and the emperor.

Running around the nearby streets were thatched roofed cafés. Further down was the mohalla called Ballimaran and at the far end of Ballimaran was Qaraar's two storeyed house called Hunar-Abaad which meant 'where skill thrives'. Behind Hunar-Abaad were the family's workshops. The house had a marble arched entrance in Mughal style and was built of red sandstone. To the left was a stable where Qaraar kept his chestnut brown horse, Haider. At the centre of the house was a rectangular courtyard with a small rose garden which his mother Zainab Begum looked after. With the coming of spring, Qaraar had moved his beddings to the terrace under the pretext of sleeping under the sky. The terrace offered an unobstructed view of the majestic Red Fort, the grand residence of the current Mughal emperor, Muhammad Shah. Beyond the ramparts of the fort were a string of large houses belonging to Mughal nobility, one of which was Abeerah's. Called Basalat-Gah, it meant 'lair of the courageous.' The name was in complete contrast to Qaraar's Hunar-Abaad, reflecting Abeerah's paternal lineage as brave warriors.

Qaraar's secret reason to move up to the terrace was to get a possible view of Abeerah's house. For a while Qaraar stood under an arch on his terrace looking towards her house. His pashmina shawl that draped around his fine Awadhi angarkha made in Lucknow, fluttered in the spring breeze as he hoped to catch a glimpse of a shimmering jewel that she might be wearing or the dance of a candle flame. Unable to detect any sign of his lover, he lay back under a clear night sky and reflected on how they had first met exactly three springs ago.

Emperor Muhammad Shah was creatively inclined and encouraged musicians. The result was the khyal, a Persian word for 'imagination', an already existing style which was now elevated further and given a more rigorous and classical style by fusing it with other musical elements.[35] It was also under Muhammad Shah that the sitar came into its own.[36] Thrilled with these musical enhancements, Muhammad Shah decided to have a lavish jashn on the auspicious day of Holi.

The Red Fort enclosed various open-air marble pavilions. The pavilion that Muhammad Shah preferred was the Shah Burj pavilion. But leading up to the jashn, Muhammad Shah's elephant went on rampage destroying the pavilion and the gardens. With only a fortnight to go until the jashn, the supreme architect advised choosing another pavilion. But the emperor was adamant. The pavilion had to be restored to exactly how it had once looked. It was then that Qaraar flung himself into the quagmire. He was then just a year shy of twenty but his heart was racing with the creative spirit. It was as if he had waited all his life to express himself.

Qaraar drew a satin curtain all around the ruins of the pavilion and went to work. Camels and horse-pulled carts meandered into the Red Fort complex with supplies of marble slabs. Qaraar's eyes and hands could only see and feel marble. Days went by but Qaraar didn't put down the chisel. Hunger and thirst struck him but drunk on the desire to create, he shunned them. Blood flew from his fingers as some tired thrusts of the chisel caught them. Every muscle in his shoulder leapt in pain but his tightly pursed lips didn't release a word. As dawn broke, he would hear sparrows in a nearby walnut tree. He would spend the entire day alternating from side to side in order to carve a skyward-facing twenty-petalled flower in marble. Qaraar's forearms were trembling by the time it was dusk, and the sparrows returned to the branches of the walnut tree. His father's men would come at twilight and light 150 candles around him as he cut into the marble. A day before the jashn, Qaraar had to be carried out of the Red Fort lying on a makeshift bamboo stretcher. But he had recovered enough to be present the next day.

It was a misty day. Every tree trunk was draped in marigold flowers. Mughal aristocracy made its way through the garden pathways to the Diwan-e-Khas, the main audience pavilion, where the emperor would make his grand entry and take his seat on the legendary Peacock Throne. Qaraar followed Faiz Ali into the Diwan-e-Khas. Dressed in a black shervani and tapering white trousers, Qaraar stood at six feet, matching his father's height. Next came the Mughal generals. Shahbaz Khan, one of the most prominent military men, came and took his place. When all had gathered, three drumbeats resounded, followed by a loud and echoing announcement of the entry of 'The Refuge of the world, Jahanpanah, Emperor Muhammad Shah.' Heads bowed and eyelids lowered. Keen to get on with the jashn the emperor enquired about the Shah Burj pavilion to which the supreme architect invited him to inspect the site.

The emperor couldn't believe what he was seeing. He walked past each pillar feeling them with his hands and then passed his fingers through the fountain. In a fortnight a ruin had been transformed into a piece of art. The chief architect explained in great length, how Qaraar had obsessively undertaken this next-to-impossible task. Qaraar stood there, hands folded, head bowed. But there was a movement he couldn't help but follow and so he raised his head gently. As the chief architect went about describing Qaraar's obsessive efforts, Qaraar's eyes saw the gentle swaying of a dupatta, partially hiding a rose-complexioned face. The face was behind the right shoulder of General Shahbaz Khan.

His eyes followed that swaying dupatta, but a sharply glittering diamond nose pin halted his eye movements. The general's shoulder obstructed the other half of the view. Finding it difficult to look away from the nose pin, he reluctantly drew them away only to be struck by the dark blue kohl around her eye. The eye that looked at him for barely a fraction of a moment, then instantly lowered itself as if to say, 'You've seen enough.' But Qaraar's gaze had been tested and he wanted more. He saw dark brown flowing hair. Some disobedient strands of hair seemed to gently touch her cheeks as if drawn to the beauty of her face. By now his desire to see the complete picture was building up like a storm within him. Taking a step back, he looked again. But she turned her face. At the corner of the dupatta, he could see that her lips formed into a slim smile. Just then Shahbaz Khan moved and Qaraar had the first full view of Abeerah's face. It was petite and roundish. Her lips were fresh peach in colour. Her nose, on which glimmered the diamond pin, was small and perfectly proportioned to her face. She had pulled her dupatta up just the right amount so as to reveal her middle parting where a diamond and emerald chaand-taara teeka sparkled. As Qaraar's eyes roamed freely on her face they reached her naturally arched eyebrows, which were strung like a bow above her hazel eyes. Qaraar whispered Hafez's verse:

> Those charming brows, arch'd like the heavenly bow,
> Arm not with such disdain;
> Drive not one, already sunk low, hopeless to mourn his never ceasing pain.[37]

Abeerah seemed to have heard that whisper. She smiled. Abeerah was of medium height with long, flowing tresses reaching her curvaceous hips. Her hands were smooth and delicate. She was General Shahbaz Khan's daughter. Motherless, she was the great joy of Shahbaz Khan and had inherited her warrior father's fearlessness. The loss of her mother, when she was five, had made Shahbaz Khan an indulgent father yet one who hadn't compromised on a classical upbringing of his daughter. He followed the Betakshi Sufi order which encouraged women to pursue an active intellectual and social life. Abeerah had arrived late to the gathering and therefore was not in the ladies' zenana section. Striding confidently through the gathering, she had found her way to her father and standing behind him had attentively heard the chief architect's description of Qaraar's recreation of the Shah Burj pavilion. Abeerah had a passion for the arts. Schooled by ustads at home, she had insisted on furthering her education in the arts and her doting father had willingly agreed. The finest teachers of Mughal miniature paintings were hired to teach Abeerah. In the prime of her youth, Abeerah was the epitome of Mughal beauty and etiquette. She knew it and so did the people who surrounded her. Her adaa was sensual yet restrained. The manner in which she did the aadaab was much spoken about. Keeping the image of a hilaal crescent in mind, she would gently curve her palm. She would then bow her head and raise the curved palm close to her forehead, ensuring that it didn't touch it. Many a Mughal noble had lost his heart to that sight. But on that day of the jashn, when she saw the Shah Burj pavilion as a creation of pain and ecstasy, she coyly inspected the creator who brought marble to life. Qaraar's long arms and slim fingers first received her attention. Moving her eyes upwards she caught sight of his long neck. She then looked at his slim, shaped Mughal beard and moustache that rested gently on a thin upper lip. Emperor Muhammad Shah was so pleased that he made an announcement. A land grant: ten acres just next to his ancestor Humayun's Tomb were to be immediately granted to Qaraar. In addition to the land grant the emperor announced fifteen bags of ashrafees to the young craftsman. The emperor's announcement was welcomed by all and a huge roar went up hailing his magnanimity.

The emperor then signalled for the jashn to begin. Almost immediately the lead singer gently shut his eyes and hummed the first tunes of the khyal composition as the sitar players struck their chords, complimenting the ascending tune. Abeerah drew the translucent dupatta across the side of her face and took small backward steps towards some distant trees. A signal to Qaraar to follow. The khyal tune, as it was meant to, ignited imagination and heightened the sense of romance and Qaraar took the first steps towards her. Amid the misty spring air and colourful hues of Holi, Abeerah looked like a passing dream. Finally, behind a large oak, he found her. The mist and colour ensured that they couldn't be seen. An intuition he knew was real, overcame Qaraar. He tilted his head, lowered it to match her height and kissed her mouth. Even more than Qaraar, Abeerah surprised herself that she didn't pull away. She didn't reason. Keeping her eyes shut, she touched the side of his face and kissed back. Qaraar felt her body rise. In the distance the vocal rendition of the khyal reached its crescendo. Qaraar and Abeerah locked their fingers in a hand hold that testified to the intensity of that moment. Her forehead rested on his left shoulder, but they didn't exchange a word. Then she left.

Sitting in her golden howdah on her elephant she looked for Qaraar. At a distance she saw him mounted on his chestnut brown horse. Qaraar looked at her, not caring for the elephant that carried Shahbaz Khan next to hers. Then with a jerk to the reins and a slight nudge, he turned his horse and disappeared.

For the next few days, Abeerah thought of how she had been solicited by her father's ilk. She had been introduced to the sons of other generals who were fast climbing the ranks in the Mughal army. On occasions, she was introduced to the idle heirs to their father's estates. And on another occasion, she met the one-dimensional son of the finance minister who spent most of his time buried in leather-bound income and expenditure journals. She had unhesitatingly rejected them all. Shahbaz Khan for all his battle scars couldn't bring himself to force his daughter. In fact, he had come to admire her indifference towards pampered landed gentry.

Qaraar though, had stirred Abeerah's sensibilities. After that first meeting, scented letters would be smuggled into Abeerah's chambers. The one taking part in facilitating this romance was Munna Mia, the disabled sidekick of Hatim Khan. He would deliver Qaraar's letters under the pretext of delivering kebabs, and for his efforts, Munna Mia would be tipped with embroidered Nawabi caps. The romance thrived and the lovers met fortnightly.

Shahbaz Khan had caught the distant look that now glazed his daughter's eyes as she would look out towards the Jama Masjid and the carved arches of Hunar-Abaad from her terrace. He had seen his daughter tilt her head and run her hands through the sides of her hair looking aimlessly and smiling to herself. Abeerah kept every letter in her jewellery box, a place she knew they would be safe. Qaraar quoted Hafez and Ibn Arabi in each letter that he wrote to Abeerah, making her feel as if their destiny had been written in the stars. In one such letter, Qaraar quoted Ibn Arabi's passion for Nizam, a lady he had fallen in love with in Damascus:

> In the fever of love, separation kills. Finding her would ease the burning… Her glance, blacksilver flash is fatal. Tender the bend of her neck as she turns… She extends a hand as soft as undyed silk in musk… She lets down her hair like a black snake.[38]

Abeerah blushed crimson by the time she read the last words. The only place she could be calmed was in Qaraar's arms. And then they would meet. Qaraar would speak a language that no one had spoken to her. The language of the Sufi. The mystical lover. Shahbaz Khan felt that his daughter was losing herself swiftly to this love. He worried about her. At the jashn, he was present when the emperor had bestowed the land next to Humayun's Tomb to Qaraar. At that time, he was impressed with Qaraar, who had demonstrated a creative drive that could stun an emperor. But what bothered Shahbaz Khan was that for three years Qaraar hadn't created anything new. Shahbaz Khan had expected Qaraar to deliver more masterpieces and acquire greater wealth, but he hadn't. All of this, combined with the now-frequent sight of his daughter pacing up and down the terrace of Basalat-Gah counting the days to go with her plaited hair before her next encounter with the wandering Qaraar, made him disapprove of the relationship.

Qaraar lying on his terrace shut his eyes, waiting for the next day when he would finally see Abeerah's face again. The wait had been painful; like the sharp slash of a Mughal dagger that refused to heal.

Qaraar watched her palanquin approach. They were meeting on his land. He stood with one arm resting on a low branch of a mango tree. On another branch he had tied the reins of Haider, his horse, whose long mane swayed in the spring breeze. Abeerah's African palanquin bearers lowered it and she emerged from it dressed in a soft yellow gharara.

For a few seconds the lovers gazed at each other. Only a portion of her head was covered with the dupatta that rested gently on her loose hair. Qaraar had many times expressed his love for her middle parting from which her hair cascaded. On the left side of her head, hung the chapka. This was a Mughal piece of jewellery studded with small emeralds and rubies encrusted in gold. She walked up slowly to Qaraar. The fingers of her left hand played with the right-hand index finger that carried a pukhraj ring.

He leaned forward and gently kissed her. Taking her hand, he said, 'Walk with me.'

'Qaraar, the mango spring flowers are everywhere,' said Abeerah looking all around.

'These are the months of hope, and love,' said Qaraar, gently smiling and lowering a slender branch, bringing it close so that Abeerah could inhale the scent of the tiny fruit flowers.

Looking first at their interlocked fingers and then at him, she said, 'My love, you have transformed this place.'

'I remember there was nothing here but a few trees and now look at it! Mango trees everywhere!' she went on.

'It's not me. Without you, this place would be bereft of beauty,' replied Qaraar.

Since the time Qaraar had been gifted the land, three years ago, both Abeerah and he had planted an orchard. Abeerah shouldered the responsibility of bringing symmetry to the tree lines. She had personally supervised each sapling as it had been lowered into the ground. Qaraar alongwith Hari and artisans from his workshop had dug canals for irrigation. Ten acres carpeted thick with mango trees was the result. After three years, during spring, the trees bore their first fruit flowers.

Continuing to look around, Abeerah was reminded of Ibn Arabi's poem that Qaraar had written for her. 'Those words were for me Qaraar,' she said as she came close and put her hand on his chest.

'But there is way more to Ibn Arabi's philosophy than his love poem,' whispered Qaraar.

'Tell me all that you know.'

Qaraar lead her into a mango grove that was so dense that only a few rays of light escaped through the branches. On the ground was a Persian carpet. He sat with his back resting against the bark of a tree. Abeerah sat with her back leaning against Qaraar's chest.

'Ibn Arabi's philosophy changed how the world perceived Islam,' began Qaraar. 'It became a faith of philosophical depth and beauty,' he added.

'Born in Spain, his life began with wandering and love for a woman called Nizam. After he died, he was recognised as the greatest Sufi philosopher,' continued Qaraar.

Abeerah's brown hair lay spread over the black shawl that draped Qaraar's right shoulder and chest. She listened intently to each word that he now uttered.

Slipping his fingers through her hair, he explained further, 'Nizam, the woman that Ibn Arabi loved became a metaphor to express his love for the Divine. Other Sufi poets like Hafez and Rumi did the same. Hafez, in particular, used his love for a lady called Shakh-e-Nabat and other metaphors like wine, the arched eyebrow, the tavern and the cupbearer to voice his love for the Divine. Rumi used the separation that the reed felt from its roots to express that pining love of the creator,' said Qaraar.

'Go on,' whispered Abeerah.

'Let's stay with Ibn Arabi for now. According to him everything material is a mere manifestation of an essential truth.'

Qaraar gave Abeerah time to reflect on what he had just said. Abeerah's eyes followed the spring mist as it began its languid approach towards the never-ending sight of trees. In a few moments, the mist had softly wrapped itself aound them with only the higher branches now seeming to float on clouds. The sight of the misty orchard pleased Abeerah.

'So this orchard and this world is a manifestation?' asked Abeerah softly.

'Yes. According to Ibn Arabi, the world is only a manifestation of the attribute of God. The world is merely nominal. It has no existence of its own.'[39]

'Did he go deeper in philosophical thought?' inquired Abeerah still looking into the orchard.

'Yes... Ibn Arabi's acquired understanding of Wahadat-ul-Wajuud, also known as "The Unity of Being", is what freed his mind. Such was his deep connect with that One Absolute Essence that he came to accept all forms of love for the Divine and that's when he wrote his most famous poem.'

Qaraar recited with great feeling.

> My heart has become a pasture for gazelles, a convent for Christian monks, a temple for idols and the pilgrim's Kaaba, and the tablets of the Torah and the book of the Quran. I follow the religion of love: whichever way its camels take, for this is my religion and my faith.[40]

Abeerah turned and looked at Qaraar. With a worried expression on her face, she asked, 'Didn't the orthodox clergy find it blasphemous?'

'Ibn Arabi didn't care for the clergy. He wrote what he felt deep within.'

'The Sufis gave us philosophies that helped man evolve. Love and compassion were at the heart of it all,' he continued.

'And God, Qaraar? What do they have to say about Him?' asked Abeerah wondering how her lover might interpret the Sufis.

'I will tell you how I understand it... Sufis have a much-favoured verse for God "I was a Treasure unknown then I yearned to be known so I created creation to which I made Myself known; then they knew Me.'"

Here, Qaraar explained further: '...and so I, Qaraar, his creation, love Him...'

'You do?' asked Abeerah with a slight smile. 'How do you show it?'

Qaraar replied, 'Ibn Arabi says, first there is Absolute Essence, then there are attributes of that Essence which have names. One of the names is mercy. When I see you, I think of His mercy.'

Qaraar continued, 'You have been merciful to me by loving me... So, by loving His attribute of mercy that manifests in you, I am loving Him. In short by loving you, I love Him.'

Abeerah felt as if she was soaring into another dimension.

'And because you see His attributes everywhere, is that why I have never seen you go to the mosque?'

With a nod he replied in an agreeing tone, 'Yes. I can love Him by loving His attributes that are everywhere.'

Abeerah shut her eyes.

The afternoon had drifted into evening. 'Natiya,' called out Abeerah. The maid came rushing following the voice. Seeing Qaraar, the maid bowed her head, lifted her hand and said, 'Aadaab Qaraar Ali sahib.'

'Natiya, bring the other servants and lay out the dastarkhwan... A philosopher needs nourishment,' said Abeerah with a slight smile.

The dastarkhwan was the traditional Mughal Indian way of sharing a meal while seated on the ground. A finely embroidered white cloth was spread and a lavish spread of shami kebabs, pasanda, korma and naan was served.

Observing that the wine hadn't arrived and that Qaraar was looking for it, Abeerah called out, 'Natiya, please bring the wine.'

The gardan surahi, a silver wine flask with its curving slender neck was brought and Natiya placed it on the dastarkhwan under Abeerah's watchful gaze. Natiya knew her place. She left the wine flask and retreated. A few months before, Natiya had approached Qaraar swaying her hips, and had tried to fill Qaraar's cup in Abeerah's presence. In response she had received a fiery glance from Abeerah. The cup filled, Qaraar leaned back and drank.

Mango orchards in spring were known to attract peacocks and three of them landed not far away. Abeerah reached out with her hand and dropped her wrist, luring them towards her with a palm full of crumbs. As the indigo-coloured birds hovered around the couple for hours, Qaraar examined this perfect surrounding as time drifted by with Abeerah in his arms. In the distance, a few house lanterns were lit up announcing the advent of nightfall. Some shepherds guided their flocks back home, the tinkering sound of bells around their necks was pleasing to the lovers as it mingled with the sound of the running waters of the Yamuna not far from the orchard. The majestic dome of Humayun's Tomb began to fade in visibility as the night descended. The lovers left the orchard agreeing to meet the next day rather than wait for a fortnight in order to visit the shrine of Hazrat Nizamuddin Auliya on a Thursday. A day considered auspicious.

At the beginning of their romance, Abeerah had met Qaraar secretly, but of late she had grown bolder and left her house at her discretion.

On Thursday evening, Qaraar rode ahead with Abeerah's palanquin following. As they passed Humayun's Tomb, Qaraar held up his hand signalling to the palanquin bearers to halt. He turned the reins and slowly came up to the palanquin, 'I'd like to show you something.'

He helped Abeerah to alight from the palanquin and then holding a glowing lantern in his hand, the two rushed up the stairs of the monument. Night had fallen and only the sound of crickets broke the silence. Initially Abeerah thought Qaraar would talk to her about the dome. But holding her hand, he drew her towards the stone screens through which they would be able to see the emperor's tomb.

Qaraar lifted up the lantern and as he drew it across, each detail sprung to life, almost asking why they had been reduced to such a sad state of neglect. Cobwebs were everywhere. A lot of the stonework was broken. But to the lovers with their gifted artistic eye, the appearance was stunning. Six-pointed stars were the central attraction. Interlocking around the stars, were hexagons and squares and the three-petal tulip shape, all intricately carved. Catching the lantern's light, the star shapes danced on Abeerah's gharara.

'This geometric work is magical,' Qaraar said softly.

Abeerah listened and examined the stone screens further as Qaraar held up the lantern.

'The Sufis of Persia and Central Asia lifted this art form to a new level. I have read about this craft in the libraries,' continued Qaraar, unable to take his eyes of the stone screens.

'It's on the other side of the terrace too,' observed Abeerah as she walked towards them.

'Often the most unappreciated are the most beautiful aspects of a monument,' said Qaraar with a slight sarcasm hinted at the unpresent Shahbaz Khan.

'Imagine this geometric work in blue-glazed tilework across domes, facades and walls,' continued Qaraar.

Abeerah looked at him in wonder.

'They exist! At the mausoleum of Quli Khan in Mehrauli, across Central Asia, Persia, Turkey… and beyond.'

'What do they call it?'

'Girih tilework.'

'Aaah.'

'Come let's go, I thought I'd show you something others usually ignore.'

The Basant festival drew crowds from all parts of Mughal India to the shrine of Hazrat Nizamuddin Auliya. The festive feel was in the air and with night descending, the atmosphere grew even more frenzied. With Abeerah veiled up to her eyes, revealing only the dark blue kohl around the rims, the couple made their way down the street lined with shops selling sweet meats and hot lamb dishes. Vendors called out to people asking them to feed the poor fakirs. Goats and chickens roamed the streets freely, running in all directions as people made their way to the shrine.

Qalandars were mystics, dressed in bright purple robes and orange beads. They brushed passed Qaraar and walked straight towards the shrine. Known to shout out the word 'Haq', which meant truth, if they felt an inner calling towards God, they often stopped in their tracks, looked heavenwards, let out the cry, shook their long hair and marched on. Their wrists were covered with bracelets and charms all the way till their forearms.

The first destination for the lovers was the small shrine of Amir Khusrau, the famed poet devotee of Hazrat Nizamuddin Auliya and then they proceeded to the master's shrine. The entire marble dome was covered in yellow flowers. Qaraar scattered some rose petals over the tomb, and then fell to his knees shutting his eyes in devotion. Abeerah followed. After a few moments they were separated against their will by the surging crowds. Abeerah sat behind a carved marble screen in the zenana section and Qaraar moved further away sitting at a distance.

In moments, the first arrivals of devotional singers, the qawwals, entered the courtyard to a huge applause. Hazrat Nizamuddin Auliya had lost himself to divine love and so his followers had given him the title of Mehboob-e-Ilahi, the lover of the great lover. Here, God was not to be feared but loved. He conceptualised this as Ishq-e-Ilahi, or the 'love of God'. So taken in were the people of thirteenth-century Delhi with this concept that they had thronged to him.

The spring air was still cool. Men walked around lighting incense sticks and their scent made the setting even more mystical. People swung their shawls around them and cosied up around small fires in the courtyard, as the qawwal*s* sang the magnetic Nami-danam-che-manzil-buud:

> I wonder what the place was where I was last night.
> All around me were half-slaughtered victims of love,
> Twisting in agony.[41]

Having heard these words, Qaraar felt a searing desire to see Abeerah. The singing, the swaying, the incense burning in the marble arches, the yellow flowers and the flickering lamps in the darkness drove Qaraar to a point where the only sight that he craved was her face.

Finally, from behind the carved marble screen, Abeerah showed her face by dropping her veil. Qaraar rose and went towards her. She left the zenana and stood by a small fire. She lifted her delicate feet from the cold marble floor, alternating them and twirling them before the fire. All seemed engrossed in the qawwali while Qaraar emerged from behind her. He took his pashmina shawl from his shoulder, spread it out and with a sweeping movement wrapped it around her from behind. He held her close.

'It's you,' she whispered without turning around and leaned back. The softness and warmth of the pashmina compounded by the intensity in Qaraar's arms made her feel like a melting candle. Qaraar felt complete: united with the eternal lover, or in Sufi terms, vasl.

The mysticism that night made Abeerah believe even more strongly in her love. The ride back towards Shahjahanabad after the qawwals had finished was painful. Filled with the anxiety of parting, Abeerah peeped out of the veiled palanquin sides to look at Qaraar as much as the dark night would allow her. As they approached the crossroads where the palanquin would take Abeerah towards her house and Haider would carry Qaraar to Hunar-Abaad, Qaraar raised his hand looked skywards and said, 'Allah bring the day of union close.'

A scented letter would surely arrive that would give the venue for the next meeting.

The days were getting warmer. At Hunar-Abaad, Qaraar's parents Faiz Ali and Zainab Begum took to preparing the house for the approaching summer. Zainab Begum in her late sixties was of Herati descent as was Faiz Ali. Slim of frame and silvering in hair, she had a fresh clear complexion that deceived her age. To Zainab, her home was her paradise and she busied herself in the task of getting the house ventilated. Servants brought in large marble cauldrons which under Zainab's supervision were filled with fresh water, rose petals and a dash of sandalwood. Then they were strategically placed, some at the main entrance and others running down a crevice-like alley adjacent to Hunar-Abaad and a few on the terrace. The objective of these innovative placements was to refresh the inhabitants, as the breeze that entered the house would be fragranced by the combination of rose water and sandalwood. The servants too played their part in cooling down the house. They ensured a turbaned Bhishti regularly visited Hunar-Abaad with his large leather bag to sprinkle water on baking stone floors.

Zainab Begum personally supervised the daily cleaning of the finely carved motifs of stems and petals on the red sandstone walls of Hunar-Abaad. In the courtyard where the small rose garden bloomed, Zainab Begum ordered the planting of jasmine knowing well that it would thrive in the harshness of summer while the roses would fade. Servants brought out the charpoys and placed them around the rose and jasmine garden in the courtyard. Here after sunset, the family and their visiting friends could lounge on the charpoys under the open sky.

One afternoon as the day warmed, Hari Das's horse driven carriage pulled up in front of Hunar-Abaad. 'Khushamdeed,' said Faiz Ali opening his arms to embrace the young Shekhawati merchant as he entered the courtyard holding a large cloth bag in his hand.

'Charan Sparsh,' responded Hari Das bowing low, touching Faiz Ali's feet and seeking his blessing. After the embrace, Hari Das with folded hands turned to Zainab Begum who was making a final selection of vegetables. With a raised hand she said, 'Jeetay Raho Hari. Live long.'

'It's good that you have come,' remarked Faiz Ali. 'Your drifter friend hasn't engaged with the trade for months. Speak some sense into him.' Faiz Ali was about to continue when he saw his son coming down the terrace stairs to greet his friend.

Qaraar and Hari embraced and reclined on the charpoys as the Bhishti went around the courtyard dousing it with generous helpings of water.

Faiz Ali too joined the young men. Servants brought out three hookahs and set them up next to each of the charpoys.

'Qaraar, I brought you something,' said Hari turning, looking into his cloth bag and pulling out a large square tile.

'An Armenian trader came in last week with this piece. He says he saw it on the floor of an old crumbling caravanserai near Samarkand when his caravan was finding its way towards Hindustan. When he showed it to me, I thought of you. I traded a bag of spices for it. Here, it's for you,' offered Hari.

'Aaah! This is just magnificent. The blue is from the lapis lazuli stones from Badakhshan in Afghanistan. Thank you, Hari.' Qaraar brought his hand up to his chest as a gesture of gratitude.

Faiz Ali seemingly uninterested blew smoke from his hookah and addressed Hari, 'What's the latest news from the arriving merchants, Hari? What do they have to say about the state of affairs in Persia?'

'Ali sahib, Nadir Shah has a tight grip on power,' replied Hari.

'So, things are settling down there?'

Hari went on to offer a detailed explanation on the state of affairs, 'Not quite, Ali sahib. Nadir Shah has got a reputation of being a ruthless savage. He is a warmonger, continuously fighting with the Ottomans and the Uzbek Khans. The word from the traders is that he doesn't take the advice of the Sufis,' Hari said all this in one breath, as if he had to get it off his chest.

Qaraar walked up to an arched niche in the wall, placed the tile inside it and turning to Hari he said, 'I have read about tile making techniques...'

Then he paused and lit a candle and placed it besides the tile in the niche. The light from the candle dazzled against the blue-glazed tile making the niche look like a shimmering sapphire encrusted in the wall.

Faiz Ali couldn't help himself and let off a tirade towards his son, 'Qaraar, all you do is read in the Mughal libraries or spend time with your poet friends. If not that, you are chiselling away with the workers and if not that, you are wandering with the general's daughter'. Faiz Ali's voice grew agitated as he elaborated on a sensitive topic, 'All of Delhi has been talking about your romance with Abeerah. Start concentrating on the trade. Start thinking about how we can buy marble more cheaply, or make plans to create a new monument for the emperor.' Faiz Ali paused for a while and rubbed his forehead that now wore the most anxious frown. Then looking at his son he continued, 'The empire might be in trouble but this emperor is a great patron of the arts and crafts. He is also encouraging the Sufis. Don't lose this opportunity. Work with the supreme architect, make a plan and get the emperor's seal on it.' Qaraar rose from his reclining position ready to verbally duel with his father but Hari Das turned to his friend and with a tight blink of the eye signalled to be calm.

Hari spoke up for his friend, 'Ali sahib, it takes time. You know how it is with creative people. They need to feel it. Right here!' he said touching his chest. 'Then they see it. Right here!' he said pointing at his eyes. 'And then it manifests itself into plans and figures and all of that. Right here!' he said pointing to his head.

'Qaraar has yet to feel it. Give him time,' urged the loyal Shekhawati friend.

'What about Abeerah?' asked a frowning and hookah puffing Faiz Ali.

'Everyone's been talking about them,' said the upset father looking at Hari Das. 'I mean from the Mughal aristocracy to the kebab sellers at the steps of Jama Masjid. The talk is everywhere. They even say that this romance is only surviving because the general is a doting father to his motherless daughter... otherwise... are you listening Qaraar, otherwise the general would have had you executed!'

'Love never only survives, Abbajaan. It thrives,' came Qaraar's defiant yet respectful reply as he added more cinnamon to the burning coal of his hookah. 'Ishq-e Haqeeqi through Ishq-e-Majaazi... is what I have with her. Loving the Divine through His beautiful creation... you won't understand it.'

'But where is this relationship going? The other day that poverty-stricken fakir... what's his name? Ah... yes, Baba Ilyas, that's it... He came up to me in his torn rags and said Abeerah is like an "intoxicated deer lost in the forest of your son's love". It's been three years you have been meeting her. This is reaching proportions like no other love story in Mughal Delhi. Tell me! What do you plan to do? Shahbaz Khan's patience will sooner or later run out.'

'I will marry her,' pausing briefly, Qaraar completed his sentence, '...at the right time.'

'Yes, my Dildaar son! Marry her! Your father and I can take a proposal tomorrow itself to her house,' said an excited Zainab Begum, who up to now hadn't bothered to take part in the conversation but now hearing her son's declaration, she dived right into it.

She announced, 'I will take a yellow dupatta, some henna which I will apply to her soft hands and your grandmother's diamond necklace as an engagement gift. Shahbaz Khan is well aware of our family's standing as the chief artisans to the Mughal court and he knows of the great respect the emperors have held us in for generations. He daren't say no,' Zainab Begum went on with great confidence in her voice. Then she lifted the lid of her paandan, pulled out a perfectly triangle-shaped paan, tucked it into the left side of her mouth and chewed on it slowly.

Clearing her throat, she continued, '...and if Shahbaz Khan does say no to the proposal, I will expose his origins. His ancestors were mere foot soldiers in the great Akbar's army. Only through war, did they earn their feathers of honour,' she concluded.

'Shahbaz Khan will say no!' interjected Faiz Ali getting up from the charpoy and flinging the hookah in a rage.

'The reputation of our family will not be in question. But it's you Qaraar. He thinks you are incapable of achieving anything!'

'She doesn't. And that's all that matters,' came a defiant reply from Qaraar as he rose from the charpoy.

'But then what's stopping you from marrying her now?' responded the father.

'I will tell you why,' Faiz Ali continued, 'it's because you know deep down that you haven't achieved what you could have in the last three years.'

Zainab Begum couldn't help herself, and she addressed her husband making a face dripping of nonchalance, 'As far as Shahbaz Khan is concerned, you don't know for sure that he will reject our proposal. My heart tells me he will accept it. He is a man with great compassion for his daughter. And as far as our son is concerned,' she said looking at her husband, her facial expression taking on a firm look, 'you need to have faith in him and in his abilities.'

'Come now it's evening. Let the young men go for their daily walk to the steps of the Jama Masjid. It will lighten their hearts. Their friends, the new poets, will be reciting their verses today,' said Zainab Begum bringing an ease to the conversation.

She walked up to them. They lowered their foreheads. She kissed them and walked them to the door. Hari Das signalled to his carriage to follow them as the two young men made their way through the winding lanes of Ballimaran towards the steps of Jama Masjid.

On seeing Qaraar, Hatim Khan, the kebab seller, who was grilling lamb skewers, came forward and gave him his right hand as a mark of respect. After shaking his hand, he brought it up to his chest and said, 'It's going to be a fun evening Qaraar sahib... your friends, the new poets are expected to turn up shortly.' Then coming closer, he whispered into Qaraar's ear, 'Munna Mia, my limping sidekick, has been delivering your letters to Abeerah Begum quite efficiently over the last few years... How about raising the tip a bit, Huzoor! From caps to gold coins? You know, he limps all the way to her house.'

There was a smile of a greedy man on Hatim Khan's face and Qaraar was reminded of what his father had said about the romance being the talk of nobility and kebab sellers. It annoyed him. He gently pushed Hatim Khan away saying, 'We will see,' and continued walking with Hari Das towards the Jama Masjid.

Ahmad Bokhari, the boot seller, waved to Hari Das and Qaraar as they walked to the steps of the mosque. They avoided the crooked boot-seller's signals.

Soon a mixed crowd of nobility and commoners gathered on the steps of the Jama Masjid. Some sat on the steps, others stood around the shops ordering their halwa from the Kaleem brothers. Mughal nobles either came on horseback dressed in their fine robes or in their open-air palanquins. Qaraar stood on an elevated platform outside Hari's shop from where he could easily see the performances. Hari stood next to him. Two Ottoman travellers on camels slowly meandered in. They were Hari Das's trading partners and had come to collect boxes of spices, yarns of silk and cotton fabric. Hari Das quickly ordered his servants to load up their camels.

Perched on top of a camel, one of the Ottoman travellers enquired about the gathering, 'What's going on here?'

'It's the sunset poetry evening of our friends, the "new poets",' replied Hari.

'Ah, yes! We have heard of this, let's stay and listen,' said one of the travellers to the other.

'In Persian?' enquired the other.

'In Urdu,' said Hari Das. 'It's a language that's gaining much prominence with the young new poets. It's a blend of Persian, Arabic and Hindi.'

'We've picked up Hindi because of our travels to this land, I'm sure we will understand the poets,' explained one of the travellers to Hari Das.

'Hari, I want her here,' said Qaraar, hands folded across his chest and looking at the gathering.

'Short notice my friend but we can try. Munna Mia!' called out Hari to Hatim Khan's diminutive sidekick.

Munna Mia looked at Hatim Khan for approval. With a slight smile and an upward twitch of the neck, Hatim Khan gave the approving signal to Munna Mia and the tiny assistant scrambled towards Qaraar.

'Take this to the General's house – Basalat-Gah,' said Qaraar dabbing the four corners of the letter with a dainty brush that had been dipped in a bottle of musk perfume. The brush and the bottle of perfume were borrowed from Hari's desk.

'A gold coin this time, Qaraar sahib!' said Munna Mia as he limped away with alarming speed holding the letter in one hand and a box of kebabs in the other.

Three young poets made their way to the steps: Sauda, Dard and Mir. Sauda was a strapping young man of twenty-five. Dard was seventeen and Mir sixteen. As the three passed by Hari's shop they stopped and exchanged a few words with Qaraar and Hari. Their friendship had grown over the last few months particularly when making fun of Ahmad Bokhari, the boot seller who sat not too far away.

'Make way! Make way!' screamed a self-appointed master

of ceremonies at the top of the steps. 'The new poets are arriving! Young they might be, but their hearts and words burn with promise!'

The crowd parted and made a passageway possible up the steps as Sauda, Dard and Mir climbed up. Just then Abeerah's palanquin arrived. She disembarked and bravely stood by Qaraar, her face veiled. First up was Sauda and just as he was about to recite, a voice yelled out from the crowd, 'Oh, here comes the emperor's elephant.' This was an unofficial surprise visit and the gathering wasn't prepared for any royal ceremonies. The swaying elephant came close to the steps and the emperor, Muhammad Shah, drew his hand out of the howdah. There was silence and all bowed.

Sauda began:

> When from the elements the human form was made, from the little fire that was left, the lover's heart was raised.[42]

The crowd roared at the delicacy of the verse. Sauda carried on.

> Glances, graces, guiles and smiles – this is my heart's price.
> Tell us what you will pay, if you want to buy.[43]

Again, the crowd went mad screaming. Just then Sauda saw the orthodox clergy make their way shaking their heads in disapproval of the poetry session. Seeing this Sauda couldn't help himself and lashed out a verse that stung them.

> Take off your turban before you go to pray, O Shaikh, lest you aren't able to raise your bowed head again…
> The pious won't stop condemning the joys of drinking wine, until he is taken to the tavern and made to taste it.[44]

The last verse and particularly the last line were so bold that silence fell upon the crowd. Then came Dard's turn, the mystic, who at a young age had begun writing about how mankind needed to be more compassionate.

If you want the joy of heart, contentment, acquire.
Never can the man of greed fulfil his desire.
God created man to further kind compassion,
There was no dearth of angels to offer adoration'
...Be it Kaaba, be it temple or school,
We were mere visitors, You, the Host that ruled.[45]

In Dard's words were profound messages and the crowd reacted differently. Instead of roaring like they did while listening to Sauda or falling silent, now they shut their eyes, swayed and smiled to themselves as Dard raised man's position above angels. 'Do good in this world and let angels adore God' – Dard's message came home brilliantly as it sank into the crowd's hearts.

Then came the turn of the young Mir, who walked up the steps gingerly, and recited.

The heart was a wondrous town with myriad thoughts aglow.
Alas, it has been ravaged by the beauteous!
My shattered heart is a sight to see
What a mansion wrecked by griefs![46]

The crowd felt Mir's deep pain. Such was the intensity of this love poet that the crowd let out a loud sigh. The diversity of the evening had left them dazed. Sauda's bravery, Dard's philosophy and Mir's melancholic pain for his lover had spun a web of contemplation and emotion around them.

Many fell over wanting to touch the young poets. The clamour to get to them was uncontrollable. The emperor's elephant blocked the winding street as nobles mounted on their steeds began reigning in their nervous beasts. Boldly the standard-bearer declared that the poetry just recited would be given tunes and vocals by the court musicians and would be recited from the Red Fort by the best singers. Then the emperor showered yellow rose petals on the crowd. The throng roared again in appreciation as the emperor's elephant disappeared.

'Let's give our benevolent emperor a title,' said Qaraar aloud.

'Yes! He deserves a title that symbolises his love for the arts,' added Abeerah.

After some deliberation in the crowd, a voice yelled out 'Rangeela... The colourful one.'

'Rangeela it is! His name shall now be Muhammad Shah Rangeela,' came another call.

Slowly the crowd started to thin out. Just then a Mughal noble named Janbaz Bakht rode up to where Qaraar and Abeerah were standing. He was a young lieutenant in the Mughal army whose father was a general like Shahbaz Khan. But there was more to it. Abeerah had punctured his ego by rejecting his marriage proposal.

Mounted on his steed and facing Qaraar and Abeerah, he thundered, 'How dare you belittle the emperor with a frivolous title?'

Hari Das in the meantime signalled to Munna Mia, who started running towards Hunar-Abaad.

'Why don't you tell the emperor? He might just love the title and may even honour you with more fake medals,' replied Qaraar.

Abeerah buried her face in her dupatta holding back her laughter.

Janbaz Bakht directed his response at Abeerah. 'As for you Abeerah, it's not befitting for you to be frolicking with this craftsman...' Then he looked at Qaraar with a sarcastic smile and completed his sentence, '...who hasn't created a thing in Shahjahanabad – word will reach your father,' said Janbaz Bakht still mounted on his horse and swivelling the reins aggressively.

'Go on,' replied a defiant Abeerah. 'He knows.'

'But he still shuts his eyes,' came Janbaz Bakht's retort. 'I will open them for him.'

Just then Munna Mia entered the fray leading Haidar by the reins. Hari Das had sent for his friend's horse knowing it would be demeaning for Qaraar to walk back on foot while Janbaz Bakht was mounted. But Qaraar went a step further. He mounted Haider and reached his hand out to Abeerah, who instead of going to her palanquin, gave her hand willingly to Qaraar. The next second she was mounted on Haider with Qaraar's arms around her.

Looking at Sauda, Dard and Mir, Qaraar held his arm up in the air and announced, 'Dinner at Hunar-Abaad and Hari bring your Ottoman traveller friends too… they will make for interesting conversation.'

With a nudge to Haider, a quick turn of the reins and a glancing look at Janbaz Bakht, Qaraar rode away with Abeerah. Hatim Khan, the Kaleem brothers, Ahmad Bokhari, the Afghan dry fruit sellers and Holar Pasha the animal trainer let out a huge cheer for the fantastic sight of the steed-mounted lovers. It seemed as if all of Shahjahanabad were celebrating them.

The dastarkhwan was laid out on the floor at Hunar-Abaad. But Zainab Begum hadn't been expecting so many. Nevertheless, she played the perfect host.

'Ah what a surprise! Abeerah, you look like a glowing moon, a mehtaab,' exclaimed Zainab on seeing the one she was sure would become her daughter-in-law. She kissed Abeerah's forehead and gave a warm embrace.

'Qaraar, how brave of you, my Dildaar son! You've brought her home,' she said, patting Qaraar's shoulder as the two entered the house.

'Yes Ammijaan, but we have some other guests too. These are Ottoman travellers… Hari trades with them,' said Qaraar as he stretched out his hand to welcome the guests in.

'Tie your camels up by the entrance and do, please, come in,' said Qaraar.

Immediately Zainab Begum drew her dupatta as a veil across her face and went towards the kitchen. These were men she didn't know, and much more cooking needed to be done. 'Get the biryani going, ensure you put the right amount of saffron in the rice and let's make some... murgh mussallam... and baingan curry... we have more guests,' she said aloud as she scurried towards the kitchen.

Hearing all the noise, Faiz Ali emerged. As his wife was passing him and heading towards the kitchen, he grabbed Zainab Begum's arm. 'Is that Abeerah?'

'Yes, it certainly is. My son has brought her home,' she replied with a shy smile but with a sense of pride, straining her neck upwards.

'Are you mad, Zainab? This is not the right way to do things. If they really want to get married, we should be going to her house with a proposal... not like this.'

'Oh, come on, let the couple be! Look how magical they look together. He, slim and tall, she, like a rose. Aaah! Just so beautiful – now go to them and be courteous,' said Zainab Begum releasing her arm from her husband's grip and walking towards the kitchen.

'Please make yourselves comfortable,' Faiz Ali said approaching the crowd who greeted him with bows.

The men settled on the charpoys in the courtyard and the hookah did the rounds as Abeerah went to the kitchen to help Zainab Begum. The aroma of crushed tomato curry with garlic, coriander and red chillies cooked over wood fire chulas wafted out from the kitchen and soon filled the courtyard.

'Tell me Huzoors,' began Faiz Ali as he closely inspected the distinctively Turkish-looking Ottoman travellers in their red fez caps and robes, and sporting light brown drooping moustaches that ran down the sides of their lips, 'What is the state of the empire in the Ottoman lands?'

One of the travellers who had until then been distracted with the fresh aromas coming out of the kitchen said, 'Not very good, Agha. After the defeat at the walls of Vienna, the empire is on the retreat. Budapest and Hungary are lost, Belgrade too has gone and constant war with Nadir of Persia is depleting the treasury. There is a sense of great depression and sorrow in Istanbul these days,' he concluded with a sigh.

'Not dissimilar to here,' added Qaraar.

The second Ottoman traveller, ran his thumb and index finger down the sides of his moustache and said, 'The balance of world power has shifted.' He immediately got the attention of all with this rather sweeping political statement. The young poets, Hari Das and Faiz Ali sat up and listened closely.

'The West as we know it has been rising steadily,' he continued. 'Europe, a land we once considered inhabited only by barbarians has changed dramatically.' By now, Qaraar too was keenly attentive.

'Through navigational mastery of the oceans, they have discovered new worlds. It all began more than 200 years ago when that Columbus fellow crossed a gigantic ocean and discovered a massive land mass. They call those lands the 'New World'. Britannia, Spain, Portugal, France, the Dutch – they have all been setting sail and exploring... while we the Easterners – the Ottomans, Persians and Indians – are now confined to our dwindling realms,' concluded the traveller, sighing and puffing at his hookah.

'But surely there is nothing in those... what are those lands called... New World?' asked Faiz Ali with a puzzled look on his face.

Qaraar joined the conversation finding it intellectually stimulating, 'Abbajaan, I have read about those discoveries.'

'The West is indeed propelling forward they sailed here too,' explained Qaraar.

'That's true,' said the second Ottoman traveller. 'But the West hasn't just acquired mastery of the oceans, they are pushing the barriers of science. Some time back, I met an Englishman on one of my journeys to Hindustan and he spoke of one Ishaaq Neeweton... or a name like that. He had recently died ... but what is remarkable is that this fellow had been studying the old Persian and Indian mathematicians and had apparently developed new theories on gravity... while all this is happening in the West, we watch with an idle spirit,' he concluded with another sigh. 'There will soon be a voyage that Britannia will send further East.'

'Further East?' inquired Faiz Ali, 'Where will they go? Fall off the earth?'

Laughter broke out but Qaraar was not amused, 'They believe that there is land beyond Indonesia,' replied Qaraar. 'In fact, if we had the vision, the emperor should sanction a joint-discovery project with the Ottoman Sultan to go beyond Indonesia and investigate what lies there,' continued Qaraar.

Faiz Ali stepped in, 'Beyond Indonesia? First let him try and save whatever is left of his empire here, my son. That itself would be a miracle.' He finished off with a laugh.

'But that's what I mean Abbajaan, we – the Ottomans, Persians and Indians – are so caught up in our inner struggles that we have lost the hunger for further oceanic and scientific discoveries. Britannia, France, Spain too have their conflicts, but they are the ones now with the desire to explore...' Qaraar replied.

Faiz Ali dismissed what Qaraar had just uttered with a wave of his hand, 'To me, the Europeans will always be playing catch up.'

'Not true,' said Qaraar. 'They have had their Renaissance. Men like Leonardo da Vinci experimented with science and art and he even tried to invent a flying machine.'

'Leonard... what?'

'Leonardo da Vinci – the Omar Khayyam of the West. A scientific genius and a painter too.'

Hearing the word 'painter', Faiz Ali looked around with a smile hoping to get an approval from the others and said, 'Oh don't tell us Easterners about art, painting and architecture. We are giants in those fields. Look at our buildings, mosques, temples, miniature paintings, calligraphy. Europeans can't match us.'

'Dinner!' announced Zainab Begum gleefully.

Displeased that the conversation was interrupted, Qaraar hoped to keep it alive, 'I am going to petition the emperor to send a voyage further...'

'Ah – let's feed these young poets who have been silent, come along,' said Faiz Ali cutting of his son's sentence.

'...East, beyond Indonesia,' whispered Qaraar to himself and finished his sentence.

All sat on the floor as the dastarkhwan was spread. The aroma of biryani, baingan curry and the murgh mussallam was everywhere. Taking leave after the meal, all kissed Faiz Ali's hand and made their way out. Qaraar walked with them to the main gate to see them off.

'Sauda, Dard, Mir, it was the most wonderful evening at the steps. When do we hear you again?' enquired Qaraar as the three poets rode out.

'Soon. Try and acquire the longing and the patience of a poet's heart,' replied Sauda as he waved goodbye.

Hari left in his carriage, while the Ottoman travellers mounted their camels and slipped into the night.

Abeerah waited in the dark alleyway just adjacent to the main gate. It was so narrow that barely a horse could pass through it, and as a result, hardly anyone used it. Qaraar had given it a name – 'Poshida kucha', the hidden alley. Qaraar walked upto her and touched her face gently.

Then he held her in his arms and without saying a word, kissed her.

Breaking the kiss, he said, 'By Allah, I have missed you – a fortnight is too long!'

'I'm here now,' she whispered, and he kissed her again.

There was rustling not too far away. Abeerah's palanquin bearers were making their moves having seen the other guests leave. She had to go.

Qaraar soaked his right hand in the rose water which shimmered in the marble cauldron and ran his fingers through her lose hair.

'Write to me soon,' then slightly lifting her gharara, she ran to her palanquin.

Abeerah resembled a pearl disappearing into the dark night. Qaraar ran into the house and up the stairs to the terrace from where he saw Abeerah's palanquin winding its way out of the silent narrow lanes. His bed was already made by the servants and he lay down trying to sleep. His mind wandered all over the place. Abeerah and her love, the state of the empire, his poet friends, the conversations with the Ottoman travellers and also what Janbaz Bakht had said – 'he was a craftsman who hadn't created anything'. He shut his eyes.

He woke up in the middle of the night. A lone minstrel fakir's distant voice was gently reverberating in his ears. Qaraar rose from his bed and looked below into the streets. A few candles and lamps lit some paths. Shahjahanabad was lost in slumber. But there was the wandering minstrel fakir Baba Ilyas emerging from a corner. He was the same fakir who had met Faiz Ali and had called Abeerah, an intoxicated deer lost in Qaraar's forest of love. Now he hummed a different tune.

'He has the skill of the lost blue girih. He has the heart of a lion. He has the generosity of the earth. Shah Rezaan, the Sufi has come. Shah Rezaan, the artist has come.'

Looking up at Qaraar who stood on the terrace, the fakir, dressed in rags, nodded, smiled and disappeared into another street.

Qaraar's spirit rose almost immediately on hearing Shah Rezaan's name. Qaraar's life was about to change. He would find his teacher. He would create.

CHAPTER 2

THE SUFI'S SCENT

Shah Rezaan was eighty-years-old and originally from Isfahan. A scholar of Sufi philosophy and literature he lived the life of a recluse. The aspect of Sufism that he had mastered was how to meditate on the divine attribute of beauty, and inspired by that, understand geometry and then create the most stunning girih tiles. With the swift decline of the Safavid Empire and the patronage to the arts dwindling, Shah Rezaan had found it difficult to relate with the emerging power dynamics in Persia. The rise of Nadir Shah and his barbarous ways convinced him that he had to leave Persia. Having found his way to Delhi, Shah Rezaan took up residence in a caravanserai just outside Mehrauli and next to the shrine of Qutub sahib.

'Take me to him,' requested Qaraar after finding Baba Ilyas, in a narrow alley, singing to some children.

'To Shah Rezaan? I saw you listening to my song last night Qaraar sahib! Come with me!' came the fakir's quick response.

At the shrine of Qutub sahib, the fakir led Qaraar into a small room in which was the trunk of an enormous neem tree. Not wanting to cut down the tree, the keepers of the shrine built the walls of the room around the tree trunk. There, Qaraar saw Shah Rezaan seated under the tree. The Sufi was sitting with his legs folded under him. His eyes were shut, and he seemed deep in contemplation also known as tassawuf. His hands were shut in a fist and rested on his knees. The fakir gestured by tapping his hands on the ground for Qaraar to sit on the floor.

Shah Rezaan had an extremely light complexion. His silver eyebrows fell over his eyelids and his trimmed white beard almost seemed to merge with his facial complexion. He kept his hair long and the white tresses fell below his shoulders. He wore a light peach robe and a light fawn coloured conical tall cap made of fur. The fragrance of the incense burning next to him filled the small room. After a few moments, Shah Rezaan opened his eyes, lifted his head and opened his shut fist. A few dates were within and he offered them to Qaraar and the fakir.

'What brings you here young man?' asked Shah Rezaan in the softest of velvet voices.

'Learned one, I wish to learn,' said Qaraar, altering his voice to make it softer than that of the Sufi.

'If you call me the learned one, I cannot teach, because I still learn,' said the Sufi. 'I am just a seeker,' he continued with a smile.

The humility of the sage struck Qaraar. He reached forward and took the Sufi's hand in his. Then he kissed it and placed it on his eyes as a mark of respect.

'It's girih tiles that I wish to learn.'

'Why do you want to learn this art?' asked Shah Rezaan.

'Because of their beauty.'

'Jawab khoob ast... Good answer, if you had replied for fame and fortune, I would not teach... Do you have access to kilns?' enquired Shah Rezaan.

Feeling left out of the discussions, the fakir elaborated about Qaraar's family background, their workshops and kilns.

'I will not teach amidst crowds. Set up kilns somewhere else,' said Shah Rezaan, lighting a few more incense sticks.

'I have an orchard and there I will set up new kilns!' said Qaraar with child like enthusiasm.

Shah Rezaan seemed pleased. 'A kiln in an orchard! Come and get me when you have it all set up. Enough for today young man – it's time for me to feed the poor.'

Rising up, Shah Rezaan made his way to a large cauldron known as a degh in which he had prepared halwa. In a few moments, scores of destitute began queuing up. The fakir left Qaraar's side and took his place in the line-up. With the glow of kindness on his face, the Sufi handed out earthen pots filled with warm halwa to the starving men and women. Qaraar took in this sight and left, all the time facing the Sufi, ensuring he didn't turn his back. He traced his steps backwards right till he got to his horse.

For the next month Qaraar went about building a kiln in the mango orchard at night with the help of some loyal craftsmen from his workshops. Abeerah visited him after a fortnight and her presence beside him encouraged him even further. Abeerah gazed at Qaraar, so deeply involved in building those kilns – and she felt that finally, Qaraar was onto something. She didn't quite know what it was, and neither had Qaraar expressed a clear outline of what he wanted to achieve by acquiring the knowledge of making girih tiles. Taking breaks during the intense days of building the kilns, Qaraar and Abeerah would sit under the mango trees looking at the young fruit bursting through their once fledgling buds. It was summer now and the couple anticipated their first harvest.

'The kilns are ready and await you,' Qaraar declared, with his right palm pressed against his chest. It was a month since he had last seen the Sufi.

'Also bring your belongings with you, please. I have built a small shack for you to stay in the orchard,' he added.

As Shah Rezaan entered the orchard he was unable to take his eyes off the beautiful tree formations. Settling into his shack, he asked, 'Who laid out these trees?'

Qaraar who was tying his horse's reins to a drooping branch hesitated to answer.

'Go on young man, there is a feminine touch to this orchard.'

'Has the fakir been saying things to you?' replied Qaraar, walking up to Shah Rezaan after harnessing his horse.

Shah Rezaan kept quiet but continued arranging his books, incense sticks and prayer beads by his floor seating.

'The one I love has laid them out,' said Qaraar looking at his orchard.

'Good. I am pleased that there is ishq in your heart. Without ishq there is nothing, we can't even start our work. Now you need to show it through your hands in the kilns. Let's get to work,' said the Sufi.

'Before we make girih tiles you first have to love the kiln, the clay and most importantly, the heat,' explained the Sufi as the two entered the kiln.

'The clay won't obey you at first. The furnace in the kiln will test you. Give the clay and kiln love and see beauty in it and you will succeed,' advised Shah Rezaan.

'For the next few months you will be focused only on brick making. Make the perfect slim Lakhori brick. Then we will progress to tiles.'

'As you say.'

Wanting to take the conversation to girih tiles, a train of thought that pleased him most, Qaraar then said, 'My friend Hari Das's spring caravan left for Persia more than a month ago via Badakhshan and I ordered sacks of lapis lazuli stones. They should come in with his returning caravan and I could use them for the...'

'Blue paste for the tiles?' enquired the Sufi, interrupting Qaraar, and continuing with a soft warning, 'Don't be over ambitious... begin with the slim Lakhori bricks,' said the Sufi.

Shah Rezaan's plan was to test Qaraar's endurance in Delhi's searing summer heat. The Sufi and the pupil went to work. As temperatures soared, Qaraar sat for hours on a small stool in the kiln, bare-chested, striving to mould clay into a perfect thin Lakhori brick. Time and again he failed, with Shah Rezaan rejecting and casting them away because they weren't slim enough. The sun beat down with enormous venom. Qaraar felt rivers of sweat drip down his forehead, back, arms and chest, forming a pool where he sat. Day after day Qaraar failed. He would start moulding the clay at dawn and present his shapes to the master by midday only to be rejected. Sitting under a tree he would break bread for quarter of an hour and then enter the kiln again. At dusk, Qaraar, with whatever little energy he could muster, would mount Haider and ride back to Hunar-Abaad. This went on for a month. Failure after failure. Then she came to see him.

Dressed in a white gharara, Abeerah wore no jewellery out of respect for, the simple hermit. Standing beside a mango tree, a fair distance from the Sufi's shack, Abeerah veiled up to her eyes and watched the Sufi reject Qaraar's bricks with every presentation. While returning to the kiln Qaraar glanced at her as she nervously played with her fingers and caressed her wrist.

'How slim they are,' thought Qaraar of her wrist and fingers.

He came close and held her by the arm and brought her to the kiln.

With eyes focused only on her slender wrist, his hands went to work.

Shah Rezaan watched this sitting at the entrance of his shack.

After a few hours on a tray he placed the moulded clay and presented them to his master.

'You have it,' whispered the hermit. 'And it's apparent that without her beauty, you can't create.'

'Now take them to the kiln and fire them in the furnace,' continued the Sufi.

The sun was at its zenith. The heat in the kiln was stifling. Qaraar entered the kiln and lit the furnace. Such was the intensity of the flames that sprang out, compounded with the summer heat, that Qaraar felt his eyelashes burn as he inserted the clay into the furnace. 'Stay close to the furnace and watch the reddening,' came the Sufi's voice.

With blurring sight, Qaraar fixed his gaze on the furnace. After an hour, the Sufi's velvet voice was heard again.

'Pull them out gently and bring them to me,' he said.

Qaraar, barely able to take the steps, stumbled and fell at the Sufi's feet. The slim bricks scattered everywhere. Abeerah rushed towards him. The Sufi looked at her. She held back. Shah Rezaan examined the bricks without touching them.

'Perfect,' uttered the gentle voice.

'Now repeat it,' he added.

The entire afternoon Qaraar did multiple repetitions of the same process. By the time it was dusk his legs could barely hold him up. Abeerah seated him down under a tree. She had questions. What was driving him? But Abeerah didn't ask. She only helped him sip some water from an earthen cup.

'Natiya,' she called out to her maid who appeared and spread the white cloth for an early dinner. As had been the practice on so many occasions, the couple shared their fortnightly evening meal in the orchard.

'Some of the mangoes are ripening quickly,' said Shah Rezaan with a smile as he inspected a few trees. The comment was also a hidden hint at Qaraar's progress.

'Might I pluck just one, even though it's not quite ripe? I will store it in a straw basket and wait for it to ripen,' requested the Sufi.

'Zaroor!' came Qaraar's tired reply, with a slight nod of his head.

'Please join us for dinner,' said Abeerah holding up her veil.

Caressing the mango Shah Rezaan replied, 'No thank you… He is ready to learn girih patterns,' summed up the Sufi as he closed the straw door to his shack.

'Abeerah!' called out Shahbaz Khan. There was a gentleness to his voice when he took his daughter's name. Having finished his military exercises, Shahbaz Khan had returned home. He stood with his hands spread out in the air. Two men were busy taking off his armour.

'Abbajaan!' came the daughter's reply as she rushed forward and wrapped her hands around him from behind. 'My Noor-e-Chashm, the light of my eyes,' exclaimed Shahbaz Khan, breaking the hug and then kissing his daughter's forehead.

'How is the emperor's army?' enquired Abeerah with a slight jest in her tone.

'Ah! We are still a reasonable fighting force,' said Shahbaz Khan, 'even though our emperor would much rather convert his garrisons into art galleries!'

Both father and daughter laughed as they made their way to the terrace of Basalat-Gah and settled under a crisp white shamiana, sipping on cool pink sherbets made of milk and crushed rose petals that a servant had just served.

'Seriously, Abbajaan, will the Empire survive?'

'Who knows my child,' replied Shahbaz Khan looking out towards the Jama Masjid which shimmered like a mirage in the Delhi heat.

'Ominous signs my child.' A frown now appeared on Shahbaz Khan's forehead and he pursed his lips.

'What do you mean?' pushed on Abeerah, as she saw her father tighten his grip on the sherbet cup. The conversation now had a tense tone.

'The winds blowing down from the Afghan mountains are carrying the stench of a jackal that has gathered a powerful force,' said Shahbaz Khan.

Abeerah looked at her father curiously as if wanting a name out of him.

In a hushed tone as if not wanting the wind to carry what he was about to utter, Shahbaz Khan whispered the name, 'Nadir.'

'He hides behind a veil. Waiting for his moment. He needs money to feed his bloodthirsty lot, and his eyes are scanning Persia which has nothing more to give him. Where will he turn next?' Shahbaz Khan seemed to be talking to himself, lost in his thoughts.

'No Abbajaan, I don't want to think about it!' said Abeerah, breaking her father's thoughts.

'O look, see who rides in, it's Janbaz Bakht!' exclaimed Shahbaz Khan, hearing the galloping sound of a horse entering his grounds.

The last time Janbaz Bakht had seen Abeerah, she sat mounted on Qaraar's horse with the craftsman's arms around her. Abeerah thought of that moment and prepared herself for any eventuality.

Walking to the edge of the parapet that overlooked the massive grounds which were part of his property, Shahbaz Khan looked below and saw Janbaz Bakht athletically jump off his horse as the general's servants took the animal away.

He then quickly turned and looked at his daughter with soft pleading eyes.

'No Abbajaan, I know that look in your eyes. My answer is still no!' said Abeerah, getting up to leave.

'O come Abeerah, stay my child. I haven't seen you for a week,' said Shahbaz Khan, still secretly hoping that Janbaz Bakht would improve his performance in front of his daughter.

The first time Shahbaz Khan had introduced the two with a hope that Abeerah might be impresed, all Janbaz did was hark about his accomplishments in the wrestling den. Wanting to please her father, Abeerah took her place at a little distance.

'Khushamdeed,' said Shahbaz Khan welcoming the guest with an embrace.

Servants brought an assortment of brightly coloured sherbets from which Janbaz Bakht chose one and gulped it down and went for another and another.

Seeing this Abeerah couldn't help herself.

'Did you lose in the wrestling den?' Her question had the sharp ring of sarcasm as it crashed into Janbaz Bakht's ears.

'Not quite, I pinned down my opponent, sat on his chest and pummelled away. Just then three of his compatriots held me from behind and I flung them with one arm…'

'Alright, we get the picture,' said Shahbaz Khan, as Abeerah smiled and shook her head.

'Tell me, what brings you here?'

'A frontier spy informs us that some of the Mughal caravans are being raided by Nadir's men,' replied Janbaz, a bit annoyed that he wasn't able to go on with his self-gloating.

'That's not a good sign,' Shahbaz Khan locked his hands behind his back and began pacing the terrace.

'Let's send out a force to teach Nadir's men a lesson. Let's kill them all!' shouted Janbaz Bakht.

'And then what, Janbaz? Invite Nadir to retaliate with all his might? Don't be brash!' These weren't Shahbaz Khan's words, instead they came from Abeerah.

'With all due respect these are matters for soldiers, not for ladies – or for that matter, craftsmen!' came Janbaz's response, while looking at Shahbaz Khan.

'Careful Janbaz,' said Shahbaz Khan. 'I know your father well. Much mutual respect between us. But there is a line. Don't cross it.'

Janbaz had hoped for another response from the general. One that would have hopefully been about wanting to know more about the craftsman and his daughter. But the father didn't give him that window, and all that could now come out of Janbaz's mouth was an apology.

'I, uh, I am sorry...' he stammered.

'It's getting late and you have given me enough to think about,' said Shahbaz Khan holding up his arm in the direction of the stairs that would take Janbaz down to his horse.

A sullen Janbaz made his way out. Abeerah came and stood by her father who had moved to the parapet overlooking the grounds. She rested her head on his shoulder and watched Janbaz gallop away. As Janbaz's horse sped through the main gate and kicked up a dust cloud, from it emerged a limping Munna Mia. He still had a while to come, having to cover the vast grounds before he could make it to the house. Abeerah watched him approach with a smile.

She knew a perfumed letter was on its way. Shahbaz Khan chose to ignore Munna Mia.

'Abbajaan, Janbaz is a sword-wielding fool who hasn't picked up a book in his life. I can't live with a man like him,' she said, with her head still resting on her father's shoulder and her eyes trained on Munna Mia.

'The same can be said about your father,' Shahbaz Khan replied with a subdued laugh, walking towards a large marble basin which had ice cubes and chilled rose water mixed in it.

'Oh Abbajaan, you know that's not true.' Abeerah picked up a fresh white muslin cloth for her father as he splashed his face.

Shahbaz Khan busied himself in some papers that needed his attention on a table that stood close by under the shamiana. Abeerah stood at the parapet and watched Munna Mia leave after he had handed over a box and bag of kebabs to the servants below. Turning back and looking at Abeerah he bowed and did his salaam repeating it five times. The bowing and salaams went on till Abeerah reached out into her silver qalamdaan, pulled out a gold ashrafee and threw it towards him. The servants came up to the terrace and delivered the box and bag of kebabs.

Not interested in the kebabs, Abeerah broke open the seal of the box and pulled out a scented letter. She read the words. It began with a verse from Bedil, a poet who had died in 1720:

> This world is the place of truth
> Time will take us to the truth
> Let me exhibit the truth
> Meet me in the circle of passion
> Feel your heart.[47]

Bedil's philosophy of the world being the place of truth was similar in essence to Ibn Sina's thinking that the human soul and body experienced joy and despair here in this world. So too for Qaraar, paradise was here in this world. In his orchard.

Abeerah looked towards the Jama Masjid searching for Hunar-Abaad's terrace. Imagining, that she saw it, she whispered, 'There he is… wearing an angarkha in the softest, white muslin.' Lost in her thoughts, the letter slipped from her hands. Just then she felt a hand on her shoulder.

'Abbajaan!' she said, her dream breaking into reality.

Shahbaaz Khan wasn't smiling as he held the letter in his hand.

Holding her by the wrist he sat her down under the shamiana.

'Leave us,' his voice was firm, and the servants scurried towards the door.

'This is why I don't approve of Qaraar. He has this hold over you. You lose yourself,' said Shahbaz Khan as Abeerah sat with her head lowered.

'I have never doubted his pedigree. It's one that enthrals emperors. But he is a drifting wave that doesn't have a shore,' went on Shahbaz Khan.

A whisper managed to come out of Abeerah's quivering lips, 'He is a thinker.'

'He is indeed but that needs direction. It's not good enough to just think. Why doesn't he write, build, create – put his skills to use?' There was frustration in the father's voice.

'He is on to something, Abbajaan,' replied Abeerah still in a hushed tone. Out of embarrassment of the letter she hadn't lifted her head.

'What is it?' The general's voice got sterner.

'I don't know exactly Abbajaan, but…'

Shahbaz Khan interjected. 'I know of the presence of Shah Rezaan in Delhi. His reputation precedes him. A great Sufi and artist. I even know Qaraar has been spending time with him. Might I remind you young lady, your father is one of the most influential men at court. I know how to keep an eye on things,' continued Shahbaz Khan, peering into his daughter's eyes.

Shahbaz Khan knew his daughter had inherited his brave

qualities and expected a look of defiance from her, but instead he witnessed a helpless watering of her eyes.

'Oh aab deedah, teary eyes! Listen, my child,' he said, enveloping her in his arms.

'You are my Zeba... my beauty. I know what love is. Your mother meant everything to me. I brought you up with these very hands; there was no room left for anyone else in my heart. My life as a soldier is on the edge. If something were to happen to me, what would be your fate? This thought keeps me up at night; you must understand me.'

Abeerah snuggled into her father's chest as he spoke these words.

Shahbaz Khan's younger brother, a soldier too, had perished trying to put down a rebellion against the empire, and he didn't trust his sister. In her mid-sixties, she had a reputation for connivance and greed. It was Shahbaz Khan's massive house that sparkled in her eyes. On many an occasion, she had tried to seize control of the household affairs during the general's absence. It had got unbearable for Abeerah as she would find her aunt lounging on the terrace ordering the servants. Abeerah had told her off on several occasions, but the woman would wind herself into the house by bribing servants and instigating domestic turmoil within the staff. She was the one who had instigated the maid Natiya to pour wine for Qaraar, hoping that the mystical lover would fall for the maid, bringing her a great source of political intrigue to feed on. It was only because Shahbaz Khan had retaliated in the most ferocious manner by instructing the gate keepers to bar her from entry after she had dared to call Abeerah 'a motherless cub fit to be a hyena's morsel' that she had since desisted from getting into the house.

'Once you are married, I know you will be secure for life', continued the father.

'But, but... I am hopelessly in love with him,' she whispered and held her father closely.

For a few moments there was silence, and nothing was said.

'Right! Then with this bold admittance we don't need you to hide behind the excuse of those kebabs from that fraudulent fellow anymore,' remarked Shahbaz Khan, hoping to lighten up the conversation.

'Abbajaan!' said Abeerah with a smile, lifting her face from her father's chest.

Father and daughter walked towards the edge of the parapet and looked towards the Jama Masjid. Shahbaz Khan held his daughter by the shoulder and said, 'His parents must come formally requesting for your hand. I won't go to them. Ramzan will be beginning in a few days, an auspicious month.'

Demurely Abeerah asked, 'And you would accept the proposal?'

'Hmm… Yes, I would if it is he who makes you happy,' said the general turning to his daughter. 'But Qaraar must promise to focus on getting new assignments from the supreme architect and…'

'Oh Abbajaan, I'm so happy!' said Abeerah, shutting her eyes and ignoring the rest of the words that were streaming out of her father's lips.

'He must come to ask for your hand soon. Something tells me, time is short,' whispered Shahbaz Khan to himself, frowning and this time looking west, towards Persia.

'Today we begin girih,' said Shah Rezaan laying out a sketch of the girih patterns on his floor mat.

'As you can see,' he continued running his finger across the sketch, 'from the star will emerge precise geometric shapes; hexagons, pentagons, octagons and then the star comes back into the pattern. The continuous repetition and interlocking of these shapes creates the mesmerising effect.'

Qaraar felt a sense of excitement rising within him.

'The key is to acquire a sound understanding of geometry,' said the Sufi. Qaraar had a basic knowledge of the subject through his childhood education but it was a fading memory. 'But before we start, I will meditate and do zikr for an hour, as you will sit beside me and watch,' instructed Shah Rezaan.

Shah Rezaan carefully picked a word from a scripture that had a list of Allah's names. Then he spread out the girih sketch before him, folded his legs under him, shut his eyes and hummed the words, 'Ya Wadud.' The name was an attribute of the Divine. It meant, 'The Loving.' Sufis did zikr, a repetition of a particular attribute they felt close to. Qaraar watched and heard the zikr for an hour as Shah Rezaan's humming remained soft and consistent. After an hour, the Sufi lifted his head and blew over the girih sketch and Qaraar's open palms.

Then the scholar sage pulled out a large blank paper, a compass, a feathered pen, a ruler and some books.

'Study these books,' said Shah Rezaan as he handed over Omar Khayyam's *Treatise on Demonstration of Problems of Algebra* in which the author's construction of a geometrical theory of cubic equations was a genuine breakthrough.[48]

The second mathematician and author that Qaraar had to study was more specific to his pursuits. The works of Abul Buzjani.[49] His works on geometry and trigonometry advanced new means of solving equations with compass and ruler. He had figured out how to construct certain types of hexagons and polyhedral. Buzjani had also written a special book on geometry for craftspeople which Qaraar had to specifically study in detail. Qaraar carried the books and sat under the shade of a mango tree and busied himself in study. At sunset when it had cooled down, Abeerah's palanquin swayed in. The muscular African palanquin bearers lowered it gently and she stepped out. Abeerah had thought that she shouldn't wear any jewellery since she would be in the presence of the simple mystic Shah Rezaan, but the unbridled ecstasy she felt before coming to see Qaraar having got the consent from her father to marry him, prevailed over austerity. She wore a sensuous sapphire choker round her neck. No other jewellery.

Sitting beside her lover she gazed at him for a while. The setting of books, compass, feather pen and ruler puzzled her.

'The mathematical works of Omar Khayyam and Buzjani. I need to study them before I can design,' said Qaraar sensing her confusion.

'It will be a month of science, spirituality and art,' he continued as the lovers watched Shah Rezaan walking in the orchard and entering his shack. He reached out for a different cap this time. It was a Sufi cap of the Qadriyya order. The same order that Dara was inclined towards. Crimson in colour, the cap had magenta flower designs. At the bottom of the cap were two black fur rolls that encircled its base. Putting it on meant it was time for the nightlong tassawuf contemplation. He then asked Qaraar to inform him if he spotted the crescent that would signal the beginning of Ramzan the next day.

As for Abeerah, she just wanted to be with Qaraar.

'Come on, study away my mystical mathematician,' she said with mischief in her voice. Then looking at Natiya and the palanquin bearers she said, 'Let's get started.'

Abeerah had decided to decorate the orchard with swings.

'Of course,' replied Natiya, an attractive woman from Bengal. Dusky skin, large eyes and full lips were the main features of her face. At times, encouraged by Abeerah's aunt, and during Abeerah's absence, she had visited her mirror and dressed herself in her ghararas and mimicked the aristocratic mannerisms of Mughal nobility. While she undoubtedly had a beautiful face, Natiya had the most sinister cackling laugh. And when she burst into it her left eyelid shrivelled up and shut. But there was more to her. Natiya had willingly become part of a more devious plan whose chief architect was Abeerah's aunt. Weaving a dream for Natiya, she told her that if she successfully lured Qaraar, Abeerah would be beyond devastated, and this would mean Natiya could marry Qaraar herself and get respectability. The aunt would then have an opening to ingratiate herself to her brother and convince

Shahbaz Khan to force Abeerah to see the folly of loving a dreamer like Qaraar and instead marry her away to Janbaz Bakht. Shahbaz Khan's large home could then become her playground once again.

But Natiya hadn't been successful as Qaraar showed no interest in her. While an intuitive Abeerah had suspected Natiya's motives, especially when Natiya had swayed her hips towards Qaraar and tried to fill his wine cup, she hadn't sacked her only because the maid had begged forgiveness and told her about the poverty of her family in Bengal whom she claimed to support. It was a lie.

The swings were made of light bamboo. Easy to hang and strong enough to carry the weight of one individual, Abeerah wanted the swings everywhere so she could entertain their common friends in the evenings.

'This branch is strong enough,' said Natiya, 'and look the other one too – hang one here,' she said looking at the palanquin bearers.

'No!' came Abeerah's response. 'You can suggest, but don't instruct the palanquin bearers to put them up. I will do that.'

'But it's…'

'Natiya!'

'As you wish.'

'Follow me,' said Abeerah as the palanquin bearers obeyed.

Seeing Abeerah busy at the other side of the orchard, Natiya made her way towards the tree under which Qaraar was studying and busy making angles and drawings with the compass and ruler. Through the branches, Natiya could see the fine lines of Abeerah's hour-glass figure now at a fair distance. She came and stood right next to Qaraar overlooking him. The maid chose a branch and played with its leaves.

'The summer heat is a killer, isn't it, respected Qaraar sahib?' she said, ensuring her dupatta dropped from her head and neck revealing her cleavage.

'Hmm, did you say something?' came Qaraar's reply, still buried in his books.

'Listen, go and ask Abeerah begum to fill my wine cup!'he continued.

Natiya felt jilted. 'Uff,' she said and stormed off.

'Qaraar sahib would like his drink,' said Natiya to Abeerah, looking at the ground and playing with the edge of her dupatta.

'How do you know?'

'He said so.'

'What were you doing hovering around him?' asked an intuitive Abeerah.

'I wasn't. He saw me and instructed me!'

'...saw me?!' said Abeerah under her breath, making her way to her lover and ordering the palanquin bearers to bring the wine cup and flask, while keeping up a fiery look at Natiya who didn't dare raise her head.

Abeerah sat next to Qaraar and poured him a cup of wine. Placing the cup next to him she looked around the orchard. A large number of trees now had swings on them, and it gladdened her heart. Qaraar was busy. Abeerah wanted his attention.

'A drink for the philosopher?'

'Dare I say I feel a bit like Ibn Sina who needed wine to write,' said Qaraar. Taking a break, Qaraar held Abeerah as she sat beside him and rested her head on his shoulder. Natiya watched from a distance, standing next to the African palanquin bearers with a growing sense of jealousy.

'My love, Abbajaan has consented to our marriage,' Abeerah said. She could feel her pulse racing as she broke the news.

Qaraar felt a burst of joy. It ran through every nerve. But then as he thought of the words that she had uttered, the grip around Abeerah loosened. Almost as if he was letting her go. Abeerah sensed it.

'Am I just... just your muse?' she said, with a dip in her voice that just a few seconds ago had the ring of ecstasy.

Qaraar was silent. Now frustration and anger began overtaking the emotions of love in Abeerah.

'We can't go on like this. We have the consent of your parents and my father too. Am I to believe you don't want to marry me?'

Qaraar kept silent and rested the back of his head against the trunk of the mango tree. Then he spoke.

'There is nothing I want more. I have loved you from the moment I saw you at the emperor's jashn… but…'

'But I know, you aren't ready,' sighed Abeerah.

A sudden sense of insecurity gripped her. Not the kind that she might lose him to another woman, but that she might just lose him to pressure.

'Give me some time,' he said.

Quickly she took control of herself and acquiesced to his request. 'Alright, take your time. But can we at least celebrate that Abbajaan has consented?' said Abeerah. Qaraar smiled and embraced her.

'It might be Ramzan tomorrow,' she said looking into the sky which had now turned an orangish purple.

'Let's look for the crescent,' said Qaraar standing up swiftly and helping Abeerah up.

They wandered through the trees hand-in-hand looking up towards the sky trying to locate the crescent. The trees were dense and full and it was difficult to spot anything. After an hour of looking, finally through the branches of one tree, Qaraar saw the slenderest of curves. The hilaal crescent.

'Ramzan Mubarak!' said Qaraar. 'Ramzan Mubarak!' came her reply and the two embraced.

Qaraar went back to Shah Rezaan's shack and out of respect for the master, not wanting to enter and disturb him during his contemplation, he slipped a note through the straw door informing him that the hilaal crescent had been spotted. Although Shah Rezaan didn't touch wine, he did not object to Qaraar's drinking, considering it free will. After a few seconds Qaraar heard the Sufi's voice from the shack.

'The holy month begins tomorrow. Here keep this with you.

Tie it to yourself or a loved one. It will protect you.' A black thread came out from under the straw door. A charm.

'Shukriya,' said the pupil from outside the door.

Qaraar went up to where Abeerah was already seated in her palanquin. Sensing he was standing next to it, she drew the curtains. Qaraar tied the black thread around her ankle. A gentle kiss to her lips and her palanquin pulled away. Natiya hated every minute of it.

For the next four weeks Qaraar's study got intense. Shah Rezaan who fasted during Ramzan, regularly supervised his progress with intermittent tests and examinations. The pupil didn't fast, but the Sufi mentor once again considered it to be free will. He was just pleased that his student was making steady progress and doing well when tested. Qaraar became a rare visitor to his own home. He had got a charpoy placed in a dense tree enclosure on which he slept under the sky. Faiz Ali had by now virtually written off his son.

Soon the day that Qaraar had been waiting for, arrived. 'From today you will learn to make tiles based on the plans of Quli Khan's Mehrauli mausoleum,' said Shah Rezaan leading the student to the kilns.

Then the Sufi continued with a smile, 'Word has reached me that your friend Hari Das's caravans have arrived with lapis lazuli. I am sending for them. After you have drawn out the patterns you will crush some of those stones. We begin the crushing when I rise for sehri,' informed the Sufi. Qaraar spent the day drawing out the sketches. The next day at three in the morning, donkeys and camels stacked with 100 large sacks of lapis lazuli stones made their way into the silent orchard. Hari came personally to deliver them. Qaraar, who was awake all night, received his friend with an embrace.

'Why, have you pledged almost all that you have earned from the restoration of Shah Burj?' Hari asked in anguish, not letting go of his friend's embrace.

Buried under a tree were ten bags of gold coins, more than half of the fifteen he had received from Emperor Muhammad Shah. Breaking away from his friend's embrace, Qaraar dug out the ten bags.

'Here, take them.'

'Not before you tell me why,' whispered Hari.

'You will see – now go, old friend!'

Hari helped offload the lapis lazuli from the camels and donkeys and left.

At 3.30 am, under the supervision of Shah Rezaan, Qaraar and some of his artisans emptied a few sacks of lapis lazuli stones into large black iron bowls. Ten artisans along with Qaraar then held aloft iron rods shaped in the form of clubs. It was still a dark night but sensing dawn was not far, the nightingale began its cry. At that moment, Shah Rezaan raised both his hands in the air and let out a resounding cry, 'Bismillah, begin in the name of God.' With an enormous thud the crushing of lapis lazuli began. Relentlessly the artisans and Qaraar smashed into the stone, uninterrupted, for four hours. They finally took a closer look into the massive iron cauldrons. It was the most gorgeous blue. To this they added water. The blue paste of lapis lazuli now had a luminous lustre and a thick voluminous look. The paste was then carried away and stored next to the Sufi master's shack and covered with white muslin cloth.

By the time it was midday, Qaraar had been instructed to mould clay in the shape of the patterns he had sketched out. But the clay didn't hold its shape.

'The clay doesn't obey you,' said the Sufi walking up to a frustrated Qaraar who sat with his forehead resting in his clay covered hands.

Several attempts followed, but the results were no different.

The Sufi pulled up a stool and sat beside the pupil. 'Open your mind! Think of the different shapes as the diversity of mankind – different races, different cultures – but when interlocked they come together in harmonious beauty.'

'You must have heard of the great Sufi, Hazrat Abdul Quddus Gangohi?' he continued.

'Yes indeed.'

'A Muslim, he was influenced by the Hindu sadhus and yoga. They say he even performed the namaz in an upside-down position probably inspired by yoga positions.[50] He was a true Sufi. Different faiths interlocked beautifully within him.'

Qaraar held onto each word.

Then pointing at the patterns that Qaraar had drawn, Shah Rezaan said, 'Diversity interlocked in beauty.'

Shah Rezaan looked skywards, shut his eyes and spoke again, 'He is the whole. And within Him is the harmony of diversity... when you create these different shaped tiles, seek to become part of this harmonious whole... the geometric tile panel will then reflect your quest for union with Him.'

Qaraar rose and went back to work with a renewed spirit. This time the clay obeyed his hands and came into the geometric shapes.

'Reach for the blue paste,' said the master as he wandered around the trees counting the mangoes and spotting a variety of birds.

Qaraar and his artisans carried the iron pots in which the lapis lazuli paste was and placed them next to the kilns. The craftsman sat next to the clay panel that now had individual pieces in stars and geometric shapes. He dipped a fine brush in the lush blue paste and painted them. With each stroke, Qaraar felt he was giving life to mud.

'Painted!' called out Qaraar excitedly.

'Fire!' came the Sufis resounding reply, who had wandered into the distance smelling the ripened mangoes.

Qaraar thrust the panel into the furnace. He watched as the flames danced close to the blue clay.

'Come away and walk with me,' came the Sufi's call.

'The mangoes have ripened, and tomorrow is Eid,' said the Sufi looking at Qaraar.

'I forgot all about them! It's time to harvest! I need to inform Abeerah,' said Qaraar signalling to one of his artisans. He quickly wrote a letter informing her that it was harvest time and that she should come and bring maids and servants for the harvest. The artisan ran out of the orchard heading towards Munna Mia at the steps of the Jama Masjid who would carry the letter.

'Let's go and see your labour of love,' said the Sufi, as they made their way to the kilns.

The tiles were ready. Qaraar strode into the kiln and pulled out the tile panel as all the artisans gathered around. As temperatures cooled and jaws dropped, the glazed tiles emerged from the smoke. Like a constellation the blue patterns sparkled. Qaraar slipped on his gloves and held the panel aloft.

'The stars of the heavens, I hold them in my hand!' he yelled.

'Take them to Quli Khan's Mehrauli mausoleum and replace the broken panel with this,' instructed the Sufi.

Qaraar ran towards Haider and mounted him but just before he was about to gallop away, Shah Rezaan spoke again, 'Meet me at Humayun's Tomb… I will get some candles and red sandstone. Together we will restore a stone screen… It'll be a long night before Eid.'

EID

'He doesn't even look at me,' said Natiya to Askari Begum, Abeerah's aunt, as she visited her at her home not far from the Jama Masjid. Askari Begum had divorced two of her previous husbands, had an affair with a cook and another affair with a general. She had spent all the meher money she had received as part of her divorce settlements from her previous husbands and was running low on cash. The house she currently lived in was a small one-bedroom hovel she had received from the general she had had an affair with, after blackmailing him with dire consequences. But now she had set her eyes on a target – her brother, Shahbaz Khan's house.

Askari Begum wasn't the greatest beauty, but despite her ordinary looks had once glittered in Mughal society with rich conversations on literature and politics. Now though, she had fallen on hard times.

'A maid will always be a maid!' sighed Askari Begum, reclining on her couch and cutting supari – with a silver cutter. Natiya sat on the floor cross-legged and heard her.

'Swaying your hips and revealing your breasts are not going to get that enlightened craftsman,' said Askari Begum spitting the red juice from the paan she was chewing into a spitula. Natiya had told her the details.

Continuing with her disparaging tone, 'Here read these – some verses of Hafez. The greatest love poet. You won't understand him for sure, but rote learn some and when you get the opportunity recite them to him. Now dafa ho!... get lost!... I have to prepare sheer khurma for that Hatim Khan.'

'The kebab seller?' enquired Natiya, with a surprised expression and her hand covering her mouth.

'He better come and spend Eid here with me, or else... I will tell his wife,' the last two sentences she spoke under her breath.

'Yes, the kebab seller,' she re-emphasised looking at Natiya, who still had the look of shock on her face. 'What am I to do? I have to lower myself to his level! My brother has almost disowned me. I'm running low on money and at least with the pleasure that damn kebab seller draws from me it ensures there is food on my table!'

Natiya continued to listen.

'That's why Natiya, if you play your part well our days will be filled with gold, silver and parties. Off you go now. I'm sure Abeerah will be going to see Qaraar today.'

'Yes, yes she is. I will be going with her. And don't worry Begum Sahib, we will get that big house and will have a good life together with Qaraar sahib by my side,' she said, unleashing her sinister cackling laughter.

Meanwhile at Hunar-Abaad, Zainab Begum had woken early to prepare for Eid. In the morning freshness, she had kept a close eye on the stirring of dishes. The cuisine ranged from Aash, an Afghan meat dish, murgh badami, to koftah in a thick tomato gravy. And for dessert the famed sheer khurma. The food was ready to be mounted onto a mini caravan of horses and mules and head for Qaraar's orchard. There, an afternoon banquet had been planned. At the orchard, the food would be re-heated in large cauldrons burning over charcoal. Qaraar had sent Zainab Begum a message that it was harvest time and he wouldn't be coming home, further requesting that she and his father should celebrate Eid at the orchard with him.

Faiz Ali sat on a charpoy in the courtyard. A servant came and poured water through a silver kettle and Faiz Ali did his ablutions for his Eid prayers which he would perform at the Jama Masjid. Then the servant helped him put on his cream shervani and a tall black velvet cap. Just then Zainab Begum entered the courtyard.

Looking at his wife Faiz Ali said, 'So he isn't coming home to wish us?'

Zainab Begum changed the topic, 'I can't wait to see his orchard bursting with fruit.' Realising that his wife had ignored his question Faiz Ali shook his head in frustration.

'You look so handsome,' continued Zainab Begum walking upto her husband and adjusting the shoulders of his shervani.

'What a day! I have to go to see my own son on Eid.' With a swift frustrated hand movement Faiz Ali brushed the air and took his steps towards his horse, that his servants were holding for him outside the arched main gate.

It was pandemonium and a rush towards the steps of the Jama Masjid that greeted Faiz Ali as he manoeuvred his horse through the crowd, guided by his two servants in front of him. A galaxy of Mughal nobility came. Some on horses, the ageing in their palanquins, and exhibitionists on their elephants, all winding their way through the narrow lanes amidst cheers from the shop keepers, fakirs and destitute who hoped to get alms after the prayers. Faiz Ali's servants helped him dismount and he made his way up the steps of the mosque. As he walked under the tall pishtaq entrance he saw the fabulous three marble domes with the inverted lotus that his ancestors had carved out. The sight filled him with a sense of pride and humility.

Then, the emperor entered with the resounding beat of the massive naqqaras. Simply clad in a humble robe he took his place behind the Imam. Faiz Ali took his place too. The prayers began, and the emperor bowed repeatedly in unison along with the others, just like a commoner. To a bird perched on the minaret the men below must have seemed like a variety of poppies bowing in submission to the one creator. After the prayers, Faiz Ali was surrounded by the alms-seeking destitutes at the steps. Baba Ilyas, the fakir who had introduced Qaraar to Shah Rezaan was there too, entertaining children with jokes and Amir Khusrau's riddles.

Suddenly the fakir saw Faiz Ali descending the steps. Rushing to him, followed by the street children, he bowed and did an elaborate salaam. Feeling generous Faiz Ali rewarded the fakir and the children with coins. Making his way towards his horse, Faiz Ali felt a tug at his arm. It was Shahbaz Khan.

'May Allah bring unending joy to our families,' said the general with a slight smile and then swiftly moved away towards his horse, mounted it and left. It was a meeting that lasted like the sight of a dashing shooting star. Faiz Ali felt a sense of confused happiness. He, too, mounted his horse and left.

At the orchard Abeerah had arrived a few minutes before

Qaraar's family and it gave the lovers the most fleeting of moments in private.

'My love you are covered in clay and what are these blue marks?' asked Abeerah, looking at Qaraar's dishevelled look, unaware he had worked all night restoring a tile panel at Quli Khan's Mehrauli mausoleum and a stone screen at Humayun's Tomb.

'I made girih tiles yesterday… it felt like I held the galaxy.'

'I want to see them,' Abeerah insisted.

'Soon.'

Just when they were about to kiss, Qaraar noticed his family and servants winding their way through the mango trees.

Almost immediately the servants and artisans took up their positions around the trees, ready to harvest. Abeerah and Qaraar glanced at each other with a smile and gave the orders. 'Begin!' Nearly 1,000 straw baskets began their wobbly dance on the heads, hips and shoulders of the fruit-pickers as they got filled with mangoes. Lunch was laid out under a shamiana and a sitar player played under it. To counter the heat servants squirted rose water in the air. Qaraar was joined by his friends Sauda, Dard, Mir and Hari Das. Faiz Ali seemed to relax a bit although he shook his head in dismay seeing his son's clay dripping clothes. He told Zainab Begum of what Shahbaz Khan had said at the Jama Masjid and it brought a smile to her face. Amidst all this Natiya chose her moments to try and get Qaraar's attention. Having failed to memorise the verses Askari Begum had given her, she stooped to vile manoeuvres which included intentionally bumping into Qaraar and desperately trying to initiate a conversation. After a late lunch, Abeerah went to the swings. There, as the evening cooled, Abeerah swayed on one shyly looking towards Qaraar. It upset her that she hadn't been able to spend time with him; maintaining a painful distance she watched her lover surrounded by his friends, parents and artisans as he took them around the orchard. She wanted him all for herself but could only watch as the craftsman explained how Shah Rezaan had taught him girih. The Sufi wasn't there, having left early in the morning for Qutub Sahib's shrine in Mehrauli where he would cook the degh all day and feed the poor. He had also taken that one mango in a straw basket.

Zainab Begum came and sat on a swing next to Abeerah's. The two had a lot to say to each other and they did. Abeerah confided in her how her father had consented to her love and Zainab Begum spoke of the incident that morning between Shahbaz Khan and Faiz Ali. To both, it was now a given that marriage festivities weren't too far away. An excited Zainab Begum applied a bit of henna to Abeerah's palm as a sign that she had been taken in by the family. Then as the sun began to fade and disappear behind the trees, Abeerah prepared to leave. She had to go back and celebrate the Eid evening with her father. Natiya's failed attempts at luring Qaraar exhibited themselves in a huffed presence as she packed Abeerah's things. From a distance the lovers looked at each other. The incomplete passion hurt.

For the next few months Qaraar flung himself into a creative overdrive. He worked closely with Shah Rezaan and some of his senior artisans, who had acquired a sound understanding of architecture after many years of working with the supreme architect of the Mughal court. Together they developed plans. Qaraar would create a Mughal Pavilion in the orchard. It would be on a patch of west-facing land where he hadn't planted any trees. Qaraar instructed for long silk drapes to surround the area from where the pavilion would rise, and work would happen behind the drapes, in secrecy.

Monsoons lashed Delhi as summer gave way to the overcast wet season. Heat and fresh raindrops mingled in the earth which erupted in a smoky scent. Through lashing downpours and faint drizzles Qaraar and his artisans made Lakhori bricks and girih tiles. But within Abeerah, a melancholic monsoon feeling surged with great force. Sitting with the side of her face in her palm she attempted at doing the impossible: counting droplets as they fell from her windowsill.

Meanwhile through most of the monsoon nights, at Askari Begum's hovel-like home, the aunt lay awake besides Hatim Khan who was fat and short with thick stubby hands and fingers. A swine-like grunt as he snored not only prevented Askari Begum from sleeping, but also made her disgusted with her situation.

'Uuh… are you awake? And why are you looking at me like that?' said a startled Hatim Khan, rubbing the saliva dripping from the sides of his mouth as he sat up in bed and faced Askari Begum.

Askari Begum's close stare at Hatim Khan had such a venomous effect that it had woken him up.

'I was thinking of how life shows different colours,' said Askari Begum with a disgusted look on her face.

'It's two in the morning, I'd better go,' said a yawning Hatim Khan.

'Okay, go – get lost.'

'Careful now! All you aristocrats, I tell you, you're so arrogant. Remember if you want to eat, be very careful with your words,' he pointed at her and tied the knot of his pyjamas.

He continued, 'We kebab sellers are at the heart of Delhi's romance. Aunt sleeps with me and the niece's romance blossoms because of my crippled sidekick. Hah!'

'Yes, but there's a difference, she loves him,' said Natiya who was until then lying on the floor. 'Who cares about love?' said Hatim Khan and stormed out into the rain.

'Ah, what a life I once had,' said Askari Begum, flinging herself back into bed and staring at the damp ceiling.

Natiya crept to the side of the bed like a viper. Rain splashed on the windowsill and ricocheted onto the bed. 'Why don't we just…' said Natiya softly.

Askari Begum rose and looked outside as if to tell Natiya that she had not yet got her attention but could, if she said the right words.

Natiya came even closer and leaning into her ear, whispered the next words with quivering lips, 'Kill her.'

For a few seconds Askari Begum continued to look into the dark drenched night. Then she tightened her index finger against the tip of her thumb. A droplet had fallen on the sill but not ricocheted onto the bed. Askari Begum tilted her head and looked at that fresh droplet. With a tensed index finger against her thumb she released the finger. The droplet was destroyed.

'Death will be easy, but the ramifications would be difficult for us. Her end will be one which will do us no harm, but only bring benefits.'

On the tenth day of November, the advent of winter was gently announced by a cool breeze that descended on Delhi from the Himalayas. These winds blew in straight after Diwali. Hari Das had finished the celebrations with immense joy and satisfaction, but on that day in November he was rushing towards Hunar-Abaad. For many months, rumours had flooded the Jama Masjid area that Qaraar was on the verge of unveiling a stunning monument. Qaraar hadn't visited home for six months. Abeerah though, had visited him every two weeks and that had been his only connection with the outside world.

Some driven by curiosity, including Holar Pasha and the Kaleem brothers had tried to creep into the orchard to get a better view. They had even got as close as the drapes but Qaraar had spotted them and chased them away. The secrecy of what the craftsman was creating had even reached the emperor who had constantly enquired about Qaraar's plans, and whilst Faiz Ali was happy with the serious dedication shown by his son, he was embarrassed when he couldn't reply to the emperor's messengers.

'Four weeks from now, on the tenth day of December is when

Qaraar says he will pull down the drapes,' said a panting Hari to Faiz Ali as he ran into Hunar-Abaad.

'I should go personally and inform the emperor's grand vazier, Asaf Jah,' responded Faiz Ali rushing towards the door.

'Who else should we tell?' Zainab Begum enquired excitedly as her husband mounted his horse and his two servants led him into the narrow street.

'Everyone in Shahjahanabad, including Shahbaz Khan,' came the answer. His horse galloped away.

On the tenth day of December this is precisely what happened. Almost the entire population of Shahjahanabad made their way to the orchard. Generals, nobility, Sufis, Hari Das and the three poet friends; all had been invited. Then there were the gate-crashers that included fakirs, shopkeepers, including the Persian carpet sellers, Ahmad Bokhari, Holar Pasha with his sloth bear, parrot and rabbits, the Kaleem brothers, Hatim Khan and Munna Mia. It was impossible to control the surging crowds in the orchard.

The emperor's procession left the Red Fort and made its way towards the orchard, but the emperor had a worried expression about him. His elephant was flanked on one side by a horse mounted by Shahbaz Khan, who also had a shadow of anxiety on his face. Rumour had it that many secret meetings had been taking place regarding the state of empire and the rising external threats. It felt like something dramatic was about to happen. But this event was an opportunity for the art-loving emperor to forget those troubled discussions and indulge in creative pleasures.

As his procession passed Humayun's mausoleum, the emperor noticed the restored stone screen. His elephant, guided ably by the mahout, swayed past the mango trees in the orchard and came and stood in front of the drapes. Amidst the crowd, Shahbaz Khan noticed his daughter's palanquin at a distance. Zainab Begum brought her palanquin close to Abeerah's and the two parted their curtains and held each other's hand in nervous anticipation.

Although Abeerah had visited the orchard every two weeks, Qaraar hadn't revealed his work to her.

The standard-bearer then thumped the ground and looking at Qaraar said, 'O! Craftsman, reveal to Jahanpanah, what you have created!'

Just then Holar Pasha rushed forward and with a floor-kissing bow in front of the elephant said, 'By your grace, some entertainment first – if I may?'

The emperor with a smile gave permission to the animal tamer.

Holar Pasha signalled to his parrot that sat on his shoulder, which then flew over the crowd and then from branch to branch. 'Yaar O Yaar! Nigah kun! Nigah kun! Look here… Look here!' the parrot said while flying. 'This is a story of love between a craftsman and a beauty that all of Delhi has been speaking about,' it quipped. 'Today his hands will be tested.' The parrot flew back to Holar Pasha as the crowd hummed in agreement.

'Now behold the somersaulting bear,' said Holar Pasha as the sloth bear somersaulted and did cartwheels.

'And now I, the descendant of Ottoman nobility present…' continued Holar Pasha, as he got carried away with the applause.

'You are no descendant of Ottoman nobility!' came a voice from the crowd. Immediately Holar Pasha looked sheepishly to identify the voice.

'…and even if you are, hide your face in shame. They say your ancestor fled from the walls of Vienna,' came another voice. The Mughals and the Ottomans had a history of collaboration and news on campaigns were shared freely. Hearing the taunt, Holar Pasha scampered away, but not before the standard-bearer had handed him a few gold coins.

'Come forth, O craftsman, and present your creation to the emperor,' instructed the standard-bearer.

Qaraar had been standing behind the drapes with Shah Rezaan. Then parting the silk drapes, he presented himself.

'I have drunk the wine of Divine love, the same as Hafez, Rumi and Khusrau,' said Qaraar boldly and with one sweeping move he pulled the silk drapes.

'I present Husn-e-Jahaan – The Beauty of the World,' he said, while pulling the drapes away and revealing the pavilion.

'Aaah!' The crowd let out a deep gasp as if they had witnessed the face of an angel.

For moments there was just silence. The pavilion was petite but stunning. It had three slim pillars made from lakhori bricks covered in girih tiles. Like a never-ending blue sky, the lustrous geometric-pattern tiles clung to every part of the pavilion. The plinth on which the pavilion stood too had girih tilework, and so did the four steps leading into it.

Then, as if woken up from a dream, the crowd rushed forward to see and touch Husn-e-Jahaan. They had to be held back by the emperor's personal guard. This privilege was only for the emperor who gently caressed the pillars and walls and then nodded at his standard-bearer.

'Twenty sacks of gold coins for the craftsman, a monthly salary of 2,000 and an appointment as Chief Artisan to the court,' announced the standard-bearer.

'Subhan Allah,' said the crowd in unison, still being held back by the emperor's guards preventing them from approaching Husn-e-Jahaan.

Seeing the emperor back on his elephant, Qaraar stepped forward.

'Holder of the Realm, may this place be one where artists can thrive; may this be a place where you can hold your festivals.'

The emperor raised his hand.

'And one more thing, Jahanpanah. Our cultural realm is shrinking. Let's sail East. I petition you to send a voyage of discovery past Indonesia. Let's discover new lands, let's take our culture there – our poetry, our art, our sciences. Let's…'

The emperor's face clouded with worry. He sighed and looked at Shahbaz Khan who was still mounted on his horse as if to say,

'Why is he asking for something I cannot give?' Then his elephant turned and left. Qaraar watched as the emperor and the elephant became a silhouette against the setting sun.

Shahbaz Khan nudged his horse forward towards Qaraar. 'You provide much relief to our troubled minds. Look at what you have created!' he said with a pleasurable sigh. Leaning forward on his horse and looking at Qaraar and then at Husn-e-Jahaan he continued, 'It can make a man like me a poet,' he said, unable to take his eyes off Husn-e-Jahaan.

Qaraar held the reins of Shahbaz Khan's horse and standing erect, but with eyes lowered said, 'Huzoor, grant me my love. Allow me to marry your daughter.'

Shahbaz Khan was surprised by Qaraar's boldness, but he had a new-found admiration for the craftsman.

'Unlike the emperor not being able to consent to your petition to travel East, this is something I can consent to. She is yours, O weaver of magic!' said Shahbaz Khan with a smile, then nudged his horse past Qaraar and rode straight up to the pavilion for closer inspection. Turning the reins he said, 'She was never mine to give, always yours.'

Crowds were now allowed to come closer to the pavilion and leave in an orderly fashion. Qaraar went up to his parents who were stunned by the proceedings. To surprise them further he told them of his recent proposal. A speechless Faiz Ali and Zainab Begum fell into his arms. To Qaraar, though, Husn-e-Jahaan felt incomplete. Abeerah wasn't standing in it.

Her palanquin was not far away. Slowly it came close to Husn-e-Jahaan and she stepped out. Leaving the couple to themselves, Faiz Ali and Zainab Begum left along with Hari Das and the poets. Qaraar watched as last of the crowd disappeared. Then he saw Abeerah standing in the middle of the pavilion. She was Husn-e-Jahaan.

Just then a rider in full gallop made his way to Shahbaz Khan who was admiring the patterns. 'Huzoor, Janbaz Bakht refuses to enter this orchard but says he has to speak with you. He is at the gate,' said the rider. Shahbaz Khan immediately rode to the entrance.

Abeerah lay down sideways in the pavilion and lit a few candles. Qaraar came up to her and gently played with her hair.

'Your father said you were always mine.'

Abeerah's face burst into a bright glow. She knew what he meant and embraced him.

She ran her hands across his chest and whispered 'Dil chee ast agar atishfishan neest… What is a heart if it isn't a blazing volcano?'

Qaraar extinguished the flickering candle flames with his palms.

At the entrance of the orchard Shahbaz Khan heard out Janbaz Bakht.

'Nadir marches towards Delhi. He has turned down all requests for parley,' said Janbaz Bakht, burning with anger and also looking menacingly at the orchard.

Shahbaz Khan looked heavenwards. 'Allah help us.' Then kicking his horse into full gallop and looking at Janbaz Bakht he said, 'Follow me to the emperor – it's war.'

There was a rustle in the branches of a mango tree. Askari Begum had smuggled herself into the orchard. Stationed at the entrance she heard her brother. Knowing now that he would soon be clashing swords in the battlefield, a smile broke on her lips.

CHAPTER 3

A GENERAL SLAYER

1739

'O Refuge of the World, Jahanpanah. You have done so much to bring back the cultural realm of the Sufi,' said Shahbaz Khan.

He was standing before the emperor in the Diwan-e-Khas, in the Red Fort. The emperor had his favourite falcon fluttering on his left arm and the bird too seemed to listen attentively. The Diwan-e-Khas was teeming with the highest echelon of Mughal power. The Grand Vazier Nizam Asaf Jah, stalwart generals including Saadat Khan and Khan Dowran, subedars and mansabdars, the provincial governors were all there. The emperor sat with his legs folded under him on the spectacular Peacock Throne.

'The Sufi mind and the multicultural diversity are sprouting once again in this ancient land. Young saplings of intellect must be protected,' he continued, as all listened attentively.

It was true. Besides the arts, Muhammad Shah had patronised mathematicians and thinkers and encouraged them to work on creating more accurate astronomical tables, the result being the culmination of a work of great scientific importance called the *Zij-e-Muhammad Shahi*. Shahbaz Khan saw this as the rebuilding of sorts of the foundation on which the Empire stood, and so the fierce desire to protect it.

'Nadir is a savage. He has no compassion for the seeking, intellectual mind, he only desires to plunder the wealth of Delhi.

His war with the Ottomans has cost him and he needs more money to fight them and the Russians. We must defeat him,' said the veteran general. The emperor rose. The falcon fluttered its wings on being discomforted. With a clenched fist and a slight nod of his head the emperor signalled his approval to go to war. The Diwan-e-Khas in the Red Fort erupted in a loud resounding victory chant, 'Fateh Badshah Muhammad Shah Fateh.' Shahbaz Khan merged his divisions with Khan Dowran's, a renowned general and statesman. Janbaz Bakht's divisions fell under the command of the Grand Vazier Nizam Asaf Jah. Campaign planning now began with great rigour and a war council was called by Shahbaz Khan the next day.

A massive tent stood erected in the Red Fort. All generals assembled and poured over the map of Northern Hindustan with the emperor at the helm. Winter had peaked and fireplaces were placed in the four corners of the tent as attendants kept the fires in the aatishdaans under close supervision, regularly flinging cedar wood, which filled the tent with an aromatic fragrance.

'Here at Karnal in the Punjab will we meet him,' said Shahbaz Khan, stabbing the map with his dagger.

Crouching over the map but turning towards Janbaz Bakht, the Grand Vazier Nizam Asaf Jah asked, 'Our total number of gathered forces?'

'Nearly one million,' came the reply in a loud confident voice.

'2,000 cannons and 3,000 war elephants, including 50,000 elite cavalry. Nadir would never have seen something as magnificent as this,' said Janbaz Bakht.

'Spy information on enemy strength?' asked the Grand Vazier Nizam Asaf Jah.

'Uh, umm…' Janbaz stuttered.

'Approximately 150,000 in total – mostly musketeers,' Shahbaz Khan interjected.

After a pause, the over-confident Janbaz Bakht said, 'Hah! We outnumber Nadir. This should be easy.'

Shahbaz Khan sounded a word of caution, 'Don't forget he has the zamburak, his mounted swivel gun, which we don't.'

'We have the elephants, cannons and elite cavalry to pummel him,' came the response from Janbaz Bakht.

'He has the speed of his artillery with the zamburak and the spies inform us of the deployment of a new musket, the Jazayerchi, in his infantry that can be loaded faster than our muskets,' Shahbaz Khan cautioned again.

'Head to head we can crush him,' Janbaz continued with his belligerent tone.

'He won't go head to head with us, he will use deception and the speed of his lighter artillery.'

'Let's get to Karnal first and then decide tactics and strategy,' said the Grand Vazier Nizam Asaf Jah.

'That's not the way to win a war, let's plan this now,' insisted Shahbaz Khan.

'The plan is simple. We hit him straight and hit him hard. Like a sledgehammer,' continued Janbaz, looking at the Grand Vazier Nizam Asaf Jah who also seemed convinced that with the enormous numbers on their side Nadir would wilt.

'Decision taken. We go to Karnal and overwhelm him with numbers. Chances are that he will run seeing us approaching,' said the Nizam Asaf Jah. Then looking at the emperor he continued, 'We will head out for Karnal immediately. The rest can follow later.' The emperor agreed. Having said what he had to, the Nizam Asaf Jah bowed facing the emperor and left the tent with him.

Knowing that his divisions were under the Nizam Asaf Jah, the supreme commander, in many ways it made Janbaz Bakht feel more powerful than Shahbaz Khan. He had also heard that Shahbaz Khan had consented to his daughters' romance and so took the opportunity to slight the general, 'We will head out tomorrow while you and Khan Dowran follow after a few days. Keep an eye on all the arrangements for the 110-mile journey to Karnal. And let's ensure we really show off the immense military might to the people of Delhi.' Saying this, Janbaz left.

Shahbaz told the fire attendants to leave the tent too. A semblance of restrained sanguinity returned to the tent. Khan Dowran approached Shahbaz Khan who stood before a fireplace and gazed at the dying flames. Sensing Khan Dowran's presence behind him, Shahbaz Khan said, 'Your thoughts?'

'Nadir is a military genius.'

'Indeed, he is, the Ottomans know that well,' said Shahbaz Khan, referring to Nadir's wars with the Ottomans.

'Tiring out his men is going to be the key to winning this war,' Khan Dowran went on.

Now Shahbaz Khan turned and faced the battle seasoned veteran.

'They are the ones who have crossed mountains and rivers to get here. He will go for a quick victory, but we need to prolong it – engage in short bursts,' continued Khan Dowran.

'Good to know we will be fighting together,' said Shahbaz Khan.

Placing his hand on Shahbaz Khan's shoulder, Khan Dowran reassured him. 'We leave a few days after the emperor and the grand vazier. It will give us time to draw up a plan and then present it to the emperor when we catch up with him.'

The next day at Shahbaz Khan's house Abeerah tightened her grip around her father's waist as the two stood on their terrace.

'No, Abbajaan! You cannot go.'

Tears flowed like a torrential downpour from her eyes.

'What will I do if something… Oh Abbajaan! No, no,' she cried.

'My Zeba… my beauty, look at me.' Shahbaz Khan gently held his daughter's tear-drenched face in his hands and lifted it from his chest.

'It's only a short campaign. We will pin him down, break him and I will be back.' His calming tone hid his true apprehension of the campaign. 'Oh! look now, here they come,' he said, trying to distract his daughter.

Faiz Ali entered the grounds of the general's house mounted

on his horse. Besides him was Qaraar mounted on Haider. Next to Qaraar was Hari, also mounted on a steed. Behind them was a silver palanquin in which Zainab Begum sat. Finally, at the end of the entourage were a retinue of servants carrying silver plates covered in velvet, hiding jewellery pieces for Abeerah. Today was the sagaii of the couple.

'How can I get engaged when my father leaves for the battle in a few days?' asked Abeerah softly.

'You will get engaged, married and live a happy life. I'm going down to receive the guests.'

Abeerah took her seat on a diwaan which had been covered with flowers. She covered her head with a dupatta and waited. Natiya stood beside her.

Rushing down the stairs Shahbaz Khan said with a smile, 'Khushamdeed, Faiz Ali sahib.'

Faiz Ali greeted him with an embrace, hiding his fear of the looming events. A few days after the unravelling of Husn-e-Jahaan, the fear of the inevitable war had become known to all in Shahjahanabad. Both fathers had met. They wanted an engagement which would be immediately followed with a wedding ceremony. After that Shahbaz Khan had insisted on a rukhsati, the ceremony when the bride would leave her home for her husband's. Shahbaz Khan wanted all this done before he rode out. But there were problems. No Qazi was available to marry the couple. Most of them were busy performing religious ceremonial duties for the emperor's troops readying for battle.

'I tried to bribe one of the Qazi's to come today and perform the nikaah immediately after the engagement, but even he refused,' said Faiz Ali, holding Shahbaz Khan's arm as they walked up the stairs.

'Let's get the engagement done.'

On the terrace, Faiz Ali and Shahbaz Khan watched as Zainab Begum took over.

'Qaraar, sit next to her.'

Zainab Begum tied jasmine flower bracelets around Abeerah's wrist. Then she fastened a diamond necklace around her neck. 'Everything will be fine. I'm your mother now. Here, take this ring and put it on her finger, Qaraar.'

He did it. Abeerah still had her head down. Both the fathers standing before the couple smiled at her but behind those smiles were storms of uncertainty.

Just then a deafening noise shattered the air. The bugles of war broke menacingly over Delhi. All rushed to the parapet to look towards the Red Fort. This was the procession of the exiting Imperial troops. The first out of the gates were the bugle blowers mounted on horseback. Their cheeks seemed constantly inflated as the menacing noise gave no sign of relenting. They were followed by the naqqara drumbeaters mounted on camels. The pounding was fierce and had a venom to it that could instil paralytic fear in even the mightiest. Close behind were the alamdaar standard bearers, 200 of them mounted, trotting in brilliant coordination and holding aloft the Mughal flags, with the Sher-e-Khurshid insignia on them. The noise from the horse hooves was like gathering thunder.

'We must win,' said the general, standing next to Qaraar knowing fully well that the others couldn't hear him because of the noise.

'I will ride with you.'

'No, Qaraar you won't.'

'These turbulent times give us a great opportunity to re-establish the innovative and fertile Sufi mind at courts not just across Hindustan but also in Persia. After years we have an enlightened emperor in Muhammad Shah and if he defeats Nadir, Persia would be his and, like he has done here, he could create a renaissance there too.'

'Yes, I know,' responded Shahbaz Khan lifting his hand gently.

In an urging voice Qaraar pleaded, 'So please let me ride with you.'

'No.'

Their whispered discussion was interrupted with a thunderous blast that sounded like 100 cloud bursts. Having fired multiple rounds of blanks, the cannons slowly made their way out. 2,000 of them grinded along. By now all on the parapet had realised that it would be impossible to leave Shahbaz Khan's house and so Abeerah instructed Natiya to make preparations so they could stay overnight. Through the entire night the exiting troops left in a grand show of strength. The noise kept them all awake staring at the ceiling and wondering what the future held. Abeerah, however, stayed up all night watching the troops, with Qaraar by her side. Witnessing the large numbers in this fighting force gave her solace that the Mughals would win.

By the time it was 7 am the next morning, the couple had witnessed the last of the million soldiers forming the infantry columns pass by.

'Did you get some sleep Abbajaan?' said Abeerah looking at her father making his way to the terrace.

'Who can sleep in these times?

Faiz Ali and Zainab Begum made their way up to the terrace too.

Settling into the breakfast table Faiz Ali picked up on the frown on Shahbaz Khan's face. He gripped Shahbaz Khan's hand, 'I will get the two married as soon as the Qazis get free, in the next two or three days.'

But Abeerah didn't agree, 'I will wait for my father's return,' she said with her head lowered.

'Abeerah...' Shahbaz Khan wanted to interject.

'No, Abbajaan. No wedding till you return.'

'Alright my child, as you wish – but please come away with us to our home as soon as your father leaves,' said Zainab Begum holding up her veil in front of Shahbaz Khan. 'Don't live here alone,' she continued, nudging her husband for endorsement.

'Yes, you are now our daughter. You have to come to Hunar-Abaad.'

'Huzoor, this is my home. The mighty Basalat-Gah and I will be here until my father returns and then after the wedding, I will make Hunar-Abaad my home.'

'But…' Shahbaz Khan again tried to intervene. He saw his daughter shake her head.

'It's ok. Let her do as she pleases,' said Qaraar standing behind his fiancé.

'I will visit her every day,' added Zainab Begum, changing her seat next to Abeerah's and caressing her face to reassure Shahbaz Khan.

After a few days, Shahbaz Khan put on his armour, kissed his brave daughter an innumerable amount of times, mounted his war elephant and left at the head of his division to merge with Khan Dowran's. Shahjahanabad would regularly get reports from riders who acted as couriers, riding back and forth from the winding, python-like army. Hatim Khan, Holar Pasha, the Kaleem brothers, and Ahmad Bokhari would all rejoice and gossip under the steps of the Jama Masjid as reports would fly back about how the confidence in the army was peaking, how a brief mock war game was held in a forest, and how the troops and generals participated displaying brilliant skills. Some riders carried back to the army letters, love notes and even small gifts from their beloveds.

Qaraar and Zainab Begum kept up their daily visits to Shahbaz Khan's house ensuring that Abeerah felt secure. In order to lift Abeerah's spirits, Faiz Ali and Zainab Begum included her in regular outings, particularly to the orchard, where together with Qaraar they held many a picnic, overlooking Husn-e-Jahaan.

Shah Rezaan kept up the regular training of his pupil on geometric stone pattern designing and girih tile-making. An opportunity arose to travel to Sikandra and Fatehpur Sikri to restore the geometric shapes on the red sandstone mausoleum of Akbar and marble screens at the shrine of the renowned Sufi,

Hazrat Salim Chishti. Qaraar insisted that Abeerah accompany him and so Faiz Ali, Zainab Begum, Abeerah, Qaraar and the Sufi master went together after placing guards at Basalat-Gah. Their caravan of horses and bullock carts reached the shrine after a week. There they spent ten bright, sunny winter days. During the day Shah Rezaan and Qaraar would work away on the stone and marble, cutting away with hammer and chisel. At Sikandra, Qaraar restored the motifs on the walls and facade. Believing Qaraar should acquire knowledge of creating geometric patterns on all surfaces, Shah Rezaan got him carving geometric designs on wood.

On one occasion as the family sat on the stone floor besides the shrine of Hazrat Salim Chishti, under a fading winter sunset and as melodious qawwals recited their poems, Faiz Ali asked Shah Rezaan, 'Why do you emphasise so much on restoration?'

Shah Rezaan leaned on his mutteqa, the staff Sufis carried with them, and with the other hand swung his shawl around him.

'Creation will always need restoration. Restoration does not need creation. Restoration comes from that insight of man that recognises the helplessness of the created and comes to its aid. Tell me now, which is more important?'

Faiz Ali thought about what had been said and pressed his palm against his chest. Hearing this philosophical conversation in progress, a reasonable crowd of people came and laid down mats and sat around the Sufi. Shah Rezaan raised his hand for people to ask questions.

'We seek God. Where do we find him? We also seek to excel in this worldly place. What about us confused ones?' a range of questions sprung from the crowd.

'I will answer by a verse from Hazrat Ali whom we regard as the first Sufi:

> You do not know it, but in you is the remedy,
> You cause the sickness, but this you don't see

You are but a small form… this you assume
You're larger than any universe, in reality
Within you are the letters spelling out, the mystery
You are the Being, you're the very Being… It:
You contain That, which contained cannot be.[51]

'Within you is Qanaat… contentment. Seek within and you shall find yourself. Know yourself and you will know Him.'

'Wah!' came the response from the crowd.

'What is the most disliked quality by God… Oh Sufi?' came a question from the crowd.

Shah Rezaan spoke aloud, 'Munafikat… hypocrisy is the worst. Even Sufis weren't spared if they were found out to be faking ascetics… having something else in your heart but showing yourself as another is the worst… Here is a verse from Hafez denouncing hypocrytical ascetics and clerics who claimed to be "Holier than Thou":

Clerics bigoted for God,
Elders who have lost the road-
These have made a tale of us
"Drunken sots and bibulous"
Let the ascetics life be dim,
I will nothing have of him;
If the monk will pious be,
God forgive his piety![52]

After a fortnight of spiritual learning and art, the family left Fatehpur Sikri for Delhi. Abeerah and Qaraar both carried a sense of calm within.

24 FEBRUARY 1739. BATTLE OF KARNAL

The two armies faced each other.

Shahbaz Khan looked at the grand vazier and said, 'His men seem tired, let him come to us and that way we can encircle him and stay clear of his zamburaks and jazayerchis.' Nizam Asaf Jah agreed with Shahbaz Khan.

Janbaz Bakht spoke, adjusting his helmet, 'I have been riding across the front line. There is no sign of those guns.'

To check this, Shahbaz Khan, Khan Dowran and the Nizam Asaf Jah undertook one last ride across their front line to try and locate those guns.

All three pulled out their telescopes and inspected closely.

The Afsharid and Qizilbash troops were Nadir's elite fighting force. So closely knit were they that the three Mughal generals holding up their telescopes could hardly see through the ranks.

'Nadir!' whispered Shahbaz Khan as he caught a fleeting glimpse of the Persian king.

'Where?'

'Behind the ranks.'

All three generals focussed their lenses. Nadir was astride a grey horse. He wore a light armour. On his head was a four cornered crimson velvet cap and his eyes had the expression of a dead man – cold and distant. A thick jet-black beard and moustache covered almost half his face.

'Whatever the provocation, we must not attack. I'm sure the zamburaks and jazayerchis are behind the front rows,' emphasised Shahbaz Khan in a firm voice, while looking at the grand vazier and Janbaz Bakht.

Just then a massive roar went up. Another Mughal general by the name of Saadat Khan suddenly opened an attack, leading his war elephant into battle followed by his infantry divisions. He was heading straight for the Persian centre.

Shahbaz Khan swung the reigns of his horse and galloped to the Mughal camp.

'How did this happen?' yelled Shahbaz Khan angrily at the grand vazier who was in full gallop besides him. No answer came.

On reaching the camp, the generals were informed that a scouting party of Nadir's army had ambushed Saadat Khan's separated divisions, which were going to join up with the Mughal army. Driven by rage, Saadat Khan had attacked and set war into motion. The rest of the Mughal army now watched anxiously as events unfolded.

War cries from both the Mughal and Persian sides erupted. Saadat Khan's men finally reached the Persian centre and struck hard. Such was the force of the Mughal infantry that Nadir's men were pushed back.

'Break the centre!' came the loud shouting from the Mughal army as they watched, thumping their lances into the ground. It seemed that Nadir was reeling under the onslaught. Nadir's men suffered for nearly half an hour. Just then Nadir sent out a cavalry to the left, feigning flight. It was a decoy. But Saadat Khan fell for it and moved left. Luring him closer, Nadir gave the order for his cavalry to part, revealing the dreaded zamburaks and jazayerchis. In complete horror all watched as a barrage of fire was unleashed. The swivel mounted zamburaks and jazayerchis pounded away relentlessly at Saadat Khan's forces. In less than half an hour, Saadat Khan's divisions were reduced to a bloody pulp.

Back at the Mughal camp, shock and disappointment descended. But there was still the massive force of Nizam Asaf Jah and the other generals. The emperor was frustrated and angry. The impulse to seek revenge for what he had just witnessed was strong and he gave orders for another attack at the centre. This time he insisted that Khan Dowran and Shahbaz Khan lead the assault. Their repeated resistance to this un-thought out mad rush was met with a rebuke from the emperor. Having no choice but to obey the emperor, Shahbaz Khan and Khan Dowran mounted their war elephants. Looking at each other and then down at their infantry and cavalry divisions, they let out the war cry.

'Yalgaar!'

Shahbaz Khan's elephant too lifted its trunk, let out a huge trumpeting noise, shook his head furiously and surged forward. Nadir waited. And when the two divisions were in firing range, he once again gave the orders for the Afsharid ranks to part and bring the zamburaks and jazayerchis into the fight. The effect was devastating. The firing sliced through Shahbaz Khan and Khan Dowran's soldiers. Horseman after horseman fell in clouds of dust before they could even reach Nadir's centre. The neighing of horses and painful yells of bullet-hit men with torn flesh filled the air.

The two general's elephants closed ranks and advanced.

Shahbaz Khan turned to Khan Dowran whose howdah was by now right next to his. He yelled out, 'Surely the Nizam Asaf Jah has witnessed this massacre and will send re-enforcements!'

The bitter truth was that Nizam Asaf Jah, would not come to join the battle. The two generals were on their own. A realisation of fight to the finish now set in. Shahbaz Khan loaded his musket and fired into Nadir's ranks from his elevated position atop his elephant. His fire hit Nadir's soldiers with lethal precision. Shahbaz Khan's musket then tracked Nadir. The shot stung through the air but it missed Nadir and hit his bodyguard instead. Almost instantly Nadir signalled his artillery to target the two generals. A barrage of bullets flew towards Shahbaz Khan and Khan Dowran. One of them caught Khan Dowran straight in the head.

All this seemed to happen in a few seconds as Shahbaz Khan watched from his elephant. Before he knew it, he heard another volley of shots in his direction. His mahout took four rounds and dropped from the head of the elephant to the ground like a freefalling stone. Seeing his trainer lying on the ground in a pool of blood, Shahbaz Khan's elephant went mad with anger running in all directions. Seeing the raging beast headed their way, Nadir's infantry let out a flurry of shots. All hitting the elephant. Shahbaz Khan leaped out of the howdah and fell to the ground. In one last gasp, the elephant got up on its hind legs like a gigantic marvel and then thudded down in a massive cloud of dust.

When the dust began to settle Shahbaz Khan realised he now stood unarmed right in front of Nadir's cavalry. It was as if the entire cavalry now focussed their attention on the brave-hearted Mughal general. One single shot pierced the air. It hit Shahbaz Khan in the stomach. He swivelled and caught another shot in his back which sent him flying face forward into the ground. With fading eyesight, Shahbaz Khan saw a lone, rider-less horse speeding towards the Mughal line. The dead horseman's foot had been caught in the saddle and the body was being dragged with great force. With the little strength he had left, Shahbaz Khan held onto the body of the horseman and was dragged back to the Mughal ranks.

Within minutes, Shahbaz Khan was attended to by medicine men. Seeing the fall of Saadat Khan, Khan Dowran and Shahbaz Khan's divisions, the Nizam Asaf Jah insisted and prevailed upon the Mughal emperor to give the call for surrender. He believed paying off Nadir to be a wiser option. In less than three hours, the Mughal army had been beaten. But Nadir refused payment. He knew that the wealth of Delhi now lay before him and nothing could alter his access to it.

The next day a heavy winter fog descended on Shahjahanabad. The people of the city were woken by a slow pounding of just one drum. The beat was heavy and prolonged. Most inhabitants rubbed away the last bit of slumber in their eyes and came out to investigate. From the fog emerged Emperor Muhammad Shah, head bowed. Behind him were the standard-bearers of the Persian Afsharid army. A beaten emperor had been sent into his city to prepare for the arrival of Nadir the conqueror the next day.[53] Silence swept Shahjahanabad as people watched the entry of their defeated ruler, in cutting cold winter shock. Fear gripped them all. Then from the fog emerged a bloodied Shahbaz Khan. As a show of conquest and humiliation, he had been put on a horse and his legs had been tied around the animal. His chest was exposed and bloody and his abdomen was almost black. Only a few sporadic gasps signalled a semblance of life.

'Aaaaaaah! No! No! My Abbajaan!' screamed Abeerah from the terrace as she saw her father and began sinking to the floor. A stunned Zainab Begum quickly gathered her senses. Holding Abeerah tight, she dragged her away from the terrace.

Qaraar mounted Haider and galloped to the procession.

As he approached the Afsharid elite, guards surrounded him. Qaraar pulled at Haider's reins who went up on his hind legs. The resultant noise from the commotion reached the ears of some of the Mughal soldiers, who explained to the Persian generals the relationship between Qaraar and Shahbaz Khan, and so disdainfully they gave consent for Qaraar to take away the dying general.

Qaraar rode into the grounds of Basalat-Gah carrying Shahbaz Khan with him. However, before they reached the entrance gate Shahbaz Khan inhaled one last time and life left him. Once in the middle of the grounds, Qaraar reined in Haider and brought down the body. Qaraar knew the entire city would soon be shutdown. Seeing his son, Faiz Ali rushed out. All afternoon the two of them dug a grave for the general and buried him. Inside the house Zainab Begum hurriedly paid and dismissed all the servants and packed the belongings of a now dazed and speechless Abeerah who sat on the floor of her bedroom. Having locked down the house, two horses headed for Hunar-Abaad. One carried Faiz Ali and Zainab Begum, and the other carried Qaraar and Abeerah. As Haider galloped past the mound of mud that testified to her father's presence as dust, Abeerah shut her eyes tight and held on to Qaraar.

The next day, Shahjahanabad wore the blanket of silence. People kept to their homes and rarely ventured out with Nadir's soldiers patrolling the streets. It was curfew. Mughal police officers, the Kotwals, also fell under the control of Nadir's men. The Mughal emperor was deeply loved in these lanes and information had started trickling out of the Red Fort of the utter humiliation he was suffering. Nadir had placed himself on the Peacock Throne, mocked at the emperor and ordered his ministers around as if they were his concubines. Most importantly, the news of the rapaciousness of Nadir's looting got out. Under threat, a humiliated Muhammad Shah had meekly handed over the keys of the treasury to his conqueror. Within hours, the dazzling wealth of the Mughals had been almost completely depleted, as Nadir gave orders to extract nearly 700 million rupees from the Mughal treasury. This included taking the Peacock Throne, the legendary diamonds Koh-i-noor, and the pink Darya-i-Noor.

Nearly 12,000 horses, 400 elephants and 4,000 camels were loaded up with loot to be carried away back to Persia. Seeing and hearing all of this, the inhabitants of Shahjahanabad felt insulted and humiliated.

Amidst all this, Qaraar spent his time with Abeerah at Hunar-Abaad. The sobbing had been non-stop for days but now she was beginning to show resilience.

'Your father wouldn't want to see you this way.'

'No, he wouldn't,' said Abeerah as she dabbed her eyes and restrained any further flow of tears. 'Without you this burden of loneliness would be unbearable, Qaraar.'

Just then a servant came in from the streets and announced, 'The restrictions have been lifted!'

'Finally! I must go and check on Hari and the poets.'

'Be careful my love.'

'Don't worry, I will be back soon.'

On reaching the Jama Masjid Qaraar witnessed Sayyid Niaz Khan, a Mughal nobleman of repute, surrounded by grain-sellers. A few hours ago there had been rumours of trouble in the Paharganj district, not far from Shahjahanabad. Some Persian Afsharid troops had gone there to fix corn prices.[54] This had infuriated the corn merchants and unhappy with the low price stipulated, they called a crowd towards the evening and assaulted the Persian troops, killing some at the granaries and even fanning out in neighbouring parts of the city, attacking them wherever they could see them.[55] The atmosphere was tense.

'Nadir's men are cheapening the price of corn in Shahjahanabad too,' said Hari Das in a tense voice as Qaraar rode up.

'The price stays the way it is!' yelled Sayyid Niaz Khan at Nadir's men. 'Go back and tell your king. I stand with the farmers of Delhi.'

Sayyid Niaz Khan had built a reputation for resistance. Over the past few hours he had raided the stables where Nadir's captured elephants were kept, killed Nadir's men and carried of the animals to a fort outside the city.[56] Sayyid Niaz Khan would spur people on to resist and encourage the rioters whenever opportunity presented itself.

'You will pay for this,' responded the Afsharid soldier hearing Sayyid Niaz Khan's defiance.

'Don't you threaten me,' came the Mughal noble's fearless response.

Just then Janbaz Bakht rode in with his guards and rebuked him.

'Sayyid Niyaz Khan! What do you think you are doing? We are trying to strike a delicate power balance between us and Nadir Shah's men.'

Qaraar couldn't help himself.

'Don't you utter a word – where were you at Karnal?'

Word had got out about the Grand Vazier Nizam Asaf Jah and Janbaz Bakht's refusal to join the battle. The crowd now seemed to train their raging eyes at Janbaz Bakht. The tension was rising and suddenly the air seemed fraught with looming danger.

Sensing the anger in the crowd, Janbaz Bakht turned his horse and galloped away.

Evening was giving way to night in Shahjahanabad. The Afsharid soldiers were 200 in number and suddenly they realised they were surrounded by more than 400 locals.

'You've looted the Red Fort and insulted our emperor,' said Sayyid Niaz Khan walking up menacingly to the commanding officer of the Afsharid soldiers.

'Let's finish them here!' yelled Hatim Khan the kebab-seller, pulling out a skewer and walking besides Sayyid Niaz Khan.

'Kill them all!' screamed Sayyid Niaz Khan.

A mad butchery took place as Qaraar and Hari Das watched on in disbelief. It seemed all the inhabitants of the winding lanes of Jama Masjid had descended on to this spot. Some bearing swords, others lances, and some with pistols. Ahmad Bokhari didn't have boots in his hands but a blood-stained curved sword. The Kaleem brothers and the Afghan dry fruit sellers were equipped with daggers also dripping with blood. Except for one all of the 200 Afsharid soldiers were killed in minutes.

'Blood below the Jama Masjid!' Qaraar rushed home and, catching his breath, related the entire incident in intermittent bursts of anxiety to Faiz Ali, Zainab Begum and Abeerah who listened without blinking.

Faiz Ali turned white as a sheet. 'What! Do they even know the consequences of this? Allah help us all. Turn off the flaming torches… who knows what will happen tonight.'

The single soldier who had escaped found his way to the tent of one of the most powerful generals in Nadir's army. His name was Mansub Qoli. The influential general heard out the soldier.

'I will deal with this matter personally, no need to inform the King,' said Mansub Qoli dismissing the soldier. 'And send in that Janbaz Bakht.'

'I believe you were there. Who led this?' enquired Mansub Qoli on seeing Janbaz Bakht entering his tent.

'Uhh…, I believe the two rabble rousers were Qaraar Ali and Sayyid Niaz Khan. Both live near the Jama Masjid.'

Janbaz Bakht watched as Mansub Qoli led 700 well-armed men into the silence of the night, and chuckled to himself, 'Abeerah, now you are mine!'

At Hunar-Abaad there was fear and anticipation of the unknown. The family ate their dinner in darkness. The occasional look at the other had only apprehension written on their faces. A knock shattered the silence. Abeerah grabbed Qaraar's hand.

Getting up he said, 'It will be fine.'

'Who is it?' whispered Qaraar coming close to the door and muffling his voice with a cloth.

'Sayyid Niaz Khan. Could I please come in?'

'Of course. Huzoor, please come in.' Qaraar lifted the heavy iron bolt that had locked the door.

All rose in welcome of the renowned noble. Shaking Qaraar by the shoulders and then looking at him straight in the eye, 'It's been a bloody day, but…'

'But what?' said Faiz Ali getting up and going over to one of the wall niches in which the Quran was. 'Are you mad, Sayyid sahib? This is Nadir Shah you are dealing with! He idolises the barbarity of Genghis Khan! It's his men you have killed.' Lifting the Quran in his hand, 'Only Allah can save us now.'

'Calm down Abbajaan, let's hear what Sayyid sahib has to say.'

'We must resist Nadir.' Sayyid Niaz Khan said in a calm but confident voice.

'Violence is not my way.'

'I know Qaraar, but times are changing. I must rush. I can leave some of my men behind to guard your house.'

'No thanks, it will only arouse suspicion, and besides, I wasn't involved in the killing. Where are you rushing?'

'We have learnt Nadir's men will be out tonight trying to punish us. I have armed most of this area. We are ready to fight,' said Sayyid Niaz Khan and left.

By now it was past midnight. Fear gripped Zainab Begum and Abeerah as they retired to their rooms. All the servants were instructed to go into the servant quarters, lock their doors and not come out. Some even went into Qaraar's adjacent stable and hid themselves in the hay. Faiz Ali flung himself into prayer, holding up a candle and reading the Quran softly to himself. Qaraar went up to the terrace from where he could get a view of all the lanes that surrounded the Jama Masjid. They were empty. Every house had extinguished their lamps. Abeerah abandoned her room, not wanting to be alone, and came up to the terrace to join Qaraar. It was freezing. Just then Qaraar saw a column of Afsharids approaching.

'Quick, lower your head, let's make our way down the stairs.' Qaraar held Abeerah's hand and took her down into the courtyard. Passing the rose garden, they opened a wooden creaking door to a guest bedroom and lay on the bed covering themselves under quilts. The window next to the left side of the bed that opened out with a view of the street had been bolted and shut tight.

A trembling Abeerah held onto Qaraar as he looked up towards the ceiling holding a jewel hilted Mughal dagger in one hand. Suddenly, the silence was shattered by screams, yells and cries from outside. Loud noises of clashing steel tore through the darkness. Many a loud thud sounded on the window next to Abeerah's side. And then, just as quickly as it had started, there was silence. For nearly ten minutes nothing was heard. But then, a movement and noise to the right caught Qaraar's eyes. He slowly turned his head and realised that he had forgotten to shut the room door. He could clearly see the rose garden. But the noise and movement didn't come from there. It seemed to come from the first floor. He looked upwards and saw a stumbling shadowy figure which instantly fell straight down into the the rose garden. Qaraar sprang out of bed, dagger in hand and went to the man who quickly rose to his full height.

Not being a fighter, Qaraar froze for a few seconds. It was only when the intruder had grabbed him by the back of his neck and began dragging him towards the door that Qaraar realised he was under attack. A scuffle broke out between the two men. It took Qaraar a few seconds to remember that he possessed a weapon – the Mughal dagger. The flashing blade slashed across the intruder's chest who let out a loud yell. This brought Abeerah rushing out of the room. Faiz Ali and Zainab Begum too came out screaming, 'Allah! Allah! Mercy!'

In one final blow Qaraar buried the dagger straight into the heart of the intruder, who fell back onto the ground. He was stone dead. Just then there was a thumping on the main door. A stunned Abeerah could hardly utter anything as she stood at the door of the room overlooking the courtyard.

Qaraar went to the main door.

In a stammer he asked, 'Who, who is it?'

'Open up Qaraar sahib, it's me – Sayyid Niaz Khan.'

Qaraar gathered the little strength he had left and unbolted the door. It was like a rushing river that burst through. Within minutes the dark courtyard was filled with 200 men holding flaming torches and arms.

'We have been looking for him. We thought we saw him climb up towards your house, and here he lies – deservedly dead!' said Sayyid Niaz Khan, inspecting and then kicking the body of the dead intruder.

Qaraar was in a complete daze. The speed of the sequence of events and now the sudden lighting-up of the courtyard compounded his confused feeling. He felt his body shaking violently. Sayyid Niaz Khan's face was right in front of his as the nobleman shook Qaraar.

'Qaraar sahib! Can you hear me? Look at me!'

All of a sudden Qaraar seemed to snap back into consciousness.

'What's been going on? Who are all of you?'

'Qaraar sahib, it's me, Sayyid Niaz Khan and this man lying dead is Nadir's general, Mansub Qoli.'

'What?!'

'Yes! It's true. He came with 700 men, but we were ready for him; we killed them all just outside your house. Except him. He ran up your wall.'

'But he was trying to drag me to my door.'

'Of course, he was. He had lost his sword and was unarmed. He would have taken you outside as his human shield, but look – you killed him!'

'Fateh! Fateh!' A loud chant went up. Qaraar looked all around. Everything looked hazy. Most of the faces he didn't recognise. Some he did. The Afghan dry-fruit sellers were now holding swords, Hatim Khan too. The rest were Sayyid Niaz Khan's guards and private soldiers.

'Qaraar sahib, from today you will be known as Qaatil-e-Salaar… the general slayer!' said Hatim Khan aloud. A huge cheer went up, 'Qaatil-e-Salaar! Qaatil-e -Salaar!'

All this was too much for the craftsman. He ran towards the room and into Abeerah's arms. She held him tight and took him into the room. There he threw up a few times.

'My love! Just lie down. I will get you some water.' A frantic Abeerah got Qaraar to stretch out on the bed.

A fearful Faiz Ali and Zainab Begum who had watched all this from a distance slowly walked past the body of Mansub Qoli.

In a trembling voice and pointing at the dead body Faiz Ali asked, 'What do we do with him?'

'Don't worry we will take it away,' said Sayyid Niaz Khan and left.

His men dragged the body out, washed away the blood stains and left too.

All night Qaraar had a raging fever and couldn't sleep. He thought of how Hunar-Abaad had been named 'A place where skill thrives' and today it was home to a murderer. The thought made him even more distressed and he had bouts of loud weeping. Abeerah, Faiz Ali and Zainab Begum sat beside Qaraar until it was dawn. As morning came Faiz Ali heard a commotion. He rushed to the terrace and spotted some people running to their houses.

'What's the matter? Tell me!'

'Nadir is personally coming with his army!'

'What?'

'Yes, they have left the Red Fort. You'd better bolt your doors!'

Qaraar had recovered with some rest and came out into the courtyard. Faiz Ali stumbled down the stairs from the terrace and briefed him.

Qaraar spoke with complete awareness of the looming calamity in a voice that was calm, but which couldn't quite hide the horrors that played out in his mind. 'It's going to be a blood bath Abbajaan…

Furious galloping interrupted Qaraar's sentence. Distracted, he ran up to the terrace. This time he had a spyglass with him and Abeerah by his side. Looking through the lens he saw Nadir riding ahead of his troops.

'He's making his way to the Sunehri Masjid,' said Qaraar.

After a few minutes he continued, 'He's climbed the terrace, and now he has drawn his sword.' Lowering the spyglass Qaraar tightened his hold around Abeerah's waist and looking at her said frantically, 'It's a sign for a massacre. You have to get out of here. You have to leave and live!'

'No!' she screamed. 'Never without you!'

Both of them rushed down the stairs to the courtyard.

Meanwhile the entire Afsharid army now attacked houses in Shahjahanabad. They smashed through doors. Dragged out women by their hair and shot them in front of their children. Pulled out men and beheaded them and then shot the children. Screams of innocents ripped the air. The old and sick begged for mercy but instead got spears and lances plunging through their chests. Nadir sat alone, sword in hand and expressionless on the roof of the Sunehri Masjid looking into the cold mist and listening to the screams. Not once did he flinch.

Seeing the soldiers approaching from her broken window was Askari Begum. Hatim Khan had spent the night with her, but now it was clear to her that Hatim Khan himself was a real threat to her existence. The Afsharid soldiers smashed through her door.

'Please, please Huzoor,' she said frantically, 'I beg you, mercy! I have a gift for you – this beast of a man,' she said, kicking Hatim Khan. 'He was the one responsible for last night. Kill him! Kill him!'

Hatim Khan turned to the woman in disbelief. He rushed for the tiny window and tried to squeeze out, but they dragged him back into the room and shot him in the head. Natiya, who was standing next to Askari Begum, screamed relentlessly seeing Hatim Khan's brains splattered all over the floor.

Stammering with fear and holding her head, Askari Begum cried out, 'Don't! Please don't! We will please you in every way possible. We will service you and satisfy your every desire... Look see how beautiful Natiya is...'

'We spare you only because you gave us this man... and your promises of service,' said the commanding officer with a smile for Natiya. Then he left. He had others to kill.

An entire regiment went into Hari's home. First to take a bullet was his ageing father, then his mother and then Hari took a bullet in his stomach. Bleeding profusely, he began transiting between unconsciousness and death. The Kaleem brothers were beheaded in two swift sabre slashes, their heads tumbling into their cooking pans. Ahmad Bokhari was shot between the eyes. The Afghan dry-fruit sellers and Persian carpet-weavers were dragged out together with their families and beheaded. All of Holar Pasha's animals were killed, with multiple stabs for the sloth bear. And after finishing off the animals the soldiers plunged their swords into a screaming Holar Pasha.

Amidst the bloody carnage, Janbaz Bakht rode up with his men, hoping to make his way to Hunar-Abaad and take Abeerah. But on seeing a Mughal ride up, the less-knowledgeable Afsharid soldiers read his movements as a threat. They dragged him and his three guards down from their horses and hacked them to death.

Where homes were heavily bolted, Nadir's soldiers climbed up the walls and descended on the inhabitants like an avalanche. Sayyid Niaz Khan was trapped in a fort not far away. Surrounded, he and his men fought bravely but it was of no use. They were soon captured and taken to Nadir, where they were executed in cold blood.[57]

At Hunar-Abaad, Qaraar was hurriedly scribbling out a road map. 'We are the last house in this lane, it gives you a few minutes extra to escape. This is a short cut through the narrowest of hidden alleys, what I call the poshida kucha. It will get you out from the rear district of Shahjahanabad. Only a single horse can fit through, but Haider knows the secret way out. Guide him well and you will be fine, now go!'

'Never, never!' said Abeerah, walking away from the table where Qaraar stood with the map in his hand.

'I promise I will meet you there. They will soon be here.'

'How will you get there? There is only one other horse, and you have your parents.'

'Just go my child!' yelled Zainab Begum.

Suddenly Qaraar reached out for a piece of cloth and grabbed Abeerah. He then forcibly strapped it around her mouth. She resisted violently, slapping and scratching Qaraar. He tied her wrists and carried her to the stable. There, he got his frightened servants to help him put her on Haider. One of the servants then opened the stable door. Qaraar quickly cut the cloth around Abeerah's wrists.

'How far are they?'

The servant who had opened the stable door looked back and said in a trembling voice, 'Almost on us!'

Qaraar slapped Haider's hind and the horse bolted out and into the secret alleyway. Qaraar tried to get back into the main house, but the servants held him and dragged him back into the hay while one servant bolted the stable door. Frantic, Qaraar parted some of the hay and crawled to a tiny window through which one could see into the courtyard. He thrust it open. He saw his parents holding onto each other. He then heard the Afsharid regiment slamming a huge log into the door.

'Abbajaan! Ammijaan!'

'Hush, hush. Don't say a word now, my Dildaar son,' said Zainab Begum.

'No!' yelled Qaraar.

Two servants held him back and pulled him away from the window. One placed his hand across his young master's mouth.

The main door of Hunar-Abaad was smashed open and came crashing down with a thunderous noise. Qaraar watched, struggling to break free as the soldiers poured into the courtyard.

'This house belongs to the one they call "Qaatil-e-Salaar"?' asked the lead officer in a chilling voice, pointing his sword at the old couple. 'Where is he?'

'We don't know, I promise… our son…'

A spear went straight into Faiz Ali's chest before he could complete his sentence and emerged from his back. The old man fell to the ground releasing his wife's hand. Zainab Begum fell to her knees holding her husband's head in her arms. The lead officer then asked for a musket. He loaded it and then at close range shot Zainab Begum through the head.

Qaraar shut his eyes tight having witnessed this horror. A soldier then noticed the small window and pointed it out to the lead officer. Running up, they shoved five flaming torches through it. Within seconds the stable was ablaze. Screams and coughs of burning servants was everywhere. Faiz Ali's horse went mad. Seeing the flames, he leapt over the barricade and started banging his head against the door. Qaraar watched as five of his servants were charred to death. The sleeves of his angarkha were also now on fire. He picked up a woollen shawl that had once belonged to one of his now dead servants and wrapped it around himself. He knew his house was the last in that lane and the soldiers would have traced their steps back from where they came. Breaking open the stable door, he mounted the horse, and took one last look at the now burning Hunar-Abaad to which the flames from the stable had spread. Then his horse entered the narrow alley.

After an hour Qaraar reached the orchard and went straight to Shah Rezaan's shack. Abeerah came rushing from behind the trees and held onto the horse's reins.

'My love! you made it!… What happened?'

'All are dead.'

Qaraar dismounted and flung himself into her arms. He wept uncontrollably as she held him tight.

'Can you both get to Merv?' came Shah Rezaan's voice from the shack.

Entering the shack and sitting before the Sufi with his head in his hand, Qaraar said, 'I… I don't know. Why Merv?'

'Nadir is everywhere… Lahore, Peshawar, Kabul… but Khiva, I know, is resisting and so if you can get there and from there onto Merv, you will survive my children. You need isolation.' Then Shah Rezaan shut his eyes and whispered, 'From the remotest parts of the world the most dazzling colour will emerge.'

'And you, master?' Qaraar asked in a quivering voice.

'My time has come.'

'What do you mean?'

'Don't worry about me. Think Merv. Isolation and remoteness are what you need. Here's a map. Now, run!'

They heard galloping. Cutting through the rows of mango trees came an Afsharid regiment. Under threat, some people of Shahjahanabad had told the Afsharids of Qaraar's orchard and the possibility that he might be hiding there. It was almost dark now. Qaraar and Abeerah ran towards Haider and mounted him. Abeerah held Qaraar tight from behind. The other horse they left for Shah Rezaan and disappeared into the maze of trees.

Shah Rezaan stood erect in front of the cavalry; his arms spread wide. This time his voice wasn't soft like velvet as Qaraar had first heard it. Instead, it had power and rage.

'Murderers! Allah says the killing of one innocent is the murder of all of mankind. You and your thug king are the murderers of mankind!'

The lead cavalry officer responded, 'Where is that Qaatil-e-Salaar?

'He is free like the wind! Go away and never return to this place of peace.'

'Tell us where he is, and you will be rewarded by the King of Persia – or else…' The lead Afsharid cavalry officer drew his sword and held it aloft.

Seeing this Shah Rezaan broke into a sarcastic smile. He walked up to the horseman. 'Ah! You come from Persia, the land of scholars. Why didn't your king put a pen in your hand instead of a sword?'

The soldier seemed puzzled at the calm manner in which the Sufi spoke.

'You talk about a reward from your king! Can he reward me with a conversation about the 'Farr' that Ferdowsi mentions in his Shahnameh as the divinely bestowed right to rule on noble kings? Maybe not, because your king is not noble!'

'Enough! Yelled the cavalry officer tightening the grip on his sword. Shah Rezaan stretched out his bare neck. In one clean slash, Shah Rezaan was beheaded.

'Burn this orchard down!' came the order.

The horsemen torched tree after tree as the orchard came ablaze. Fire was on every branch. As the night sky lit up, Nadir's men spotted the lovers mounted on Haider and gave them chase. Qaraar guided Haider in a zig-zag fashion, desperately moving from behind one tree to another as flaming branches fell around them. By now, the fire had spread over the ten-acre orchard and was so intense the Afsharid soldiers feared being burnt alive. They galloped away, but not before one Afsharid soldier thought he chanced upon a clear shot. While riding he strung a single arrow. It rung out through his bow and pierced Abeerah's back. She didn't utter in pain, just tightened her grip around Qaraar and rested her head against his back. Haider now stood on the western side of the orchard, right in front of Husn-e-Jahaan. The blue, girih tilework caught the reflection of the orange flames all around and dazzled as if it was its last gasp. As Qaraar dismounted, in dismay he saw Abeerah collapse.

Qaraar looked skywards, 'Ya Allah! No! Why?' Abeerah was losing consciousness. He carried her in his arms and took her inside Husn-e-Jahaan. After pulling out the arrow from her back he laid her on the ground.

'You always wanted to go East my love, now go north-west, to Merv!'

Frantically Qaraar spoke, 'This wound will heal Abeerah. I will heal it.'

Just then Askari Begum emerged from the burning orchard along with Natiya, beating her chest in animated profound grief. 'Hai Hai, my niece!' she said, running up towards Husn-e-Jahaan. 'We thought this would be the only safe place, so we made our way here. We hear, Qaraar, that your father still lives.'

'What?'

'Yes! It's said a wounded Hari went in and saved him. You better go and make sure. We will look after Abeerah, and besides, this place isn't safe anymore. We will take her to Humayun's Tomb. Meet us there after you bring your father,' said Askari Begum seating herself next to Abeerah and taking her head in her lap.

'No! I won't leave her!'

Abeerah whispered in a faint voice, 'If he's alive, get him here.'

'I am not leaving your side.'

'You must. He is alive, didn't you hear?'

'It couldn't be... I saw it with my eyes – the, the spear went right through...' Qaraar hid his face in his hands as his voice trembled.

'What if it's true, will you forgive yourself?'

'And you? I will never forgive myself if something were to happen to you.'

Trying to moisten her parched throat, Abeerah said softly, 'They are here with me, but there, he and a wounded Hari are alone.'

Qaraar thought to himself, 'It's late. The soldiers must have surely left by now.'

'Let me first get you to Humayun's Tomb. This place will soon be ash,' he said looking around as flames approached Husn-e-Jahaan. After laying Abeerah down under a frangipani tree in the gardens of Humayun's Tomb and kissing her forehead Qaraar left for Shahjahanbad.

Making his way through the poshida kucha he entered the rear district of Shahjahanabad. Hunar-Abaad had collapsed and through a gaping wide hole, he saw the most dreadful sight. Faiz Ali and Zainab Begum were deformed charred corpses. Qaraar let out a scream of anguish. Unable to look at the grotesque figures, he nudged Haider along whose hooves and ankles were soaked in blood from the streets. There was wailing and crying as he entered the winding lanes choking with dead bodies. Jackals were already feasting on open wounds. Some men who identified their dead tried to chase away the beasts but the stubborn jackals bared their fangs in defiance. Helplessly the distressed folks watched their dead being eaten in front of them. Finally, Qaraar made it to Hari's shop.

Having been shot in the stomach, Hari was holding onto his last breath. Qaraar held his friend's head in his hands.

'Hari, Oh Hari,' he wept.

'Death is everywhere,' whispered Hari.

'The poets?' Qaraar asked.

'D… Don't know.'

Hari stammered on. 'You must leave Delhi.' He then pointed to two men who were until then hiding behind a table, but who quickly scrambled out.

'We are Uzbeks and want to flee. Nadir hates us. That's our bullock cart. All the goods in our caravan are burned. We hid ourselves under the dead in this house.'

'Where are you headed?' asked Qaraar, coughing because of the stench.

'Bokhara. Nadir's hold is not yet that strong there.'

Wiping his tears and caressing Hari's head, Qaraar asked, 'Can you get me to Merv?'

'Very remote. But we can get you to the Murghab. From there you will have to go on your own.'

'I have a map. I will take my chances. How much?'

'What do you have?'

'This ring.'

'How many of you?'

'Three. Abeerah, me and Hari.'

'Do you think it's safe to leave now?'

'Yes, I have just come from Humayun's Tomb. I need to go back for Abeerah.'

'Let's leave now!'

'Hari! Hari! No!'

Qaraar hadn't realised, but Hari had died with his head on his friend's chest. Laying Hari's head down Qaraar went and tied Haider to the rear of the Uzbeks bullock cart, then he climbed into it and covered his head and face. He looked back. The sea of dead bodies presented their last gory sight. 30,000 inhabitants of Shahjahanabad had been massacred by Nadir's men.[58]

After an hour in the bullock cart Qaraar was back at Humayun's Tomb.

'Where is she?' yelled Qaraar at Askari Begum.

'My niece! My niece! What can I tell you Qaraar?' said Askari Begum, burying her face in her dupatta. 'She insisted we go back to the orchard. She said she was dying… it was her last wish to see Husn-e-Jahaan, she insisted.' With each word Qaraar had a sinking feeling in his heart. 'So, so, O Natiya, you say, it's too much for me.' Natiya continued, '…so we took her there.'

'You what?'

'It was her last wish and then, and then she couldn't run back as the flames chased us.'

'No! No!' Qaraar ran towards his burning orchard. The two Uzbek traders ran behind him and got hold of him.

'There's no time, we have to leave.'

'Abeeraaaaaah! O Cursed world! Look at my love, she goes up in flames! He said looking at his burning orchard. 'Abeeraaaah! My life… it, it leaves me. All is lost.'

Qaraar fell to his knees unconscious.

The Uzbeks lifted him and put him into the bullock cart. Quickly they sprinkled some water on his face which barely revived him. Qaraar buried his head in his chest. His body, an embryonic curl. The Uzbek cracked the whip. The bullock cart made its way north-west.

PART II

CHAPTER 4

WHO LIVES WITHIN?

Qaraar's way out of Hindustan wouldn't be the conventional route of passing through the Khyber Pass, which linked Hindustan to the rest of the world. Almost every caravan and army used this Pass to enter and exit Mughal India, but the Uzbeks knew that Nadir now controlled it. His regiments, henchmen and spies were in every village leading towards Lahore, Kabul and beyond, into Persia. In Delhi, however, having cleaned their blood-drenched swords, Nadir's men were tired after the massacre and returned to their barracks, unintentionally helping the travellers and their escape out of the city walls.

In the Afsharid army there was divided opinion regarding the Qaatil-e-Salaar. Some believed he had been burned alive in the orchard. Others were convinced that the arrow that hit Abeerah had penetrated both and that the lovers died together on horseback. Yet others believed he was alive. Over the next few days, speeding Afsharid couriers began sending out imaginary sketches of him, along with a bounty headline. The cart carrying Qaraar, though, had left Delhi's villages just in time.

The bullock-cart made its way north of Delhi, taking great care to avoid towns and cities. Sticking to forests and the countryside where the Uzbeks hunted rabbits and antelope at night, they made their way through the densely wooded and remote Lahul Spiti Valley on the foothills of the Himalayas. From here the remoteness of the Himalayan range began and the plains of Hindustan were behind them. Throughout, Qaraar burned with fever. He lost weight and his eyes sunk into the hollows of his skull because of a lack of sleep. Most nights he would wake up weeping or hallucinating that Abeerah and Shah Rezaan were by his side. On other occasions, the image of his parents' torched bodies would haunt him. As weeks passed, just lying and weeping in the cart, his beard grew in length and touched his chest and his hair became winding tresses. The Uzbeks nursed him and fed him what they hunted in the forests.

A few hamlets hidden in mountain mist and inhabited by local tribes of Lahul Spiti provided some much-needed shelter. The Uzbeks traded whatever little they had, including some boots and hats for food and a few days rest in local temples and houses. During these short stays, always frightened at the slightest noise, they offered their services to work in the apple farms owned by the tribes. This way they earned some money and saved it for the months ahead. They insured they didn't stay too long in a hamlet-a maximum of a week. While these villages were remote and the tribes given to their own customs and had been generally left alone by rulers of Delhi, word was beginning to reach them about Nadir's massacre and any link to that horror needed to be avoided. The three men left Lahul Spiti after replacing their bullocks with horses at one village, to help in the arduous months ahead. After a slow climb into the Himalayan hills, braving heavy snowfall and avoiding the Kashmir Valley, they ascended into Ladakh and then into the picturesque Zanskar Valley.

Massive mountains now presented themselves. Here, by the clear waters of the Zanskar, they broke their journey again for a few weeks. The Uzbeks fished fresh trout and cooked it on a fire by the stony banks, nourishing themselves and a sick Qaraar. Soon they made their brave move to climb higher into the Himalayas and then into the Karakoram range. Snow lashed as diligent hooves ploughed their way through and ascended into the peaks. Haider resolutely kept pace tied to the rear of the cart. The horse watched his master lying under quilts and on occasions when Qaraar opened his feverish eyes, he locked them with those of his faithful steed as if sharing a common thought of drifting into life's unrevealed future.

After a month of tough climbing, the little cart reached a peak at the bottom of which lay the Karakoram Pass. On top of the peak was a desolate, windswept and whitewashed Buddhist monastery, which seemed to merge into the snow and sky. There was only one middle-aged, crimson-robed monk who lived there. With a beaming smile, a scratch to his bald head and a low bow, he let them in. In true Buddhist hospitality he cooked warm meals for the travellers, fed soup to Qaraar from his own bowl and hands, chanted prayers for Qaraar's health and blew those prayers into the high mountain winds. In the snug conditions of this isolated monastery, nursed by warm cosy fires and quilts, Qaraar recovered steadily. After a month's rest, Qaraar finally got to his feet, stepped out of the monastery and looked into the mountainous vistas. They were so high up on the peak that Qaraar could see clouds floating below him. Looking down, Qaraar enquired softly, 'Where does this pass lead?' – his first words in months.

Walking up to his guest and giving a carefree spin to the Buddhist prayer drums with his hand, the ever-cheerful monk said, 'Below to the west is Gilgit, Baltistan, Afghan lands, Bokhara, Khiva, Samarkand and beyond.'

'But look! Below to your right is Tibet, from where I come,' he said excitedly, with a little jump.

Qaraar's eyes searched for Hindustan to the south. There was a misty blue look to those mountains beyond which was his homeland. It now seemed so far away after months of travel.

Looking at the distant blue peaks and the triangular yellow and red Buddhist prayer flags that fluttered from a pole, Qaraar whispered, 'This place feels like the roof of the world.'

Draping Qaraar with a new shawl the monk said, 'It is. Feel the sky within you. Feel free – inhale.'

The sky was a sharp cobalt blue. The same colour of the girih tiles he had once made. Qaraar shut his eyes, pulled the shawl closer and inhaled, hoping to find peace. For a few seconds he did. Then an image of Abeerah burning in Husn-e-Jahaan flashed through his mind. He opened his eyes wide. 'Abeeraaaaah!' he yelled out into the never-ending empty space that lay still and cold in front of him. His voice didn't come back as an echo. The mountains seemed to have buried his lover's name in their chests, and they lured him towards them to meet her in a final union. Tears rolled from his eyes as he shut them again and walked towards the edge of the terrace. Stretching his arms out sideways, he flung his head back and was about to let himself go…

'No! This is not the way!' The Buddhist monk had rushed to the edge and pulled the craftsman back, who was only seconds away from descending to sure death.

Sitting Qaraar down on the floor he said, 'Whatever it is from the past that took you to the edge of that terrace, you must leave behind; and the only way you will do that is to continuously travel. Keep absorbing, may your heart become a sponge.'

Turning to the monk in a weak voice Qaraar spoke, 'I am empty.'

'You will become full. Now go, your caravan awaits you!'

This time, Qaraar didn't lie in the cart, but instead he mounted Haider who delighted in his master's recovery by rising up on his hind legs. Qaraar rode behind the Uzbeks as they descended and entered the Karakoram Pass. Qaraar looked back. The monastery with its fluttering Buddhist prayer flags faded into a snowy distance. Making their way through the Pass they were dwarfed on both sides by sky-kissing mountains, resembling wise sages with their snow clasped peaks that looked like silver hair. After weeks of riding, climbing, and bearing terrible altitude sickness, they looked below into the fabulous Gilgit and Baltistan regions. Rich in alpine forests, turquoise lakes and freshwater streams, Gilgit and Baltistan had come under Nadir's sway. From a distance one of the Uzbek's spotted an Afsharid standard fluttering below in a village. In order to keep these remote parts in control, a bunch of Afsharid soldiers would go in occasionally and camp there as a show of strength.

'We must stay in the forests for a few days,' said one of the Uzbeks, changing course and guiding the horses into the high alpine tree lines.

'We need essentials from the village,' said the other.

'Going into the village is only possible when Nadir's men have left.'

Once they had settled at a safe distance, Qaraar started to talk.

'How far is it to Merv?'

'Another month, if we are lucky.'

'This journey is like my life – aimless.' Qaraar covered himself in his shawl and quilts and walked up to Haider whose reins he tied to a low alpine branch.

'We need a fire, or we'll freeze to death,' said one of the Uzbeks.

The other reproached his friend in a hushed but angry tone, 'Absolutely not! If Nadir's men see a fire in the high forest, it will raise their suspicion.'

'Let's huddle together and cover ourselves with as many quilts as we have, and sleep in the cart.'

Silence like never before descended on them. The only sound was their breathing. They remained like that for two weeks, with icy night winds their only audible companion. Until one day it got unbearable. The travellers had consumed all the food they had picked up from the monastery and had also come to loathe each-other's role as transmitters of body heat. Finally hunger and desperation got them to leave the safety of the cart. As night fell the three went looking for food. Holding daggers in their hands they trudged through the alpine forest and snow hoping to find a small animal or bird. There was nothing. Just when hope was giving way to anguish, one Uzbek saw a snow leopard glide away. Known for its shyness, the travellers had disturbed it. The snow leopard left its half-eaten prey and vanished. The carcass of the mountain goat, it's victim, was still fresh, and the starving travellers fell upon it ravaneously. Later they dragged the carcass to the cart.

Qaraar was revolted by this savage act of which he had been part. Disgusted with himself, he thought of his cultivated upbringing and what he had just done. Wiping the blood off his mouth he flung himself into the cart, shut his eyes and slept. Dreams varied. One was a deeply thoughtful and disturbing one. Usually, Abeerah sat in front of him on Haider and he wrapped his arms around her, but why hadn't he done so when they galloped from the Afsharids in his orchard? If only he had sat behind her, he would have been struck by the arrow and not her. Meanwhile the starving Uzbek's had given into their hunger and had lit a tiny fire. On it they grilled the smallest pieces of the dead animal and consumed it hurriedly. Some meat pieces were gobbled down before they had been cooked. Flames reflected on their bloody faces. Then they spoke in hushed whispers, revealing their sinister plans.

'He is in deep sleep.'

'Yes, but speak softly.'

'We have brought him back to health – a job well done.'

Turning and looking at Qaraar, 'Now he will fetch a handsome sum.'

'Where should we sell him?'

'The transiting slave market not far from Khiva and Merv.'

'How much do you think we will get?'

'500 dinars.'

'Aha!' said one of the Uzbek's rubbing his hands in glee and flashing a toothy smile.

Nadir's hatred for the Uzbeks because they resisted him was well known and that was the only reason why the two hadn't handed over Qaraar in return for a reward. The two Uzbeks feared that if they approached Nadir's soldiers, along with Qaraar, they too might lose their heads.

'Look down in the village! Nadir's men are leaving,' said one of them excitedly.

'Just what we needed. We leave tomorrow.'

At dawn, having seen the last of the Afsharid's leave, the two Uzbeks descended swiftly into the village, bought some food using the money they had saved from working in the apple farms, and as quickly as they had descended, went back into the alpine forest. Heading north they were soon in the remote Badakshan Valley.

Realising where he was, Qaraar asked his Uzbek travellers to stop a while. In the valley lapis lazuli was in abundance; a few were scattered on the arid landscape. Qaraar dismounted and picked one up. He gently felt its texture and thought of Shah Rezaan's words. 'From the remotest parts of the world the most dazzling colour will emerge.' Overcome with an emotion that stemmed from being trapped in a rudderless existence, he flung the stone into the winds. The travellers then headed further north. The Pamir mountains were a daunting prospect. Treacherously steep, blizzards slammed into them with enormous velocity. The three men urged their beasts on. Looking down and watching the pebbles that Haider's hooves had stumbled on fall and vanish, Qaraar felt an emptiness. On one occasion the velocity of the blizzard was so strong they had to take shelter in a small mountain cave. Shivering and trembling, they watched helplessly as snow covered the cave's mouth.

Days passed in the soul-destroying cave. The only sound was moaning from cold. Huddled and shivering in his damp quilt, Qaraar watched despondently as icicles on the roof of the cave grew longer. At times, the silence was so loud that it put him to sleep. The nightmares continued in which he saw Mansub Qoli. 'Why did I kill him? He was unarmed. He just wanted to use me as a human shield.' Qaraar mumbled these words in sleep. Even in the freezing cold he would wake up dripping in sweat. While examining his dreams, he loathed himself for becoming a murderer. Nights went by battling these demons. Eventually the blizzard seemed to lose its bite giving the inhabitants of the cave enough time to slowly clear the snow from its mouth and scramble out.

Haider, who had until then been trembling outside along with the other horses, had become skin and bone. The journey through the Pamirs lasted an excruciating three weeks. Eventually they descended the Pamirs and turned left. To the south was Vaksh, the birthplace of Rumi. Qaraar looked at the map Shah Rezaan had scribbled out for him. It wasn't the clearest, but the dead master had made it a point to mark out Rumi's birthplace. It seemed so desolate. 'From the remotest parts of the world the most dazzling colour will emerge.' Qaraar again turned these words over in his mind. It was true. From remote Vaksh, Rumi's father moved to Balkh town and then later towards the Ottoman lands of Anatolia. Emerging from the isolation of Vaksh, Rumi bloomed in Anatolia.

It was from these lands of northern remote Khorasan, which included Vaksh, Balkh and Merv, that a constellation of Sufis had emerged. Their influence in that region had made it a cauldron for spiritual thought. As he rode, Qaraar felt each mountain and dust particle speak to him about the lost Sufis of that region. From Ibrahim Adham Balkhi, the eighth century prince who gave up power for the life of a spiritual ascetic, feeding the poor from what he earned as a labourer; to Shaqiq, 'the thoughtful', who when cornered by Harun-al-Rashid, the King of Baghdad, made him realise that his kingdom was only worth a drink of water, if he the King was stranded in the desert in front of a water-carrier, who demanded his Kingdom in return for quenching the King's parched throat.[59] Then there were the ninth- and tenth-century thinkers, Bishr and Sayyari, also from Merv, who lived by the belief that 'the highest spiritual merit was earned by serving mankind,' and who urged pilgrims making their way to Mecca to give their money to orphans instead, and earn more spiritual merit than a pilgrimage. Sayyari spoke about union with God and understanding that He unites through His attributes. Sayyari's thoughts were similar to Ibn Arabi's.[60]

Qaraar thought pensively, 'Isolation and remoteness were the two words Shah Rezaan used before he gave me this map. Besides safety in isolation, there must be a purpose for me in Merv.' As they approached Rumi's birthplace, he felt as if the poet spoke to him through the winds. Rumi had found the Divine through Shams Tabrez and similarly Abeerah had been Qaraar's link to the Divine. Now without Abeerah he felt the seething pain of separation from both her and the Divine as he recited Rumi's verses.

Sighs a hundredfold
From my heart arise;
My heart, dark and cold,
Flames with my sighs
Happy was I, in the pearls heart to lie
Till lashed by life's hurricane, like a tossed wave I ran.[61]

'Did you say something?' asked the Uzbek.

Wiping the tears from his eyes he said, 'Rumi was born just south of here. Look, you can see Vaksh – it's right there!'

'Who cares!'

Qaraar noticed the sudden rudeness in the voice of the Uzbek and also that they seemed to be heading further north.

'We need to head east towards the Murghab, that's where Merv is. Why are you going north?'

'Keep your mouth shut, and ask no questions of us,' barked one of the Uzbeks.

'Huzoors, we need to follow the map!' pleaded Qaraar.

The two Uzbeks stopped the cart and walked up to Qaraar, who had also dismounted and presented the map for them to study. One Uzbek pretended to analyse it, whilst the other came from behind and struck Qaraar with a huge staff, in a heavy blow to the back of his head. Qaraar fell unconscious. His mouth, hands and legs were tied, and he was loaded into the cart. The ring that Qaraar had promised to give the Uzbeks on reaching the Murghab was roughly pulled off his finger. Haider was tied to the rear of the cart and the Uzbeks carried on north.

For the next two weeks Qaraar remained tied, with only the cloth around his mouth being taken off for force-feeding. The travellers skirted around Samarkand and Bokhara and left Khiva behind, finally arriving at an obscure village called Darvaza, half-way between Khiva and Merv. It had a habitation of only 50 souls but was where the annual transiting slave market was held. The Uzbeks took up temporary residence in a Turkic tent made of brown Bactrian camel skin and waited for the next day when the slave traders would arrive. Darvaza, just for the day, would be teeming with thousands. At daybreak, that is precisely what happened. Hundreds of Tajiks and Turkmens stormed in, their horses kicking up massive dust clouds. There were some Arabs, a few Portuguese, the odd Spanish slave trader and an East European slave trader too. All prepared to bargain, haggle, fight and kill if need be. Soon all gathered below a high wooden platform.

The Portuguese, Spanish, Arabs and Turks whipped their African and Persian slaves who climbed up with chained ankles and wrists. As a loud roar went up, the auction began almost immediately. In minutes, all were sold.

The Uzbeks watched all this from afar, standing just outside the tent, gulping down their koumis, a fermented drink made from mare's milk. Wiping the liquid from their moustaches, one of them yelled out.

'We have an exotic specimen – from Hindustan!'

'Bring him out!' went up the roar.

The previous evening the two men had forcibly trimmed Qaraar's beard to a mere stubble. His long hair was cut down to shoulder length. Shackled in chains at the wrist and ankles he was thrust out of the tent. The crowd cheered. He was put up on the platform.

'Look at this stunning Hindustani,' screamed one of the Uzbeks. 'Give us a demonstration that you value beauty! Come on! Make an appropriate offer!' he continued.

'But he doesn't have muscle!' came a voice from the crowd, 'How will he carry stone?'

The one thing the Uzbeks had forgotten to do was tie Qaraar's mouth while leading him out. A mistake. Things would change dramatically. Raising his head and looking at the crowd and then at his own state and what was befalling him, Qaraar spoke.

'O people of these lands!' There was silence. They had never heard a slave speak.

'I come seeking the mind of Omar Khayyam. He was once with you, not far from here. He lived in Merv.'

The crowd remained silent.

'There, Omar Khayyam worked in the libraries,' pointing with his chained hands southwards.

'I come seeking the mind of Rumi and Ibn Sina both born in this region.'

There continued to be silence.

Qaraar held his interlocked fingers and wrists to his forehead in frustration and shut his eyes while words flowed out of his mouth. 'They roamed these lands, free. Weren't they your guides once? O you people of a lost realm! Do you even know what I'm talking about?'

A puzzled look was on many faces.

Then he opened his eyes and continued pointing at them unleashing a verbal assault at the pathetic state of man. 'What have you become today? Slave traders, treacherous traitors? To the hell with the lot of you! Hang your heads in shame!' he said, looking at the two men who had brought him here.

He uttered these words secretly hoping that what he had said might enrage the crowd, and some crazed Central Asian would string an arrow that would pierce his heart. His eyes searched for that deadly arrow. One that would free him from this state of abject misery. 'Come on,' he thought to himself, 'finish me here. My love awaits me.' He shut his eyes, anticipating the piercing yet joyous pain of freedom. It never came.

Instead, the crowd seemed to disperse.

Walking past the two Uzbeks one from the crowd said, 'No-one wants a thinking slave. Get him out of here.'

'Don't want to buy this fellow. He will be hard work!' said another, and the crowd completely thinned.

A deep voice suddenly rang through. 'I will buy him for 100 dinars.'

It was an East European slave trader who had sat at a distance, surrounded by his fierce-looking bodyguards watching this unusual spectacle. His name was Aalf Olsson and he was of Viking descent. Tall and broad chested, he had long blonde hair tied in plaits that rested on either side of his chest. Sparkling blue eyes that bore testimony to his Viking heritage completed his appearance. For centuries, the Vikings had come down the Volga that opened into the Caspian Sea with captive slaves and sold them at various ports. The word 'slave' came from the fact that the ones who were sold, were Slavs.[62] Sailing down the Caspian, the main transaction points for this slave trade was the town of Akil, and then the Persian town of Sari at the bottom of the Caspian Sea. As it was, Darvaza could also be accessed from Sari and so after his business dealings in that Persian town, Aalf Olsson would make his way to the transiting slave market at Darvaza, hoping to pick up a few good bargains.

Aalf Olsson took great pride in his Viking ancestry, particularly their legendary ship building and fighting skills. His ancestors had become slave traders but he didn't enjoy it. Although illiterate, the desire to learn burnt within him. Because of his trade he had learned to speak a very basic Persian and his visits to Persia had encouraged him to explore more. On this fateful day, Qaraar had impressed him.

'Maybe 200 dinars?' said the Uzbek with a toothy smile,

knowing well that there wasn't a chance of him getting 500 dinars now that demand for Qaraar had plummeted after his performance on the platform.

'150,' said Aalf Olsson walking up to the Uzbeks, surrounded by his giant, blonde-haired bodyguards.

'Uhh hmm,' then looking at the menacing guards, the Uzbeks stammered, 'D… done!'

'…but he has a horse too, that chestnut brown one in the distance.'

'A slave with a horse! Ha!' laughed Aalf Olsson. 'Another 5 dinars for the animal.'

The money was flung at them and Qaraar was lowered from the platform as the Uzbeks disappeared from sight.

Having made his purchase, Aalf Olsson headed towards the Caspian alongwith his bodyguards and the other slaves he had bought. For the next few days Aalf Olsson watched his new purchase with curious eyes as Qaraar walked besides his horse in chains, with his head lowered. 'A slave, meant to clean rubbish and die in wilderness, is this what you had in mind for me?' thought Qaraar repeatedly, thinking of Shah Rezaan.

Setting up camp, Qaraar was given his list of chores: cut down trees and bring firewood, clean the boots of the bodyguards and wash clothes in freezing river waters. Faltering on many occasions he felt the Viking whip lash across his back. All this went on for a few weeks until one night the seeking intellect in Aalf Olsson got the better of the slave-trader in him. Seeing Qaraar making girih patterns with his fingers in the sand he walked up to him.

Sipping his locally brewed liquor from a wooden cup and tossing his blonde tresses behind him, Aalf Olsson spoke, 'I have seen these patterns.' Qaraar kept quiet. Then looking at the patterns he erased them with his chained hands.

'Why did you do that?'

'The angles weren't perfect.'

'Angles?'

'Geometric patterns need correct angles… you won't understand,' Qaraar exhaled a sigh.

'Then make me.' Aalf Olsson's voice became softer and he sat on the ground besides Qaraar.

Qaraar was surprised by the curiosity, but he felt a sense of wanting to share his knowledge. He explained the girih pattern work in detail. Aalf Olsson gaped and listened carefully. All night Qaraar explained basic geometry and tile-making. When the first rays of the sun appeared as a crimson border of a dark cloud, both young men felt the gentle strands of a possible friendship.

Looking at the rising sun, rubbing his eyes and letting out a loud yawn, Aalf Olsson said, 'Will you teach me to read and write?'

'Will you take me to Merv?'

'You are my slave and in no position to make demands.'

But seeing Qaraar's head drop, he said, 'I'll take you to Merv, but you must teach me.'

'Agreed. Now, tell me, where have you seen these patterns?'

'Samarkand, Khiva, Bokhara, Isfahan, but they are in a terrible condition.'

Qaraar felt a strange emotion, as if through mist, a road was appearing. It wasn't quite visible but he felt there was a path for a new life.

After just two days of travel they crossed the white Murghab and reached Merv.

Dun-coloured mountains surrounded Merv, and wisps of white clouds circled around them. But there was nothing left of this once incredible city. Just ruins. A few ancient walls seemed to speak to the travellers, telling them tales of past intellectual grandeur. They passed the bricked mausoleum of Sultan Sanjar, the twelfth century Seljuk King of Khorasan Persia, which was in a great state of distress, with gaping holes in the walls and a collapsing dome.

The pitiable condition of this once intellectual bastion reminded Qaraar of his own state. Still in chains and running in order to keep pace with a horse-mounted Aalf Olsson, who regularly tugged at the chains making Qaraar stumble, the craftsman couldn't take his eyes off the broken walls of Merv. Aalf Olsson kicked his horse into a gallop. The slave could no longer keep up falling face forward in the dust and getting dragged along. Being rendered such treatment, Qaraar uttered a few lines from the famous poem *Tears of Khorasan*.

> The characters of this script are dry as bosoms of the oppressed
> …At the doors of the ignoble the well born stand sad and bewildered
> In their hands the virtuous are captive and bound.[63]

Sultan Sanjar had made Merv the epicentre of learning. The great poet, Anwari had also been encouraged to live and work here. But in the early twelfth century, wild tribal horsemen had attacked Merv, defeated Sultan Sanjar and destroyed the city, and upon seeing its destruction Anwari had written *Tears of Khorasan*.

Forced to get back on his feet by the galloping horse, Qaraar began to run besides his mounted master. As the travellers circled around Sultan Sanjar's mausoleum, he recited a verse from Omar Kahyyam's *Rubaiyyat* in honour of the mathematician poet.

> The worldly hope men set their hearts upon
> Turns ashes – or it prospers
> Like snow upon the deserts dusty face
> Lighting a little hour or two and was gone.[64]

'What is this that you are reciting?' asked Aalf Olsson.

Qaraar didn't answer.

'There is nothing here, only dust. What do you want to do here?

'I see what you don't.'

'Halt!'

Aalf Olsson stopped his guards from riding further. He dismounted.

Now he was angry. 'Why did you want to come here?

Looking around desperately, Qaraar suddenly spotted a tiny brick room close to Sultan Sanjar's mausoleum. The room didn't have a door and was part of a ruined caravanesarai which was once a resting lodge for travelling Sufis. Qaraar rushed into the room, struggling with his chains. On the floor was a small carpet. It was dusty, but on its right corner rested a Sufi cap of the Qadriyya order – exactly as the one that Shah Rezaan used to wear. He grabbed the cap and clutched it tight. 'You were here! You lived here some years ago!' The left corner of the carpet fluttered due to the wind that rushed through. Qaraar lifted it. There was a note. He read it and held it close to his chest.

> Whoever might visit here, should try and restore these walls. Every brick counts. But if you can't do it all, don't worry. It's a sign; it means the walls want others to share in the pleasure of reviving beauty.

The hidden meaning was clear to Qaraar. It was from this remoteness and through the restoration of the walls of Sultan Sanjar's mausoleum that the restoration of his life would begin. He ran out of the brick room and into Sultan Sanjar's mausoleum. Here, he inspected the crumbling walls closely; 'Shah Rezaan, you were restoring this wall, you worked here!'

Stammering in joy he said, 'I… I know what I have to do. I have to restore the walls of this mausoleum and then…' He looked at Aalf Olsson who had followed him in and was listening attentively. 'And then you said the girih patterns in Khiva, Bokhara, Samarkand and Isfahan are in a bad condition? Right?' Aalf Olsson wore a confused look on his face but nodded in affirmation. 'Then I have to go and restore those girih patterns there. That's the direction for my life.' Qaraar didn't care that Isfahan was in Nadir's Persia. He felt a strange calling to immerse himself in restoration and that feeling overtook fear.

Aalf Olsson was soon surrounded by his bodyguards. One of them spoke.

'Lord we must not agree to this. Let's take him across the Caspian and sell him to the Russians. Let's be done with him.'

Looking at Qaraar, Aalf Olsson spoke in a firm voice, 'We had agreed that I would bring you here but not to stay.'

'If you want to learn to read and write, we stay!' said Qaraar.

Aalf Olsson grabbed Qaraar by his neck and shook him, 'You cannot blackmail me!'

Qaraar managed to get a few words out of his choking throat. 'Do you want letters in your head or just barbaric thoughts?'

Aalf tightened his grip around Qaraar's throat. Grinding his teeth, he said, 'Slaves don't bargain.'

The next few words that Qaraar managed to get out would take root in Aalf's hidden but fertile mind. 'Aalif is the first letter to enlightenment in Urdu and Persian… and you are Aalf. So close but yet so far,' Qaraar managed a sarcastic smile.

The words had the desired effect and Aalf's grip weakened in the face of truth. Releasing Qaraar, he walked away and had some time alone, pacing up and down.

'How much time do you need?'

Qaraar kept inspecting the bricks, 'I don't know – as much time as it takes.'

Qaraar turned and looked at the approaching Viking descendant. There was a calm determination on Qaraar's face which made Aalf Olsson stop, and turn to his men.

'We camp here.'

'A few more things,' added Qaraar. 'Please send your bodyguards to nearby villages to get me enough materials to build a simple kiln, and a regular supply of clay. Also, cut these chains,' he said, holding up his arms.

'You cheeky craftsman from Hindustan!' Aalf Olsson cut the chains.

'And you, a Viking descendant, will learn Urdu and Persian from this slave. Your lessons begin tomorrow at first light.'

'Fine,' – but when he saw Qaraar looking at Haider, he quickly added, 'but don't think I will allow you to ride your horse; slaves don't have that privilege. I will ride and you will walk.'

'Agreed.'

Having built straw shacks for the bodyguards and other slaves, for the next two autumn months, Qaraar restored parts of the walls of Sultan Sanjar's tomb. The surroundings were so remote that the kiln he made was not the most functional and the clay supply that the bodyguards brought in was intermittent. After a few false starts, Aalf Olsson began making progress in learning Urdu and Persian alphabets. Slowly Qaraar taught him grammar and sentence formation. Impressed, some of the bodyguards also joined the tutorials. Haider also got his master's attention. Returning from nearby villages the guards brought fresh apples, carrots and grass for him and Qaraar fed him personally. In no time the horse recovered his strength. The one thing that was working in Qaraar's favour was Merv's remoteness and so he was safe. The silence and solitude also helped him recover emotionally. In working on the brick walls, he had found a cause, and in Aalf Olsson a pupil. The two young men spoke about their past. Aalf Olsson told Qaraar of his small village on the banks of the Volga where he once had a wife, who died from the plague. He expressed his love for prostitutes and ships with great passion. Qaraar spoke about Abeerah, his life in Delhi, Shah Rezaan, and the massacre, but not the fact that he was a wanted man. Aalf Olsson hadn't quite won his trust in entirety. Qaraar felt that by continuing to be seen a slave of a deadly lot he could get into Khiva and Bokhara. He now wanted to work on the blue tiles there. Merv, Khiva, Bokhara and Samarkand were all a ten-day ride from each other. When Qaraar told his master of his intentions, Aalf Olsson thought it might be financially beneficial.

The Khan of Khiva had the reputation of being a scheming and brutal man. But he had a love for the arts. His palace was the Kunya Ark, Aalf Olsson had seen it and knew that it needed much attention. The most beautiful part of the palace was the Khan's personal residence, with its exquisite geometric blue tile and woodwork. But all knew it was past its glory days and the crumbling roof and tiles were a symbol of the turbulent times in this part of Central Asia. Aalf Olsson hoped to make a fair amount of money if Qaraar could successfully restore the tiles and roof.

Leaving the slaves behind at Merv with some guards to watch over them, Aalf, Qaraar and a few guards left for Khiva. After a few days of dusty riding, with Qaraar in a bamboo cage, they reached the gates of Khiva. Just before entering Khiva, Qaraar was pulled out of the cage. They entered the city with Aalf Olsson on horseback and Qaraar on foot, leading his master's steed. The bazaars were bursting with activity. Young men sat on the shop floors selling the brightest melons and plums. A few carpet shops were there too, and a line of butchers. Old men sat by the streets stroking their white beards, adjusting their furry caps and keeping an eye out for anything new and imaginative. Occasionally a street dog would be scolded, sending it scampering for cover. Aalf Olsson and Qaraar headed straight for the Kunya Ark Palace.

'Let us in. The Khan will be pleased with what I have to offer,' said Aalf Olsson to the guards.

'Gum sho. Get lost!'

'This slave of mine is a craftsman and can restore parts of the palace. If you don't allow me in and the roof collapses on the Khan, believe me I will ensure his family knows you didn't allow us in. You will be skinned alive.'

The guards opened the door and Qaraar led Aalf Olsson's horse in.

The Khan sat on a chair which was on a crimson Persian carpet. He wore the famed Bokhara boots and the enormous fluffy black chugirma hat, the strands of which flew in the air. Attached to his waist was one of the broadest and longest swords the two young men had seen. The Khan's hands were twice Qaraar's, who observed them with concern. He looked the true manifestation of his ancestor Genghis Khan. Next to him was a bowl of grapes and cut slices of melon. Behind him were the fiercest-looking guards; their hands menacingly placed on the hilt of their swords. Even Aalf Olsson had a moment of hesitation.

Nudging Qaraar as the two stood in front of the Khan after bowing, he whispered, 'You better be good at this restoration stuff or we'll lose our lives. Now, speak up!'

'Great Khan, your brilliant roof with these fabulous patterns is falling to...'

'Tell me what I don't know. Where are you from?' roared the Khan, after swallowing the grapes his teeth had massacred into a pulp.

'I can restore the woodwork on the roof and the tiles around the Ark. I specialise in blue geometric patterns and tiles.'

'Geometric patterns and tiles!' said the Khan, looking all around at the falling blue tiles and the eroding woodwork. 'How do you know this artform? The last of the Persian masters have all died,' he sighed, but this time chucking some melon pieces into his mouth. The sweet syrup dripped down his lips and he slurped them back.

'The last of the lot taught me.'

'You didn't answer my first question – where are you from? You speak Persian, but don't quite look it,' he said, tilting his head, making his eyes small and focusing in on Qaraar's face.

'From, uhh... my forefathers were from Herat.'

The Khan's face lit up. 'Herati! Herat Shahar Khaylee Khoob Ast! Herat is a great city!' But almost immediately a frown appeared on his face, '...that monster Nadir holds it now.'

Just then one of the Khan's advisors rushed in and whispered something in his ear. The Khan's face turned red with rage.

'Nadir sag ast! Nadir is a dog. I say his name and bad news

arrives! Send out the scouting party and kill those Afsharids if they are encroaching. I have to go, craftsman.' Then rising from his chair, he said, 'I will give you my artists and workers to assist. You have one month.'

Qaraar and Aalf Olsson bowed, 'My Khan.'

A warning tore through the hallway and struck hard in their ears like a thunderbolt. 'If you don't deliver, I will have dried straw thrust through your fingernails, then have them pulled out and your fingers fed to the stray dogs of Khiva... and that goes for you too, Viking.'

The Khan rose to leave.

Aalf Olsson grabbed Qaraar by the arm.

'You better make this work,' Qaraar brushed his arm off.

'And if I deliver?'

Turning swiftly and looking back at Qaraar, '200 dinars.'

Aalf Olsson smiled.

The original plans were shared with Qaraar and for the next month Qaraar and his team worked day and night. Lapis lazuli was easily available, but the main problems were the Khan's other craftsmen who didn't have knowledge of how to recreate the precise geometric patterns. So Qaraar took it upon himself to make them. His experience in restoring the geometric patterns in stone in Sikandra, at Akbar's mausoleum, held him in good stead as the principles were exactly the same. Here too in Khiva, like in Sikandra, the six-sided hexagons and six-pointed stars were the heartbeats of the pattern. The only difference was that in Sikandra they were carved out as stone screens and here in Khiva they were in blue tiles.

Painstakingly, Qaraar sketched out their perfect angles on scrolls. The crushing of lapis lazuli was left to the Khan's craftsmen, but the firing of the tiles was done by Qaraar. The inlaid geometric pattern on the wooden roof then got Qaraar's attention. This was a complicated pattern, particularly the eight-sided octagon in the centre, within which was an eight-pointed star, within which was another smaller star. Once the main octagon with the two stars within it were restored, the pattern would have to be repeated into smaller octagons with yet smaller stars within them, in an interlocking fashion to give the impression of a never-ending pattern. It took days. There was nervousness all around as the month's end approached. On the last day just before sunset, the Khan made his way to inspect the work. Qaraar hung from the ceiling with his back to the ground on a pulley contraption he had invented. The last touches to the centre star within the octagon were excruciatingly difficult. The Khan drew the curtains apart and entered the reception area. But before he took his first step, Qaraar came crashing down, as the pulley gave way.

The Khan saw this sight of a falling Qaraar, 'What is…?' but he couldn't complete his sentence. All around him the restored blue tilework sparkled in spectacular glory. He looked up at the roof. It was majestic in its restored form. 'By Allah, you are a genius!' whispered the gaping Khan still looking around.

A velvet bag with 200 dinars was handed over to a relieved Aalf Olsson. The Khan of Khiva then sent a message to the Khan of Bokhara, who also ruled Samarkand and wanted specific restoration done on the geometric tiles in the magnificent Shah-e-Zinda shrine in that city. In the next three days, slave and master were on their way to Samarkand. Aalf Olsson now had a profound respect for Qaraar and allowed him to ride into Samarkand on Haider. For the first time after the massacre in Delhi, Qaraar felt joy.

On a bright day, Samarkand's mulberry tree avenues were a welcoming sight. As Qaraar rode past them, he plucked a bunch. Riding together, Aalf Olsson and Qaraar shared the fruit. Almost immediately they entered the glorious Registan square, the architecture and craftsmanship of which was spellbinding. But nothing had prepared them for their meeting with the Khan. On meeting him, they were promised 200 dinars or a gruesome death, and the chilling punishment was announced with great delight by the Khan's standard bearer. First, the Khan's falcon would gorge out their eyes and then it would be death by drowning. Aalf Olsson seemed less worried this time and shrugged his shoulders nonchalantly, even winking at Qaraar. The Khan caught that. Seeing this demonstration of over-confidence, he tripled the work: the geometric tilework on Ulugh Beg's Madrasa and Ulugh Beg's observatory which had once been thriving schools for students of astronomy and theology, would also have to be restored for no additional rewards. If just one building was restored they would get nothing, but the promised death. Aalf Olsson ran towards the Khan trying to plead for more time but with a wave of the hand he was dismissed. Qaraar's speed and quality was on test.

The Shah-e-Zinda avenue of mausoleums had blue tilework everywhere. Legend had it that it was the mausoleum of a Sufi who although dead, was alive in spirit. The girih patterns were predominantly on wall panels and Qaraar managed to finish restoring these to perfection. Then he moved onto the geometric designs on the Ulugh Beg Madrasa and wove his magic there restoring every geometric tile to perfection at break neck speed which took him to his final destination – the Ulugh Beg observatory. This was once the centre for the study of astronomy in the world and it stimulated Qaraar even more. The finest mathematicians studied here in the fifteenth and sixteenth centuries, but Qaraar saw just a handful of students. On one of his breaks he met the Chief of the Observatory having a rest on the open porch.

'Huzoor why are there such few students?' Qaraar said, having been lowered by the workers that operated his pulley contraption.

The chief closed the buttons of his turquoise gown embroidered with wine creepers and lounged back on the yellow cylindrical cushions.

'We haven't had a full house of students here since many years,' he said, yawning out of evident boredom and resting his chin on his hand.

Putting down his tools and dusting his clothes that were covered with clay, 'Why not?' asked Qaraar.

The Chief scratched his beard. 'There's no interest in education.'

'I understand there is strife in the region, but study must continue,' said Qaraar.

'In such turmoil rulers and politicians don't support the sciences and arts.'

'That's not true. In Hindustan Muhammad Shah did, and he did so even while his Empire was crumbling. There is no excuse for not learning.'

'O well,' said the chief, his hand done with scratching his beard and now caressing a dusty metal instrument meant for the study of planets. 'Maybe Muhammad Shah should have won at Karnal, he would have marched right through Persia and these lands and brought about a renaissance.' Then looking at Qaraar he said, 'The only interest seems to be in bloodshed. All the young are continuously recruited to fight.'

'Each day I knock on doors urging parents to send their children to study. I even offered to teach for free,' he continued.

'But?'

'Doesn't work.'

The next day Qaraar came up with a brilliant idea to make geometry fun for the children of Samarkand, hoping it would arouse their curiosity to learn more.

Qaraar and Aalf Olsson went into the bazaars and bought almost all of the much-desired Uzbek caps in Samarkand which came in bright colours and shapes. Then they bought all the delicious melons. The Viking descendant and his bodyguards cut slices and placed them in little plates, and each plate was placed next to a cap. All this outdoor activity on the steps of the great Ulugh Beg Observatory soon attracted a crowd. Qaraar cleared the porch and with a chalk, drew out the geometric tile patterns of the facade he was restoring. He left some easy angles to be calculated by the children. As a clue he wrote out the basic equations on the side. All the children had to do was to calculate the correct angle and write it on the side of the equation. The original plan, which had the complicated solutions and angles, Qaraar kept safely tucked in his pocket. On a piece of cloth Qaraar wrote in Persian, 'A free cap and a slice of melon for any child who can work out the angles!'

Rosy-cheeked, clamouring Samarkandi children of all ages gathered around, seeing these strange things happening.

'Now then, listen up! It's a beautiful bright Samarkand day and we are going to have some fun!' roared Aalf. 'This is how it works…'

'Get in line!' interrupted the bodyguards. 'In an orderly fashion now!' The children were crowing around, bursting with curiosity.

'You see that slave of mine?' The giggling children strained their necks and saw a waving Qaraar sitting, legs folded, on the wooden platform which was part of the pulley contraption.

'He has written something out for you to solve on the porch. If you can calculate it and write the correct angles,' – there was hushed silence – 'then,' with a wink Aalf Olsson continued, 'you get a cap, a plate of melon and you can pull the ropes with my men to take that slave into the air to work on the tiles! Up and up into the sky he will fly! Agreed?'

Before he could finish the sentence, the children ran to the porch where the simple equations were written out for them. The teenagers who had dropped out of school had a basic understanding of geometry. Some angles were solved with the help of additional clues from an amused chief. The children who got the angle right gulped down their melons, put on their new caps and ran like mad to the pulley contraption. Then, along with the Khan's workers, the children pulled at the ropes sending Qaraar into the sky.

'Up into the sky will the slave fly!' yelled the children as they pulled at the pulley contraption. Qaraar worked on the tiles through the day and was lowered by the children whenever he wished.

This carried on for days as the 'Flying Slave' became his title.

Qaraar asked, 'Now, tell me children, isn't geometry great?'

'Yes!'

'Look up and see what I have completed. Fun, isn't it?'

'Yes! Yes!'

'And there's more! You can learn about Nizam-e-Shamsi... our solar system, just go and spend time with the Chief of Observatory... and maybe one day you will become famous Sitara Shinasees... astronomers like Ulugh Beg.'

From then on, a steady line of Samarkandi children began streaming in regularly to the Observatory.

On the day of inspection, a huge cheer went up in the Registan square. 'Long live the flying slave! Long live the flying slave!' After receiving 200 dinars, Qaraar and Aalf Olsson rode out of Samarkand amidst wild cheering.

'I want to go to Isfahan and work on the tiles on the Darb-e-Imam shrine,' declared Qaraar.

'To get to Isfahan we will have to cross the desert. It will take us two and a half months just to get there!'

'Let's leave now, but we won't get paid there. Nadir is on campaign.'

Aalf Olsson thought it best not to oppose the idea. 'We'll make more money in due time,' he thought to himself.

Driven by his creative spirit, and in quiet opposition to the mindless barbarism that Nadir was unleashing in the region, Qaraar wanted to bring some beauty to Isfahan. Qaraar thought to himself, 'This is my way of opposing Nadir's ways.' After two and a half months of riding through the desert having disguised themselves as turbaned Heratis, with intermittent breaks in different date-palmed oasis where Qaraar continued with Aalf's Persian and Urdu lessons they reached Isfahan. Here, there was a nonchalance towards restoration. It was also considered an impossibility for a fugitive from Hindustan to make it into the heart of Persia and so Qaraar's presence was insignificant.

In Isfahan, Qaraar restored the tiles on the façade of Darb-e-Imam shrine to geometric perfection. The craftsman was sending a subtle message to Nadir, 'Bloodshed and ego will always be beaten by freedom of mind and creativity. Here I am in your city, inspiring beauty, while in mine you spilt blood.' During breaks, Qaraar and Aalf wandered the streets of Isfahan. Carpet weavers complained about dwindling business. Nothing new was being taught in science colleges. When they asked about new philosophers and poets the people of Isfahan drew a blank. In coffee shops, they overheard conversations only about the Sunni-Shia divide and how Nadir's obsession to make Persia a Sunni Empire was consuming him. Here, it was only about studying Islamic jurisprudence and trying to prove which school of law was the divine one. To Qaraar, the Sunni-Shia arguments lacked intellectual stimulation. According to some, Nadir's latest religious obsession was to get the Ottomans to accept the Jafari Immamiyah as the fifth legal sect of Islam, and he had been prepared to go to war against them too.

After some months in Isfahan and its surrounding areas, Aalf Olsson and Qaraar crossed the arid desert again. It took them another two and a half months to reach Bokhara. Amidst cheering crowds that showered rose petals on them, Qaraar was welcomed as the 'Flying Slave'. His accomplishments in Samarkand and Isfahan through travellers had found its way to Bokhara. In this city, he restored the tile work on the most majestic buildings – the Nadir Diwani Khanqaah and the Nadir Diwani Madrasa and picked up another 200 dinars.

'Many adventurous months behind us!' said Aalf Olsson sitting on a dust dune, having come back to Merv.

'You are a rich man, Aalf.'

'Rich with letters in my head', Aalf said with a smile and put a cloth bag in front of Qaraar. As it made contact with the ground, the clash of metal resounded. 'I have taken the 155 dinars I paid for you and your horse… this is yours. And as for you,' he said, placing his hand on Qaraar's shoulder, 'you are a free man.'

Qaraar opened the bag. 300 dinars. At that moment he knew he could trust the descendent of the Vikings. They rose and embraced. Both knew this was now a friendship that would last a lifetime. Hari was back in Qaraar's life in the form of Aalf. Qaraar looked at some of the other slaves that were with them in Merv. They had been under the watchful eyes of Aalf's bodyguards for the many months the new friends had travelled across Central Asia and Persia. Their pathetic condition concerned Qaraar deeply.

'Free them too. All humans are equal before God…'

Mounting his horse, Aalf signalled, 'As of now craftsman, I'm off!'

'To where? I wanted to tell you something important.' Qaraar wanted to tell him that he was a wanted man.

Swivelling the reins, 'Well, go on then!'

'Over a drink when you are back… where are you headed?'

'Not too far – just to the closest brothel!'

'Hah! I should have known.'

Qaraar reclined on a dust dune and watched Aalf and some of his guards disappear into the sunset. It had been a year and half since he had fled Delhi. Qaraar lit a fire as night descended. The greyish blue smoke from the fire wound its way skywards and vanished. The silence was soothing. Merv looked like a crater in the moon. In its ravaged state was an inexplicable beauty and Qaraar felt a sense of serenity within.

In the distance he saw five Bactrian double-humped camels making their way. They were Herati travellers who on seeing the fire Qaraar had lit came up and gently requested a few moments of warmth. With a smile Qaraar invited them.

'Some raisins, Huzoor,' the leader of the travellers, an old and wrinkled faced man offered Qaraar as a gesture of thanks.

'Who are you and where are you heading?'

'I was once the chief of the atelier of Kamaleddin Behzad the fifteenth-century artist of Herat… with chaos everywhere no one visits, so we are heading to Samarkand to show the works of the master.'

Qaraar sat up, 'Could you show me?'

The old man pulled out a miniature painting from his cloth bag. This was Behzad's cataclysmically melancholic work – *The burial of the great thirteenth century Sufi, Fariduddin Attar*. Attar, had written the famous poem – *Conference of the Birds* in which he told the story of each bird's quest to find the king of birds, the mythical Simurgh. To find their king, the birds had to undertake an arduous flight to the mountain Taar. On reaching the mountain, they discovered an inward realisation that the best resided in each one of them, and it was actually the search to understand themselves which was more important than finding a king.

Attar, an elderly man of eighty, was captured and then murdered by the all-slaying Mongols in 1225. Behzad had painted his burial with great emotion. A man wearing a blue robe had ripped it in mourning. But what Behzad did in the middle of the painting signified love and defiance. He painted a tree rising from the middle of the painting. A tree without leaves, almost lifeless, signified winter and Attar's death. But as if urging the eyes of the interested to climb branch by branch, at the topmost branch he painted a little nest. The nest had two small eggs and two birds perched on a branch next to it. And at the bottom of the tree was the slain Attar's grave. To anyone with a fertile imagination Behzad had communicated what he had felt. A Sufi could be physically murdered, but his philosophy of love would always find new life.

'This is exquisite,' said Qaraar admiring the painting as its sumptuous colours sprang to life when he held it next to the fire.

'Is this why you took this remote route, for fear of being robbed?' He continued.

The old man smiled but didn't say a word. Qaraar sensed his helplessness in these times. He reached into the cloth bag that Aalf had given him, pulled out 100 dinars and gave it to the surprised and speechless traveller.

'The pleasure of holding this painting in my hands is worth it. I wish you well.'

The travellers left. As they faded from sight, one amongst them sang the epic love poem *Laila Majnun.* His soothing voice – full and deep, had the dull but sensual, forlorn call of solitude of the Khorasan desert dunes. A realisation made its way into Qaraar's consciousness. He hadn't thought of Abeerah for a while. Qaraar lay back on the dune looking into the starry night. In the remoteness of deserts where God spoke to man, Qaraar felt his conscious state melt and he entered a dimension of divine contemplation. He thought of what his role was in this world and what would be his khidmat-e-khalq – the selfless service to mankind. He shut his eyes and began a zikr, repeating one of Allah's names, 'Ya Wadud' – the Loving, just as Shah Rezaan had done. He slept soundly.

Aalf's loud, earth-shaking voice shattered his sleep. 'Wake up! Wake up!'

'What is going…?'

'Get up now! Mount, and let's get out of here!'

It was dawn and Aalf was shaking Qaraar violently. Qaraar rose to his feet and looked around. Aalf's men were mounted.

'Why didn't you tell me you are the wanted Qaatil-e-Salaar?' holding Qaraar by his arm Aalf dragged him to Haider.

A surprised Qaraar stammered, 'I was going…'

'Forget it! We have to ride now.'

Qaraar mounted. So did the slave trader, who while holding the reins of his horse with one hand thrust a spyglass towards Qaraar with the other.

'Look! Afsharids! Nadir is attacking the Khan of Bokhara.'

Qaraar focussed. The Afsharids and the Khan's men were clashing fiercely. These were the frontier lands of the Khans and Nadir was trying to breakthrough.

'We were returning early this morning and saw masses of Afsharids riding towards Bokhara. Some held sketches of you, under which was written Qaatil-e-Salaar, whilst others held sketches of me.'

Qaraar looked at Aalf.

'Yes! You! And me! But you aren't the only reason for Nadir attacking Bokhara. He's had enough of these Khans holding out and is finally out to subdue them.'

Qaraar looked into the spyglass again. The battle was raging with great intensity. The two Uzbek's who had sold Qaraar had fallen into Afsharid hands in a dodgy tavern. Drunk, they had boasted about the secret route they had taken out of Hindustan and how they had sold the Qaatil-e-Salaar to a Viking descendant at the transiting slave market. The two Uzbeks were grabbed, taken to the local Afsharid commander who had them flogged publicly until they gave the exact description of Qaraar and Aalf to the sketch artists. They were then shot dead.

'Afsharids are coming in our direction!' Qaraar hastily put down the spyglass and swivelled Haider's reins.

The guards pulled out spare horses and the chained slaves were asked to mount. The reins of those horses were then quickly tied to theirs. Dust clouds from the approaching Afsharid horsemen were like menacing storms. Aalf screamed, 'Towards the Caspian!' All kicked their horses into a full gallop. Qaraar and Aalf sped past Sultan Sanjar's mausoleum, Qaraar briefly managing a smile. 'I'm leaving some pleasure for others in reviving its beauty,' he thought.

The friends soon broke into open desert. Qaraar looked down. The ground seemed to be disappearing under Haider's hooves at great speed. Galloping next to each other they had to yell to be heard.

With his hair flying in the wind, Aalf asked, 'If we make it to the Caspian, do we sail towards the Ottoman lands?'

Loosening the grip on the reins so that Haider could gallop even faster and getting into a crouching aerodynamic position with his head and back leaning forward, Qaraar yelled back, 'Yes! They rode like men possessed.

CHAPTER 5

PATTERNS OF THE HEART

Aalf Olsson and Qaraar soon doubled the lead they had on the chasing Afsharids. It helped that Qaraar and the slave traders rode light, whilst the Afsharids gave chase clad in heavy armour, which slowed down their horses considerably. Aalf Olsson also knew this land between Merv and the Caspian Sea like the back of his hand, having taken that route to the transiting slave market every year. He knew every shortcut and which were the friendly, or hostile, villages that dotted the landscape – but the Afsharids didn't have that knowledge. The two friends, the bodyguards and the slaves first rode straight into the Kopet Mountain range and lost the Afsharids in the maze of hills, ravines and rivulets, as the armour-clad Afsharid riders struggled to climb and turn. They briefly stopped at crumbling caravaneserais where their horses could be fed and watered.

Finally, after five days of blistering riding and clever navigation they made it to the coastal village of Ekerem. Here, in this unassuming village by the sea, hidden in a secret bay meant for local Turkic fishermen, Aalf kept a boat well stocked with food and wine. It was big enough to carry horses and his men. Along with the boat, he also kept a Persian with a title of 'Captain of the Ship' and a small Turkic crew. After sailing down the Caspian, he would normally disembark at the sea-town of Sari, at the south end of the Caspian, but this village of Ekerem, on the south-east of the Caspian, was his secret escape route out of Central Asia if things turned bad. Today, his insightful contingency plan had come in handy.

The large boat built on the northern banks of the Volga had a Viking shape to it. It was a piece of ancestral heritage that Aalf took great pride in, and he showed it off to Qaraar with immense joy.

'It's brilliant,' approved Qaraar marvelling at the rugged Viking design.

'Isn't it?' said Aalf Olsson, running his right palm across the wood, with a beaming smile. 'This is what we were known for.'

'Lord, we must sail – now!' came the voice of one of the guards.

'Kashtee bharo!' Aalf instructed his men in his newly acquired knowledge of Urdu.

Greatly amused, Qaraar abided by the instructions. He guided Haidar into the water and then onto the ship. Hooves of other horses splashed into the Caspian's waters and then onto the gangway. Within minutes they were sailing. The tough Turkic crew showed real muscle as they got stuck in with the slaves in the lower deck rowing with immense power and strength. The Afsharid naval threat was still very real. Sitting on deck with the captain, Qaraar and Aalf pored over a map of the Caspian as waves lashed the sides of the boat.

'Nadir controls everything, Azerbaijan, Georgia and even Armenia. Baku is right here,' said Aalf, pointing at the port.

'Where is it that you really want to go, Lord?' enquired the Persian captain of the boat, a bit frustrated at not being involved in the sailing plans.

Aalf ignored the captain and addressed Qaraar instead.

'We must get to the Ottoman lands and so let's keep going north and then cut west when we have passed Baku and Izberbash's latitude… then we can disembark in Sulak in Dagestan.'

'From there my friend,' Aalf looked at Qaraar, 'there is a slender land corridor that will take us into the Ottoman lands leaving Armenia to the side.'

Qaraar and Aalf shook hands.

'Got it?' Aalf asked the captain.

Uhh... yes.'

Aalf pulled the captain by the back of his neck and forced his head to focus on the map.

'After we disembark, you will sail up the Volga and into Europe. Got it?'

'Okay, my Lord!'

Tightening his grip on the back of his neck, Aalf said, 'Do not, I repeat, do not sail back down the Caspian.'

'Okay, okay,' the captian croaked.

The sailing was in near perfect conditions and the vast expanse of seemingly never-ending waves filled Qaraar with happiness. He had never laid eyes on a sea before. Having lived all his life in Delhi, the closest he had got to natural flowing water was the Yamuna and more recently the Murghab, but never the sea. Excited like a child, he spent hours on deck taking in the sights of waves, dolphins and the odd flying fish. Despite knowing full well that he was a fugitive, the sight of surging Caspian waves gave him a sense of freedom. He looked around and saw the variety of people he was surrounded by: Viking descendants, a Persian captain, Turkic crew, African slaves and himself, a Hindustani. All in one boat. Watching the boat rise and dip in accordance with the varying sizes of waves, he recited the famous verses of the fifteenth century mystic, Kabir.

> As the bubbles of the river are accounted water and blend with the water of the ocean,
> so the man who looketh on all with an equal eye, shall become pure and blend with the infinite.[65]

Then seeing the diversity around him, another verse left Qaraar's lips. The words of Shek Isa, a seventeenth-century Sufi scholar who had written commentaries on Ibn Arabi's works.

Were the heart of a single drop to be dissected,
From out of it comes hundreds of oceans,
All gods; all beloveds, all actors and all universalities are the theophany of His attributes.[66]

Sitting on deck, he watched the sun that seemed to ascend and descend over the surging waves. After a few hours, some of the Turkic crew came on deck with a seafood dinner of crab, shrimps and grilled sea bass. Both friends settled in to savour this welcome meal after five days of hard riding.

'Thanks to you, I'm a fugitive too,' Aalf said while cracking open a crab.

Rubbing his bottom, he continued, 'My arse is sore from the riding!'

Choosing to ignore Aalf's crude demonstration, Qaraar said, biting into a shrimp, 'I don't know what the future holds, but there is a rising sense of adventure.' The sound of lashing waves against the ship seemed to agree.

A smiling Aalf nodded and called out loudly, 'Bring out the wine!'

For Aalf, it was always about selling humans, fighting his way out of tricky situations and living a life of a vagabond with his bodyguards. He hadn't respected any of his peers for this business, but now he had a friendship with someone who had a reputation for intelligence and bravery, and an inheritance of love and loss. Sharing life's adventures with someone whom he could relate to as a friend and teacher was something that had come to excite him. The sun disappeared into the Caspian waves, turning the blue waters orange.

'Urdu and Persian lesson time!' said Qaraar, ensuring that his voice rose above the noise of the waves.

'Bring it on master!' came the brave response from Aalf, who struggled to his feet as the boat bounced around.

'Sunset! What is it in Urdu and Persian?' asked Qaraar looking at the orange sky.

'Ghuroob-e-Khursheed,' came a confident answer.

'Well done... Now give me the line for one intoxicated in divine love?'

'Sarshaar-e-Ishq!' came another confident reply.

'Well done again!' Qaraar smiled.

'And you? Who are you?' asked Qaraar.

'Just a drunk... a Baaday Khaar', laughed Aalf.

The waves climbed higher and crashed against the boat with even greater force, overflowing onto the deck.

'A verse from Hafez now, but write it down!' Qaraar pushed his student.

'Get me Kaagaz-Qalam,' Aalf instructed one of the Turkic crew members who scurried down into the cabin and came back with a lantern, paper and pen.

On a wobbling deck, the Viking descendant wrote as his servant held the lamp up for him.

That, that is not the flame of love's true fire
Which makes the torchlight shadows dance in rings,
But where the radiance draws the moths desire
And sends him forth with scorched and drooping wings.
The heart of one who dwells retired shall break,
Remembering a black mole and a red cheek, And his life ebb,
sapped at its secret springs.[67]

'Subhanallah!'

'Thank you master. Ask me more!'

'Her dark tresses.'

'Siyah zulf,' said Aalf, but before Qaraar could compliment him, he had something more to say, 'But I can do better master.'

'What do you mean?'

'Please reveal yourself!'

Qaraar watched on curiously holding onto the mast of the boat.

From the cabin emerged a beauty. She had sharp features, piercing blue eyes, naturally deep red lips and long jet-black hair down to her waist. She made her way to the deck and sat by Aalf's feet.

Looking at her Aalf said, 'She was at the brothel that night.' Not taking his eyes off her, he continued, 'Her name is Hova. An Armenian Christian. She was sold to the brothel. I heard her story in that smoky room; paid off the brothel keepers...'

There was silence.

Aalf turned to Qaraar, 'I thought of your words – *all humans are equal before God...* I'm in love and I brought her with me for a life of an equal.'

In the frenzy of escaping from the Afsharid soldiers, Qaraar hadn't noticed this beauty who had been covered in men's clothing during the flight. She rode amongst them and was now part of their camp.

There was that genuineness in Aalf's eyes that used to be in Qaraar's when he looked at Abeerah. Qaraar spotted it immediately as the Viking descendant put his palm on the beauty's head, which rested on his knees. She looked up helplessly and then lowered her eyes. After a moment's pause, Qaraar let out a huge unabashed laugh.

Stumbling and walking up to Aalf, 'The slave trader with a heart as soft as a rabbit's ear! A lover! So that's what you've become!'

Then looking at the beauty he said, 'Make your hair into chains of love around his wrists.'

Qaraar gulped down a glass of wine as the beauty was lifted to her feet and tenderly embraced by Aalf.

Looking at Hova, Qaraar was reminded of Sarmad the Armenian poet in Dara Shikoh's Sufi circle. He recited a line:

> If Sarmad is the body: the soul, is in whose hand...?

Almost instantly, Hova turned back and completed the verse from Sarmad.

And if the arrow is the heart, the bow is in whose hand?[68]

'You know him,' nodded Qaraar in approval.

'Our greatest!'

The lovers left.

Qaraar stayed on deck. The captain came rushing up and spoke nervously, 'The lights of Baku are in the distance.'

Qaraar grabbed the spyglass with one hand and continued to sip wine with the other. It seemed his anxiety had been replaced by the sense of adventure. 'O well – keep sailing.' There was a callousness in his tone. 'The sea is too rough for any Afsharid ship to come out and give chase,' he thought to himself.

The captain left.

Alone on deck Qaraar thought about how love resides in everyone's hearts, whether a poet, a craftsman or a slave trader. He thought about the power love had to make people better human beings. He slept on deck that night.

After 10 days of sailing, some of which was slow as the winds disappeared, they docked in Sulak, guided in by Russian fishermen. But as they disembarked there was uneasiness amongst the guards.

Looking at Aalf, one of them spoke, 'Where do we stand in all this?'

'You are with your Hindustani friend and Hova. You have Nadir's men looking for you. We haven't sold any of these slaves on-board. God knows where we are headed! Now that you are a fugitive, we can't do any slave trading. We aren't taking this any longer!' he raged.

While this was a rebellion, the guard had an important point. The lives of the guards depended on the selling of slaves and it had been an exceptionally long time since they had either bought new slaves or sold the ones they had. Looking at the slaves the guard continued, 'This stock is getting old. We need to dispose of them now.'

'Quiet!' said Qaraar hearing this mockery of humanity.

'This is the lowest that man can fall to!' he continued in anger.

'We are on the run because of you, with nowhere to go,' came the guard's defiant reply.

'Enough!' roared Aalf. Then sighing deeply, 'Maybe the time has come after all.' Turning to Qaraar he spoke softly, 'Maybe I was waiting for your presence in my life to give me the courage to do what I am about to.' He felt a sense of lightness as he spoke the next words. 'For years I have been carrying this burden, but now I know it's the right time to let go.'

The guards looked at him with surprise. 'You are all free to go. I will no longer be a slave trader. The captain will sail up the Volga. You can go with him and then do as you please. You don't have to accompany me.'

Then looking at the slaves, he said, 'My last order as your Lord is to free these men. They were bought under my command and as my last command I release them.'

'But!'

'It was my money which bought them. Now cut them free.'

The chains around the slaves' ankles and wrists were cut, and the men ran in all directions.

'Those of you wanting to join us, can join as free men,' said Qaraar, as he mounted Haider.

'What about money?' asked one of the guards.

Aalf distributed all he had. Qaraar looked into the little bag of dinars. There were only 100 dinars left. Qaraar pulled out 50 dinars and handed them over.

'We are almost bankrupt,' said Qaraar continuing to peer into the bag.

'But my conscience is rich!' replied Aalf. Then he yelled out, 'Come forward if you will join us!'

Just two of the 50 guards stepped forward. They went to the ship and pulled out provisions that could sustain them, then mounted their horses and rode up next to Qaraar. These two men were the best in the newly acquired knowledge of Urdu and Persian having joined Aalf for his lessons. They were also brilliant carpenters, having worked on building Aalf's ship. Aalf and Hova watched the boat sail up towards the Volga delta. That life had now left Aalf. It reminded Qaraar of how his own past had left him.

Qaraar said reassuring words. 'Let it go. We will be fine. In the Ottoman lands there is much restoration work to be done.'

'Into Anatolia – the Ottoman lands!' cried Aalf as he kicked his horse into a full gallop.

After another month of cautious riding they slipped through the slender mountainous corridor that took them into the Ottoman lands. And after a few more months where the riding changed from cautious to carefree, they reached Lake Van. Spring of 1741 broke, with clear blue skies framing the hills, which were entirely covered with tall, dark green cypress trees.

Lake Van, surrounded by hills and ruins of Armenian monasteries, became the playground for the Viking-Armenian romance. Hova hid in the ruins and Aalf chased her around like a love-struck puppy. Qaraar and Hova also struck-up a friendship, cemented by their mutual interest in Sarmad's mystical poetry. The travellers, though, had to be mindful of their resources. Days of fun under the Anatolian sun gave way to more serious thoughts and conversations of subsistence. They had to find work. Leaving Lake Van behind they travelled further west until after a few days they spotted an old, brown mud-walled caravanserai. Tying their horses at the stables, they entered the main building. An ageing, stocky Turk greeted them in Persian.

'Khushamdeed. How many rooms?'

'Four,' replied Qaraar, as he handed over the last of the dinars they had.

'There you go,' said the smiling host giving them their keys. 'Some kebabs are being grilled in the main room, if you wish to have an early supper.'

The travellers took their seats on the floor, which was covered with distinct Turkish carpets decorated with depictions of cypress trees. At a distance were some other travellers, with their back towards Qaraar and busy sipping raki. Waiting for their kebabs to arrive, Qaraar overheard one of the travellers recite a verse.

> This time again, the spring has gone in vain,
> Flower after flower sprang, but you my love never came.[69]

The traveller then complimented the poet.

'What a great poet this young Sauda is. He writes so brilliantly in Urdu and Persian.'

The words felt like a cool breeze as they entered Qaraar's heart.

'Sauda!' Qaraar leapt to his feet in excitement and ran straight to the traveller who had his back to him.

Stammering in excitement, 'Huzoor, where did you hear this? Did you recite Sauda's verse?'

The traveller turned and looked at Qaraar and immediately put down the raki he was sipping.

'Sir, it's you! Qaraar Ali!'

Qaraar looked blankly.

'Don't you recognise me – us? We are the Ottoman travellers whom you entertained in your house in Delhi.'

After a few seconds, he said, 'Of course! How are you?'

'We should be asking you that.' The other traveller walked up and embraced Qaraar.

'I… I am alright. But you said you heard these verses – Sauda, is he…?' Before Qaraar could finish his question, one of the Ottoman travellers replied in excitement.

'Yes! He is alive and so are the other two poets, Dard and Mir.'

Qaraar's heart leapt with joy.

'But coming back to you Qaraar Ali sahib, we heard of the great tragedy that befell your family.'

Immediately Aalf walked up and placed his hand on Qaraar's shoulder.

'This is Aalf Olsson.'

'Salaam.'

'But you must know a few things. You are celebrated in Delhi as the great Qaatil-e-Salaar! In fact, people in Delhi are writing songs in your praise as the great craftsman warrior!'

'What?'

'Yes! It's true. There are myths and legends about you even in Khiva, Samarkand and Bokhara as the famed fighter who is in disguise as a craftsman-slave.'

Aalf added to the conversation, 'That is believable. We were there until last year and he made quite a name for himself as "The Flying Slave" until Nadir attacked.'

'How do you know everything that's going on there?' Qaraar asked turning to the Ottoman travellers.

Signalling with his hand for all to sit down and enjoy their kebabs which were ready by now, one of the Ottoman travellers elaborated. 'We went back to Delhi… Oh, let me start again! Nadir put Muhammad Shah back on the throne of Delhi and left to fight the Khans of Khiva and Bokhara. We went to Delhi hoping to reignite trade with the Mughal emperor and that's where we heard about everything. On the way back we heard of the happenings in Khiva, Bokhara and Samarkand.'

Enjoying his kebab skewer Aalf raised his head briefly and said, 'But Nadir hates you Ottomans. How did you manage to come back?'

'We are traders sir, not soldiers. Kings need us whatever our race, religion or colour.'

'True,' agreed Aalf with a nod of his head but not slowing down on the devouring of his kebabs.

'Did I hear you say Muhammad Shah is ruling Delhi and the Mughal Empire is intact?' asked Qaraar with increased curiosity.

'Yes and no. Muhammad Shah is back on the throne, but the Mughal Empire is at its weakest.'

Qaraar frowned. 'After all the loot that Nadir took away it's no wonder that the Empire is weak.' But then a thoughtful smile broke on his face, 'My poet friends that have survived will keep the literature alive.'

'And where will you go? You can't go back to Delhi because Muhammad Shah will hand you over to Nadir, as will the Khans of Khiva and Bokhara – so where to?' inquired one of the Ottomans.

'I don't know. I'm looking for work – tile-making and restoration,' said Qaraar playing with the edge of a cylindrical Turkish cushion.

'You are in the right place.'

'What do you mean?'

'Head west. You will pass tall grasslands and eventually reach Konya. The master lies there – Rumi.' All listened carefully. 'His mausoleum is bursting with creative energy. Painters, poets, musicians, potters, calligraphers. Stay there and you will not just survive, you will thrive. We must leave now.'

'Where do you go?

'We head north-west to Istanbul.'

All embraced each other.

RUMI'S MAUSOLEUM, KONYA

After riding through grassland that towered above their horses making navigation difficult, they broke into hilly countryside dotted with yellow tulips and purple pansies. From there they descended into Konya.

'Yes, we need tile-makers – come on in,' said the tall, thin chief host of the Sufi tekke, which adjoined the mausoleum.

Explaining the tekke layout, the chief host took them around. 'There at the far end, after the tulip garden, are your quarters. Next to them are the kilns. To the left are the workshops of the calligraphers, to the right are where the potters work, and this right in front of us is the door to the sama khana.'

'Can we…?' Qaraar was hoping to visit the music room.

'Not now, but tomorrow.'

A curious Hova asked, 'Why tomorrow?'

'Every Thursday we celebrate the life of the master, but tomorrow is special. It's his Urs, the day his soul merged with his lover – God, and so the celebration will be extra special.'

'Coming to the tiles, which ones need restoration?' asked Qaraar.

'Make new tiles,' said the chief pointing at the minaret.

'Yes, Huzoor.'

'Lodgings and meals will be taken care of. Besides the tiles for the mausoleum, you are encouraged to make small toy tiles which can be sold at the bazaars we have on Thursdays. You will also help out in collecting wood from the forests, picking the igde fruits and cooking in the kitchen.'

'I'd love to cook,' came Aalf's eager response.

'I'll collect firewood,' said Hova.

The next evening the music room was bursting with people. Christian monks, Jewish rabbis, Sufi scholars, tradesmen, women, old, young, rich and poor. All were One here. Fifteen men entered. They were dressed in white collarless robes known as tennures. On top of the tennures they wore woollen flowing cloaks called the destegul. Their heads were graced by the long sikke caps, which were made of solid tanned carpet fabric. At the base of the sikke, they had wrapped a destar, a white ribbon specially knitted from cheesecloth. To the sweet sound of the kaval, the long Anatolian flute, they whirled. Qaraar swayed gently watching them. As the whirling reached its crescendo a chorus of deep male voices sang Rumi's poem:

> Oh brother, you are nothing but your thoughts
> The rest of you is merely skin nd bones
> If your thought is a rose, you are a rose garden
> If your thought is a thorn, you are fuel for the fire.[70]

After an hour of whirling, the chief host brought an end to the evening saying, 'This is a life-long journey within to find love.' Making his way outside, Qaraar felt a calming of the heart and mind. The bustling bazaar outside was teeming with people. All seemed to be moulded in Rumi's mystical cast. A sense of kindness and harmony in diversity was everywhere in Konya. The inhabitants seemed to have abandoned the hammer of the judge. No one took the moral high ground on the other. People greeted each other with warmth like never seen anywhere else by the travellers. Finally, Qaraar saw Rumi's massive raised tomb known as turbe. At the head was a large winding green turban. He bowed his head, kissed the tomb and sat on the floor in quiet meditation throughout the evening.

The friends settled into monastic life with ease. Impressed by Qaraar's congenial manner, after a few months the Chief host transferred his position to him and instead took up running the library of Rumi's works. Qaraar busied himself in tile-making and welcoming people into the mausoleum. One of his favourite chores was going into the nearby hills looking for the igde plants. Standing about eight metres high, their flowers had the most wonderful honeyed fragrance. The igde fruit that hung from the branches had a thin brown skin which when peeled revealed the feathery soft white flesh. It was so soft that it would melt immediately when it entered the mouth, releasing a sugary sweet flavour. Qaraar would go foraging with his Viking assistants and would return with baskets bursting with igde. He would welcome new visitors with these fruits.

Aalf found great joy in cooking in the kitchens. He went shopping at the local farms every morning with the cooks, picking fresh vegetables and choosing meat. He chopped, cut, mixed, stirred and served daily meals with his own hands to everyone in the monastery. Scholars to beggars, all ate from the dishes he prepared. At Rumi's mausoleum, the once fearsome slave trader walked head bowed before the poverty stricken who would gather at meal times, serving each hungry human with joy and kindness.

Such deep inner satisfaction did Aalf feel that he didn't see it as a duty but a pleasure. Hova took great care of the tulip garden in the main courtyard, nurturing and nourishing its varied varieties.

One group of artists in the mausoleum were masters in the art of paper-marbling, a 300-year-old Turkish craft found mainly in Anatolia. Hova developed a keen interest in this art form and studied diligently under the residing artists. It was one of the most unique crafts where gum extracts were used to paint the most delicate looking flora, fauna and landscapes. Months of practice made Hova an expert and she soon held exhibitions in Konya. With Qaraar as the tile-maker, Hova as the paper-marbling artist and Aalf as the brilliant chef, the three found a new life and meaning. As a troupe they soon started holding regular exhibitions of their own. Every Thursday the area around the mausoleum took on a carnival spirit where Qaraar, Aalf and Hova put up their stalls. People flocked to see and buy Qaraar's tiles which now came in various formats – girih, blue with floral depictions, and children's toy tiles with figures. The two assistants who were once Aalf's bodyguards worked at a local carpenter's shop and made small ships as toys to be sold every Thursday. Qaraar even gave the troupe a name: 'Bashinday-e-Duniya.' It meant 'Citizens of the World'. It was true of them: a Hindustani, an Eastern European and an Armenian, living in Turkey.

'Let's increase the knowledge of our troupe and add to our skills,' said Qaraar one evening as they sat next to the tulip garden.

'What do you mean?' asked Hova watering the tulips.

'Aalf, you have a great way with kids and families – I saw you with them in Samarkand.'

'So?'

'Well, Nasroddin Hoja was a great thirteenth century Anatolian Sufi – his wit and stories are quite well known...'

'Go on.'

'Why don't you study his works and when we have our exhibitions, enact them for children and adults?'

'Great idea. It'll add a new dimension to our work.'

After a few months of reading Nasroddin Hoja's works with help from the Chief of Libraries, Aalf came out one Thursday dressed like him. He put on a wig with silver hair and a silver beard. He puffed himself up with a pillow then tied a large white turban around his head and rode into the bazaar on a donkey which was Nasroddin Hoja's favourite ride. He then stationed himself next to the troupe's stall.

Children immediately surrounded the stall.

'Tell us some stories of Hoja! Now! Now!'

'Here you go,' said Aalf adjusting his turban.

A neighbour came to ask Nasroddin for his clothesline so he could dry his clothes. Nasroddin said, "I'm sorry, I'm drying flour on it". The neighbour said, "But how can one dry flour on a clothesline?" "It's easier when you don't want to lend it," he replied.[71]

The children and parents roared in laughter.

Seeing Aalf kick his donkey into motion, a child yelled out.

'Hold the reins of that donkey! Don't let him go!'

'Please one more! Please, please!' Nearly fifty children surrounded Aalf and the donkey.

Bringing the baying beast back to the troupe's stall Aalf gave in to the children's pressing demands.

'Alright, calm down, one last one, listen carefully,' said Aalf.

"One day a man fell from a roof and on to Nasroddin. Poor Nasroddin broke his neck. People came rushing up to him, including a scholar of logic, who asked, 'What lesson have you learned from this?' Looking up at the scholar, Nasroddin replied, 'I have learnt to shun theoretical questions that people like you ask; If a man falls from the roof, will his neck be broken? He fell, yet I broke my neck – so I don't believe in logic.'"[72]

Smiles, laughter and claps immediately followed.

The Bashinday-e-Duniya troupe soon left Konya and travelled to nearby villages received by adulating crowds. Every evening they would return to their quarters at Rumi's mausoleum, a deeply satisfied and content lot.

One day two opportunities came up at the same time. One was to restore the blue tilework in the inner sanctum of the mausoleum, and another was to restore the geometric-patterned blue tiles at the Alaeddin Mosque not too far from the mausoleum. The Alaeddin mosque also contained the tombs of Seljuk Sultans of Rum.

'Which one would you like to begin working on first?' came the question from the now Chief of Libraries.

Qaraar responded in a flash, 'To work on the tiles of the master's mausoleum will be the greatest honour. Sultans will have to wait.'

For the next few months Qaraar worked exclusively in Rumi's mausoleum glazing each tile to perfection. Once this had been completed, he moved onto the Alaeddin Mosque's geometric patterns. Here, he hung from the ceiling under the majestic dome with the help of his pulley contraption effectively managed by the two assistants. After three months of hard work the result was astonishingly beautiful. Even here in Konya, like in Samarkand, Khiva and Bokhara, people gathered all around in admiration of the finished work.

Satisfied after the restoration work one evening, Qaraar was sitting by the tulip garden when he heard a voice.

'I heard your answer three months ago to the Chief of Libraries.'

Qaraar saw an elderly dervish. He was a calligrapher of great repute from the Naqshbandi Sufi order. While the origins of this order were in Bokhara, travelling calligraphers of this sect often took lodgings at the tekkes in Rumi's mausoleum. Going with Rumi's philosophy, all were welcome. This elderly dervish had learned and exclusively worked on the Hillye-Serif calligraphy styles, a unique kind of calligraphy work done on gold, turquoise and cobalt backgrounds. Qaraar had been so busy with his tilework that he hadn't taken notice of this new resident.

'Huzoor.'

'It was the apt answer – Sultans must wait.'

'Thank you.'

Seeing the calligrapher seated on the floor poring over his labour of love, Qaraar asked, 'Might I enter the calligraphy rooms?'

'Of course, do come in.'

Aalf and Hova followed and they sat on the floor in front of him. On closer examination they saw the robe the calligrapher wore was unique. It had Rumi's poetry all over it.

'Did you calligraph these verses on your robe?' Qaraar enquired, taking a closer look.

'Yes, this way the master's words stay close to my heart!' replied the Sufi calligrapher with a charming smile. 'So, you are from Hindustan?' he continued, dipping his pen into black ink.

'Yes Huzoor. Have you been?'

'No, I haven't, but my grandfather visited it,' the calligrapher continued with his illustration seemingly undistracted and quite easily multitasking.

'How come?' Qaraar held out his palm, filled with little igde fruits.

'Umm, thank you!' Then, after gulping down the fruit and putting the seeds in a little wooden cup, he continued.

'Well, Dara Shikoh the Mughal Crown Prince had heard of him and invited him to teach him calligraphy along with other Turkish and Persian calligraphers.'

'That's fascinating.'

'So, coming back to your answer "Sultans must wait" – it's good to know that you can make a distinction between Sufism and power.'

Qaraar realised that there was a meaningful conversation to be had and so he enquired deeper, 'But Huzoor some Sufi orders did play a role in politics… Your order, the Naqshbandis advice kings regularly.'

'Yes, you are right, son,' came the Sufi's answer, but raising his eyebrows he explained further. 'We do provide advice and guidance but for the good and that too when we are sought out. We declined positions at court that wielded daily power.'

'So, do different Sufi orders engage differently with politics?' Qaraar enquired.

'Indeed, the Chishtis and the Mevlavis, for example, completely disassociated themselves from courts and kings... and I'm beginning to get more inclined towards this way... that's why I keep coming here... to the master.' The Sufi said pointing at Rumi's mausoleum.

Aalf probed further, 'But Huzoor, aren't power, religion and politics important?'

Smiling and now continuing to move his calligraphic pen in what seemed a beautiful rhythmic movement, 'Not to the Sufis. They aren't.'

'Why?'

'When power and dogmatic religion become political, it becomes a heady mix and brings out the worst in man. It makes him untrustworthy.... and the Sufis stay away from those men,' said the calligrapher forcefully.

Having known Qaraar well now, Aalf brought a dimension to the conversation which he knew would interest him even more. 'Why don't the orthodox clergy and the Sufis get on?'

The calligrapher reached out for another ink pot, while rising slowly and supporting his knees he answered, 'The Sufis applied an esoteric, mystical and inward meaning to the verses of the Quran which related to renunciation, satisfaction, hope and poverty. For them it wasn't a rule book to be imposed on others, it was about undertaking a journey within oneself. Their main aim being to rid their lives of hypocrisy.'[73]

All listened intently to these words as the Sufi calligrapher brought his fresh ink pot, placed it on the floor, wrapped his robe, folded his legs under him and sat in front of his incomplete work.

Then he minutely inspected the range of calligraphic pens around him. While examining one with particular interest he continued, 'The clergy unlike the Sufis were mere administrators of law and they denounced the Sufi mystics as ignorant of the law – in turn, the Sufis criticised the clergy for being externalists and formalists.'[74]

Seeing the conversation was getting interesting, Qaraar rushed to a niche in the wall where a teapot and some glass cups were kept. He came running back hoping not to miss out on the words. Pouring deep red, Turkish tea into the small curved cups he served it first to the calligrapher, 'Go on, Huzoor.'

Sipping the tea slowly and pleased with having chosen the correct pen, the calligrapher dipped it into fresh ink and continued, 'Only when the individual self and ego is lost, the doors to illumination of the heart are opened and the Universal Self is found.'[75]

'So, the rulers used to seek out the Sufis, not the other way around?'

'Yes, and when the rulers spent time with them and learned from the Sufis it made them compassionate and enlightened. It also meant fewer wars.'

'Wars!' yelled Aalf, flexing his muscles.

'War is never an option for Sufis, but wars did happen and continue to happen, but when undertaken by rulers under Sufi influence, they did their best to be humane.'

Aalf snorted into his tea, 'Humane in war?'

'Difficult I know, but there are examples. Hazrat Ali, made it clear that in an unavoidable war, the old, women and children wouldn't be harmed. Homes wouldn't be burnt, and neither would trees and saplings be uprooted.'

'Really?' asked Aalf in disbelief.

'Yes, even here in Anatolia.' The Sufi calligrapher adjusted his artwork and then continued. 'Seljuk Sultan Keyhusrev defeated the Greek King Alexius III in 1196 and took many Greek prisoners. But then see what he does next – he listened to the Sufis when it came to the treatment of prisoners. He treated them so well that it shocked the Greeks. He personally brought bread and firewood for the prisoners, gave them land for cultivation and provided them seeds and eventually freed them.'[76]

'And in most cases when rulers were influenced by Sufis, they directed their resources to sciences, arts and social improvement,' said Qaraar caressing the Turkish carpet with his hand.

'Indeed,' said the Sufi calligrapher focusing his eyes on his work.

Aalf asked, 'Does that mean that when the dogmatic clergy got close to the rulers it made them short-sighted and bent on the imposition of the rules of religion?'

'Now you've got it!'

Seeing his audience in rapt attention, the calligrapher continued.

'When Rumi passed into the arms of God, at his burial Christian and Jewish monks wept. A weeping Greek priest said, "He was like bread and we were hungry... have you ever seen a hungry person run away from bread?"[77] So you see this is Sufism: it brings people together, unlike power that divides.'

'So, one should not aspire for power?' asked Hova.

'According to me never! There was once a man called Parwana. He lived in the thirteenth century. The most politically astute man, always power broking between the Seljuks and the Mongols. He got this title because he was like a moth attracted to a flame. He, the moth. Power, the flame.' All listened carefully as the Sufi calligrapher lowered his voice, his tone hinting that something outrageous would soon be heard. Then he continued, 'Parwana double-crossed and did everything he could to stay in power. He tried to get an audience with Rumi many times trying to seek his blessings, but Rumi avoided him. Eventually fed up with his games, the savage Mongols killed him, then boiled and served his flesh at a banquet.'[78]

'What?!' gulped Aalf, spilling hot tea on himself.

'Careful now, don't boil yourself for a banquet!' said the calligrapher.

All laughed.

'Anyway!' Getting up from the floor he said, 'Here is a little gift for you – I love the name of your troupe.' The Sufi presented them with a gold-bordered panel with the troupe's name written in the most exquisite calligraphic form in black ink on a turquoise cloth.

'Thank you Huzoor – such an honour!' Qaraar bowed and kissed the Sufi's hand.

'This will be our Alam, our standard, and we will hold it aloft as we enter cities and villages,' Qaraar said with great excitement.

'I must leave now,' said the Sufi rising slowly with difficulty.

Aalf asked him, 'Where to?' and rushed to help.

Catching his breath, he said, 'Istanbul. The sultan will be coming to me.' Holding onto his mutteqa staff and then looking at Aalf with a grateful smile, 'To my khanqaah. He's been craving to see my work. Finally, I have spared some time for him.' Then with a wink, 'I have kept him waiting for many years.'

'Let me help you with your luggage.' Qaraar walked the Sufi calligrapher to his horse.

The troupe soon gained a reputation. From the villages around Konya, word spread north. Qaraar's brilliant restoration of tiles at Rumi's mausoleum and at the Alaeddin Mosque enhanced their fame. Even the Sufi calligrapher stopped over in Bursa on his way to Istanbul and made a recommendation on their behalf. The Yesil Cami Mosque, had once sparkled with some of the most exquisite girih tilework, but now was in the worst possible condition. It was evident that here too in the Ottoman lands, constant conflict with Europe in the west and Nadir in the east meant diminishing funds for cultural upkeep.

The Sufi calligrapher recommended the troupe's name with a special mention of Qaraar's restoration skills, highlighting the fact that since they worked in villages, they wouldn't be too expensive. Within a month of the calligrapher's departure from Konya, the troupe was invited by the Qadi of Bursa to come and restore its girih tiles. The money on offer was meagre, but the troupe hoped that Hova's paper marbling sales and Aalf's performances would supplement it.

The troupe had spent more than two years in and around the Konya region. Qaraar wanted to remain in Konya but the Chief of Libraries convinced him that a craftsman should never turn down an offer to restore beauty. It would be like a doctor refusing to attend a patient. Repeatedly kissing the turbe of the master, teary-eyed the troupe left for Bursa with gratitude in their hearts.

They rode north. Aalf took his baying donkey with him. A guide from Konya accompanied them. The road to Bursa was a dangerous one, swarming with highwaymen and bandits. The most dangerous part was the unavoidable, desolate, long narrow pass through Sultan Dagi, above Egirdir leading out to the ruined fortress of Myriocephalum. At the mouth of the pass, the guide looked around unsurely.

'Dismount!' he said.

'Why?' asked Qaraar.

'Shhh. Speak softly!'

The guide took the invitation of the Qadi of Bursa, made two holes on the edges, strung a thread around it and put it around Qaraar's neck.

'Wear it on your chest, if the bandits attack.' Everyone paused and looked up at the high mountains that overhung the narrow pass they were about to enter. 'They will see the invitation immediately and know that you are poor craftsmen.'

'What makes this place so eerie?' asked Hova, holding tightly onto Aalf's arm.

The guide explained the history of the pass. 'In 1176 the Byzantine King Manuel's army came down from Constantinople with a massive force, determined on crushing the Seljuk Sultan Kilic Arslan. Walking in a single file, the army entered this pass. The sultan, though, had astutely placed his men on the mountain tops and from there, like thunderbolts, the Seljuk Turk's arrows struck Manuel's army. Stones and boulders were also hurled down. It was slaughter in the crevice like pass and the Byzantine army was crushed under lead and stone.'[79]

The guide gulped, 'They say if one listens carefully, the screams of dying men can be heard even today. Some say that skulls are still...'

'That's enough, let's proceed,' said Qaraar interrupting the guide whose words were frightening Hova.

Cautiously they entered the pass. It was so narrow that hardly any light penetrated through it. The guide recited prayers as he led the way. The pass's haunting history soon came alive as Qaraar spotted a dusty helmet and then a brittle skull lying in the undergrowth.

'Man's duality revealed yet again,' Qaraar thought to himself, 'From the humanity experienced at Rumi's mausoleum, to the barbarity in the dreadful pass.'

On arriving in Bursa, the Qadi immediately took Qaraar to the site. The girih tilework at the Yesil Cami Mosque proved to be extremely challenging. For days, Qaraar sat by the walls with compass and pen. The shapes weren't forming. So intricate were they, so specific their angles and the remaining clues so obscure, that Qaraar failed a few times. In frustration he drew a cloth all around the site, so that people couldn't mock at his repeated failures. The hexagon mosaic had to be remade with individually cut pieces of monochrome tile fitted together to form a pattern. A multi-pointed star in the centre added to the challenge. It took Qaraar a year to restore these wall panels and the geometric open work screen facing the mihrab. But when the day to reveal the walls came and he drew the cloth, the invited gentry – that included the sultan's minister of culture – felt his magic. Elated by what he had seen, the minister of culture soon sent Qaraar the ultimate invitation.

The card read thus:

We, the Arts Council of Istanbul, invite
The Bashinday-e-Duniya troupe to be part of
the annual celebrations to mark the fourteenth year of the reign
of Sultan of Sultans,
Commander of the Faithful, Lord of the Universe
Sultan Mahmud I.
Make yourself known at the mighty Topkapi Palace
by presenting your credentials to the Sultan on 30 May 1744.

Sealed
Ministry of Culture

It was the annual cultural event when the sultan met with the creative world in his Empire. If he found the works or performances outstanding, he invited the select few to be part of his inner circle of the creative arts.

'I don't want to go. I'd much rather go back to Konya,' said Qaraar flinging the invitation away.

Aalf picked up the card. 'Not going will be an insult to the sultan and believe me, we can't afford that!' he laughed.

'Sultans, emperors, we should stay away from them – didn't you hear what the Sufi calligrapher said?' Hova agreed with Qaraar.

'But we aren't pursuing a political career in his court, just demonstrating our skills,' insisted Aalf, walking up to Qaraar with the invitation.

Aalf continued in a comforting voice, 'Qaraar, you worked for Muhammad Shah so why this conflict?'

'That was another time. I don't want to be anywhere near power.'

'Listen. We present our credentials, and come back.'

'What if we get selected into his inner circle?'

'So what? We carry on with tilework, paper marbling and me – well, I just love riding that baying donkey like Nasroddin did!'

Qaraar smiled.

Aalf looked Qaraar in the eye. 'I know you want to stay away from palaces and power but just because we go to a sultan doesn't make us power brokers.'

'Alright.'

ISTANBUL

Qaraar, Aalf, Hova and the two assistants stood on deck. From the boat, the vistas of this glorious city on a clear day were majestic. Chirping seagulls glided over the pristine waters of the Bosporus. The Hagia Sophia loomed on a hill to the right. The hill itself seemed to rise from the sea. The Blue Mosque was to the left. In between the Hagia Sophia and the Blue Mosque were avenues of lush green cypress trees and tulip gardens which encouraged people to stroll through them. Far beyond were dense untamed pine forests. As the boat approached the main docking bay, the troupe caught sight of the glorious Suleymaniye Mosque and hidden behind cypress trees was the Topkapi Palace, the sultan's residence.

They leapt off the boat.

Even Qaraar felt the infectious air of Istanbul, and the troupe roamed around the city with a sense of bursting excitement. This was the seat of the mighty Ottomans that Qaraar had read about in the Mughal libraries in Delhi. This is where East and West embraced. The troupe settled into their lodgings provided by the Ministry of Culture in the multicultural area in Galata, above a stone tavern called Tas Nerduben which actually meant 'stone steps.[80] It was owned and run by a Greek who on realising the troupe had been invited by the minister of culture gave them free drinks for a week.

The famous Galata Tower was built in Byzantine times, and the area around it was a magnet for aspiring singers, actors, playwrights and artists. The troupe loved these surroundings.

Hour after hour under the tower young songwriters and singers sang their latest verses, their tunes mingling effortlessly in the breeze. The elders stroked their beards and shut their eyes taking in the words, as the young held each other swaying gently to the melody. Romance in Galata was like none other in Istanbul. The surrounding cafes seemed to overflow with a sea of bright red fez caps and multi-circular crisp white turbans resting on heads that bobbed in appreciation of young talent.

Looking out of the window for a brief moment Qaraar felt a tinge of nostalgia, the surroundings reminding him of Delhi.

'We need to go shopping,' said Aalf placing his arm on Qaraar's shoulder.

'Yes, yes, let's go!' Hova rushed up from behind and hugged Aalf.

Hurriedly the three made their way down the steps, into the lanes and towards the shops. The bazaar was reverberating with noise. The most prominent were the Mudejar bread-sellers who sold their famous fine white francala bread. The Mudejars were the last of the persecuted Moors of Spain to flee that country after the Spanish re-conquista. They made Istanbul their home and in particular, Galata. As the three friends passed their shops the Mudejars yelled out, even grabbed them, insisting they sample their bread. Other Turk confectioners showed off their large glass jars with thousands of coloured candies, flavoured with musk and ambergris. Further down were shops selling compasses, watches and lenses.

Finally, they got to the cheapest clothes shops.

'How's this?' Aalf asked, putting on a fez cap.

'You look like a Turk alright,' affirmed Qaraar, lifting his eyes briefly from the clothes he was interested in.

'I'll take one,' said a delighted Aalf in Persian. Although the official language in all of the Ottoman lands including Istanbul was Turkish, most people understood Persian and even spoke it rather eloquently.

'A kaftan for me – that light blue one please.' Qaraar put it on.

'And you look like a sultan!' quipped Aalf.

'Hoja... respected one, put on this white turban. It will look wonderful with the kaftan,' urged the shopkeeper, hoping to increase his business. Hoja was a rendition of the Persian word Khwaja which meant 'learned one or teacher,' but was now being used in Istanbul as a general term of respect.

'Alright then, tie it for me,' said Qaraar.

'There you go! If not a sultan, a noble pasha for sure.'

For a second Qaraar thought of Holar Pasha. He dismissed the thought.

'Look my love! How do I look?' Hova emerged from the rear of the shop with a lady assistant wearing a white sheer gomlek, a chemise and an ankle-length red outer robe called an enteri. This was combined with flared pants called the shelwer, in yellow.

'A Turkish beauty!' said Aalf joyously.

The three eventually found themselves in the square between the Hagia Sophia and the Blue Mosque. Aalf and Hova held hands and ran carefree in the tulip gardens. Suddenly Qaraar saw Aalf on one knee and he held up a ring. Before he could react, Hova let out a joyful yelp and nodded her head vigorously.

They ran up to Qaraar.

'I asked her to marry me – and she said yes!' said Aalf catching his breath and holding onto Hova's hand.

'Hah! From slave trader to Persian poet, to actor and now to a domesticated husband! Come here you big Viking!' The two men embraced.

'Here, keep this ring and don't forget to give it to me tomorrow.' Aalf had discreetly bought a simple metal ring from the clothes shop earlier.

The next day the troupe went to the oldest church located in Galata, where after being baptized into the Armenian Church, the Viking descendant under frescos of the Virgin and baby Christ, married Hova. The friends spent that evening under the Galata

Tower, listening to minstrels and later in Tas Nerduben, the stone tavern under their lodgings where they drank themselves silly and danced on tables.

On 30 May, in the front grounds of the Topkapi Palace a loud voice roared in Turkish and then in Persian, 'He who is, Commander of the Faithful, Custodian of the two Holy Mosques, Sultan of Sultans, Sultan Mahmud I appears. Your heads shall remain lowered.'

It was déjà vu for Qaraar, who couldn't help but think how elaborate and similar the descriptions of the Emperor of Hindustan had been. 'What has all this pomp got you, O Sultan or you, O Emperor?' he pondered. 'Nadir defeated one and plundered his city, and now this sultan watches over a reduced Empire.' It made Qaraar uncomfortable. The sultan took his seat and the order was given to look up. The sultan had a dark brown beard till his chest. His eyes were drooping and his neck seemed to have been forcibly jolted into his back creating a pronounced hunch. On his head rested a round turban that resembled an enormous white cloud. After a few troupes had performed, the voice of the sultan's standard-bearer echoed:

> Bashinday-e-Duniya, present yourself!

The two ex-slave traders held the standard of Bashinday-e-Duniya aloft as the other three followed. First up was Aalf on his donkey with stories of Nasroddin. The sultan smiled, but only slightly. Then Hova presented her marbled papers. The sultan raised his eyebrows. Finally, Qaraar presented girih tile panels. The minister of culture seemed to be struck by an idea. He called for a halt to the presentation and whispered something in the sultan's ear, to which he got a beaming response. The sultan left. Immediately the minister of culture signalled to the standard-bearer who made an announcement.

'You have been selected in the inner circle. The rest are

dismissed.' A disappointed murmur ran through the rest of the troupes as they began making their way out.

'You!' said the sultan's standard-bearer amidst the thinning crowd. 'The tile-maker! The minister of culture has instructed that the girih scrolls in the palace will be studied by you, and then you will create a pavilion for the sultan – all in girih tiles.'

'I…'

'The chosen site is within the Topkapi Palace complex, the space behind the Sultan Ahmed Library,' continued the standard-bearer, pointing in its direction.

Before Qaraar could say anything, he added, 'Your study will begin tomorrow. Kilns will be set up for you. You will also work closely with the Supreme Architect. Deliver the pavilion in two years,' after saying this, the standard-bearer went his way.

For a few moments the troupe looked at each other in silence, utterly confused. Just then a familiar voice rang through.

'Well done!' It was one of the Ottoman travellers who had dined with Qaraar in Delhi and then at the caravanserai in Anatolia.

Putting his arm around Qaraar, 'This means great rewards, fame and fortune!'

Stammering, 'Th… thank you Huzoor.'

'But also, a warning – if you don't create a stunning pavilion…'

Qaraar, Aalf and Hova looked at him with apprehension.

'Well, let's just say it won't be pleasant.'

'Pleasant? He'll lose his head!' yelled Aalf. 'Anyway, what brought you here?' he said, petting his donkey.

'I don't live far from here, just overlooking the Bosporus actually.' Looking around at the troupes dismantling their stalls, he added, 'I was hoping to find some interesting Turkish delights to take back to Hindustan with our caravans at this gathering.'

'And?'

'Nothing really, but I'm sure we will see more of each other, now that you are in Istanbul. O, and to reciprocate your hospitality in Delhi please accept my invitation for supper, two Friday's from now.' He scribbled down his address and left.

That night as the friends retired in their lodgings, there was a strange restlessness amongst them. Once again it seemed their life hung by a thread. Qaraar lay in bed thinking. It was clear to him that he was a brilliant restorer, but to create, he needed to fall in love. 'How will I create?' Qaraar shut his eyes and hoped he would find answers in his dreams.

No answers came in his dreams. In fact, a loud knocking at the door shattered his sleep the next morning and every morning after that. The Supreme Architect would personally come and take Qaraar to the Sultan Ahmed Library within the inner courtyard of the Topkapi Palace. This was the exclusive library of the sultan. Surrounded by tulips and roses from the outside, the interior of the library, where only silence lived, was soul-stirring. It had an exceptionally high ceiling held aloft by magnificent pillars and glazed blue tiled walls. Large rectangular stained-glass windows were high above. On the floor were seating arrangements of cushions and mattresses. Here, seated on the floor in complete silence, with light filtering through the high stained-glass windows, Qaraar studied the 97-foot Topkapi girih scrolls.

In order to get to the Sultan Ahmed Library from the main gate of Topkapi Palace, Qaraar would have to walk through a small garden. One evening after two weeks of study, and on the Friday when the troupe had been asked to their traveller friend's for supper, he heard a woman's voice while returning from work.

'Where do you go, almond eyes?' It was followed by giggles.

Qaraar looked behind him. A bunch of elegant women were huddled together, as the most finely dressed of the lot held up a red veil revealing only her brown eyes.

Adjusting his notebooks he replied, 'To my lodgings, my lady.'

So elegantly were they dressed it was apparent to Qaraar these were ladies of court.

'And then?' came another question from the brown-eyed one, to which all the ladies burst into giggles yet again.

Qaraar seemed puzzled. 'Well… then for supper with a friend. And who are you my lady?'

'Me… me, you ask?' The giggles around her grew in volume. 'I'm just a passing abr, a… cloud!'

'And you?'

'I'm a tile-maker – a restorer.'

'So, you bring things back to life?'

'I restore beauty.'

The lady dropped her veil. She was in her mid-twenties.

Qaraar noticed she was endowed with fine features. A beauty for sure. She looked deep into Qaraar's eyes. Her voice softened.

'I have heard of you. You and your troupe are in the inner circle now, and I have been watching you every day.

Qaraar decided to walk away.

'Don't you dare turn away!'

'What's going on here?' The loud voice of a guard resonated in the small garden.

'Nothing, Hoja.' Qaraar continued walking.

Later that night at the Ottoman traveller's simple home overlooking the Bosporus, they discussed the incident. Lounging on one of the cylindrical Turkish cushions, the host declared, 'Stay away from her. She is the sultan's youngest cousin. Fiery in temper and known to be a man-eater!' he said, having heard the description from Qaraar.

Aalf got into the discussion. 'No distractions… please make that pavilion!'

'I still don't feel it.'

'You won't feel your head falling like a ball into a bucket, either! You know it happens really fast… swishhh – just like that,' said Aalf with an elaborate demonstration of the hand slicing his neck.

Qaraar's reply to Aalf's demonstration of his possible decapitation was typically mystical. 'There was something in her eyes… While the words that came from her mouth were frivolous, her eyes reflected pain, I think.'

Changing the topic, the host opened a wooden door. 'Come now, let's go to the garden.'

The garden was tiny. At the edge were steep cliffs that dropped straight into the Bosporus. It was evident from the arriving guests that the Ottoman traveller enjoyed the company of creative people. He himself was not wealthy, just comfortable – and the people that came in were of the same standing. Amongst them, was a Mudejar from Spain. When the Mudejars fled to Istanbul fleeing persecution in Spain in the fifteenth century, they brought with them knowledge of unique arts and creative forms including playing the Moroccan drums. Settling into conversation, one of them, dressed in a typical Moorish robe, walked up to Qaraar who was caressing the delicate white jasmine petals.

'We heard about you being chosen into the inner-circle Mubarak! My name is Saad-ibn-Khalid.'

'Well, let's see how it all goes!' The two men shook hands and kissed each other's cheek.

'We heard you are a tile-maker with a speciality in geometric patterns,' said Saad with curiosity in his eyes.

'Yes.'

'Those star and geometric patterns are on the wooden roofs in the Alhambra-Andalusia too.'

'Indeed, I have read about them.'

'There is some great tile work in Andalusia. I wonder if they still glisten under the Spanish sun?' Saad said with a melancholic tone, looking west towards the lost home of his grandfathers. At that moment both Qaraar and Saad felt a sense of similar loss.

'How long have you been here?' Qaraar asked.

'I was born here, but my great-grandfather was one of the last Moors to be forced out of Spain in 1614.'

'He must have had memories.'

'He left as a boy and passed on stories of glorious Moorish Andalusia to his son and he onto my father.'

'Are your parents here?'

'I'm an orphan.'

'Ah and now for some entertainment!' The Ottoman host stepped into the garden followed by two youths dressed in traditional Turkish attire. They led in a small bear, a rabbit and parrot.

'Holar Pasha!' cried out Qaraar without thinking.

'What did you say? Holar Pasha?' came an equally quick response from one of them.

He rushed up to Qaraar and grabbed him by the shoulders. 'How do you know that name? He's our father!'

Qaraar felt a surge of excitement which was followed by immediate caution. 'Best they don't know Holar Pasha's fate,' he thought to himself.

Then stammering for thoughts, he said, 'He… he… lives in Delhi and does animal tricks like you!'

Lowering his head and sighing with relief and then lifting his head up with a big smile, the young man said, 'You bring peace to our hearts knowing that he is well.' Pressing Qaraar's shoulders tightly, there were now tears streaming down the youth's face. 'He left so many years ago, unable to bear the taunts…' Qaraar put his arm on the young man's shoulder. 'Let it be. Just know that he has a new life of peace and anonymity.' Then looking at the Ottoman traveller who frequented Delhi and who could have known of Holar Pasha's awful fate, they exchanged a look which meant the secret would remain buried in their chests.

'What are your names?' asked Qaraar, seeing that the youth was now in control of his emotions.

'I'm Izzet and that's my brother Hikmet.'

It had been a life of misery for the two. Everywhere they went with their animal tricks in Istanbul they were ridiculed, and a few coins thrown at them if someone felt pity. At times they did acrobatics but that didn't stop the ridicule and didn't increase the coinage. Izzet and Hikmet were stout. Although young, both had receding silver hairlines because of the hardship's life had flung at them. But that night when the two young men performed their tricks the gathering didn't mock. In fact, they applauded. The coins received weren't flung at them, but instead given in their palms. They pressed it against their chests in a show of gratitude.

'Come and see us at our lodgings whenever you wish, or even better drop by the Sultan Ahmed Library where I work,' said Qaraar to the youth before they left.

'Hoja we are honoured. We don't remember anyone speaking kindly to us,' said Izzet.

'Don't worry about all that. Spend time with us.' Qaraar felt deep compassion for them.

For the next few months Qaraar changed focus. Instead of pursuing plans for the pavilion with the Supreme Architect, he spent time with Holar Pasha's two sons. A vigorously nodding Aalf and Hova agreed that their animal tricks and acrobatics should be added to the Bashinday-e-Duniya troupe when Qaraar made this suggestion. With their association with a troupe in the inner-circle of the sultan, the taunting in Istanbul reduced for the youths. Such was the spirit of Rumi's kindness that descended on all of them that on a clear day they went into the forests and released the animals and the youths decided to focus on their basic acrobat skills. After a few wobbly attempts they became quite good. Qaraar made little tile toys in the kilns and the troupe went all around Istanbul performing and showcasing their crafts with great success. Seeing this growing success even Saad, the Mudejar, joined the group. His added dimension were paintings and sketches of Moorish Mudejar buildings in Andalusia, which sold well too. Besides this, he also played the Moroccan drums which brought music into the troupe. Bashinday-e-Duniya was now a truly multicultural troupe. Looking at them Qaraar thought, 'Like a Sufi girih pattern our diversity interlocks us in beauty'. But after some months, a strict order from the Supreme Architect was received at the lodgings. He was angry. They were behind deadline to deliver the pavilion. And besides the Supreme

Architect, another person waited for Qaraar at the Topkapi Palace – the sultan's young cousin.

'You and your troupe have been galivanting around for almost a year and we are behind schedule.' Then, flinging scrolls at him, the Supreme Architect said, 'Here, study these design plans for the pavilion and tell me how you want the tilework. Let me know when the tiles will be ready!' he added, storming out of the Sultan Ahmed Library.

Alone in the silence of the library, Qa'raar spread out the plans. Deeply engrossed in study for a short while, it was only a shapely shadow falling on to the scrolls that interrupted his thoughts. Then the shadow seemed to speak.

'You have kept me waiting so long!' There was anger and frustration in her voice.

Qaraar rose and turned, 'I have been busy.'

'Busy, did you say? I am royalty. Bow and show some respect.'

She was now so close he could almost hear her heart beating. He walked away.

'You are the first one to avoid me. Yes, reject me.' Her words felt like fire.

'I don't reject you.'

In a flash she was in front of his face again, 'Then why this aloofness, tile-maker?'

She held him by his kaftan and pulling him close. 'I have waited for a year since I last saw you and you have been going around Istanbul with your troupe, never once casting a thought for this one.' There was a sudden mellowness in her voice.

'My lady...'

'My name is Gul Khatun. Say it!' Now her voice grew fiery again.

'Gul Khatun.'

'No... just Gul. Say it!'

'Gul.'

Qaraar pulled away and stepped back. She advanced. Qaraar's backward steps hastened. Her forward steps gained momentum. Qaraar moved like lightening towards the door, lunging for the handle. It was locked. Then his hastened steps took him towards the window as Gul followed him. She chased him through the library. From window to window. Door to door. Finally, out of exhaustion she fell in his arms.

Panting profusely, she said, 'Look what you have made me.'

'Reminds me of Yusuf and Zulekha in Behzad's fifteenth-century painting – you know of it?'

Still panting, in his arms and smiling, 'A little bit. Did they make it?'

'Doesn't matter. What matters is something else.'

Now she had a soft almost helpless look on her face. Both settled on the floor. Catching his breath, Qaraar spoke, 'In the Haft Awrang the Sufi meaning of Zulekha's search is explained. It's love she seeks. Initially Yusuf's physical beauty enthrals her, but when rejected, out of anger she accuses him of all sorts of things.' Gul rested her head on Qaraar's shoulder and listened intently. '...but with time, her desire to love him transcends physicality. Eventually she loves him for the beauty of his soul, and when they come together, they merge into the Divine. What matters is true love.'

'Where can I find it?' She pressed her forehead against his shoulder.

'Let it come to you.'

'I have been waiting for so long.'

'When it comes to you it will glimmer with three attributes of the Divine – kindness, sincerity and truth. Look out for those, and when you love him for those attributes, you will know how to love the Divine too'

Qaraar felt he could ask more, 'What happened in the past?'

'He betrayed me when I couldn't be the person he wanted me to be.'

'What do you mean?'

The sun's rays flooded through the large stain-glass windows of the Sultan Ahmed Library and bathed the two in its warmth. Looking all around the high ceilings, she said, 'Well, you know, all the pomp and show that comes with being royalty. He wanted me to dress in a certain way, speak in a way that pleased others. It was too regimental.'

'Then it wasn't true love.'

'I was more into the outdoors, loved being in the country – doing things with my hands.'

'But you do flaunt your royal lineage, like you did with me.'

Her eyes moved from the ceiling and then looked at Qaraar. Sighing and smiling, 'Oh that's just an act – you saw through it.'

'Don't you want to know who he was?'

'Doesn't matter, he hurt you... that's not the path of true love.'

'But I will tell you who it was... The minister of culture.'

Gul continued, 'Well... anyway... after that, I went crazy!'

They laughed.

'I have never felt this light before.'

Gul now knew the love of her life wouldn't be Qaraar, but a serenity seemed to descend on her.

As they got up to leave the library, Qaraar gave her his hand.

Helping her up he said, 'Rumi says carnal ego gets in the way of true love. Overcome ego and love will find you.'

Their friendship grew and Gul began spending more time with the troupe. When Qaraar couldn't accompany the troupe for their performances, Gul went with them instead. She displayed Qaraar's tiles on his behalf. Gul loved being with the troupe. It was freedom. Then it happened. One day Gul was able to get permission for the troupe to visit the shrine of Gul Baba in Budapest. Gul Baba was a much-revered Sufi by Christians and Muslims alike and for his Urs celebrations, the Habsburgs gave special permission for pilgrims to travel from the Ottoman lands. Gul meant 'rose' and she had been named after this great Sufi.

After weeks of travelling, the troupe reached Budapest. On a little hill next to the shrine of Gul Baba various stalls were assembled, and the area was bursting with festive spirit. When it came for the Bashinday-e-Duniya troupe, the two acrobats led the way. Hikmet did splendidly and was showered with coins. Gul noticed that instead of keeping all the coins for himself, Izzet ran towards the destitute and gave them some. Pure kindness of heart. Then came his turn for doing acrobatics. Against the backdrop of Saad's drumbeats Izzet's attempts to walk the tightrope in mid-air failed as he slipped and fell. The crowd jeered. He got up and tried again. Saad increased the volume of his drumming, but the acrobat failed again. Gul watched with trepidation as the jeering and taunting got even louder. Izzet dusted himself down, got back up on the tightrope and walked. Saad's fingers played on the drums as each beat followed his steps. He continued cautiously, with his toes gripping the rope with fear.

Veering slowly he somehow reached the middle of the rope and looked down catching Gul's eye. There was only truth and sincerity in his eyes when mockery was at its sharpest. Gul's heart absorbed it and reflected love back. Effortlessly, while still looking at her, Izzet completed the other half of the tightrope walk. The crowds' jeering turned to cheering. How fickle they were. At the shrine of the hermit Gul Baba, Gul the royal princess had found true love. Izzet held out his arms. She rushed to him and they embraced – and from then on, they would be inseparable.

Meanwhile, at the Sultan Ahmed Library, things were getting nasty.

'We have just a year to go and you haven't even made your tile plans. What are you up to?' shouted the Supreme Architect.

'I just don't feel it,' said Qaraar.

Grabbing Qaraar by the upper half of his kaftan, 'I don't care about your feelings! We need to get the pavilion done – get on with it!'

'In the same way that ishq can't be forced, neither can creativity.'

Qaraar pushed down the Supreme Architect's hands and walked away towards the gardens.

After a while a loud voice was heard, 'Lower your head, drop your eyelids to the floor. Sultan of Sultans, Commander of the Faithful is making his way!'

The Supreme Architect had gone and complained to the sultan about Qaraar's disinterest and the impossibility for the pavilion to be ready by next year. The sultan accompanied with his minister of culture was now storming towards him. He was in a rage.

CHAPTER 6
TURQUOISE

The minister of culture was a lean-looking man with hollow cheeks and high cheekbones. A drooping light brown moustache fell over his lips in a typical Turkish style. His eyes were set deep into their sockets and he had a voice that sounded like the creaking of a door. He now declared the chilling consequences of failure: the site in the Topkapi Palace compound designated for the pavilion, where some preliminary digging had begun, would be Qaraar's grave. He would be buried alive, and all members of his troupe except Gul Khatun would meet the same fate. The sultan and his entourage then left, fuming. Qaraar felt as if a massive stone had been placed on his chest. He thought he had left behind violence and threats from men possessing wild egos and power.

For more than three years, in Ottoman lands he had roamed free, immersed himself in what he had loved, created a troupe of artists and performers and had emerged from the ghosts of his past. His work in Merv, Bokhara, Khiva, Samarkand, Isfahan, Konya and Bursa was not just the restoration of brick and tilework on buildings, but through those works he had restored his desire for life itself. To him, each tile and brick had become a symbol of restoring the lost art and intellect of the Sufi. But now he faced a situation that went against the very essence of creativity: force and violence. And carrying this burden on his shoulders, he was expected to create.

That night at the Tas Nerduben tavern, the Bashinday-e-Duniya troupe met.

Candles flickered on their table, gently illuminating their dark corner. Misket, the Bulgarian wine, did the rounds, their cups being filled by an attendant. There was silence.

Aalf was seated next to Qaraar. 'You have changed our lives,' he said putting down his glass and breaking the silence. Aalf's two guards who had worked diligently as Qaraar's assistants nodded vigorously.

Opposite Qaraar sat Gul and Izzet, holding hands under the table. 'If it wasn't for you, I wouldn't have found him,' said Gul looking at Izzet with tender eyes.

Saad and Hikmet said in unison, 'Indeed you have given meaning to our lives.'

Hikmet continued, 'Through you we got respectability – what more can a man ask for?'

Hova who was sitting on the other side of Qaraar put her hand on his shoulder, 'You are the glue that binds us together.'

'Yes, but…'

Just then a loud noise of thundering hooves against the stone alleyway was heard. In a second, the wooden tavern door was forcibly thrust open and in rushed the soldiers of the minister of culture. Grabbing Gul by the arm they dragged her out.

'No! No!' She stretched out her arm to Izzet who reached desperately.

'It's house arrest for you!' screamed one of the soldiers. Aalf, his two guards, Qaraar and Saad rose in a rush spilling wine all over the table.

'Stay there you bloody troupers. One move and we have instructions to starve her. She'll only get fed if you start work towards building that pavilion!' The soldiers vanished with Gul, leaving Izzet chasing the galloping horses through the dark, winding alleyways. Eventually, exhausted, he fell to the ground.

The next day Qaraar went straight to the site. With his friends' lives under threat, he would now force himself to create. His sketching at times was interrupted by conversations the soldiers had amongst themselves. One afternoon they revealed the minister's true motives.

'This is all to ingratiate himself even further with the sultan,' whispered one guard biting into his kebab roll.

'Is it? Tell me more!' egged on the other, chomping away at his kofte.

'The sultan is fed up of his grand vazier and is going to sack him.'

'Why?'

'The sultan wants peace with Nadir, but the grand vazier hasn't been able to come up with a mutually agreeable treaty.'

'Go on...'

'Well, to distract the sultan from the gloom after the loss of Belgrade and Budapest, it was the minister of culture's idea to get a pavilion made and dedicate it to the sultan.'

'Aha!'

'And then after all that flattery, he will make a claim to the post of grand vazier.'

'Really? And then?'

'This minister of culture is no culture enthusiast – he wants war.'

'More war? We are already fighting Nadir on our eastern borders!'

'Well they say he wants all out war against Nadir in the East and he wants to retake Budapest and Belgrade in the West.'

'No! A war on two fronts!'

'Hey tile-maker! Get on with it! Don't you dare slow down your sketching.'

The rest of the troupe had been banned by the minister from travelling and participating in fairs until such time that the pavilion was completed. The two acrobats pitched tent under the Galata Tower and slept there. Saad moved into the lodgings with the troupe. Fear grew amongst them about lurking death. Aalf kept up the brave front encouraging Qaraar, and also uplifting the spirits of the troupe by his enactments of Nasroddin Hoja. Many weeks passed in the lodgings peering out of their window and listening to the young singers below the tower. Hearing the love strains, Izzet pined for Gul. Gul's captivity in the Topkapi Palace was stifling. She knew Qaraar worked at the edge of the garden opposite the Sultan Ahmed Library and so she would often stretch her neck from her iron bared window hoping to get the slimmest sight of the craftsman.

One morning, before heading out to the site Qaraar found Izzet sitting below the Galata Tower with his head buried in his hands.

'Write something for her,' said Qaraar.

'You could lose your head.'

'I could lose it for not completing the pavilion too. I might as well lose it trying to help lovers.'

'Here, let me give you verses from Hafez.'

Qaraar took the love note and reached the site.

Looking out into the Bosporus waves which were restless and turquoise in colour, Qaraar suddenly turned to the guards who had dozed off and yelled.

'Turquoise!'

'What?' said one, rubbing sleep off his eyes and adjusting his turban.

'The sketches are done, and I need turquoise!' Seeing their puzzled expression, he added, 'Go and get the minister of culture.'

The two guards scampered off.

Qaraar rushed to Gul's window and threw the love note.

Gul came rushing.

'It's from him?'

'Yes. And don't worry, we'll get you out.'

She read Hafez's verses penned by Izzet.

Falcon of sovereign renown, high nesting bird of lofty gaze
The corner of affliction town, befits thee ill to pass thy days…

Lost… I roam, craving she would come
Where shall I thy phantom see,
Where, dear nymph, a glimpse of thee?[81]

Gul held the verses close to her chest and shut her eyes.

Qaraar rushed back to the site and waited for the minister of culture.

'What do you mean turquoise?' roared the minister as soon as he came.

'All the girih tilework will be in turquoise,' said Qaraar in a voice feigning excitement.

'There is no turquoise in Istanbul. Well, surely not in the quantity to cover an entire pavilion,' said the minister as soon as he arrived.

'Now listen, all my drawings are based on that, see!' Qaraar showed of his scrolls. The entire facade, every pillar, even the floor and plinth had girih tile sketches on them.

'You want to please the sultan, don't you minister?' There was a hint of sarcasm in his voice.

'Of course.'

'Then this pavilion must be unique… all in turquoise!'

'But that amount of turquoise can only come from Nishapur in Persia.'

'Go get it!' said Qaraar now full of confidence, knowing well that the momentum of the conversation was with him.

'I will not make the girih tiles unless I get turquoise! Do you hear? And you can chop off my head for all I care!' yelled Qaraar.

'Nishapur is under Nadir and we are at war with him, we can't just go in and get turquoise from those mines!'

Qaraar put his nose up in the air and looking down at the minister said, 'Very well then. I will tell the sultan you dashed my plans for the most glorious and unique pavilion.'

'How dare…'

Before he could finish his sentence Qaraar walked up close,

'What will also be revealed is your secret desire to become grand vazier and your flattery of the sultan with this pavilion.'

'No! Listen. Give me some time!' The minister left.

The minister found himself trapped. Secretly he began a correspondence with Nadir's cultural office in Isfahan requesting access to the turquoise mines in Nishapur. The response was fiery. It came from the orthodox clergy who were now in charge of everything cultural, and their loathsome attitude towards a Sunni Ottoman Empire was reflected in their scathing letters that ranged from abuse to sarcasm. What Qaraar had done successfully though, was to buy time for him and his friends to reassess their situation.

'You aren't going to build that pavilion, are you?' asked Saad, in the lodgings, sitting with his drums between his legs. Aalf sat reclining on cylindrical blue Turkish cushions, his wife curled in his arms. Izzet, Hikmet, Qaraar and the two assistants sat on the Turkish carpet on the floor with their legs tucked under their thighs.

'We have got time,' said Qaraar, his hands folded across his chest and looking out of the window at the Galata Tower.

'Time for what? Eventually they will want results,' replied Saad.

Qaraar sighed and put his head down for a few seconds. He didn't have an answer. 'We need to escape.' Saad's voice had conviction in it.

'And go where? asked Hova in a nervous voice.

'No! We are not going anywhere without Gul,' said Izzet in a firm voice.

'We are not going to leave Gul behind,' said Qaraar with a reassuring look at Izzet

Saad struck his drum. A rich bass sound resounded. 'We've got to escape to Spain.'

'What?' screamed Aalf.

'That's impossible,' said Hikmet. 'How will we get there and what will we do there?'

'A few weeks ago...' Saad looked around hoping he had everyone's attention.

'Go on,' insisted Qaraar.

'Well, a few weeks ago a boat arrived from the Mediterranean and I met some of the travellers. Most of them spoke of Crown Prince Ferdinand of Spain who will very soon be king.'

'So? Aalf asked in a slightly annoyed tone not knowing where Saad was going with his thoughts.

'Well,' responded Saad calmly but also striking a drum beat with a smile '...it is said that the crown prince is an enlightened man and a patron of the arts and they are already calling him, 'The Learned.'

'But what about the Spanish hatred for you folks – the Moors?' asked Aalf bluntly.

'Spain has always been our true home,' said Saad. 'It's said that some Moors were so convinced of returning back to Andalusia that for several years they hung the keys to their Spanish homes on their doors in Morocco.'

'But they will kill you there! You can't go back. As recently as 1728 there was a case of persecution of an alleged Moor,' said Hikmet.[82]

'I consider it a lost home. Besides, much time has passed since the Reconquista and expulsions. I'll risk it.'

'Let's get to the basics here. Who were these people you met Saad? And what will we do in Spain?' Qaraar tried to bring some focus into the conversation.

'I was coming to that. The travellers who came off the boat from the Mediterranean were Venetian merchants who had come for diplomatic meetings with the pashas, who are the sultan's chosen diplomats. The Venetians and Turks have a love hate relationship. They trade and they fight. One of the servants of a Venetian diplomat who I befriended got me an opportunity to play drums for them one evening. They seemed jolly folks and very knowledgeable about Spain since they sail to that country for business too. I spoke with them at length about the state of some of the buildings in Spain. It seems Prince Ferdinand has a deep desire to restore old buildings, so you – Qaraar – can find tilework there if we can get to the Prince's court. We on the other hand can find work in little villages and towns.'

Having heard all this intently Hikmet spoke, 'We go where Qaraar goes. What future do we have here without him?'

'None whatsoever!' shot back Aalf in his typical fashion. 'A life of ridicule!' Then putting his hand on Qaraar's shoulder, 'What do you say?'

'What are the choices? I give in to a man drunk on power and build a pavilion so that he can flatter the sultan? And also watch Izzet and Gul suffer in separation?' said Qaraar.

'You didn't answer how we would get there,' said Hova, looking at Saad.

'There are large Venetian ships that actively trade in the Aegean and Mediterranean Seas, but they don't get deep into Ottoman waters. We must smuggle ourselves on-board.'

'How exactly do we get onto that boat?' asked Aalf.

'There are human smugglers who operate smaller boats between the Bosporus and the Aegean. We will need to get onto one of those small boats first which will then take us to the bigger Venetian ship in the Aegean... and then into the Mediterranean headed for Spain,' Saad struck a drumb beat again. The sound of which made him think he had reached Spain.

'Human traffickers!' Qaraar said in anguish.

'Yes.'

Sensing adventure and feeling an adrenaline rush Aalf leapt and sat besides Saad. 'And how often do these smaller boats come to the Bosporus?'

'Every few months.'

'How does the boatman manage to dock in the Bosporus?'

'Bribes.'

They all looked at each other. Then everyone fixed their gaze on Qaraar.

After a few moments, Qaraar looked at Saad and said, 'Spain it is then…' And immediately turning to Izzet and reassuring him, he continued, 'but not without Gul.'

AUGUST 1746

The onus of delivering the pavilion was now on the minister. He was embarrassed at not getting the turquoise but continued trying to find ways to smuggle in the stones by getting in touch with smugglers and bandits. In the Topkapi Palace, Gul had been under house arrest for many months. Once a week, Gul would be allowed to leave her quarters. Under strict supervision she would go for walks in the tulip gardens between the Harem, the Baghdad Pavilion and the Sultan Ahmed Library. At those times Qaraar would bring in Izzet, disguised as his assistant. The two men would sit in the Sultan Ahmed Library and at times even besides the open-air site, pretending to refine the girih sketches and plans. This would be the time when Izzet and Gul would exchange looks. Gliding past the gardens surrounded by guards, Gul resembled the flower surrounded by thorns.

Most nights, Saad, Aalf and Qaraar secretly visited the Golden Horn, the primary inlet of the Bosporus into Istanbul to keep an eye out for the little boats that came in after midnight every few months. One night, Saad spotted a bobbing little boat coming in. A scruffy Bulgarian sailor looked around cautiously and then anchored. Jumping out of the boat he looked a picture of vile villainy. His front two teeth were black as the night. He was bald and had the neck of a powerful leopard. Hastily he was surrounded by a few Ottoman guards who vanished almost as soon as they had arrived clutching onto their bribes.

Saad, Qaraar and Aalf emerged from their hiding place in a dark alleyway.

'Who are you?' asked the sailor in a muffled voice.

'Musicians, craftsmen, performers,' stammered Saad.

'What do you want?' He grabbed Saad by the neck.

'Spaa...'

'What?'

Aalf was about to attack him, but Qaraar held him back.

Holding his neck that had just been released from a vice-like grip, Saad continued. 'We want to go to Spain. Can you get us to the large Venetian ships in the Aegean?'

The sailor looked around them and then at Aalf and said, 'This Viking is no performer.' Coming close to Aalf he said, 'I know his lot – you must be a bloody slave trader.' The two men eye-balled each other.

'He's a performer.' Qaraar separated the two men. 'Can you get us to those boats or not?'

'How many of you?'

'Nine.'

'Fifty gold pieces. For that, yes, I'll get you into those ships bound for Spain.'

'We don't have that kind of money!' whispered Saad.

'Forget Spain then.' The vicious man made his way to the jetty, jumped into his little boat and began untying it.

Qaraar rushed to him. 'Is there anything else we can pay you with?'

'Silver. One hundred pieces.' The boat was about to sail away. 'Ah but let me guess... you don't have that either! Hah!'

Qaraar ignored his retort and said, 'We also have horses.'

'How many?'

'Two.'

Aalf interjected, 'And a donkey.'

'Another twenty gold pieces.'

'But how will you fit them in this small boat?'

'I will get a slightly bigger one. You will be surprised by the resilience of animals if they want to travel with their masters.'

Qaraar quickly hastened to ask, 'If we arrange something, how do we find you?'

The boat was pulling away. The sailor turned and looked back. 'The jetty down the promenade of the Blue Mosque. Same time. Exactly a month from now.' His boat sailed away.

Aalf embraced Qaraar. 'You never wanted to leave Rumi's shrine. We had peace there! I forced you into coming here.'

'It's alright.'

'No, it's not. We were doing well there. Now there's all this mess. You and the calligrapher Sufi were right – we should have kept away from power brokers like that minister.'

'Look at it this way, we would never have met the acrobats, bettered their lives or even met Saad and added him to our troupe.'

Saad came up to them.

'A month from now we escape. We have something to work towards!' said Qaraar putting his arms around Aalf and Saad.

From then on, for most nights the troupers didn't sleep well. The deadline to deliver the pavilion was approaching too. Qaraar, Aalf and Hova by now had grown used to living the life of constant travel, uncertainty and upheaval. But Saad and the two acrobats had never lived in such anxiety and began cursing their luck. At the lodgings, Qaraar did everything to ease their stress. On occasions he read Omar Khayyam's philosophising *Rubaiyat's*, seated on the Turkish carpet as the acrobats and Saad listened carefully.

> Let whoso make or buy,
> my clay with long oblivion is gone dry:
> But fill me with the old familiar juice,
> methinks I might recover by and by.[83]

The pretence of continuing to work on the site had to continue.

'We escape 5 September 1746.'

Izzet wrote his note to Gul with approval from Qaraar. While no real plan had yet materialised to free Gul, it was a date, and everyone in the troupe believed in it. Izzet dropped this note as his lover approached, surrounded by her guards during one of her walks. Gul picked it up pretending to caress a tulip. Her heart leapt with joy.

Back in her royal apartment she saw her parents. They were busy with her seven brothers, as it had always been since she gained consciousness in life. She, the youngest and only girl, had been completely ignored. It was as if she hadn't existed. Life had only revolved around how her brothers could ingratiate themselves with the sultan and increase their landed estates.

On innumerable occasions and at many state functions she hadn't been spoken to. Her parents had even forgotten her name on many occasions, until reminded by their maid that the young lady's now deceased grandmother had named her Gul after Gul Baba the Sufi saint of Budapest. Countless nights had been spent in muffled sobbing on her pillow out of sheer loneliness. Now again she watched her family immersed in political discussions that could benefit the seven brothers. Her disappearance wouldn't be noticed. Looking at her family at a distance she whispered Ibn Arabi's verse to herself.

> Those held deep in my heart where are they gone?
> You saw their phantom. Have you seen their true form?
> How long have I been searching among them… for them
> To be secure with them, but never with them secure
> Could be my happiness is strung between near and far
> May these eyes rest in them
> May I ask after them no more.[84]

Gul casually got up. Pulled out a small bag. Put three pairs of simple clothes in it. And waited. Every day all she did was look at that small bag. At times she would pick up *Diwan- e- Hafez* which she had by her bedside. So deeply revered was this book that it had a legend attached to it called the Faal. Across Turkey, Persia and

Mughal India it was believed that by opening the Faal one could get an indication of what the future held. It was thought that if one was in an anxious and troubled state but meditated with a pure heart and called for divine help, opened the book with shut eyes and placed a finger on a verse, that verse would guide that person towards their future.

Gul did exactly that and placed her finger on a verse. Then she gently opened her eyes and read:

> Dark is the stony desert, trackless and vast and dim
> Where is hope's guiding lantern? Where is faith's star so fair?
> What is the truth shall light me to heaven's strait thoroughfare?
> Where, O heart, thou hastest? …See what an adventure is thine unending quest.[85]

Gul held onto the word 'adventure' and took solace in it. Days and weeks passed. Amidst whispers and hushed tones, the troupe discussed how to raise the money to get out of Istanbul. Nothing of substance emerged from those discussions. With just a day to go Hova wept uncontrollably out of anxiety. The acrobats became frantic and cried too.

'Turquoise!' yelled the minister of culture wearing a wicked smile. 'Here it is.' Three bags thumped onto the ground besides Qaraar who had been pretending to refine his drawings besides the pillars of the pavilion which were now complete.

'Now then! Get on with it!' said the minister kicking the sacks which he had managed to smuggle in from Nishapur.

'Has the cat got your tongue, craftsman?' asked the minister looking at Qaraar who wore an expression of surprise.

But before he could launch into a threatening tirade, a nobleman came rushing towards him.

'Agha! The sultan wants you right away!'

'Catch your breath you fool. What's the matter?'

'The relentless fighting with Nadir is to end!'

'What?'

'Yes! The sultan and the grand vazier have signed a peace treaty with him.'

'That damn grand vazier will take the credit for bringing peace. I won't let it happen – we need war.'

'No Agha, you can't do anything. The treaty I believe is already sealed. It's even got a name.' He gulped and panted profusely.

'What is it called?' The minister grabbed the nobleman by his neck.

'The Treaty of Kerden.'

'That damn grand vazier has got one up on me... Aaarggh!' The minister let go of the nobleman's neck in disgust.

'What happens to your chances of becoming grand vazier?' asked the nobleman sarcastically.

'Aaarggh!' With his hands tearing at his turban the minister continued. 'All my plans have gone to dust. Now with this peace treaty the sultan will only listen to the grand vazier!'

Qaraar and Izzet heard it all and exchanged glances.

The minister then rose. The look of despair was replaced with burning rage. He looked at the turquoise sacks and then at Qaraar.

He ran up to the sacks. 'It's all because of these!' he yelled. 'And all because of you!' He pointed at Qaraar. 'All my time has gone into sourcing these bloody stones.' He kicked the sacks in fury. 'What's the use of this damn pavilion now? No use at all!' he shouted.

'The sultan would like it finished,' said the nobleman.

'I don't care!' shouted back the minister.

'Calm down Agha, you must go and see the sultan and the grand vazier.'

'What for?'

'Well there is apparently going to be an exchange of prisoners and wanted men, and the grand vazier and sultan want your opinion.'

The minister dropped his head and shook it vigorously.

'Is that all that I'm fit for? Discussions on prisoner exchange?'

'Apparently there is one that Nadir's ministers are very keen on. They captured a Persian boatman who worked for some Viking descendent…'

'So I'm now supposed to find Vikings?' sneered the minister.

'Let me finish Agha. This Viking slave-trader whom the Persian boatman worked for in the Caspian Sea helped a Hindustani escape across the Caspian. And this Hindustani is a killer of repute.'

'Killer?'

'Yes, he is a famed killer also known by the title Qaatil-e-Salaar because he killed one of Nadir's generals in Delhi.'

'Go on.'

'Well, Nadir's men interrogated the Persian boatman who said he last saw them in Dagestan, and there is a possibility they entered Ottoman lands.'

'Qaatil-e-Salaar – an interesting title.'

'There are legends about him in Central Asia as being some flying slave who they say is also a craftsman, as well as a brave fighter. People back there are writing songs about him.'

Qaraar who was not far and pretending to work on his plans felt his heart sink.

The minister looked at the nobleman with a curious expression on his face.

'This killer has a dual personality?'

'It seems so.'

'Do they have any sketches of this man who has hoodwinked Nadir?'

'They do and they will send it to us in a few days.'

'Let's go see the sultan.' He turned quickly to Qaraar and Izzet, and then looked around at all the unfinished digging and pillars on the site. 'Whatever comes of this is no concern to me now,' sighed the minister. Then he looked at the guards. 'There is nothing left for you to do now, so come with me.' He left with the nobleman.

Rising up from his haunches Qaraar whispered under his breath, 'We told that Persian boatman not to sail down the Caspian!'

'What are you muttering?' asked Izzet.

'Nothing.'

Qaraar went back to the lodgings and in a quiet corner briefed Aalf about what had happened. The next day they were to escape. After some thinking Aalf insisted he had a plan and should be taken back to the construction site as soon as possible. There were still a few days for the sketch to make its way to Istanbul, but only a day left to rescue Gul and meet the human smuggler at the Golden Horn. Aalf refused to reveal his plans.

The next day the troupers woke at dawn. Qaraar, Aalf and Izzet left for the Topkapi Palace taking their daily route of sailing out towards the Golden Horn. After being frisked at the entrance as was the norm, the three arrived at the site. It seemed completely abandoned. There were no guards surrounding it. In fact, the only guards on duty were the ones under Gul's window.

'There look at those,' said Aalf pointing at the three sacks filled with turquoise. Overnight they had just been left by the site. 'That is our ticket to freedom!' He had a smile and a look in his eye that reflected his anticipation of now having a real chance to escape. The previous night the guards had heard the nobleman say that the sultan wanted the pavilion completed and so they had left the sacks the way they were.

'Fill up!'

Qaraar looked at Aalf in disbelief, but quickly realised that this was the only way out. Hurriedly they stuffed their pockets with turquoise. Some were large squares and others rectangular. Aalf pulled out three large cloth bags he had folded and hid in the inner pockets of his large kaftan. The three flung the bags choking with turquoise across their backs, and then slowly made their way to Gul's window. Five guards stood there with hands on their scabbards.

'Halt! That's how far you will come to the window!' shouted a guard.

'Agha I just wanted to say....' Words stuttered out of the lovelorn acrobat's mouth.

'Kam goh, Speak less!'

Hearing the acrobat's voice, Gul came rushing to the window. Holding desperately onto the iron bars she said, 'I have been waiting!'

'Gum sho! Get lost!' All five guards now surrounded the three men.

Before the situation got out of hand, Aalf stepped forward. He spoke in a hushed voice. Opening the kaftan, he nodded his head as if calling the guards close.

'Agha look inside.'

'What for?

'Yak Nazar... One look, Agha.' He came closer to a guard, winked and again opened his kaftan.

They peered into his inner pocket. Their eyes lit up.

'As you know, this is for the pavilion. We are taking it for crushing. Why don't you take some and let her out,' he hurriedly added, seeing the eyes of the guard rise and meet his after their longing look at the stones. 'Only until evening Agha – after dinner she will be back.'

The five guards looked at each other and huddled, whispering away.

Then they nodded in agreement. Handful of turquoise was handed to each guard and Gul's door unlocked.

She ran out and flung herself in Izzet's arms.

At the lodgings, Gul was welcomed back with hugs, kisses, laughter and music. Hikmet did some cartwheels for her and Aalf's two assistants carried her on their shoulders to the first-floor lodgings. All hugged and shrieked with joy as she came up the stairs. In Gul's honour, Saad and Hova sang an Arabic and Armenian love song as she entered the lodgings. Gul had never experienced affection like this from her own family.

Aalf and Qaraar, though, stepped outside the lodgings to discuss escape plans. Both feeling anxious, tensions rose between them. Qaraar insisted the troupe leave now and hide in the garden next to the Blue Mosque giving them access to the jetty. He convinced that since the garden was so close to the Topkapi Palace the guards wouldn't suspect the troupe would hide so close to it. Aalf thought it would be too dangerous.

The tension got to Qaraar and he uttered words in anger he would soon regret. 'I am the master restorer. It's because of me we are who we are. I am the one who you should listen to.'

Surprised at these words Aalf gave in. By sunset the troupe and their animals were in the garden behind the Blue Mosque. Fear gripped all, but they took comfort in the fact that they were together.

The troupe watched the sun disappear behind the six minarets and five domes of the Blue Mosque. The air chilled and the Istanbul sky turned into its famed pink against the backdrop of which sea gulls glided. Gazing at the Blue Mosque, Qaraar felt a magnetic lure. Excusing himself from the troupe he entered the mosque.

Instantly he felt humbled. The might of the Divine manifested itself in the interiors. The ceiling was so high it dwarfed Qaraar completely. Clinging to the walls were 20,000 handmade Iznik tiles. High up, almost as if yearning to reach the apex of the dome, were nearly 200 stained glass windows with the most sumptuous colours – red, cobalt, green and yellow. Lowered from the ceiling were massive circular iron chandeliers carrying thousands of oil lamps, which created a dazzling effect when their light fell on the glazed tiles.

In flowers, fruits, creepers and cypress tree shapes, the tiles spoke the language of beauty. Such was the radiance emanating in the interiors that it stunned Qaraar. This never-ending tile journey seemed to look down at Qaraar and ask, 'Can you create this?' He fell to his knees right under the main dome. He, the master tile restorer, was now nothing but a speck. He lowered his head and shook it in regret of the words he had used earlier towards Aalf. After what seemed like hours, he raised his head and with damp eyes looked upwards. A verse inscribed on blue ceramic glistened in the light from the oil lamps.

> God is the light of the heavens and the earth, the example of his light is like a niche within which is a lamp, the lamp is within glass, the glass as if it were a pearly white star lit from the oil of a blessed olive tree, neither of the east, nor of the west, whose oil would almost glow even if untouched by fire. Light upon light. God guides to his light whom he wills. And God presents examples for the people and God is knowing of all things.

Qaraar was aware this was a verse that Dara Shikoh had spent a lifetime analysing. The power of the verse was such that it seemed to keep Qaraar on his knees. He felt the hair on his arms rise and an inexplicable stirring. Here was craftsmanship at its peak but it couldn't have reached this zenith without Divine guidance, he thought to himself. With his head bowed, he stuttered, 'Is a slight flickering of your light within me? For now, neither am I of the east nor of the west. Neither do I know what is to become of me...'

Then he heard rushing feet on the soft crimson carpet. 'Qaraar! Come on, we must go – the guards are coming!' said Izzet who had come running in looking for him. Rising up and looking up one last time at the mighty dome, he hastened out of the mosque and into the garden.

It was late by now and a full moon had taken its place in the night sky. 'They are all over the place,' said Saad, his voice trembling with fear.

'Hush! Lower your voice and stay low,' said Aalf as they all lay down and hid behind the tulip clusters. Haider and Aalf's horse were also forced to get down on their knees. Luckily the horses didn't burst into a disobedient neighing. Aalf tied his donkey's mouth shut and lowered him too. Some guards rushed past the garden, but none chose to go in. As Qaraar had predicted, they didn't think the troupe would dare hide in the vicinity. Most of the guards were making their way to the boats to get them across the Golden Horn and into Galata.

Lying on his stomach in the grass, Qaraar placed his hand on Aalf's shoulder. 'I'm sorry,' he whispered.

'Hush now master-restorer, you will get us killed!' whispered back Aalf with a smile.

Qaraar dropped his head.

'Even the best can fall from grace,' said Aalf nudging Qaraar, who looked back at him sheepishly. 'Apology accepted!' Their friendship wasn't brittle.

After a few more moments of anxious hiding in the garden, all of them slid down the slope and onto a rough muddy promenade. Qaraar led Haider, Aalf led his horse and Hikmet led Aalf's donkey. Between the three animals walked Gul, Hova, Izzet, Saad and the two assistants, with great caution. By this time, it was close to midnight. The full moon bathed the Bosporus and the Blue Mosque in silvery light. As the troupe made its way to the jetty, they saw a few guards approaching from the east. Aalf and Qaraar tugged at the reins and slowed down the horses, guiding them into the thickets. This was the only way to the jetty and their hopes of getting to it began receding as more guards hurried down the slope and onto the promenade. The troupe clung together pressing their backs to the slope. Their breathing was heavy, and the crisp air made their breath visible in the form of wisps of smoke. The silvery full moon exposed everything on the promenade and the Bosporus. In the distance, swaying on the water, they spotted the boatman. He had come with a larger boat to accommodate the animals. Behind his boat was another large boat making its way to the jetty.

Just when all hope seemed lost of getting to the jetty, Aalf heard some rustling in the thickets behind. A large band of dervishes belonging to Rumi's Mevlavi order descended down the slope. They were a sight to behold. Nearly fifty of them were making their way towards the jetty. The second large boat was meant to carry them to Antalya, and then they would undertake the land journey by camel to Konya. Each wore long white robes with a large camel brown belt around their waist. Around their necks were light green Hadjibaktash stones, with twelve edges. They wore these as inspiration from the Bektashi dervishes of Sari Saltuk Babadag in Romania, a shrine they had recently visited.

'This is our chance! Let's join them!' said Qaraar.

As they approached, he said, 'Salaam, Dede can we come with you?' Dede being the Turkish form of address to a Sufi leader.

All fifty dervishes surrounded the troupe. Then the dervish leader who had the gentlest look in his blue eyes looked at Qaraar with a testing expression that prompted Qaraar to recite Rumi's verse:

> This drunkenness began in some other tavern...
> Meanwhile, I'm like a bird from another continent sitting in this aviary...
> the day is coming when I will fly off.[86]

The dervish leader placed his hand on Qaraar's head and said 'Shireen zabaan, shireen zindagi... sweet words, sweet life.' Then he looked at his followers and nodded. Nine of them opened their small cloth bags and pulled out a spare white robe, the troupers rushed into the thicket and came out dressed as Rumi's dervishes. The fifty dervishes closed ranks around the troupers and walked towards the jetty passing the unsuspicious guards as the leader pulled out his kaval flute and played it gently. As soon as the large boat arrived, the leader signalled for the dervishes to board.

From the deck of the dervishes' boat Qaraar signalled to their boatman, who sailed up slowly behind them. Both boats then sailed gently out of the Golden Horn. Once out of sight of the guards on the jetty, the Bulgrian boatman sailed up besides the dervish boat and lowered a plank. Everyone looked around in anticipation to see who would be the first to venture on this hazardous crossing. Waves relentlessly tossed both the boats around. Nervously Qaraar led Haider on the plank amidst anguish-filled sighs. Gul dug her fingernails deep into Izzet's hand. Hova turned her neck and buried her face in Aalf's chest, unable to keep her eyes on Qaraar and Haider. Saad bit his lower lip hard. The assistants and Hikmet covered their faces in their hands and peered out of parted fingers.

Qaraar spoke gently to Haider, caressed his mane, and carefully took the first few steps onto the plank. Haider followed as Qaraar balanced. As both the boats rose and fell like the tunes of a symphony seemingly orchestrated by the waves, Haider pulled back. He shook his head vigorously in fear and refused to move any further. Stranded quarter-way down on the plank, Qaraar lowered his centre of gravity by going down on his haunches. Slowly the steed raised each hoof and followed Qaraar. Then all of a sudden Haider slipped. A huge sigh went up as Haider's one leg went into the moonlit, silvery waters. Qaraar swung his arm around the horse's neck as his heart sank at the thought of losing Haider. After what seemed like hours of agony Qaraar looked up at the skies and called out to Khwaja Khizr, the great Sufi mystic of the seas. No one knew his exact date of birth or death, but legend had it that his powers were known to rescue the lost and distressed and guide them to safety.

'Ya Khwaja Khizr Imdaad… Oh Khwaja Khizr, come to my help!' screamed Qaraar desperately with his arm around Haider's neck, both still precariously perched on the swaying plank.

A few moments later the entire dervishi boat reverberated with the call for help from the mysterious Sufi. 'Khwaja Khizr Imdaad' was the call. Every dervish came on deck holding out their hands heavenwards. The reverberations had such an effect that all of a sudden Haider pulled his leg out of the water, stood up and took slow but steady steps and entered the other boat behind his master.

Aalf led his donkey out onto the plank and into the other boat reciting the call for help. The rest followed successfully.

After all had settled in and waved the dervishes goodbye, the voice of the smuggling boatman sounded like the crack of a whip on soft skin 'Where's my gold?'

'We don't have gold,' said Aalf.

'Silver then?' asked the boatman rubbing his two front black teeth with his index finger.

'Don't have silver either.'

'Descendant of the barbarian Vikings! I'm taking this boat right back to the jetty – there you can die like dogs!'

'We have thirty turquoise stones. Will that suffice?'

'Thirty turquoise stones?' said the boatman in an angry but puzzled tone.

'Here.' Aalf held out his hand with stones.

Then suddenly the boatman caught sight of the bags in which the turquoise stones were kept and lunged for them. 'I want them all!'

'Don't even think about it!' said Aalf pulling him back by his shirt.

The boatman screamed. 'We had a deal! Now that you are paying me in turquoise, it means three bags full of those stones.' Then looking at Aalf closely he added, 'You must have stolen those stones – I'm going to take the boat back,' went on the boatman.

Aalf calmly responded, 'If you do, I will tell the guards that you were with us in stealing the turquoise, and then you can spend your entire life trying to prove to the sultan that you didn't.'

The boatman's expression suddenly changed to reluctant acceptance. 'Fine, thirty stones then,' he said, snatching the turquoise from Aalf.

Qaraar lay on deck as the boat pulled towards the Marmara Sea. The night was a clear one. The only sound was the slapping of the oars against water. He looked back. The Blue Mosque was already far in the distance.

Gul and Izzet sat at the other end of the deck. She too looked out towards disappearing Istanbul. 'They won't have even noticed that I've left,' she thought of her family. Like most previous occasions, it was true – her family hadn't noticed her absence. But instead of feeling melancholic, Gul's face shone with the light of freedom and joy. She rested her head against Izzet's chest. Her refined education as a royal princess meant she had learned a fabulous number of languages. She was fluent in Turkish, Persian, Arabic, French, Italian and most importantly, Spanish. And now with Spain as their destination, she would begin basic Spanish lessons for the troupe during the voyage.

Qaraar still looking at the waves felt something in the pockets of his flowing dervish robe. To his surprise he pulled out a small cloth bag. Gul and Izzet curiously looked on from the other end of the deck. When he opened it, he found it bursting with dates, the famous igde fruit, some bread and a few apricots. Excitedly he dug into the other pocket and yet another small bag emerged in his hand. It contained some cheese and grapes. Seeing this, Gul and Izzet did the same and found these little treasures too. Each trouper had the same little bags in their robes. Delighted, amongst much laughter on deck, a little midnight picnic ensued as Aalf and the others joined in with their supplies. Thinking this to be a gift from Rumi, they looked heavenwards and thanked the great Sufi.

After hours of hard sailing and cautiously watching Ottoman battleships sail by, the boat left the waters of the Bosporus and Marmara seas and entered the waters of the Aegean. Turning south by late afternoon the next day they passed the island of Lesvos. For the next five days, they sailed past a cluster of islands that appeared sprouting out of the crystal-clear waters of the Aegean – Chios, Samos and then Patmos. While passing the remote island of Patmos, Aalf somehow managed to convince the boatman to drop anchor. The island was under Ottoman control but was so small and remote that only a few guards and a tiny patrol boat were present. Considering the troupe harmless dervishes of the Rumi order, the

Ottoman patrol allowed them onto the beach. They knew that cross-cultural exchanges often happened between the Rumi order and Christian monks. Hova had heard of this island as it was here that the Christians believed that the Apocalypse was written by St John the Baptist.

On top of a steep hill was the cave in which the manuscript was rumoured to have been completed. A Greek Orthodox monastery was perched on the hilltop. At the base of the monastery were a clutch of simple stone houses belonging to local shepherds and fishermen. Hova insisted on a visit to the monastery and the troupe trekked up spending some calm hours there. On their way back they were invited by a shepherd into his simple home. They communicated through Hova who being Armenian also knew basic Greek. There, in the shepherd's little house, they broke bread and drank wine with him. The simple hospitality of the Greek warmed their hearts and filled their bellies. On their way to the boat, while walking along the pebbled beach, they overheard the fate of the minister of culture being gossiped about by the lone patrol guard, who received courier messages every week to ten days. The minister had lost all control of himself, screaming and yelling in the streets. As punishment for his ill temper and for not being able to complete the pavilion, he was first flung into the dug-up hole which was on the site. Then he was sacked and banished from Istanbul. Apparently, seeking penance for all his political misdeeds, he was heading to Rumi's mausoleum in Konya. Aalf and Qaraar couldn't help but share a smile.

From Patmos, the boatman turned west and after another five days of sailing he anchored at the island of Idra. Here it was apparent that the Ottoman hold was weakening. Venetian and Spanish ships were seen in the far distance. This was where the troupe finally felt free. Gul was the first to fling herself into the transparent waters. The entire troupe then dived in and swam carefree, laughed unabashedly and felt the true spirit of freedom surge within them.

The Venetian merchants had stormed into world prominence in the early eleventh century. Trading in slaves and in other commodities helped them build connections and networks across the Dalmatian coast which propelled their influence along the Adriatic Sea and beyond.[87] The Italian communities had permanent merchant settlements in Constantinople and in other cities in Byzantium, and as a result the Venetian merchants were well established even along the Mediterranean for many centuries. Just off the island of Kythira, south of the Peloponnese and north of Crete, in the Ionian Sea, the Bulgarian boatman handed over the troupe to a Venetian merchant ship. The massive three-deck ship carried large cargo including livestock, spices, silks and textiles, and was part of a larger merchant convoy of ten ships. It had a massive central mast on top of which fluttered the Venetian insignia of the winged lion of St Marks, in yellow against a deep red background. Enormous white square sails swollen with wind hung all around. The route had been charted. First, a brief stop at the headquarters – Venice, then back down the Adriatic with a stop in Sicily and then non-stop through the Mediterranean to Spain.

The boatman left, warning the Venetian merchant and owner of the ship that Aalf was a tough negotiator. Aalf negotiated two bags of turquoise for the troupe to be dropped off in Cadiz, Spain. The other bag he successfully managed to retain. They would have to share their quarters with cooks, cleaners and other labourers, but would not do any of the chores, again negotiated by Aalf. As the troupe settled in, they noticed the true might of the Venetian merchants, as no sooner had their ship and the rest of the convoy sailed out of Kythira, when a large number of smaller, armed boats surrounded them as an armed escort. They looked deadly. Equipped with guns and known as the Venetian galley they were made for swift assault. After sailing up the Adriatic, they reached Venice. As the ships pulled in, massive crowds waved and welcomed the convoy. Sailors and merchants disembarked and flung themselves in the arms of their loved ones. Some of them were meeting after years of being away. The troupe got off too and savoured the sites of this incredible floating city with its timeless little bridges and narrow lanes. At the massive St Mark's Square, Qaraar watched with great pleasure as Gul and Izzet and Aalf and Hova ran around hand in hand. Saad, the other two assistants and Hikmet spent their time looking at the enormous cargos being loaded into ships for the onward journey to Spain and enjoying the vistas of the snow-capped Alps in the distance.

After just a day in Venice, they boarded again and sailed down the Adriatic and then into the Ionian Sea. Soon they docked in Syracuse, Sicily. Here, Qaraar watched an open-air exhibition that captured his imagination. It was taking place near the docks. The artist was a forgotten fifteenth-century Sicilian master called Antonello da Messina and his paintings had been brought from Palermo for display in Syracuse. In *The Virgin Annunciate,* Antonello da Messina had painted the moment when Gabriel announces to the Virgin she would bear Christ with such simplicity and purity that Qaraar was spellbound by its beauty. The subtlety with which the Virgin raised her hand when interrupted while reading, but still delicately holding onto her scarf, bearing just a semblance of a smile – captured the ethereal moment with striking brilliance.

The other painting Qaraar's eyes devoured was the painting of *Saint Jerome in his Study*. Many symbolisms formed part of the painting as was explained on the board below it, in Latin and Arabic, and further explained by Hova. Saint Jerome was seen reading a book which symbolised knowledge. A peacock at the bottom represented immortality of knowledge. A lion behind Saint Jerome was the one from whose paw he had pulled out a thorn and the animal's gratitude signified kindness. Back on-board the ship and leaving Sicily behind, Qaraar couldn't help thinking how when man was inspired by religion's true spiritual teachings of peace, kindness, a genuine quest for knowledge and a belief in the unity of man – like in the case of the *Saint Jerome painting* – he could create beauty. On the other hand, when overtaken by greed and hunger for power, the same man could bring about violence and death like in the case of Nadir. He was convinced now that the Sufi calligrapher was right: it was best to serve mankind through knowledge and spiritual quest, without aspiring for power. That is what he would do in Spain.

The ship captain announced in a loud clear voice that there would be no more stops. It was now straight to Cadiz. Qaraar looked out into the Mediterranean. Close to the ship, the sea was a lapis lazuli blue and as his eyes looked further out, it turned turquoise. The sea itself resembled a blue tile with different shades. The warm Sirocco Mediterranean breeze swept in, lifting his spirits. These serene moments were interrupted with a cheerful Saad making his way to the deck.

'Excited?' Qaraar asked, holding onto the rails and looking at Saad with a smile.

Saad took a deep breath. 'Yes, my forefathers lie buried in Spanish soil. I feel like I'm returning home.'

PART III

CHAPTER 7

NOTHING BUT ONE

The Solano breeze, blew warm and gentle every summer across Andalusia. Between Cordoba and Granada, where vast hilly lands were draped in sunflower fields and olive groves, the wind kissed their petals and leaves, then rose and lost itself in the hills. Through the year the pine trees had a light green freshness to them as they stood daintily against the sky. Amidst this carpeted quiet landscape of flowers and fruits, Catalina sat in solitude most afternoons under the clear blue Spanish sky and read poems and love stories. These were the works of Ibn Mutadid and Ibn Mutamid, the eleventh century father and son Moorish kings of Seville. Scattered all around Andalusia were tiny whitewashed villages, nestled between the hills and olive groves, looking serene and calm. Catalina lived in one such tiny village called Zahara de la Sierra, which was almost equidistant between Cordoba and Granada, but closer to Seville. The white houses of Zahara de la Sierra wrapped themselves around a hilltop Moorish castle and overlooked the rocky 'Eagle Mountain' which got its name because of the birds that nested on its summit. Under the 'Eagle Mountain' too local farmers grew oranges and olives. Catalina's father was a humble village farmer. Catalina had started to look after the family's plot of land, growing olives and sunflowers, whilst her father concentrated his efforts on his tiny grape field. Her mother was given to prayer, stitching clothes, and looking after Catalina's ten-year-old brother. The family's modest stone house was at the edge of the village, beyond which were fields and mountains.

Catalina though, had an enquiring mind. She had a keen interest in studying although she had abandoned school at a young age to help her mother make simple clothes and sell them in local markets. She was twenty-four and had been hailed as the beauty of her village. Her hair was a light blonde colour and resembled strands of silk with her eyes being a very light green. She had a well-defined jaw line that made her peach complexioned face look delicate and petite. Catalina's lips were a natural deep pink. She had a long smooth neck, at the base of which a thin silver chain with a delicate cross rested gracefully. Her shoulders were well proportioned and slim.

She chose her spot carefully in the afternoons to read the works of the Moors. The place was usually an isolated one. The legacy of the Moors in Spain from the eighth century to the fifteenth century had been one of scientific and literary progress. A battery of philosophers and scientists had sprung from Andalusia and blazed the intellectual pathways. Ibn Rushd, or Averroes as the Spanish called him, had become the leading authority on Aristotle. Ibn Khaldun, one of the greatest social scientists, had advised the kings of Granada and his study on the rise and fall of empires and society were groundbreaking. He had made history, a science. The Moors had pioneered watermills all around Andalusia that led to a green revolution. They had organised the wonderful kingdom of Cordoba which was the marvel of the Middle Ages, and which, when all of Europe was plunged in barbaric ignorance and strife, alone held the torch of civilisation and learning, bright and shining before the western world.[88]

Cordoba was that majestic city where seventy public libraries had fed the minds of scholars and half a million books had been gathered together for the benefit of the world.[89] Seville had been nursed carefully by the Muslim Moor rulers too, making it the epicentre of weaving, with close to 16,000 looms, from which numerous elaborate products sprung.[90] Students flocked from

France, Germany and England to drink from the fountain of learning which flowed only in the cities of the Moors.[91] Such was the fertility of mind that the Moors even encouraged women to devote themselves to serious study, and the female physician was not unknown amongst the people of Cordoba.[92]

The practical work of the fields, the scientific method of irrigation, the arts of fortification and ship building were brought to perfection by the Moors.[93] Even when it came to religion, the ruling Muslim Moors had permitted the Christians of Spain to retain their own laws and judges, practise their faith and keep governors of their own, while administering their districts.[94] When it came to religious toleration, instead of persecuting the Christians and forcing a compulsory conversion upon them, the Moors left them free to worship whom or what they pleased.[95] Similarly, when it came to land tax, which varied according to the productiveness of the soil, the tax was assessed equally for Christians, Jews and Muslims.[96] Spain's fertile provinces, rendered doubly prolific by the industry and engineering skill of the Moors bore fruit an hundredfold. Cities innumerable sprand up in the rich valleys of the Guadelquivir and the Guadiana, whose names and names only would commemorate the vanished glories of their past.[97]

However, the sheer vengeance of the reconquista between the thirteenth and fifteenth centuries, concluding with the fall of Granada in 1492, had meant not only the defeat and subsequent expulsion of the Moors, but it also fuelled hatred towards their literary and intellectual accomplishments. All this meant that reading the works of the Moors had to be done in secrecy. Catalina who had been deeply saddened at losing out on a formal education quenched her thirst for knowledge by reading. She usually managed to get hold of the translated works of the Moors by bribing travelling private librarians of other cities with free grapes and olives when they broke their journey in her tiny village.

Catalina's favourite spot to read was at the edge of her olive grove, from where the sunflower field began and beyond that were open vistas of majestic mountains. One afternoon, Catalina settled into her quiet spot and pulled out the works of Ibn Mutadid. The breeze flicked her hair as she opened the leather-bound book. It whispered to her as it climbed up into the olive trees and made the slender branches rustle above her. She smiled to herself and read in a hushed tone.

> A gazelle's are her eyes, sun-like is her splendour
> Like a sandhill her hips, like a bough her stature
> With tears I told her of my love for her
> And told her how much pain I suffer
> My heart met hers knowing that love is contagious…
> Oh hour how short thou wast in passing
> But your sweet memory will linger forever.[98]

She felt as if the words had climbed deep into her heart. The breeze that had seemed nestled in the olive branches above her rustled those branches again, as if it were signalling a new beginning. Then, like a spark that flew from the sun, she saw and heard a thunderbolt bursting through at the far edge of the sunflower fields. Something was moving so fast she could only see the dust rising in the distance. She felt her heart had beaten so fast it had stopped. Her eyes caught a fleeting glimpse of the steed. It was chestnut brown. The intensity of that moment was such that she broke into a sweat. Catalina tightened her grip on the book and ran into the house, shut the door hard and rested her back against it, breathing intensely.

That night, sleep evaded her. The moment of having read the verse and then witnessed a flash that was like a shooting star, kept her awake. She twisted and turned, trying to reason. But reason seemed destroyed at the doorstep of intuition. She feared it, but she wanted that moment back. She waited anxiously for dawn to break, and then for the afternoon when she could go back and sit at the same spot. When that moment arrived she carried the works of Ibn Mutamid, the son of Ibn Mutadid. With fear intermingled with desire she opened the book and read.

> The dwelling of fierce lions and of beauteous maidens
> What lion caves they were…
> And those nights spent on the river dam
> With a girl whose armband was like the curve of the crescent!
> She would pour out wine for me with her glances.[99]

The sunflowers swayed. Catalina read on. It was an account of Ibn Mutamid and his Christian wife from the north of Spain. Homesick, he had found her weeping one day for the winter snows she thought she would never see again in Andalusia. Moved by the tears of his wife, overnight Ibn Mutamid assembled an army of gardeners who planted a forest of almond trees in blossom just outside her window. The next morning Ibn Mutamid led his wife to the window and said, 'See my love, there is your snow!'[100]

Catalina lifted her head from the pages and looked up towards the sunflowers. At the very edge of the swaying field, in the distance, she saw the chestnut brown horse standing sideways. It was calm. There was silence. Only the rustling of the sunflowers could be heard, along with the occasional chirp of the Spanish nightingale. Like the sunflowers, the horse's mane swayed in the breeze. Her eyes worked their way up towards the rider. She saw his knee-length tan, dusty torn boots and under a neat and tight light brown turban, his face. Qaraar.

He had been looking into the distance, not at Catalina. Then he slowly turned and looked at the Spanish beauty. Surrounded by sunflowers, here in the heart of the West, Haider and the rider stood boldly for all that was of the East. Drawn to him, hesitantly Catalina took a step. In no time she was in the middle of the sunflower field. Still mounted, Qaraar looked at the gentle shape of her hair, as a few stray silk-like strands landed softly in the shape of a crescent across her forehead. Not far from him now, Catalina seemed lost in his gaze. But then the mind spoke in an unsettling whisper to her.

'A Moor… a Saracen! Here!' Fear gripped her and she dropped the book. In an instant she turned and ran back towards her house, shut the door and ran to a window from which she peered out. Qaraar dismounted and walked up to the spot where Catalina had dropped the book. He turned the pages. Under each Arabic line, was a Spanish and Persian translation. Qaraar became swiftly engrossed in reading. Still holding the book, his eyes glued to the words, Qaraar sat down in the middle of the sunflower field. To Catalina, watching from the window, it seemed that the rider had disappeared into the earth. The sunflowers were so tall she couldn't see him. Only Haider was visible. Catching her breath and calming herself down she decided to go to him again.

Qaraar, who was marvelling at the words, felt her presence standing at a reasonable distance. And that's where she remained. After a few hours of an excruciating wait Catalina saw him rise, mount his horse and ride away. She rushed back to the spot where he had been sitting and reading. The book was still there. But peeping out of one of the pages was a fluttering bookmark. It was a piece of soft white muslin cloth. It was a sign that he would come back. The next morning, she went out and placed a bunch of grapes, olives and cushions next to the book. He arrived again at the same time. She watched him dismount and disappear under the tall sunflowers only to emerge after a few hours and gallop away. This continued for a few days with Catalina waiting eagerly for the afternoons. Grapes and olives found new companions in cheese, bread and peaches. Yet she dared not speak with him.

Then a thought occurred to Catalina. 'Once he finishes the works of the Moor kings of Seville, "the rider" won't return.' Worried, for days she paced up and down her little house. Her parents noticed the finger biting and frown on her face. She stumbled at times while walking, placed a few wrong stitches to the clothes, and even pierced her delicate fingers with a needle, sucking hard to stop the blood flowing but her mind always thinking of ways to keep him coming back. Finally, she managed to bribe some librarians and get her hands on more books.

Overjoyed with her new acquisitions, she knew she would continue to see the one she thought of as a Moor for a longer period. When Qaraar appeared next, he found a note: 'O Rider! Ibn Rushd to follow.' And after he had finished the works of the kings of Seville, in the same spot he found Ibn Rushd's commentaries – his devouring of Andalusian literature continued in the sunflower field. Ibn Rushd's commentaries on Aristotle riveted Qaraar's mind. Such was the eloquence and depth of the understanding of the Greek master that Qaraar had to read each paragraph three times. It took time to understand why the twelfth century Ibn Rushd had opposed the tenth-century Ibn Sina. Ibn Rushd believed that everything had to be proved through physics and not metaphysics which Ibn Sina had used.[101] Even for the interpretation of the Quran, Ibn Rushd believed it should be a philosopher who should interpret it rather than a religious priest or clergy.[102]

By now Catalina knew the rider had a mind that thirsted for intellectual drink. In her thoughts she changed his name from 'the rider' to 'the reader.' Her confidence in him grew. When he had finished Ibn Rushd's work, she placed Ibn Khaldun's *The Introduction* and *The Book of Observations* on his reading spot. Yet after days of reading, there had been no interaction between them. To Qaraar, when he investigated deeper in his heart, he was craving to see her. Within Catalina, curiosity to know more about the reader grew immensely. While placing Ibn Tufayl's iconic *Hayy ibn Yaqzan* she placed an empty glass and a bottle of wine. Then she waited. The reader appeared as usual and settled into the cushions under the sunflowers. When he left, Catalina went to the spot. The wine bottle was almost empty.

Qaraar, having soaked up the works of these great Andalusian writers, now couldn't wait any longer to engage with Catalina. One afternoon she walked deep into the sunflower field and stood right in front of him. The timing couldn't have been better. Qaraar was just about to finish Ibn Tufayl's work. He was on the last page. She saw him reading the last few sentences. Qaraar rose to his full height and held the book out towards her.

Struck by her beauty, his words came slowly in Spanish. 'Tienes mas a dar… Have you more to give?'

'I have given all…'

Then she continued, her green eyes locked into his brown ones. 'Who are you, O reader, and how do you speak my language?'

Qaraar smiled to himself, 'Another name – the reader.' Looking at the empty wine bottle he said, 'Qaraar Ali. I have been in Andalusia for more than a year – enough time to learn your language.'

'And how do you survive here Moor? The last of you were expelled on a boat in 1614 and you are hated here,' she whispered, coming closer to him and putting down his outstretched arm that was holding the book.

'Not a Moor – I come from Hindustan.'

'Hindustan…' She came even closer and looked at his features and his muslin tunic. Years had taken its toll on the fabric which also had rips across the chest – pieces torn off by the reader for bookmarks.

'That explains the muslin,' she said feeling the soft white fabric. 'I have read of muslin.'

'Why are you here?' she continued. By now she was so close Qaraar could admire the natural pomegranate blush on her cheekbones.

'We move from village to village trying to get work.'

'Why haven't I seen you in my village?'

'You see me in your sunflower field.'

'And so you didn't enter the village?'

'No, I entered the field of knowledge, which you set up for me.'

'You said "we" – didn't your compatriots miss you?'

'They know me well.'

'Now having read all that I can give, what else reader?'

'My craft takes me to Cordoba tomorrow and then onto Granada.'

Catalina didn't like what she heard. He wouldn't be here tomorrow. Her face reflected it immediately. Her green eyes seemed to dull.

'Why must you go?' Her lips were now close to his.

'A craftsman must be true to his art and to his promise.'

The sun began its slow downward trajectory.

'Will you come to see me?' Qaraar placed his hand on the side of her face and she shut her eyes.

'What will you do in Cordoba and Granada, reader?' She had her head on his chest now.

'Restore the geometric woodwork and tiles in the Cordoba mosque.' Catalina looked up at him. By now she was in his arms. 'Then the same at Alhambra-Granada.'

She didn't understand but kept quiet for a while.

'So, you must be a master in geometry.'

'Don't know about being a master, but I have studied it deeply.'

Qaraar felt love soaring within him and he kissed her.

'You didn't answer. Will you come to Cordoba?'

Catalina put her face back on his chest. After a few moments she spoke.

'You are Muslim?'

'Yes.'

After a pause, he continued, 'One who enjoys his wine like Ibn Sina and one who believes in his philosophy.'

She asked, looking at him, 'You know I… I am Christian. What will happen to us in the hereafter?'

Qaraar interjected, 'I live by Ibn Sina. Everything is in this world. The rational intellect prevails even after the body is gone. It feels just peace.'

'Is he the one who wrote *The Canon of Medicine*?'

'Yes.'

'Was he a doctor too?'

'Yes.'

'I will come and see you.'

She turned and kissed him. Her slim arms wound around his neck like a necklace of pearls. The sun disappeared, leaving only an orangish deep purple sky with the slimmest crescent. Below the hilaal crescent, bright like a diamond, was the planet Venus. They were them.

CORDOBA, 1748

Since arriving in Andalusia more than a year ago, the Bashinday-e-Duniya troupe had not met with success. Having docked at Cadiz they had taken up residence there for a few weeks and tried to get some opportunities at local exhibitions. Not much came their way. Fearful of drawing unnecessary attention, they didn't exchange the last turquoise bag for cash. They paid in stone, often using large amounts to bribe people to seal their lips about Saad. He was strikingly a Moor and so easily identified by the Spanish. Soon the troupe, which also had other Muslims like Qaraar, Gul, Izzet and Hikmet in it, began pulling back from being at the forefront of scouting for jobs. No one wanted to see Islamic tiles, listen to the Moor's drums, see paintings of restored old tilework on Muslim buildings of the East, the marbled papers or listen to the tales of Nasroddin Hoja. It was Aalf and Hova who took the lead. Aalf worked for a while with an ironsmith making swords and lances and Hova took up a job as a house cleaner in a merchant's house in Cadiz. But that too didn't last long, as other maids working for the merchant discovered the faith of the rest of their friends. When confronted, Aalf agreed to leave Cadiz and even paid those maids more than half of the turquoise he had for not revealing their secret.

The troupe then made their way into the Andalusian mountains. Gul who was making a brave effort in adjusting to the ways of a travelling nomad took ill with regular bouts of food poisoning but yet continued in her optimistic manner. With her constant sickness though, she had to take a break in teaching the troupe Spanish. Bribing always helped, as it did when hiring a country thug to teach them the language; once again paying in turquoise. On the outskirts of the tiny mountain village of Gaucin that overlooked the Mediterranean, hungry, and with no money, for days the troupe slept on empty stomachs under the sky and outside the village limits. Matters reached such an awful state that every night two members of the troupe would sneak into the village and bring back scraps of food from the garbage sites.

Things got even worse as it became ever so difficult to hide Saad's Moorish origins. Time and again the troupe would have to surround him in a protective circle to hide him and prevent any physical harm. It was apparent to Qaraar that Saad's romantic illusions of a life in Andalusia were precisely that and sooner than later things would get completely out of control. But it was in Gaucin that the troupe's luck changed. One night, while sneaking in for food, Aalf and Qaraar got caught by five giant-like guards of a powerful and wealthy merchant. Aalf gave them the last turquoise stone that he had, but instead of freedom got punched and presented in front of the merchant. It turned out that the merchant was an enlightened man whose heart and mind were without prejudice. The merchant had his country house in Gaucin but enjoyed connections at court. It was he, who on hearing about Qaraar's skills, suggested his name to King Ferdinand VI to restore the wooden geometric patterns at the Grand Mosque of Cordoba, and restore the tilework and decaying geometric patterns on the roofs at the Alhambra. Not just that, the merchant even got them a decent advance.

The troupe made north for Cordoba months before their anticipated date of arrival in the city, out of fear that the king might change his mind, but they were compelled to take a longer route to avoid bandits. Destiny worked its magic. After days of riding, they reached a small pool of fresh water with which they refreshed themselves and their animals. Immediately in front were large rocky mountains. Through a slender gap between two mountains they saw a hill on which was perched the Moorish castle and the village of Zahara de la Sierra. Guiding their horses through the slender gap between the mountains they approached the village. On the outskirts of the village, Qaraar caught sight of Catalina. She had been plucking olives in her grove. Almost instantly he felt drawn to her and on his request, the troupe carried on to Cordoba while he stayed back and became 'the reader.' In Cordoba the troupe's quarters were modest, but right on the banks of the Guadalquivir. Now Qaraar, too, arrived in Cordoba, his heart filled with love but also with anxiety that he may never see Catalina again.

'You've found her, haven't you?' asked Gul having recovered from her food poisoning bouts and sitting under an orange tree in the courtyard of the Grand Mosque besides Qaraar as he looked at the crumbling wooden patterns.

He recited Hafez:

> So sweet perfume the morning air
> Did lately from her tresses bear,
> Her twisted musk diffusing hair –
> What hearts calamity was there.[103]

'I hope she will come.'

'There's nothing quite like it, is there?' said Aalf, peeling an orange he had just picked from the tree.

'Like what?' asked Saad.

'Being in love,' replied Aalf.

'I don't know. I'm just content taking in the sights of this mighty heritage of my forefathers,' replied Saad gasping at the beauty of the Grand Mosque.

'Go in and take a look,' said Aalf chewing on the orange slice.

Saad hesitated, knowing full well that as a Moor he wasn't welcome in the mosque that was now a cathedral.

'Go on Saad,' said Hova. 'If you wish, I will come with you.'

'No.'

'Oh come! We are under the king's protection! Let's go in and see this marvel,' said Hikmet, who was lying under one of the many palm trees that also dotted the courtyard garden.

Aalf signalled to the king's guards, five of whom had been designated to the troupe. They formed a protective circle around the troupe as they made their way inside.

The beauty was such that Saad's feet betrayed his eyes. He stumbled and widened his eyes to take in the architectural wonder. The red striped arches were typical of Moorish architecture and when looked at from a distance came across like an illusion. The very next day Qaraar got to work, focussing first on the woodwork that needed restoration and after toiling all day, each evening he would wait under the orange trees hoping to see Catalina. But she didn't come.

Having restored the woodwork, he focussed on the tiles. These were in different colours – yellow, green and black. While working on them, the desire to see Catalina reached its peak. The tiles were positioned below a resplendent Christ and everytime he completed a star shape, she would seem a galaxy away. When the tile panels were complete Qaraar fell to his knees under Christ. 'When I can see you in her, why does she not show herself? She is but a manifestation of your light.' Yet she did not come.

On completion of the project, Aalf received the money on behalf of the troupe. From the window of their quarters, as all packed to leave for Granada, Aalf watched Qaraar as he walked along the stone bridge over the rushing waters of the Guadalquivir. Pacing up and down, looking at the moon, the mighty river and some wandering people, verses of Hafez left his lips.

A mountain sea, moon clouded o'er,
And nigh the whirlpools awful roar –
How can they know our labour sore
Who pass light-burthened on the shore?[104]

GRANADA

The Sierra Nevada mountains experienced their first snow fall. Qaraar looked out towards them from a balcony in the Alhambra, having completed his restoration tasks. Just one tile needed to find its right place. He had made it but hadn't yet put it into the panel – instead it lay on the floor beside him. Stretching out his hands horizontally he stood under the arch taking in the fresh mountain air coming down the snow peaks. Then he glanced at the tile panel that he hadn't completed. It reminded him of the geometric designs on the stone screens on Humayun's Tomb in faraway Delhi.

The similarity in design of the tile panel to the stone screens at Humayun's Tomb included the star, the six-sided hexagon and some polygons. But the tulip design was different. While Humayun's Tomb screen had three petal points, here there was an additional petal point to the flower. The echo of his past reached even here in Spain. The last tile that needed to be inserted into the panel was the one with the four-pointed tulip design. Qaraar looked at it and then turned his face away, fixing his gaze on the snow peaks.

A few moments later a delicate wrist holding the tile came in front of the view of the mountains.

'I told you I would come.'

'Where to, from here?' Words came from Qaraar, in a mix of joy and anger for having had to wait so long.

'Come back to Zahara de la Sierra.'

'So that you can keep me waiting there too?'

'So that you can survive.'

Qaraar turned his face towards the mountains.

Catalina brought her face in front of his.

Both were under the arch when she caressed his face with one hand and said, 'Reader – now become a teacher.'

Qaraar looked at her closely.

'Such knowledge within you – don't you want to share it?'

'My time has gone.'

'Your time has come.'

She led him with one hand, and they went to the tile panel. Qaraar bent down with her and together they both put in the last tile. The panel was complete.

'You from the East are masters of mathematics,' said Catalina as she nestled into his arms on the floor. He wrapped his arms around her.

'I have got you a job as geometry teacher to the children at my village school.'

'How did you manage that?'

'It's taken months of persuasion; I'm being selfish, keeping you close.'

'Is that why you didn't come and see me for so long?'

'Yes.'

Qaraar gently lifted her chin with his fingers and kissed her.

'How have you come now?'

'With my father, to sell his grapes and olives.'

A few miles outside of the village of Zahara de la Sierra, Qaraar and Aalf bought two tiny pieces of sloping land next to each other from the money they made after the restoration projects. Qaraar's name didn't sound Arabic and so the deal went through hastened by the fact that two desperate and utterly poor peasants wanted to dispose of their land and move to Cadiz for better opportunities. The plots of land had unrestricted views of the hilltop Moor castle, the whitewashed village and to the right the rocky 'Eagle Mountain.' Charmingly, Qaraar's little plot had a ruined stone barn on it. The troupe put a thatched straw roof on the ruin and made it their home. Straw demarcations meant a separate room for Gul and Izzet and for Aalf and Hova. The others, including Qaraar, slept on the floor in the main area. Gul, the Turkish princess, had impressed all with her complete devotion to not just Izzet but to the whole troupe. She slept on the floor with her man. She ate, without fuss, the frugal food that was made available and encouraged her lover to learn more acrobatics and card tricks so that he could earn more money.

Aalf bought some local goats and hens which he kept on his land. Saad kept himself confined on Aalf's plot helping in making yoghurt and butter and looking after the goats, and Aalf kept him protectively close to him so that no one dared attack the Moor. Sometimes Aalf would get on his donkey and go to nearby villages to sell milk and yoghurt. Soon his enterprising nature earned him and his assistants a job at the local bakery too. Accompanied by Aalf and his assistants, Hikmet and Izzet, now feeling safe, did acrobatics and juggling along with card tricks that impressed the locals of the remote village.

Every morning Qaraar woke up and went to the escuela, or school. Among inquisitive Spanish children who had never seen a Hindustani before, he taught geometry. From the school he could see Catalina's olive groves and sunflower fields. But he didn't see her most weeks. Some days he would be lucky to see her under the olive trees. Seeing him distracted by the Spanish beauty and his compass faltering, his students would break into unabashed laughter.

On many an occasion after giving lessons, Qaraar would not go back to the barn, but instead he would wander away for long walks on his own. He was aware he was getting esoteric in nature. His inward journey gave him peace. There were moments when his ego had been awakened. In those moments he once was Qaraar Ali – the renowned craftsman who had been the chosen hand of emperors, khans and sultans. His hand had brought life back to the majestic buildings from Hindustan to Spain. That voice told him he was the greatest of restorers; he was the one to which every brick and tile should bow. That voice mocked at his current status as a mere geometry teacher to fledgling minds in a remote village. Where once he had been paid in sacks of glittering gold, now he only got the smiles of children and a handful of coins. There had been a time when he had been the love of a woman who had shimmered in diamonds, sapphire and emeralds. Now he was the love of a peasant's daughter who appeared in simple stitches. How he had fallen, said that voice arrogantly within him.

But then as that voice rose menacingly, another voice within him overtook it and subdued it forever. The voice of the Sufi. During his walks, in the wilderness, climbing mountains and shrubbery ridges which took on the look of pink velvet in the Spanish sunset, the verses of Rumi left his lips drowning his ego completely.

See how in pride they go
With lifted head,
Till fate with a sudden blow
Smiteth them dead...

Flowers every night
Blossom in the sky;
Peace in the Infinite
At peace am I.[105]

What makes the Sufi? Purity of heart;
Not the patched mantle and the lust perverse
of the vile earth-bound men who steal his name.
He in all dregs discerns the essence pure:
In hardship ease, in tribulation joy.[106]

Then his own words reached deep within him.

'A true Sufi gives all he has – these are your greatest moments. When a child's sterile mind stirs with a thirst for knowledge because you have planted a seed there, you shall find yourself standing right there, with a water canter. This is your contribution to mankind, your khidmat-e-khalq: nurture these saplings.'

Taking in the natural beauty of Andalusia during those regular walks Qaraar had destroyed his ego in entirety. He felt he had entered a stage of fanaa. Most Sufi's believed this was attained only through ascetic practices, meditation and isolation, but Qaraar believed he had got there by finishing his ego with deeds that helped others. An inexplicable peace had entered him. His heart felt like a polished mirror where he could see Him and himself as One. Even Catalina had merged into the One who he now saw within. Alone in the Andalusian mountains Qaraar went deeper into contemplation on how to widen his khidmat-e-khalq with deeds of goodness. The more he thought of doing good, the closer he felt to his creator and the closer he felt to his creator the more intense flashes of ecstasy he felt within.

From then on, his teaching days at school took the form of love.

'How far is Hindustan?' asked Diego, a ten-year-old boy rubbing sleep off his eyes.

'Oh, very far.'

'Tell us, show us!' said Enrique, another ten-year-old, who was also Catalina's brother.

'Beyond the seven seas.'

'Seven seas!' A loud voice went up in disbelief.

'Well, let me show you,' said Qaraar kneeling down on the stone floor with a large paper.

He began sketching a map. 'Here we are in beautiful Andalusia.'

'Aha.'

'...and this is the Mediterranean Sea.'

'Aaah.'

Guiding his fingers to perfection, '…and now here are the Adriatic and the Ionian Seas.'

'Hmmmm.'

'From then on – as you can see as I draw – this is the Aegean Sea and then the Sea of Marmara.'

'Next to Turkey?'

'That's right, but my Hindustan is further away.'

'Further than Turkey?' enquired another boy in utter disbelief. His name was Alfonso.

'Yes. Just watch my fingers now, Alfonso.'

'Here is the Black Sea.'

'Black? Is the water really black?' asked the children, jumping all around Qaraar as he drew.

'I don't know – I haven't crossed that one!'

'Black! It is black!' yelled Pablo, an eight-year-old with floppy light brown hair who flung his head back and laughed uncontrollably 'Black Sea is Black' he went on.

'No, actually it's not – but let's carry on. Here children, is the Caspian Sea – and further south-east are – the lands of Hindustan!'

'Hindustan!' sighed the children, running their fingers behind the pencil as Qaraar drew the Pamir Mountain range and then the first outlines of Hindustan.

'So how many seas did you count?' asked Qaraar.

'Hmmm… seven!'

'That's right!'

'So you come from across the seven seas,' sighed the children in disbelief, looking at the map.

Alfonso poked Qaraar's hand to see if he was real.

'Well yes, but I only crossed six – I didn't cross the Black Sea.'

'The teacher from across the seven seas!' yelled Enrique with his hands up in the air.

The children laughed and ran around Qaraar.

Then Enrique spotted his sister in the olive grove.

'Ven aqui! Ven aqui! Come here! Come here to the window,'

he said to Qaraar, pointing at her saying with a smile, 'Go and talk to her!'

Over the days, the children had picked up on Qaraar's anxiousness hoping to catch a glimpse of Catalina from the window. 'Go! Go!' shouted all the other children, as Qaraar broke into a smile.

Putting down the pencil he left the classroom.

His giggling pupils ran to the window.

'Here, let me help you,' said Qaraar taking a straw basket from Catalina's hand.

Picking the olives the two walked through the dense grove.

'You've settled in well, reader,' she said demurely.

'How can I be settled when I long to see you?'

She turned, dropped the basket and quickly looked around. The school had disappeared into the distance, the giggling of the school children had been replaced by the rustle of the Solano breeze in the olive trees. She wrapped her arms around his neck and kissed him. These secretive meetings continued for a while.

Qaraar's rather innocent drawing of the route he had taken to Spain led to a new opportunity. One day the head of the school saw Pablo engrossed in it. Coming close, he inspected the sketch and was struck by the detail of what was almost the entire known world. When Pablo told him it was Qaraar who had drawn it, the very next day Qaraar was made an offer to teach elementary geography. Education in remote Spanish villages was poor. Knowing this, the head of school welcomed anyone with knowledge to come and teach at the local school, but there weren't many who had come forward. In fact, the staff strength was only two. Qaraar taught mathematics and geometry and another taught Spanish. Qaraar accepted this new opportunity, with which came additional money.

At the ruined barn Qaraar found Gul to be a tremendous source of information. The Turkish princess now came forward and helped Qaraar in drawing maps. Crouching over the floor and surrounded by candles the two of them drew and sketched away. Izzet sat beside

Gul and learnt, adding to his knowledge. Gul's detailed drawings of the European continent, its rivers, mountains and seas were one set. The second set were maps of eastern Europe and the Balkans. Qaraar sketched out maps of Persia, Central Asia and Hindustan. Over a period of one week they had mapped out most of the known world including the Atlantic Ocean and the new world. Gul, began accompanying Qaraar to the school to assist in the geography lessons and seeing her devotion, Qaraar gave all the earnings from the geography lessons to her. He knew well how much Gul and Izzet needed the money and he felt a great sense of satisfaction in helping them. She excelled even further giving demonstrations about fossils and botany. Such was the passion with which she taught that eventually Qaraar convinced the head of school to give Gul an independent job as geography and botany teacher. With a steady income now, Gul and Izzet felt a sense of self-esteem.

Just when the troupe thought they had settled into Andalusian coutry life, the inevitable happened. Catalina's father found out that Qaraar and Izzet were Hindustani and Turk Muslims, and Saad was a Moor. He had overheard her speaking to a friend. In minutes his wrath descended on her. She was flung into her room and the door bolted. Axe in hand he stormed into the barn.

'Infidels! How many of you?' He screamed in a mad rage.

'We are under the protection of the king!' screamed Gul as she rushed and stood in front of Izzet, who was the father's intended target.

'You were… but with his work done, you are no longer,' roared the enraged father as he raised his axe.

'No!' Hova rushed in front of Gul and held up her pendant. A cross.

'I am Christian,' she said clutching the cross firmly with one hand and with the other pushing Gul behind her. 'You will have to kill me to get to them.'

The colour on the father's face grew blood red. He left them alone and rushed out of the door making his way to the school.

Qaraar was busy teaching. Catalina's father stormed into the classroom and rushed towards him swinging his axe in the air.

'I'm going to send you to the fires of hell!' He grabbed Qaraar by the collar and raised his weapon menacingly.

Enrique, Diego, Alfonso and Pablo ran towards the two adults. The rest of the children got up and rushed towards them too. In seconds Qaraar was surrounded by twenty children. Some latched onto the raging father's arm and tried to pull it down; others clawed him.

'He is our teacher! Stop!' they yelled.

'Put it down, father,' said Enrique bravely as he attacked his father's hips, punching them with all the fury his little fists could unleash.

But with one massive swipe the father had all the children on the ground.

'After I'm done with you, I'll get that Moor too!' The father raised his axe for one telling blow.

Just then Aalf's deep baritone came booming into the room.

'No! You won't!'

Hova and Gul had rushed to Aalf's plot where he was feeding his donkey and goats and told him about what had happened at the barn.

Aalf and his two Viking assistants grabbed the father. They tackled him to the ground and disarmed him.

Rising from the ground and held by the two Viking assistants, the father's struggles to break free seemed utterly futile.

'Now, listen to me!' roared Aalf looking at the father.

'You so much as lay a finger on Qaraar and you'll lose your head.'

'He and that Moor are infidels,' came the father's sharp retort, accompanied by saliva shooting out of his mouth.

Holding onto the father, one of the Viking assistants thundered into his ear, 'They are our friends!'

Gasping for breath and yet still being held, the father said,

'You… you all won't last long in Andalusia when word gets out.'

'We'll take our chances,' snapped back Gul, peering her head out from behind Aalf.

'Besides, think of the consequences of killing him. We might not be under the king's protection now, but word will get out that you killed a man who had worked for the king – then you and this obscure village of yours can bear the legal consequences,' Gul said it all in one go.

Then, embarrassed by his father's behaviour, the bold ten-year-old Enrique walked up to his father. 'Leave my school, and never come here again!'

The Viking assistants pushed the father out of the school.

That night while everyone slept, Qaraar heard a noise in the barn. Choosing to remain still, Qaraar opened his eyes slightly and saw movement in the far corner. Saad and Hikmet slowly rose in the dark, covered their heads with their shawls, dropped a note, made their way out and disappeared into the night. Something in Qaraar let them go.

Qaraar waited for silence, got to his feet, and read the contents of the note.

'I saw the misty blue mountains of Morocco from Gaucin. They call me. I will be safe there. Hikmet and I will play the drums and do acrobatics. Without me, all of you will be safe. Bashinday-e-Duniya will always live on in our hearts.'

'I hope they make it to Morocco,' thought Qaraar looking out into the night. The next morning a sense of loss was felt by all the troupe members. Izzet wept for his departed brother and Gul consoled him. Aalf held the note tight to his chest. Saad and he had become close, milking goats, making yoghurt and Aalf had taken it upon himself to personally protect the Moor. He felt he had let him down. The next few days were spent with a feeling of self-speculation and introspection.

Meanwhile at Catalina's house an intense debate raged. The unlikely hero being little Enrique.

'Why have you locked up my sister for days?' Enrique boldly raised his finger while questioning his father who towered over him.

'Question me any further and I will lock you up as well.'

'Juan, the girl hasn't seen sunlight for a week,' said Almudena, Catalina's mother, while sorting out the olives in a basket and addressing her husband with a slight firmness in her voice.

'Until now the villagers don't quite know of her love for that man,' he said. 'The day they find out who he is, they will either kill him or throw us out with him.'

'He is respected in the village! He is a teacher, not some axe-wielding mad man,' quipped Enrique.

The father stormed towards the boy.

'Slow down Juan!' Almudena came in between the two. 'All those children that stood up and protected him, are children of the village. If he's got the children's adulation, he cannot be a bad person.'

'So, what are you saying?'

'I'm saying, let's get to know him a little.'

Juan looked at Almudena.

'I'm told he is someone given to…' Almudena paused and thought a bit, then spoke again. 'Su – Sufism… yes, that's it! He has the mind of a Sufi.'

'Sufi?' enquired Enrique with an intrigued look on his face. 'I like the sound of it – Sufi! Sufi!' he said with a smile.

'What is that? And how do you know?' growled the father.

'They are Muslims, hungry for spirituality and science. Our daughter told me.'

'So you've known about them?'

'Yes, someone has to.'

'Sufi… Sufi… Sufi… I love the word!' Enrique continued.

'Well, he's still Muslim.'

'Listen, let's not fool ourselves. The Muslims had the most vibrant culture in Andalusia.'

'Yes, but the villagers...'

Almudena now came straight upto Juan. 'We live for ourselves, not for society. We live for our happiness and the happiness of our children, don't we? And besides, not even the entire village would be able to harm a hair on his head with him being watched over by those giant Vikings!' She said the last sentence looking at Enrique and mischievously winking at him.

The mention of the Vikings made the father gulp in fear.

'Well alright, if he is like one of those...'

'Like a Sufi!' added Enrique, helping his father complete the sentence.

'Yes... then let's meet him.'

Enrique stuck out his open hand. His father put Catalina's room key in it.

'What do you do with such a vast amount of olives?' asked Qaraar as he and Juan strolled in the olive grove. Both men had started taking morning walks together before Qaraar's teaching began at the school. Qaraar preferred solitude during his evening walks which were moments of contemplation for him, and so he met Juan in the mornings.

'Some I sell, but most I use to make olive oil,' said the father.

Then pointing at a tiny wooden mill, he said, 'That's the mill where I crush them for oil.'

'And the grape field?'

'Well, I don't make wine here. I sell the grapes in Cordoba and Granada.'

'If you need me to help in the olive grove and with the grape harvest, I'd be happy to.'

Juan could sense Qaraar's genuine love for nature.

'Why don't you help out for an hour each evening?'

'With pleasure.'

Catalina would visit Qaraar.

'How many baskets have you filled with olives, reader?'

'Ah, well, ten today.'

'Look how beautiful they are,' she said lifting a few dark purple ones and a few green ones in her hands.

'Here taste them from my hand.' She fed him a few from a basket that had marinated olives.

'Help me get rid of the leaves.' Both would work together.

On other occasions Qaraar helped build and whitewash knee high stone walls around the grove so that goats couldn't get in from Aalf's plot. In the mill, Qaraar and Juan would begin crushing the olives. The oil, fresh and deeply fragrant would be emptied in wooden casks to be sold later in surrounding villages. When the harvest season for the grapes arrived, Qaraar would be seen in the fields gathering the fruit. Later with permission from Juan he took a few vine creepers and formed an arch, at the entrance of his plot and soon clusters of grapes hung under those arches. Another year passed by engaged in these country activities. On many occasions he would even accompany Juan on his horse-pulled cart to Cordoba and Granada for the annual grape harvest markets, helping out in the sale. These journeys would take days. During one such journey to Granada, Juan and Qaraar bonded over conversation.

'Look at these ruins,' said Juan, guiding the horse with one hand and pointing to a Moorish castle. Many of these ruins dotted the Andalusian landscape and spoke of their glorious past. 'How the mighty Moors fell,' Juan continued, as the horse-driven cart slowly passed the ruin. 'Wonder how it all happened,' he said, scratching his head.

'They lost asabiyya,' said Qaraar looking at the ruins.

'What's that?'

'According to Ibn Khaldun, asabiyya, or group solidarity, and a sense of energised belief in identity, drove them to great heights, but when they lost that sense of group solidarity, the downfall began.'

'Why did they lose that solidarity?' asked Juan.

'Not just them. According to Ibn Khaldun all empires rise and fall when they lose asabiyya. The more the once attacking conquerors from the countryside get confined to leisure and urban city life, the more they lose focus on empire building.'

'So urban life and leisure helps destroy empires?'

'Well, sedentary life and stability occurs with the building of urban societies – and it's during periods of stability that the arts, philosophy and refinement of thought takes place. So urban living and leisure time does have its benefits, but it does make an empire vulnerable when the refined society loses its hunger – it then falls prey to other tribes who are driven by solidarity to create a new identity.'

'So, it's a cycle?'

'Exactly. According to Ibn Khaldun, each dynasty goes through five stages: conquest on the basis of group solidarity, then a powerful ruler, after this there is a period of wise rule, this is followed by over-confidence and indulgence in luxury, and finally the dynasty falls to another tribal group.'[107]

'This can also be true to families and the rise and fall in their fortunes,' Juan's voice had a sombre ring to it now.

'Yes, it can.'

'It happened to my family,' said Juan, now deeply moved. 'My great-grandfather went to the Imperial court as a leading jurist and acquired great wealth and power, grandfather stabilised it, but my father was a drunk and lost it all – and now there's me. I just sell grapes in the markets of Granada.'

'Oh come, it's not all that bad,' said Qaraar. 'Learn to see the beauty in what you have.'

'Difficult when you know about what once was.'

There was silence as Juan guided the horses and they passed another ruined Moorish castle.

Then looking at Qaraar, Juan asked, 'How do you know so much about Ibn Khaldun?'

'He was here in these lands advising the kings of Granada in the fourteenth century... then he left Spain to teach in Cairo. He lies buried in a Sufi cemetery there.'[108]

'But how do you know his works?'

'Your daughter. She gave me his books to read.'

Juan was silent for a while.

Then he asked, 'How will you treat my daughter?'

Qaraar looked into the clear blue Spanish sky and said, 'Just how the fifteenth-century Sufi Borkluce Mustafa advised – to treat Christians like angels.'

The answer left the father speechless.

Months passed and the relationship between Juan and Qaraar changed from animosity to tolerance and then acceptance. One day back in Zahara de la Sierra, Qaraar did what he had been wanting to for a long time. Under the arch of vine creepers below bunches of grapes, he asked Catalina to marry him. She flung herself in his arms. Such was the sincerity with which Qaraar asked and the change of feelings Juan had towards him, that her father said yes even before Qaraar could finish the question. There were concerns, though, of the religious differences between the couple.

A meeting was called to discuss this sensitive topic and the venue chosen was the shack on Aalf's plot.

'You will have to become Christian,' said Juan surrounded by the troupe members.

'You should not,' said Aalf as he and his assistants stepped into the shack. Juan hadn't seen Aalf since the time of the incident at the school and developed sweaty palms just seeing Aalf.

'Why do you have to convert?' continued Aalf, placing a sack of hay on the side.

'Well, there can't be a wedding then,' said Gul. 'Am I right?' She looked around. 'I for one don't need marriage, I'm happy to live in sin,' she laughed, and looked at Izzet.

'Here in Andalusia unfortunately Qaraar will have to embrace

Christianity if there is to be a wedding,' Almudena clarified for all present in the shack.

'Nothing wrong with that,' said Qaraar.

'But why should you? You are who you are,' emphasised Hova shaking her head and shutting the door of the shack to prevent the goats from entering.

'Listen all,' Qaraar said, standing up. 'If Sarmad the great Sufi who lies buried in Delhi could be an Armenian Jew, a Muslim and a Yogi Hindu, why can't I carry multiple faiths in my heart?'

Everyone was silent.

'I love you for who you are – you don't have to,' Catalina spoke and held him from behind.

'I open my heart to the Lord,' Qaraar said stretching his arms out.

On the day of the wedding a simple baptism ceremony was to take place at the local church. The entire village gathered outside to see the spectacle, but they weren't allowed inside. That was a request Catalina's father made with all, including his closest friends, so as to respect the young easterner. Just before the ceremony Catalina's father went up to the priest and whispered something in his ear. Water was sprinkled on Qaraar's head, and a robe put around him. The distant crowd let out a huge cheer. Once it was done Catalina entered, accompanied by little Enrique, wearing a simple white dress which she had made herself. She took her place besides Qaraar who wore his muslin tunic, the torn parts patched up by Catalina. Aalf followed and stood behind the groom with a simple ring that Qaraar had bought in a nearby village market. The exchange of vows took place and Qaraar slipped the ring onto Catalina's finger. Another roar went up outside the church.

After the ceremony the couple went to the barn which the troupe had decorated with azahar, the flower of the orange tree blossoms. The gentle fragrance mixed with the fragrance of the Dama de Noche (lady at night) flowers, lured the couple into the barn's seductive environment.

The rest settled into Catalina's parent's house to celebrate. After much singing and dancing, Catalina's father walked up to Aalf.

Aalf looked at him with disdainful eyes, holding him responsible for Qaraar's conversion.

Catalina's father couldn't look Aalf in the eye. Then all of a sudden, he did.

'It didn't really happen,' he said, gulping down a glass of wine in one go.

'What do you mean?'

'The baptism – it didn't really happen. How could I get him to convert, when there's such true love in his heart?'

'Go on.' Aalf was curious.

'The priest mumbled some other verses, but not the ones for baptism.'

'What?'

'Catalina came to me a few days before the wedding. She couldn't bear the fact that he had to convert to have her. I couldn't see my daughter that distraught… so, I told the priest to put on a show rather than recite the correct verses for the baptism.'

'How did the priest agree?'

Now the father had a twinkle in his eyes. 'He is my brother and loves Catalina as his own daughter.'

'Ha ha! You are worthy of an embrace, Spaniard!' Aalf put his arms around Juan and swung him around in glee.

'Who knows about this?' he asked.

'Catalina, you, me and my brother – best to keep it amongst us.'

'Yes, yes, of course. Let's drink to man and love!' Aalf held up his glass.

The next day Qaraar and Catalina woke to the gentle fragrance of the azahar orange blossom flowers. Qaraar looked at her beautiful face, radiant in the sun as she lay in bed. He gently ran his fingers through her hair. He felt a union with her like never before. She turned towards him and ran her hand across his chest. The contentment she felt was deeply satisfying.

Both walked to the main door and looked out at the land in front of them. Then they stepped out and looked behind at their barn.

'It's our home,' said Catalina resting her head on his shoulder.

Qaraar deeply inhaled the fragrance of the orange blossoms. He felt a sense of permanency and a sense of home and belonging. 'It is our home, but much can be done,' said Qaraar rushing in and putting on a shirt.

'Where are you going?'

'Come with me, let's create!' Qaraar seemed overcome with enormous energy.

'Look at this wonderful land – it's empty! I want to plant an orchard here.'

He ran towards Haider and mounted him.

'Wait for me!' Catalina rushed towards him laughing with excitement and joy.

Leaning down from Haider, Qaraar gave his hand to Catalina and swung her onto the steed. She sat in front of him and the horse galloped out.

'Where to, my love?' she asked, her hair flying in Qaraar's face as they made their way into the village.

'To each student's house.'

'Why?'

'You will see.'

First, they stopped at Diego's whitewashed house. His father had a cart which Qaraar harnessed to Haider, and Diego jumped into the cart. Then they stopped at Catalina's parent's house to get Enrique, who also jumped into the cart. Then at Pablo's, Antonio's Alfonso's and the rest of the school children. The cart was soon filled with twenty children as they went through the narrow lanes of Zahara de la Sierra cheered on by the parents. The next stop was a plant nursery.

'Come on children, pick twenty orange saplings,' said Qaraar as the children rushed in to choose their little plants.

'Get some bougainvillea too!' said Catalina.

'All in different colours?' asked Pablo, quickly turning for approval, with his hair flicking across his forehead.

'Yes, yes, go on now!'

'Oh Alfonso, also get some cans of whitewash.'

Back at the barn work began in earnest.

'Each of these saplings will carry your names,' Qaraar said looking at the children who were holding them in their small hands with the most excited looks on their faces.

'Yes, what you hold in your hands is an extension of you,' reiterated Catalina.

Qaraar took off his shirt, lifted a pickaxe and shovel and began digging. As he dug, sweat dripping down his forehead, Catalina noticed the scars on his back for the first time. The lash from a whip was from when once he was a slave. It was then that Catalina realised that she didn't know much about Qaraar's past. He hadn't told her, and she hadn't asked.

Taking a break, wiping the sweat off his forehead and leaning on the pickaxe, Qaraar yelled out to Aalf who was herding his goats on his land within earshot.

'Come and give me a hand. I'm planting an orange orchard!'

The Viking descendent leapt over a few shrubs that separated his land from his friend's and came rushing with additional pickaxes.

The two men dug hard, mud flying everywhere. But Catalina continued to observe the scars on Qaraar's back. As he raised his pickaxe, Aalf saw Catalina's fixed gaze on the scars. Through the afternoon and early evening digging and planting carried on till last of the children had left with soiled hands and their hearts teeming with excitement of having planted an orange orchard.

It was evening and Catalina knew it was time for Qaraar's walk. She wiped his chest, gave him a bottle of water to carry and kissed him. He left.

'My men and I gave him those scars.' Aalf dropped his head in regret and sat by the entrance of the barn.

'You?'

'I was a slave trader once. He was... he was my... I can't even utter it.'

Catalina looked on in disbelief.

'He changed my life. Made me a better man,' Aalf said looking into the distance as Qaraar's silhouette against the sunset disappeared.

'It's a painful past. Both his and mine,' he continued.

Over a period of a month Aalf revealed all to Catalina. Every evening when Qaraar left for his walks after watering the orange saplings with the children, Catalina would ask Aalf to come and tell more. There was such loss and joy in their life's journey that Catalina couldn't hear it all in one go. By the time she had heard it all she had fallen even deeper in love with the man whom she still addressed as 'the reader.'

The barn got the craftsman's attention too. He whitewashed it with love. Each day a little. It was a warm evening in August 1749 when only a tiny bit of the outside of the barn needed whitewashing. Qaraar was about to give it his attention, with Catalina by his side, when Gul, Izzet, Aalf and his two assistants came rushing towards him.

'He's dead!' blurted out Izzet, bending and resting with his hands on his knees.

'Dead? Say it properly,' said Gul, looking at Izzet and then at Qaraar.

Pushing her hair at the back, she shouted, 'He was murdered, stabbed to death! Blood gushed from every pore.'

'Who? Who?' asked Catalina.

'He died the way he deserved,' added Aalf kicking the ground. 'Blood must have been everywhere.'

'Who?' asked Catalina again.

Gul continued. 'His own men killed him, while he slept in his tent. Twenty of his guards entered and stabbed and stabbed and stabbed,' she said with vengeance and repeated hand movements.

'Out with the name now!' Catalina caught Gul by the shoulders and shook her.

Izzet now took over. 'He attacked my country several times – such war and destruction he brought upon us.' Then he realised he was standing in front of a man who had personally borne the onslaught of a massacre.

'Will you please tell me who has been killed?' Catalina yelled.

'Nadir! Nadir has been murdered!' said Aalf. 'He begged for his life in the end… "Take all I have but spare my life" were his last words,' he continued.

All looked at Qaraar. Catalina and Aalf walked up to him. Aalf placed his arm on his friend's shoulder. Catalina embraced him.

But the man who had lost everything to the butchery led by Nadir in Delhi didn't react.

'Aren't you happy, Qaraar? Finally, justice has been done,' said Gul.

'How did you find out and when did this happen?' asked Qaraar.

Aalf explained, grasping Qaraar's shoulder tight. 'I had sent one of my assistants to Cadiz to purchase some utensils, and there he met some merchants who told him. It happened two years ago, and the news has only just reached us – can you believe it?'

Catalina looked at Qaraar. 'Your past…' But before she could finish her sentence Qaraar dipped the brush he had into the tub, then with one stroke he swept the brush across that part of the barn that needed to be whitewashed.

'I have swept the past aside.' He put down the brush. It was time for his evening walk, but instead he took steps towards Haider.

Mounting the steed, he signalled to Catalina who walked up to him.

'From now on we ride together every evening, as One.'

She gave her hand to him. 'I will sit behind, my hair will distract you.'

'No. Never behind me. Always in front.'

Qaraar wrapped his arms around Catalina and Haider galloped out of the fledgling orange orchard. Haider's pace increased as the two looked up at the ruined Moorish castle on the hilltop of Zahara de la Sierra. It soon became a blur as Haider galloped towards the 'Eagle Mountain' putting a fair distance between them and the inhabited world. Deep within Qaraar had forgiven Nadir.

CHAPTER 8

FROM THE MOUNTAIN FLAME

SEMANA SANTA AND EASTER SUNDAY, 1752

By now, Qaraar was the much-respected mathematics and geometry teacher, and Gul the passionate geography teacher, who were both welcomed everywhere they went in the village, even at gatherings during the elaborate Semana Santa – Holy Week – before Easter. The teaching jobs, and in Qaraar's case the additional money from the sale of the olive oil, ensured a steady income for them both. Gul and Izzet had moved out of Qaraar's barn and rented a tiny house in the heart of the village.

During Semana Santa every evening the cathedral at Zahara de la Sierra, and the plaza outside the cathedral, would transform itself into an oasis for the spiritually inclined, with dancing candle flames and echoing hymns. A few days before Easter, the statues of Christ and the Virgin were lowered in the cathedral so that the village folk could come and kiss the hands of the statues.

Catalina and Qaraar stood in the village square holding up flaming torches every evening. For the entire week as evening fell, a line-up of priests dressed in purple, and on other days green robes, with their heads covered with conical caps, would lead the procession to sombre music, swaying lanterns and through a shower of petals thrown by the onlookers. Behind the priests were the pasos. These were large floats on which life-sized wooden statues telling the story of the Passion of Christ and the events leading up to crucifixion were placed. Christ in all his glory, and in all his suffering that he took on for mankind, came alive on those floats as Qaraar and Catalina watched them roll through the narrow, cobbled streets of Zahara de la Sierra.

Catalina had watched with great respect and admiration as Qaraar had accompanied her for all the processions. But something within her felt he must be told that he wasn't baptised. Qaraar had shown virtually no reaction to the baptism ceremony, as if it hadn't really mattered to him. For Qaraar, like Ibn Arabi, Sarmad, Dara, Borkluce Mustafa, Rumi and the other great Sufis, all faiths were equal in their quest for the Divine. It was their belief, and Qaraar's, that one could only find Him through the inward journey – therefore a baptism for Qaraar actually symbolised an addition, a new dimension of spirituality. The dogma of conversion didn't arise in his mind, because to him, spirituality had risen above the ritual and the ceremony.

But Qaraar hadn't spoken to Catalina about how he felt. On the other hand, Catalina had numerous thoughts about how Qaraar might perceive her parents, particularly her father. Juan had prevented the baptism from happening but Qaraar was unaware of that. At nights Catalina lay awake, her thoughts racing while she looked at Qaraar sleeping soundly. 'Does he think my father is a bigot? Does he think I am small-minded and given to petty religious laws? Does he love me less?' She had to tell him that he hadn't been baptised, and that her family had accepted him for who he was and so she waited for the right moment to tell him.

Two days before Easter Sunday, Qaraar and Catalina invited their close friends, Catalina's family and a few villagers for Easter lunch at their barn. Catalina had busied herself for days before, in simple decoration of her house. She had tidied the interior with help from Gul and Izzet. She brought a spare wooden table from her parents' house and placed it in the middle, on top of it were fruit bowls filled with peaches. From the windows she hung cobalt blue curtains symbolising the Spanish sky, which her mother had made as a wedding gift for the couple. She swept the floor exposing the robust stone which gave the barn a clean and rustic look. Carefully she cut a few yards of simple cotton cloth and with needle and thread began stitching herself a knee length white dress. Then she stitched a sash in indigo blue that she would tie around her waist and finally she stitched a translucent mantilla with white lace as a border that she would drape gently around her head. Seeing the dress in its complete form, it represented truth, purity and simplicity to Catalina. Its then that she decided that she would tell Qaraar the truth on Easter day itself. Worried about how Qaraar might react to the truth, Catalina decided to distract herself and plunged into preparing for the Easter lunch. She spent time tending to the pink and purple bougainvillea planted just outside the whitewashed facade of the barn by gently lifting the creepers and ensuring they wound their way across the building. Hova and Izzet had placed chairs and a table from where people could get a fantastic view of the orange trees, the majestic ruins of the Moorish castle and the towering mountains that surrounded Zahara de la Sierra. Knowing well that the lunch would carry on into the evening and night, Aalf's two assistants placed tiny lamps on the arched entrance and under the orange trees.

Easter Sunday arrived on a clear day in April. In the morning, the entire village had gathered at the cathedral, including Qaraar and Catalina. Leaving their orchards behind on the slopes of Zahara de la Sierra, some old village folk climbed slowly up the winding narrow streets, taking regular breaks and leaning against walls to catch their breath. Seeing this, Qaraar and Aalf took out their horses and the donkey to give them a ride. These were the gestures that had earned Qaraar the love of the villagers.

All finally gathered and the cathedral reverberated with hymns. Qaraar sang along, and it was at that moment Catalina decided to tell him about his supposed baptism that never happened. While the hymns grew in volume and Qaraar's voice mingled with the others, Catalina came close to him and whispered, holding his arm.

'Reader!' She still addressed him as such. Then she gulped and went on, 'You weren't baptised. You don't have to sing along.'

Catalina felt as if an enormous weight had been lifted off her chest. For a few moments Qaraar fell silent. He didn't sing. Catalina didn't know what his next reaction would be. Then after a few moments, he sang again. When the hymns reached their crescendo, Qaraar's voice complimented it with a passionate surge. Catalina hoped to get some reaction from Qaraar, but there was none at that time.

After the service, as they stepped outside the gate of the cathedral and into the plaza, Qaraar, sensing Catalina's anxiety, finally answered back. 'To me, dogmas of religion have never mattered.' He had a warm smile on his face.

Catalina held his arm firmly, turned and kissed him. She felt a renewed sense of joy. Then she placed her head on his chest and spoke softly, 'I was afraid you loved me less.'

Qaraar held her close and a verse from Rumi left his lips,

Let the beauty we love be what we do.
There are hundreds of ways to kneel and kiss the ground.
Out beyond ideas of wrong and right, there is a field.
I'll meet you there.[109]

They kissed again. Catalina's joy was uncontrollable, and she had a surging desire to share it with everyone. Eagerly she started inviting the entire village to the barn for the Easter lunch.

First, she went to her uncle, the village priest. Holding onto his arm excitedly she said, 'Padre, please do join us for lunch at the barn.' On hearing an initial hesitant, but eventually agreeing 'yes', she moved on to others. The head of school was next, 'Lunch at the barn,' she said beaming. He too accepted with a nod. Then she ran to the parents of Diego, Pablo and Alfonso inviting them all.

'You better get to the kitchen,' said Aalf looking at Qaraar. 'The way she's going, she's going to need help,' he laughed.

'Better leave now,' said Qaraar running towards the barn.

Then he quickly turned and looked back at Aalf. 'And what do you think you are doing waiting here?'

'I, uh.'

'Well, get going with me, Viking. I will need your help.'

'I'll go and get some more straw mats and cane chairs from the shack and meet you at the barn.'

Meanwhile Catalina ran to every home, knocking on their doors and inviting them. Every child at school was invited, and soon the main street filled with people. Some poked their heads out of their windows hoping to receive an invitation.

'It's at the geometry teacher's barn,' shouted the farmers and potters to each other, having been invited.

'Should we bring some food with us?' yelled out some of the parents from their tiny windows, as Catalina, holding up her white dress, floated from home to home.

'Not necessary,' she said, nonchalantly waving.

Then she went to the butcher.

'What would you like Senorita?' he asked, pulling out his sharp knife.

'Nothing. I just wanted to invite you to lunch at the geometry teacher's barn.'

'Me?'

'Yes. Please come!'

'Uh, okay,' said the surprised butcher.

'Oh!' said Catalina, remembering he had a little daughter, 'Bring the little one too.'

Hearing all the commotion in the main street, Gul and Izzet popped their heads out of the window of their rented house.

'What's going on Catalina?' asked Gul excitedly, moving the bougainvillea pot that was outside her window so she could get a better view.

'The village is coming for lunch!' said Catalina, looking up.

'The entire village?' laughed Gul.

'Yes! Yes!'

Gul rushed back inside. 'Izzet, get dressed! This is going to be quite a party; she will need our help.'

At the barn Catalina flung the door open and seeing Qaraar busy chopping tomatoes she rushed over and held him tight from behind. Sighing, she said again, 'I'm so happy.'

'Now, we have a village to feed,' he laughed.

Her eyes immediately widened, and she brought her hand to her forehead. 'That's 200 people! Aah, what have I done? What do we do now?'

Just then Aalf entered the barn holding a sack in his arm and a wooden tray in the other.

'I have got cheese.'

'What's in the sack?' asked Catalina curiously, walking towards it.

Aalf bent down and opened it. 'Fresh eggs laid by my hens and more bread from the bakery.'

'So many eggs!' said Catalina, 'But yes, that's great, thank you.'

Then Catalina went frantically looking around the kitchen.

'Great! We have lots of chickpeas and spinach for the stew.'

Hova, Gul, Catalina's mother and Izzet then entered the barn, each holding a sack of potatoes.

'Oh Madre, what do I do?' Catalina rushed to her mother. 'The entire village is turning up!'

'Silly girl,' laughed Almudena. 'I know. I met most of them as I came up here.'

'But don't worry,' continued Almudena, finishing tying an apron around her waist and then beginning to fasten one around Gul. 'They say they are all bringing dishes.'

'What a relief!' Catalina breathed more easily.

'Yet let's not rely only on their dishes – let's put up a good show,' said Hova wrapping an apron around her waist.

'Right,' said Almudena, 'We'll make lots of tortilla and for that we need eggs, lots of eggs.'

'We have them in this sack here,' said Gul investigating inside.

The friends flung themselves into cooking up a feast. Eggs were cracked, potatoes and onions peeled for the tortilla, chickpeas and spinach stirred for the stew. Qaraar began reading up on the recipe for torrijas from a book that Catalina's mother had brought. These were honey-soaked breads cooked with eggs. They sounded delicious and Qaraar got straight into it. Soaking some of the bread in milk and whipped eggs, he then fried them in olive oil, flipping them regularly.

Soon the guests arrived with a large-heartedness typical of any peasant population, bringing food with them. Qaraar and Aalf kept the regular flow of tortillas coming fresh from the kitchen. Gul and Hova went about serving wine, olives and cheese. Catalina worked away at her chickpea and spinach soup bringing it out regularly in brown clay bowls. Diego's father, Rodrigo, who was the famed village guitarist and played in the plaza outside the cathedral every evening, had come with his guitar. His music added romance to the setting. Amidst much laughter and pockets of chattering guests, Qaraar walked around his orchard.

As Qaraar past one group he was stopped by the head of school and butcher, who had been involved in a conversation about bettering children's education.

'I don't want my son to become a butcher.'

'Nothing wrong with that,' said the head of school. 'It's good that you want them to aspire for more though – what do you think Qaraar?'

'I know your son. He's doing well in mathematics.'

'I have a daughter too, over there in the far corner of the orchard.'

Qaraar saw the butcher's daughter running around the orange trees with Enrique and Diego.

'Why haven't I seen her in school?'

'Well, my daughter wants to be a doctor and the boy wants

to be a soldier,' said the butcher, biting into his tortilla. His eyes glimmered when he said 'soldier.'

'Daughter a doctor! That's wonderful!' Qaraar said.

'I will get her married though,' went on the butcher.

'Why? Let her study!'

'Girls don't become doctors,' continued the butcher, his mouth filled again with another huge bite of tortilla.

'Why not?' Qaraar asked. 'In Cordoba, during the Moors, female doctors were the best in Europe. Did you know that?'

The butcher looked blank. The chewing on the tortilla slowed down. Then looking at the girl playing, Qaraar continued, 'She should be the custodian of that Andalusian legacy.'

The butcher gulped.

Qaraar patted the butcher on the shoulder and moved on. He picked up a tray that had many bowls of chickpea soup and walked around serving the guests. When he reached the village priest he was welcomed with a broad smile.

'Qaraar, this is Senor Cristobal, the head teacher of the school in Oleva, the village close by to ours,' said the priest picking up a bowl. 'He has some good news for you.'

The head teacher of Oleva also picked up a bowl.

'I have heard of your work in teaching mathematics and geometry here. Will you teach at our school,' he said slurping the soup.

'I mean, afternoon classes perhaps, after your morning classes here?' He continued. Then looking at Catalina, he added, 'Don't worry, you will be back to your beautiful wife before sunset!'

'With great pleasure. Thank you, Senor.'

Just before moving on, Qaraar asked, 'Do you teach geography?'

'Not quite.'

'Geography is one of the most important subjects,' said Qaraar. 'It opens new horizons in children's minds. It gives them the power of imagination – it will make them explorers.'

Something changed in the head teachers mind and he reflected as guests kept walking upto Qaraar and picking soup bowls from the tray he held. The head teacher of Oleva then sighed despondently, sipping wine. 'Yes, we Spanish were once great explorers. We sailed across the oceans and discovered the new world.' The head teacher seemed lost in his thoughts. Then he saw Qaraar smiling at him. 'Why not! Let's teach geography to the children,' he said with a determined voice.

'That's wonderful! My friend Gul who is right there,' said Qaraar pointing her out, 'She and I will come across every afternoon and teach at your school.'

'Brilliant!' The head teacher put down his soup bowl and glass of wine and shook Qaraar's hand with great gusto.

Diego, Enrique, Alfonso, Pablo and all the other children now surrounded Qaraar.

'That's my tree isn't it, teacher? It has my name on the bricks,' asked Pablo, his hair flopping on his forehead.

'Yes, why?'

'See, I told you,' said Pablo in an angry voice, pointing to another child. 'He didn't believe me,' he cried.

'Well, you all have trees with your names on it.'

'Yes, but the chalk had faded on the bricks that surrounded mine,' complained Pablo again, making a sorry face.

Holding Pablo's little hand, Qaraar walked with the children towards the trees. When they were in the middle of the orchard he said, 'These are your trees and you have to look after them. No use saying they are mine and not helping them grow. When was the last time you came around and watered them Diego, Pablo, Enrique and all of you? I have been watering them for you.'

Diego dropped his head. His lower lip stuck out in a sad expression. 'Sorry I haven't come to water them.' Enrique too dropped his head and so did the others, 'We are sorry.' Qaraar looked at the fallen, sad faces. He smiled. 'It's alright, but from today, you must come every day and water your trees.'

'Yes, yes, we will!' yelled Diego.

'Let's start now,' said Alfonso.

'Okay go to the barn, fill up some canters, cups, whatever you can find and water them – go on!' Qaraar laughed. The children leapt with joy and ran towards the barn, coming out minutes later with water canters and jugs filled to the brim. Each one began watering their tree.

The sun was setting, and its faint glow fell on the mountains around Zahara de la Sierra. The little lamps around the orange trees and the arched grapevines at the entrance shimmered amidst the bursting earthy fragrance of the soil being drenched in water by the children. People began making their way home. Qaraar and Catalina stood seeing off the guests and thanking them for upholding Catalina's wish for an Easter lunch for all. The children left too, with promises of coming back every evening to water the trees. When all had left, Aalf came up with two cane chairs. He placed them facing the barn and the looming Zahara de la Sierra hill. The ruined Moorish castle on top of the hill turned a pale orangish yellow as the two friends took their seats and admired the view. Catalina rubbed Qaraar's shoulder and made her way into the barn.

Sipping his wine and looking up at the Moorish castle, Aalf said, 'We pulled it off.'

Qaraar looked across the knee-high stone and shrub wall that divided the two plots. 'Your farm is doing well.'

'Yes, I love it,' said Aalf, turning and looking at his hens and goats.

Qaraar sipped his wine. 'The journey continues – from slave trader, to poet, actor and now farmer.'

'But it should end here,' said Aalf still looking at his farm. 'I love this place.'

Just then a Spanish nightingale flew in, dabbed its beak into one of the water canters the children had left behind, and flew into the orange trees. 'Yes. It's home,' said Qaraar looking at the bird and his barn.

Then turning to Aalf he asked, 'How's your Persian and Urdu going?'

'Every morning, I read a page of Hafez,' emphasised Aalf.

'Let's hear something.'

Aalf recited.

The earth with pearls and rubies gleams
Where thou hast poured thy wine;
Less than the dust are we, it seems,
Beneath thy foot divine.
Hafiz since we may never soar
To ramparts of the sky,
Here at the threshold of this door
Forever let us lie.[110]

'Indeed, Here let us lie,' said Qaraar with a sense of belonging to his new home.

Then looking at Aalf, he asked, 'Do you think Saad and Hikmet made it to Morocco?'

Aalf sat up. 'He shouldn't have left.'

'It would have been impossible for a Moor to continue here.'

Just then Aalf's two assistants jumped over the shrubs and walked up to the friends. 'We'd like to say something.'

'Go on,' said Aalf.

Gathering some courage one of them spoke. 'We have got jobs in Cadiz, the shipbuilding port,' he stopped.

'And we would like to go.' The other helped the first finish the sentence. Aalf now stood up.

'It's been difficult for us since we moved to Spain. You have been very kind, but the farm doesn't make enough to sustain us all.'

It was true. Selling yoghurt, cheese, eggs, milk and working part-time at the village bakery wasn't enough to sustain Aalf, Hova and the two assistants. The two assistants had even taken up temporary jobs with local carpenters, making toy models of

Viking ships, and had tried to sell them at the plaza outside the cathedral but sales were negligible. There had been nights when Aalf gave his food to the two assistants and he and Hova had slept on an empty stomach. On other days, the two assistants had done the same. Both men had often wondered how long this could go on. When Aalf had sent them to Cadiz to buy utensils and other things, it was then that the two had met the chief carpenters of workshops for leading shipbuilders. Both men had vast carpentry experience in the past and had worked extensively on Aalf's ship in the Caspian, and so spoke about their skills. Hearing this they had been offered the jobs.

Aalf paced around the orange trees. He had known the two men since childhood. They had spent most of their lives on the slave trade. His worry was they might be going back to it. Qaraar walked up to Aalf and there was now a fair distance between them and the two assistants.

'Spain has been at the forefront of slave trading. I don't want them slipping back into that inhumane business,' Aalf whispered to Qaraar in a worried tone, as the two assistants spoke to each other at the far end of the orchard.

'Maybe it's a genuine job offer,' said Qaraar.

'Well, the only way to find out is if we ride with them to Cadiz and see for ourselves. Will you come with me?'

'Yes.'

The two friends walked up to the two assistants. Aalf looked at them fondly. 'Go if you must and start new lives.' There was a smile on their faces. 'But we will come with you to Cadiz, I have some work there.'

'When do you need to be in Cadiz?' enquired Qaraar.

'Three days from now.'

'Let's leave tomorrow at daybreak.'

All men agreed. Aalf and the two assistants went over to the shack on Aalf's plot and Qaraar retired to the barn. There he told Catalina to inform the school that he would be away for a few days, but Catalina insisted on going to Cadiz with him. Hova would inform the school.

Like all empires, Spain had been mighty and bloody. In 1491, Queen Isabella of Castile and King Ferdinand II of Aragon as husband and wife ruled all of Spain. Most of the Moorish cities had been taken, but in the south one sparkling jewel still hadn't lost its oriental lustre: Granada. It was Granada that became an eclectic city under the Moors, attracting Sufis from Persia and Hindustan. Hajji Ali and Hajji Rashid from Hindustan had settled in Granada and added to its spiritual intellect.

Surrounded and choked from all sides by the Spanish forces of Isabella and Ferdinand, Granada was still gasping. Although shackled in despair, in a last dash to revive its fortunes, in December 1481 the Moors strode out of Granada and took a frontier village. That move would signal their end. The name of the village they took was Zahara.[111] Later 'de la Sierra' would be added to its name. Isabella and Ferdinand now had a pretext to invade the emirate of Granada.[112]

The Moor King of Granada, Boabdil, looking beyond the magnificent gardens of his fabled Alhambra palace saw the siege tents surrounding his city. Compelled, he signed the treaty of surrender. With regards faith, the treaty was implicitly clear: 'Their Highnesses [Isabella and Ferdinand] and their successors will ever afterwards allow King Adilehi [Boabdil]… and all the common people, great or small, to live in their own religion and not permit that their mosques to be taken from them, nor their minarets, nor their muezzins, nor will they interfere with the pious foundations or endowments which they have for such purposes, nor will they disturb the uses and customs they observe.'[113]

On 2 January 1492, the people of Granada awoke to see the banners of Castille flying over Alhambra.[114] King Boabdil, after handing over the keys of Granada and Alhambra to Isabella and Ferdinand, mounted his horse and, along with his courtiers and family, rode out into exile towards the Alpujarras mountain range. Such was the pain rising in the Moor king's heart, that before entering a narrow mountain pass, he turned the reins of his horse for one final look at Granada. The sigh that left his chest had such anguish in it that it would be remembered in perpetuity as the 'Moor's last sigh'. He wept uncontrollably. His mother, though witnessing this helplessness of her son, remarked with words that had a scorpion's sting: 'You cry like a woman for what you couldn't defend like a man.'[115]

Within four months of taking Granada and the fading of the Moorish king, Isabella and Ferdinand, on 17 April 1492 gave consent to Christopher Columbus to sail out West and then towards India and China.[116] Instead of finding a new route to India and China though, this incredible ocean enthusiast and sailor – would discover a new world and lay the foundations of the Spanish empire in the Americas.[117] In time, the discovery of the new world would shift the global balance of power completely. The West would become unquestionably the most dominant, with colonies in North and Latin America and Spain would become the centre of the world for more than 200 years.

Besides gold and silver from the new world, Spain's other major source of revenue came in the form of slave trade. Encouraged blatantly by Columbus,[118] it soon became a policy whereby the Spanish could take slaves from anyone who did not welcome the king's captains on their shores in the Caribbean and the north coast of Latin America.[119] The investment from these riches went into building a mighty military, the most powerful in Europe and the first to bear the full onslaught of this power were the indigenous people of colonised Latin America. The Incas and the Aztecs were swept aside in the face of this superior firepower as the Spanish military might relentlessly landed on the shores across the Atlantic.

In time, Spain broke the treaty that Isabella and Ferdinand had signed with the last Moor king, Boabdil. The Moors that had chosen to remain in Spain under the protection of that treaty faced the ominous prospect of forceful conversion to Christianity. Such was the speed and ferocity of the forceful conversions that up to 3,000 Moors were said to have been converted in a single day, and in some cases Moors were killed and robbed on their way to being baptised.[120] Once converted the Moors were called Moriscos. But this was not enough for the Spanish authorities in the sixteenth century; they spied on the Moriscos to see if they had really embraced their new faith. The authorities believed that although converted, the Moriscos still held onto their original faith.[121]

And so, in 1609, under instructions from the then King Philip, who accused the Moriscos of heresy and apostasy,[122] the Moriscos were officially told to leave by village headmen. Panic struck the towns and villages as forceful deportations began. This mindless madness continued unabated. In total a staggering number of 350,000 Moriscos had been forcibly expelled.[123] Spain, their home where they had lived for generations, a land, they had nurtured with their hands with such love that the soil had danced with sugar cane, lemon, orange, rice fields and coffee. A land, where philosophy and science could be heard in the winds. A land that they had ordained with exquisite architecture like the Grand Mosque of Cordoba, the Madinat-az-Zahra and the Alhambra Palace. That land was no longer theirs.

By the seventeenth and eighteenth centuries, Spain's decline had set in. Overstretched and damaged by foreign wars and ruled by decadent monarchs, the Empire began to come apart. The economic impact of the expulsion of the Moriscos had been catastrophic, with lasting effects; a drastic drop in population in the countryside meant abandoned farms and arid lands. The exodus had transformed the most florid part of Spain into a dry and desolate wasteland with lands left unattended for decades.[124] But besides the expulsion of the Moors there was another factor that wrecked the Spanish rural economy in the seventeenth century. It was the deadly plague. Such was the horror that an estimated 1.25 million inhabitants of Andalusia perished.

By 1750 though, Spain was ruled by the Bourbon Kings and some sense of relative progress had been established. Spain would never be the giant power that it had been, but under the Bourbon Kings it stabilised. Under Ferdinand VI, urban Spain became the primary focus. Some Spanish scholars in city universities realised that the expulsion of Moors was inhumane, and a catastrophic mistake. They also recognised that the Moors intellectual legacy was an astounding one that Spain should embrace. Spanish scholars had begun translating the works of the Moors and particularly began studyng the Sufi Ibn Khaldun's works on the role of the state in times of an epidemic and how it should be managed. While ports and cities grew, in the villages, peasants were poor, and their lands were still reeling from the effects of not having been tilled regularly because of the low population. Village education suffered immensely and schools didn't exist in most villages. Meanwhile, every merchant in the ports, large or small, was obsessed with shipbuilding, to increase commerce from across the Atlantic. Lucrative jobs in the shipbuilding industry meant that a large number of farmers acquired carpentry skills and left their villages for ports like Cadiz. Thousands and thousands of ships, which were called the galleons, were built and lined up at the harbour in Cadiz and sailed out regularly into the ocean to trade with the Americas.

It was this sight of the never-ending galleons that Qaraar and Catalina saw as they rode into the Cadiz port, mounted on Haider. Located halfway between the Mediterranean and the Atlantic Ocean, Cadiz had one of the most strategic locations for trading. This was the first time Qaraar had seen such an enormous display of passion for ocean voyaging. Qaraar took in the sight of these ships with complete astonishment. Even the horizon seemed conquerable with the number of galleons that were in the docks. He looked out into the Atlantic Ocean beyond which was the new world. 'How right were the Ottoman travellers.' He thought to himself about the conversation that he had had with them; 'the balance of power has surely tilted to the West.'

Aalf's assistants led the way to the factory of the merchant who had offered them a job. The factory, that was jostling for space along with the other shipbuilding factories, was located not too far from the docks. The portly merchant stood outside with his hands on his hips. On seeing the two men approaching, he broke into a smile and with a wave of his hand welcomed them into the factory.

'How many people do you employ?' asked Aalf, after being gingerly introduced and looking at the massive number of carpenters sawing away at wood.

'Five hundred,' said the merchant confidently. 'Come, let me take you around.'

The smell of chipping and wood being sawed was everywhere. Shaved wood pieces fell from tables and landed on the floor. Massive sketches of the ships made in this factory were on the walls. 'These are the magnificent galleon ships that we make,' said the merchant pointing at them.

Aalf walked up to one of the sketches with Qaraar and Catalina following close behind. 'This is a majestic ship.' There was a tinge of sadness in Aalf's voice, thinking about how his Viking ancestors had once been the most revered shipbuilders in the world.

'How long does it take to make one?'

'Six months to a year.'

Looking at the bare-chested workers sawing away in a synchronised repetitive motion, Qaraar asked a question, hoping to steer the conversation towards understanding the business interests of the merchant. 'What do your ships trade in across the ocean?'

'Ah! Well… I don't actually engage in any trade with the Americas. I just make ships.'

Aalf felt a sense of relief. His assistants wouldn't be involved in slave trading. Looking at them he said, 'They are good honourable men – treat them well.' The merchant smiled and nodded.

'Could we sail out into the ocean?' Catalina asked, hoping to bring a sense of celebration to the conversation that had until now been quite interrogative of the merchant.

'Of course! Follow me!' The merchant led the way to the docks, walking briskly.

The bustle at the docks was enormous. Large ships were being loaded with guns, ammunition, food and even Spanish families could be seen boarding the ships.

Pointing to the families the merchant said, 'They are settlers – going to make the new world their home.'

'Where exactly?' asked Qaraar, walking quickly and trying to keep pace with the merchant.

'That ship goes to Chile, and that one in the middle goes to the Caribbean islands – and that one on the right of that is off to Mexico. We have been settling those lands for over 200 years,' said the merchant with a sense of satisfaction.

The silvery cold waters of the Atlantic lashed against the small boat that the merchant got organised. All jumped in. As the boat sailed out of Cadiz and into the Atlantic, Qaraar looked at the ornate baroque mansions of wealthy merchants encircling the Cadiz coastline. In the balconies were merchants looking through their spyglasses and telescopes, hoping to catch sight of their returning galleons filled with tobacco, silver and slaves.

The small boat wobbled on the Atlantic as larger ships created waves. The enthusiastic inhabitants on the larger ships that were heading out to the new world were bursting with excitement at the prospect of a new life, and when they saw the small boat below their ship, they looked down and waved enthusiastically.

'Let's open this,' said the merchant with a calm smile. He had brought a bottle of wine with him. A huge cheer went up from Aalf and his assistants. 'To new beginnings for these two good men,' said Aalf.

All raised their glasses. Qaraar looked into the waves.

'If we kept going, we would reach the new world, wouldn't we?' asked Catalina.

'You'd die before you got there. This is not a river, lake or sea – this is an ocean,' said the laughing merchant.

'Great discoveries, and what a rise the Spanish have had,' said Qaraar holding Catalina in his arms and sipping the wine.

'We are well past our rise. The ones that are rising are there.' The merchant pointed northwards.

'What do you mean?' Catalina asked, dipping one hand into the cold Atlantic waters and then splashing Qaraar's face.

'Britannia, Britannia my friends. That tiny island across the Bay of Biscay has risen. They are everywhere! In the new world… in…'

'That's right. They are in Hindustan too,' said Qaraar finishing the merchant's sentence. 'They trade there through their East India Company and are ambitious for more.'

'Indeed, they are ambitious,' said the merchant resting one arm on his large stomach. 'They will soon have an empire the likes of which the world has yet to see.' He filled his glass with more wine. Then he smirked, 'Some say that the English are trying to fly.'

'Fly?' Aalf couldn't help himself. 'I'm not drunk, am I? Say that again!' He gulped down his wine.

'Da Vinci tried to invent flying machines in Italy centuries ago, so it's not surprising that Brittania would have a go,' Qaraar added to Aalf's astonishment. 'If they do fly, what a discovery that would be for man,' Qaraar thought to himself, and then realised another possibility. 'If the West dominates the skies like they do the oceans now, the East will soon be so far behind in innovation.' After an hour of enjoyable sailing in the ocean, the portly merchant signalled to the boatman to turn around and head back to the Cadiz port. Having said fond goodbyes to the two assistants and being assured that the two would visit them every few months, Aalf, Qaraar and Catalina left.

Before going back to Zahara de la Sierra, the three took a diversion and made their way to Madinat-az-Zahra, the ruined palace complex a few kilometres from Cordoba. This magical palace was built by Abd al-Rahman III in the tenth century and its ruins still echoed of its past grandeur. Built into a hill with terraced layers and lush sprawling gardens on each terrace, it featured horseshoe arches opening into halls and gardens, with sunlight streaming through the high windows. The Madinat-az-Zahra Palace became the ultimate symbol of Andalusian architecture for centuries. Even now in its ruinous state, as the three rode through its proud arches and terraces they could feel the mystical call of its once magnificent past life. Each terrace still had elements of the gardens, with viaducts through which water had once flowed and irrigated the flowers. The views of Cordoba in the distance made them pause and gaze at the city.

'Maybe one day you will build me something like this,' said Catalina, resting her head against Qaraar's chest as they rode through the ruins.

'I am not a king, my love,' he laughed. 'Just a reader, remember?' She laughed. The three camped there for four nights. Here in these abandoned and remote settings while Aalf and Catalina slept, Qaraar kept awake at nights in deep contemplation. He sat under the arches and thought about existence. Like the character in Ibn Tufayl's *Hayy ibn Yaqzan,* in isolation, he explored ideas about logic, faith and fate. The twelfth century writer, Ibn Tufayl's character *Hayy* who was marooned on an abandoned island finds himself and his relationship with existence around him through rationale and reasoning. The power of reason differentiated him from other creatures on the island and ultimately he sees the entire cosmos, its elements and living things and heavenly bodies in a single unity. In complete contrast to philosophers that championed reason and logic, like Ibn Tufayl, there was another twelfth century mental giant, Al Ghazali. Qaraar deeply thought of Ghazali's works too which represented a completely different dimension of thought. This stalwart thinker had written the *Incoherence of the Philosophers.* Ghazali was scathing of those who spoke only about the merits of logic and reason. He shifted the argument towards the heart, faith and inspired intuition. He spoke of mysticism as the source of all knowledge thereby reducing the status of rational intellect. For Qaraar there had been no logic for the murder of his family in Delhi, but faith and fate had brought him a new life. And so Qaraar asked himself, 'For mankind was faith, fate and learning through inspired intuition to be considered more important than logic and reason? But then he thought of his role in this world as a mathematics and geometry teacher which was based in logic, and it was through his teaching that young dormant minds were stirred. Surely logic cannot be weaker than faith and fate, he thought. In fact, he told himself, an awakening and development of an understanding for rationale and logic was vital – but then so is the importance of building faith and creating a deeply spiritual and kind soul, driven by the intuition for doing good.

In his mind, as he sat under the ruined arches overlooking the vast Spanish vistas covered in darkness, Qaraar concluded that logic and inspired intuition for good could live together in man, and that philosophers who had separated the two had missed out on the pursuance of a unique path – one which could enrich the logical mind and the spiritual soul. Quite like the path, Omar Khayyam had chosen. That path once trodden, is salvation in itself Qaraar told himself. There is no destination, just the path and the journey undertaken. Qaraar's heart felt like a shimmering diamond. After being camped for four nights at Madinat-az-Zahra they rode into Cordoba, where after resting a few days they headed back to their village.

Back at Zahara de la Sierra, Qaraar had a new student waiting for him – the butcher's eight-year-old daughter, Maria. Standing in the olive grove outside the school, holding onto her father's finger, and smiling shyly at the teacher, she was the first girl to attend the village school for decades. A new orange tree was planted in her name in the orchard. While Qaraar had been away in Cadiz, the students had visited the orchard every morning to water them. That continued even on his return and the trees grew quickly.

After teaching in the morning at the school in Zahara de la Sierra, Qaraar and Gul – who had bought herself a horse – would ride out to the village of Oleva where they would give afternoon lessons. So impressed were the local villagers and head teachers of the schools that Gul very astutely used her charm and reputation to get Izzet a job at both the schools too. Izzet's experience as an acrobat meant he was physically well endowed and had a good knowledge of exercises to help keep bodies supple and fit. The job he got at both the schools was that of a physical instructor and gymnast. Until now, Gul had supported Izzet, but with this new job Izzet felt a sense of renewed self-confidence.

Catalina and Hova struck a strong friendship, particularly over dress making. Hova joined Catalina and her mother in stitching clothes bringing a new dimension of Armenian fashion. Village life was filled with occurrences that provided entertainment and reason for chatter. One such moment was the case of the farmer's hen and the butcher's knife. Aalf, who took great care in raising his hens and selling their eggs, had come to love the birds with a great passion. Every morning he would count them and feel a sense of pride. One day he realised a hen was missing. The poor hen had stumbled out of the farm, made its way across a few orchards, onto cobbled street and meandered in the vicinity of the butcher's shop. Flapping away in distress and not knowing where it was, the hen attracted the attention of the butcher who promptly stepped out and grabbed the fluttering bird by its neck. Without having to pay for it, here was a bird presenting itself to its fate. Looking around gingerly hoping that no one had seen him, the butcher rushed back inside his shop and locked the hen with others that were shortly due to find themselves under his knife.

'Where is that beauty?' yelled Aalf running into the twisting village street.

'Has your wife left you?' asked Rodrigo the guitarist, peering out of his window.

The streets were so narrow with houses on both sides that neighbours often chatted across by opening their windows. Gul, who lived opposite Diego's parents, opened her window on hearing her neighbour. 'What's the matter?' she asked.

'Aalf's wife has left him,' replied Rodrigo with an expression that craved more intrigue.

Having heard Aalf's desperate wailing, by now most of the village had gathered in the street. Struck by utter despair Aalf trudged down the street and unknowingly paused outside the butcher's shop, with Gul who was now with him. The butcher, having sharpened his knife, went to the cage in which he kept his hens. Just then Aalf happened to look in that direction and saw his lost bird jostling for space in the cage. 'There she is,' he shouted in unabashed joy. 'Release her you monster – that's my hen!'

The butcher was having none of it and holding up a knife came back strongly at Aalf. 'Back away Viking, or I'll spill your guts.'

Gul rushed to Aalf. 'The hen? That's what you've been crying for?'

'Yes. That beauty. She's unique because of two distinct indigo feathers – look,' he said pointing out the feathers.

'Listen, butcher, let her go,' Gul said in her humblest tone. 'You've got so many other hens.'

The butcher ignored her.

'Never seen such love for a hen before,' said one villager to another. 'Maybe the hen loves him back too – look at her eyes!' A huge roar of laughter went up.

Aalf began walking menacingly towards the butcher who noticed the move, and immediately rushed to the cage, pulled out the hen and slammed it down on the chopping table. Suddenly, the frightened bird flapped away and started to do something quite odd. Wiggling its head, the terrified bird gently dabbed its beak at the knife that the butcher held close.

'Look, the bird kisses your knife!' said Gul with elation. 'The hen that loves the butcher's knife – it's a phenomenon!' she continued.

This not just distracted the butcher but also got the crowd interested. The curious village folk now gathered closer to witness this unique demonstration from the bird. In no time they were all clamouring into the shop. 'How can you now kill the one that kisses your blade?' said Gul with a tone that hoped to ignite guilt in the butcher. By now the hen began doing the dabbing quite frantically. The butcher, too, hadn't quite seen anything like this before.

Gul seized the opportunity. 'All eggs laid by this one are yours, butcher – and she lays a lot of them.'

The butcher wasn't impressed. 'Huh.'

Aalf, realising it would be smart to get the support of the villagers, declared with gusto, 'And one egg for every child in the village for the next month!'

The crowd erupted in Aalf's support. This meant free breakfast for the children of the village for a month. 'Release that knife-kissing bird – now!' they shouted.

Noticing that the butcher was distracted, Gul slipped in behind him and in one quick move pulled the bird from his loosened grip and ran right out of the shop. Holding it up in her arms, the crowd shouted in appreciation. The butcher realising it was a lost cause looked at Aalf. 'All eggs from that one are mine,' he said putting away the knife. 'And one for Maria every morning for the next month,' Aalf added with a smile, as he ran towards Gul.

In contrast to village life, the Andalusian vistas wove an intense charm around Qaraar. Every evening before the sun went down, Catalina would wait under the arched grapevine entrance for his return from Oleva. He was never late. Just as Rodrigo struck his guitar chords in the village plaza and the nightingale sang its sweet song in the orchard, she would see Qaraar approach on Haider. Seeing him riding up towards the arched entrance Catalina would rush into the barn, and fetching a canter, she would pour fresh water which he would splash across his face after dismounting.

Refreshed by her love, both would mount Haider and go for their evening ride into the Andalusian mountains. It was this time that they came to treasure. Sitting on top of the 'Eagle Mountain' amid silence, they would look below into the distance and with a spyglass spot their orange orchard. On most occasions Catalina would pack a simple supper of chopped tomatoes, lettuce, cheese, bread and olive oil. Overlooking the magnificent views, Catalina rested her head on his shoulder and smiled as Qaraar spoke of his experiences in school; about young boys who tried hard to get the attention of girls, about the beauty of geometry and mathematics, and about the brilliant progress Maria, the butcher's daughter, was making.

Many evenings passed lost in conversation watching the sunset. The arresting scenery would have another element added to it when the couple would light a fire and lie under the night sky, gazing at the stars and at each other, both knowing well that they wouldn't return to the barn for the night. More and more nights were spent on the mountain top sleeping under blankets, by the fire and beneath the stars. To the villagers of Zahara de la Sierra, that high mountain spot where the fire burnt came to symbolise Qaraar and Catalina. Sitting in the plaza while listening to the guitar, or on the terraces of their homes, the villagers raised their glasses most evenings and celebrated the romance of the couple burning high up in the mountain. They even gave that mountain fire a name, Fuego de Montana. Qaraar called it Koh-i-Sholah, the mountain flame. At night Qaraar would wake up and sketch next to the fire, his fingers moving with speed and precision.

One such night, as Catalina lay asleep in Qaraar's arms, her face shining as it caught the light from the fire and listening to the distant guitar from the village below, Qaraar recited Rumi's verse.

My entire life has come down to three words
I burned, I burned, I burned...
Be silent my tongue, since my heart is burning,
Your heart will burn too, if I speak of my burning heart.[125]

Then he covered her and rose. A force to create overcame him and he felt a deep desire to express his love, one which he hadn't for years. Qaraar rode down the mountain at great speed towards Aalf's shack and sneaking in, he woke him. Qaraar whispered into his ear and both picked up axes and rode out towards the forest that surrounded the mountains. In the dead of night, they chopped away at cypress trees. When their task was finally finished, they sat amidst a pile of cypress logs in the forest, and Qaraar divulged his ambition.

'There, right on top of the mountain. That's where I'm going to build a gazebo for her.'

Then he held out a sketch book for Aalf. The design was simple with four pillars and a triangular roof, but when Aalf turned the page he was stunned with the elaborate design planned for the interior of the roof. Geometric shapes that repeated and interlocked with exquisite stars would ordain the interiors.

'I can feel it galloping in my fingers,' Qaraar said, looking at Aalf who was gazing at the roof patterns.

'When do we start?'

'I will need the logs smoothed out for the pillars and the others sawed out in the form of the triangular roof.'

'Let's go to the local carpenter tomorrow.'

At the barn Qaraar told Catalina of what he would be undertaking. It meant he would be working through weekends and at nights on the mountain top. She heard him and kissed him. From then on, a steady trail of horses and mules, that included Aalf's donkey, could be seen winding their way up the mountain carrying wooden pillars, the triangle-shaped roof, saws, tools and food. Qaraar lost himself in work. With day being devoted to teaching, Qaraar would begin work after sunset surrounded by twenty burning torches. Gul, Izzet, Aalf and Hova alternated in lighting those torches every evening. Now to the villagers seated in the plaza below, the entire summit looked like it was on fire. Curiosity got the better of some of them and they visited Qaraar on occasions bringing provisions. Rodrigo rode up and played the guitar for Qaraar some nights, on others Juan and Almudena came up and watched the teacher in the role of a craftsman. The butcher and priest too came riding their mules, one bringing fresh chicken legs that Catalina would grill on the fire, and the other bringing the Bible and praying for Qaraar's successful venture.

Visitors came and went, but Catalina never left the site when Qaraar worked through the night. Most nights he worked tirelessly on the roof panels carving out the stars, other geometric shapes and triple triangular tulip forms as individual pieces. The deeply concentrated effort meant that most nights fatigue and exhaustion turned to pain that erupted in his sinews as if molten lava had been poured in them. But it was in his moments of great physical pain that inspiration flashed. Catalina had her back to him. She lay sideways against the night sky. Above her right shoulder a star sparkled. Then she rose and flicked her hair with her hand, bringing them onto one side. Next, she slowly began making a plait. Effortlessly she interwove her golden hair with ease and beauty. Seeing this, Qaraar's hands began moving on the wood again, easily interlocking stars into the pentagons, hexagons and the triple triangle tulip petals. Such were the nights submerged in the creative spirit.

After months of work the magnificence of the roof was shyly peering out. Hesitantly, it seemed to think to itself if it could once again dare show itself under the Spanish sky. After all, it was the design of the Moors. Mesmerised by what was coming to shape, Catalina thought about the origins of this passion that resided in Qaraar's heart. She thought with wonder about the East. There was a craving rising within her, but she knew well through her conversations with Aalf about the deep scars and wounds that the East had left on Qaraar. Yet, she had become restless. One night as Qaraar chipped away at wood, Catalina gathered courage emboldened by Aalf's presence and asked.

'Reader, I want to see Delhi. Will you take me?'

Aalf, who was nursing the fire so that his friend could work comfortably, turned and looked at the craftsman. The noise of relentless woodworking ceased. Qaraar rested one hand on the panel and from the other, the chisel dropped. He dropped his head and his wavy hair fell across the sides of his lowered face. Then Qaraar murmured as if speaking to himself, 'Delhi is desolate.' His breathing increased with anxiety as he took the city's name. The past had the sting of a thousand wasps.

Catalina walked up towards the roof panels. 'Such beauty – this art you carry within. I want to see where it all began for you.'

'Is it not enough to see it emerge here?' Qaraar's head was still lowered.

'You know all about me, you have seen my country – now I want to see yours.'

'See me, and you see my country.'

'But I want to sense it.'

'I am it. It is me.'

Aalf added to the conversation. 'I'd like to visit Hindustan too. We don't have to go through Persia; we could just sail right down the Atlantic to Africa, and then up into the Arabian Sea to Goa.'

'I won't go,' Qaraar shot back. He had stopped working and walked towards the edge of the mountain.

'Hindustan is your core, Qaraar. It's also why I love you, because it shines in you. I want to see that land.' Catalina walked up to him.

'No, I will not go.'

'Word from some of the merchants in Cadiz is that the Mughals are still on Delhi's throne…'

'Barely,' Qaraar interrupted.

'Mughal splendour! Oh, please let's go!' Catalina insisted.

'Leave me.' Qaraar turned and walked to his roof panels and sitting on the floor, began working again. Aalf mounted his donkey and rode down the mountain. Catalina sat by the fire all night making tea for Qaraar and wiping the sweat from his back as he toiled until dawn.

APRIL 1753

'The oranges are bursting through,' yelled Pablo to Diego from his window. Both rushed down into the main street.

'Let's go and pick them all,' Diego said while running alongside Pablo. It was a magnificent sight. The trees with their dark green leaves and vivid orange fruits against the backdrop of the whitewashed barn – the entire setting looked a picture of beauty. Seeing the children rushing in, Qaraar and Catalina stepped out and decided to meet them in the middle of the orchard.

'Pick, pick, pick! I want to pick them!' said a jumping Maria who stood next to the tree that had her name on the bricks surrounding its base.

'Yes, yes – pick you will, but after a word,' said Qaraar who was surrounded by the children.

'But…' continued Qaraar, 'You will keep half and the rest you will distribute to the poor and hungry.'

The Spanish countryside was still poor and many farmers lived in abject poverty. Some even begged outside the cathedral in the plaza.

'Also, if there are homes in which there is someone unwell, you must go there and give some oranges too,' insisted Qaraar. 'Generosity and giving to the needy will bring you satisfaction like no other deed'. He continued

Initial exuberance gave way to silence amongst the children.

Then after having absorbed what had been said Alfonso spoke with enthusiasm, 'Yes, we will! Oranges for the hungry and sick.'

All the children then ran towards their trees to get the fruit. After a while of working with the children, Qaraar stepped back and sat under a tree. Aalf walked up to him carrying a piece of paper.

'A letter from Saad,' Aalf said with a big smile, while handing it to Qaraar who grabbed it hurriedly and read.

> Hikmet and I live in Tangiers. We have Moroccan wives and are happy and content. Too many Moroccan drummers here so I'm not unique! I work in a stable breeding the finest Arab horses. Our master races them in Fez. Hikmet, too, works with me. There is a white horse, tall and proud. He protects all the other horses from snakes: I have given him a name – "Aalf." Then there is another horse, who is the fastest with the most intense eyes. He keeps to himself yet has a way that makes the new horses our master purchases feel at ease. I have given him a name – "Qaraar."

Qaraar ran out of his orchard and went straight to Gul's accommodation and handed the letter to Izzet, who read it with joyous tears rolling down the side of his face. Each day since his brother had left had been torturous for Izzet. Every evening he would look south towards Morocco with a prayer on his lips hoping that his brother had made it along with Saad. Walking back to the barn Qaraar saw the children leaving with baskets of oranges. Some parents had come to help carry them back. As he walked past the parents, he saw in their eyes their admiration for the Sufi philosophy of generosity. He overheard the children telling their parents that before they took the baskets home they wanted to stop and give some to the poor that sat in the plaza outside the cathedral.

That evening as Qaraar worked on the mountain top, Catalina asked, 'You loved her deeply, didn't you?'

Qaraar continued working.

'Is that why you don't want to visit?' she continued.

'Aalf has been talking to you.'

'Someone has to tell me about your past.'

'Yes, I loved her, but she faded.' Qaraar stood up, faced Catalina and continued, 'And another love rose.'

Catalina wound her arms around his neck. 'We don't have to go, I just wanted to see your origins.'

'My design is almost done,' Qaraar stepped aside.

'It's stunning. What more needs to be done?'

'The triangular tulip petals and the final star.'

Catalina whirled between the four pillars. She whirled and smiled to herself. Then she stopped and walked up to the roof panels that had not yet been mounted on the pillars and inspected them closely. She shut her eyes and ran her hands over the shapes. Then she opened her eyes and hesitantly asked Qaraar, 'Why don't you…' but then she didn't complete her question.

'Go on,' Qaraar walked up to her.

'Nothing.'

'You must speak your mind.'

'Why don't you add a sunflower?'

'That would…'

'Don't worry, let it be… I just thought…'

Looking at the roof panel Qaraar said with reluctance, 'It won't be an original geometric design then.'

'I know – forget I ever suggested it,' she said leaning her back against a pillar and playing with her hair.

Qaraar held her by the waist. 'You understand, don't you? I can't.'

'I do.' She lifted her neck bringing her lips closer to his.

He kissed her.

'Look reader, I brought you something,' she said, walking up to the cloth bag in which she had packed food. She pulled out a book and held it out for him.

'The works of Hamda bint Ziyad!' Qaraar exclaimed in disbelief holding the leather-bound book.

'You know who she was?'

'Yes, I do. She was one of the greatest female Andalusian poets.'

Catalina played with her plait and explained, 'Her father was a teacher and she was his only child…'

Qaraar listened intently. 'Her father gave her the most refined education.'

'Read it O reader, read to me,' she said, leaning her head against the pillar.

Qaraar opened the book and read.

> Tears have betrayed my secrets in a valley whose beauty is striking;
> A river surrounds every meadow and every meadow borders every valley.
> Among the gazelle, a black fawn stole my mind, after stealing my heart
> When the tresses are loosened, I see the full moon in the black clouds
> As if dawn had lost a brother and in sorrow, clothed itself in mourning.

'How enlightened you once were,' Qaraar thought to himself about the Moors of Spain. He put the book down and they kissed.

The next morning Qaraar met Aalf in the orchard and told him to make arrangements to sail to Hindustan. It would be a long voyage from Lisbon, in humble accommodation on-board the largest Portuguese ship they had ever seen. The entire village would turn out to see them off. Not believing the assurances he gave of his return, the children wept to see their teacher leave, and ran alongside his horse. Gul and Izzet decided to join them too. Qaraar's love for Catalina was such that to please her he had decided to come face to face with his past.

CHAPTER 9

FRESH SOIL

1754

Their ship docked at Goa in February and the mild winter surprised Gul, Hova and Catalina. After spending a week with a Portuguese merchant who had a house in Goa, and with whom they had made friends during the voyage, they made their way north by joining a protected caravan carrying fabrics headed for Delhi. Aalf and Qaraar rode, while the rest travelled in a wobbling bullock cart.

While Gul, Catalina, Hova and Izzet chatted constantly about Hindustan, and the possibility of meeting Izzet's father Holar Pasha – whose fate Qaraar hadn't revealed – Qaraar's emotions were completely different.

Every hue of Hindustan evoked a melancholic mood in him. When the caravan got lost, they followed the smoke emanating from the tiniest of village huts. At dawn, riding past poor peasants cooking over their charcoal chulas under the open sky, and with the scent of freshly made chapatti, filling the air, Qaraar felt at one with the surroundings and yet he felt a distance. After a month and a half of riding they reached Ajmer in Rajasthan. Here they broke the journey for a fortnight at the shrine of the Khwaja, Hindustan's greatest and most revered Sufi saint. The friends were fed and given accommodation by the caretakers of the shrine known as khadims, dressed in crisp white kurtas and black velvet caps. Opposite the shrine was a tree that attracted hundreds of chirping sparrows at sunset, under which Qaraar sat with Catalina looking at the white dome of the mausoleum and pensively thinking about Delhi.

The air coming from Delhi weighed heavy on man and beast. While approaching the city, Haider got into a frenzy, neighing wildly, getting up on his hind legs and dashing around in circles. The memory of the massacre and the ride down Ballimaran emerged like a frightening ghost, shattering the horse's sensibilities. Qaraar spent hours calming down his faithful steed. It was late at night when they entered Shahjahanabad. Qaraar knocked at a door which had Musafir Khana written on it in Urdu. The small two storeyed guest house was new and one that Qaraar didn't recognise. After repeated knocking, the owner released the iron-chain, yawned, took an advance, then nonchalantly pointed in the direction of their rooms at the top of dimly lit stairs. Exhausted, the friends retired for the night. But Qaraar lay in bed looking at the ceiling. He turned and looked out of the window into the dark night. At a distance he saw the faint outline of the minarets of the Sunehri Masjid. The haunting moment of Nadir raising his sword to signal the massacre from the terrace of that mosque seemed to blend into the air, carrying with it the smell of blood even after fifteen years. But then Qaraar felt as if the winding lanes of Shahjahanabad were beckoning him, as if they concealed a secret which they now wanted to reveal. Quietly he stepped out of the room. Just as he was about to leave Catalina woke. She had sensed the restlessness in Qaraar. He turned and looked at her.

'The night has something to tell me.'

'I will come with you.'

Qaraar pulled out a black shawl and wrapped it around him and another cream one around Catalina. Then they mounted and rode into the lanes, only Haider's hooves breaking the night silence.

'Where are we going?' Catalina turned her head and asked Qaraar.

'Where my mind and hands take us.'

As they rode Catalina took in the dark outline of the Jama Masjid to the right and the emerging Red Fort to the left. Qaraar's hands seemed to instinctively guide the reins when he heard a faint humming of sorts, which seemed to come from one of the lanes. Deciding to follow the sound, as they came closer the words became audible.

> O destiny why art thou elusive? The one that obeyed, but plotted, thou hast raised to be like a Queen! And the one that had Queen-like demeanour, thou hast flung into the abyss of despair… such is thy might, O destiny.

Qaraar heard these words as Haider came up to the man who had uttered them. He was dressed in rags with dishevelled hair that merged into his long unkempt beard completely hiding his facial features. The darkness of the night made it difficult to recognise him, as he lay in the middle of the street. The man had lost one of his arms as his empty sleeve swayed in the breeze. Qaraar looked closely. 'Baba Ilyas?' he whispered to himself in disbelief. The fakir had survived the massacre but had lost an arm to Nadir's men. Qaraar thought of dismounting, but just then the fakir turned and looked towards him with jaded eyes.

'That horse, I recognise it – or maybe not,' he sighed. Saying this he turned sideways and fell into a deep slumber. Qaraar swivelled Haider's reins and gently rode out of the lane not wanting to wake the sleeping fakir.

This was Catalina's first encounter with a fakir, and she wanted to know more.

'What an extraordinary man! Who was he?'

'A fakir – given to the unknown, yet leading his life in the known world.'

'Such men exist even today?'

'In Hindustan, Persia and Central Asia they do – even today.'

As the conversation progressed, something made Qaraar

think about Baba Ilyas's words. What were those words exactly? He played them out again in his mind. What did he mean? Then as if he had witnessed a flash of lightening, Qaraar yelled out, 'Is she alive? Abeerah! Are you alive?'

'What?' Catalina held him close.

'I think she is alive!'

'What do you mean?'

'His words – "the one that obeyed, but plotted, thou hast raised to be like a Queen, and the one that had Queen-like demeanour thou hast flung into the abyss of despair." Is…?'

Qaraar kicked Haider into a full gallop towards the houses that lined up next to the Red Fort. It was well past midnight but as they approached the houses there was a different vibe. Music could be heard; the tabla, the sitar and the singing of romantic Urdu and Persian ghazals was streaming out from one of the houses. There were large crowds gathered that included some drunks, some high on opium; others had knives drawn and brawled openly in the street, and yet others had flower bracelets around their wrists, kohl in their eyes and twirled their sleek moustaches. They stood outside Basalat-Gah.

'Do we have to go here?' Catalina asked in a fearful tone.

'This cannot be!' Qaraar spoke to himself as he looked at the garishly lit and decorated front of Basalat-Gah.

Catalina managed to get a few words out of her now parched throat. 'My love, why… why are we going in here – into, into this brothel?'

'Hey you!' shouted one of the men, smelling his flower braceleted wrist and giving a crooked smile. 'Are you a new pimp? And this beauty you have with you, have you come to sell her? Let me have a closer look!' The man approached the horse-mounted couple. 'Ah, she is European and in her prime! We can do with one of those specimens!' He laughed, holding onto Haider's stirrup.

'How much do you want for her?'

'Zabaan pay lagaam! Rein in your tongue!' Qaraar threatened

and kicking the man with one leg he spurred Haider on with the other, as the horse galloped into the open grounds of Basalat-Gah which was teeming with pimps, prostitutes, drug peddlers, cheap liquor sellers and awful musicians. Qaraar rode past the mound in the centre of which was the brave Shahbaz Khan's grave – the one that he had dug himself. Even here, people were lounging on it and haggling for a night's price with some desperate pimp trying to strike a deal. He dismounted, helped Catalina off and tied Haider in front of the main gate. By now Catalina had sensed this was Abeerah's house as they rushed up the stairs. They passed dimly lit rooms, and saw silhouettes of naked bodies through translucent curtains, increasing the sense of foreboding in Qaraar. Bursting onto the open terrace Qaraar finally saw a familiar face – Munna Mia, the once sidekick of Hatim Khan.

Munna Mia looked at Qaraar for a few seconds in disbelief. He blinked hard and then rushed to him. Limping in the wildest manner he flung himself at Qaraar and embraced him with an intensity that said so much.

'Qaraar sahib,' he wept. 'Qaraar sahib, it's you! I can't believe my eyes it's you.' Qaraar responded to the embrace with initial coldness, but then seeing genuine tears rolling down Munna Mia's face, relaxed a little. 'We thought you, uhh, that night... I shudder at its thought... we thought you were dead!'

'What's happened here Munna Mia?'

'Tragedy, Qaraar sahib, but we must not speak here lest we be heard – come with me.'

Munna Mia led them to a corner of the terrace under a small shamiana. There he lit a fire and sat on his haunches on the floor after he made Qaraar and Catalina sit on a charpoy. Warming his hands in front of the fire, he spoke.

'Give me time, Qaraar sahib and let me say it all.'

'You have all the time.'

'That night – that horror-filled night after the massacre, when you and Abeerah Begum were in your mango orchard,' he gasped for breath. 'On the insistence of Askari Begum and Natiya, you left to bring back your parents, who were already dead.'

'Yes, yes I know. Go on,' said an impatient Qaraar, as Catalina placed her hand on his, not understanding the conversation in Urdu but clearly sensing Qaraar's anxiety.

'When you returned to Humayun's Tomb you were told that Abeerah Begum had been burnt alive in your orchard, but...'

'But what?' Qaraar's voice got agitated.

'But she hadn't. They... those two female demons, they tied her hands and mouth and hid her behind a tree in the garden and told you she was dead. When the Uzbeks took you away, they brought her back here and nursed her back to health – only to...'

Catalina felt Qaraar's palm close into a tight fist under her hand.

'...only to tell her that you had been found up by Nadir's men and killed. Within days Abeerah Begum lost her mind. She, she became uncontrollable...' Munna Mia looked at Qaraar closely and whispered, 'She is chronically depressed and mad. We have to sedate her otherwise she will kill herself.'

Tears left Qaraar's eyes and he shut them tight while translating into Spanish.

'How do you know all this?' Qaraar asked.

'They mocked about it. First, because of her beauty they wanted to make her a prostitute in her own house and service Nadir's men, the way Natiya did ensuring her own safety. Then realizing she had lost her mind and that wouldn't be possible they forcefully made her sign away the house to them.'

'No!' Catalina gasped after Qaraar, barely able to keep his equanimity, held his head in his hands and muttered some words to her in Spanish.

'Without any income and after the utter devastation of the massacre, Askari Begum took charge of the house. But then... oh what a woman, what a woman that Natiya turned out to be.' Qaraar kept his head in his hands as all this was being said, while Catalina rubbed his back consoling him.

'She began a slow poisoning of Askari Begum and within months she was dead and flung in a drain. Now Natiya was in control of Basalat-Gah and she made it into this – this brothel!' he said, looking around.

'And how are you here?' Qaraar barely managed a few words with his head still lowered.

'What life could I have had after the massacre and the killing of my master, Hatim Khan? I had nowhere to go, so I became a pimp here for Natiya…'

'Where is Abeerah?'

'O Qaraar sahib, has time jaded your eyes?' Munna Mia turned his head left. Qaraar followed Munna Mia's eyes towards the end corner of the terrace where only an outline of a figure could be seen in the dark night. The figure sat on the floor, had its back towards them and the head was covered under a thick coarse black cloth. Qaraar rose slowly, looked at Munna Mia who nodded approvingly, and then walked up to the figure. Bending down, Qaraar looked at the face that was now partly covered with the cloth.

'Abeerah.' She didn't look at him. Qaraar sat on the cold marble floor next to her. 'Abeerah, look, it's me – Qaraar.' She slowly turned her face and looked straight at Qaraar, expressionless. For moments that seemed years they looked at each other. Her face was pale, her neck shrivelled, the strands of hair that peeped out of the cloth were dull, her eyes had no life in them, but they looked at him. Then her eyes rolled up and she began shaking her head and banging it against the wall in front of her.

'No!' Munna Mia rushed and held her back. Being in a state of shock Qaraar was unable to react. 'No, Abeerah Begum. Stop.' Munna Mia continued and made her drink water from a mud cup. Qaraar rose from the floor and took a few steps backwards. He felt deep sorrow. Catalina rushed to Qaraar and held his arm while both watched as Munna Mia nursed Abeerah with genuine care and affection.

'See how you bleed,' Munna Mia lifted her head and looked at her forehead. He dabbed a cloth that soaked the blood. 'Please don't do this,' he begged as Abeerah made a mad dash for the wall again smashing her head against it. 'No, Shhh, calm down my love,' said Munna Mia. Just then Qaraar noticed a ring on Abeerah's finger. It was a simple metal one.

Munna Mia held Abeerah's head close to his chest and she began calming down. Then he covered her head with the black cloth and walked up to Qaraar who was still looking at the metal ring on Abeerah's finger. Noticing Qaraar gazing at the ring, he said, 'I… I… had to… I had to marry her. When I started working here,' he continued, 'Natiya tried to get Abeerah Begum to lure customers, but soon realized it would only damage her business. She thought of killing her, but two things made her stop. Firstly, I married Abeerah Begum as soon as I discovered the plot to kill her,' Munna Mia paused.

After a moment of silence Qaraar asked, 'And what was the second reason that Natiya didn't kill her?'

Munna Mia took a deep breath and then looked left. Catalina and Qaraar followed his eyes to a curtained room behind which they saw a silhouette. After a few seconds the silhouette came out as a human form, walked up and stood by the fire. She was fourteen years old. She had almond-shaped eyes and naturally shaped arched eyebrows. She had a faint beauty spot right in the middle of her lower lip and her thick beautiful wavy hair hung down to her hips. In her hand were two books. The works of Bedil and Khusrau. It was evident she loved reading. Qaraar noticed that around the girl's ankle was the black thread that he had tied to Abeerah's. 'This is the second reason. Your daughter, Qaraar sahib. Yours and Abeerah Begum's daughter, Sana.'

Qaraar remained silent, trying to understand all that was being revealed on this fateful night. Then he thought to himself, 'It was the night at Husn-e-Jahaan.' After looking at the girl for a few moments he felt an explosion of love, the kind he couldn't explain, and he wept uncontrollably. Then he felt the clasping of two other arms around his waist and the resting of a face against his back. He gently turned and saw Sana holding him with an expression in her eyes that said, 'Take me away from here.'

'She knows you are her father. I told her,' Munna Mia explained. Qaraar looked closely at Sana's eyes. They were exactly like his.

'Sometimes she would say that maybe her father is alive, and I would say maybe he is – and look, you are here now Qaraar sahib.' Munna Mia wiped the tears of his face.

Qaraar held Sana, with her head tucked under his chin. 'But Qaraar sahib,' Munna Mia continued, 'you must take her away from here. Natiya has tried several times to…' Qaraar raised his hand. By now Catalina, without being explained, had understood it all intuitively.

'We must take her away,' Catalina said with a smile and caressing Sana's head.

'You won't face resistance from Natiya now. She is fed up of mother and daughter: one she knows is no use to her and recently she has written off Sana too. Your daughter has her mother's fiery nature, which has kept Natiya at bay, and she has your love for knowledge, so Natiya is just tired. Take her away soon,' he said.

'Sana, will you come with us?' Qaraar asked, looking at his daughter with tender eyes.

'Yes, Abbajaan.'

Catalina came and embraced Sana from behind.

Just then they heard a thud. 'Abeerah!' yelled Munna Mia running up to her. He shook her desperately but there was no response.

'Ammijaan!' yelled Sana. No response. Qaraar and Catalina rushed up too and tried to get Abeerah to look at them, but life had left her. Munna Mia and Sana wept unconsolably holding onto the lifeless body. Qaraar had no more tears to give, but his mind wept for the one who even in death had left him the most wonderful gift.

'Abbajaan, I want to leave right now. There's nothing for me here, please let's go.' Sana showed great resilience.

'Not before I do my duty.'

Munna Mia knew what Qaraar meant. He looked out of the terrace. The grounds of Basalat-Gah were empty.

'We can ride out easily.'

'Good, let's leave now.'

Munna Mia rode out with Abeerah's body and Qaraar led Haider out carrying Catalina and Sana. After an hour they reached the graveyard for nobility known as Mughalia Kabrastan. Stumbling over graves, Qaraar and Munna Mia finally found what they believed was a peaceful spot under a large neem tree. Picking up shovels they dug hard and eventually lowered Abeerah's body. Munna Mia as Abeerah's husband stood in front of the grave and raised his hands for the fatiha, while Qaraar took a few steps back honouring both man and departed wife. It was Munna Mia's moment with Abeerah.

The wind picked up and dust particles from Abeerah's grave flew in the air. Qaraar whispered verses into the silent night. Words of Hafez.

Wither fled, wild deer?
I knew thee well in days gone by,
When we were fast friends, thou and I;
Two solitary travellers now,
Bewildered, I and thou
We go our separate ways, where fear
Lurks ambushed, front and rear…

Give never the wine-bowl from thy hand,
Nor loose thy grasp on the rose's stem;
Tis a mad world that the fates have planned…

Then come, I bid thee; let this fragrant scent
Of fairest hope, and soft content,
Bear to thy soul delight eternal…[126]

By the time they got back to Basalat-Gah it was five in the morning. On the terrace they saw the sight of a patrolling Natiya. She looked closely at Qaraar. 'That's you? Ha ha!' Her crackling laughter echoed. '...and that daughter of yours is with you too I see. Take her and get lost.' Munna Mia dismounted the horse that he had shared with Sana and took it into the stable. Sana now mounted Haider and sat in front of Catalina and both defiantly looked up at Natiya as Qaraar turned the reins and walked Haider towards the main gate.

'Ha ha, there they go!' yelled out Natiya. 'Your ancestral house is mine, Sana, it's mine, and it is something you will never have.'

A fiery answer came from Sana just as Haider stepped out of the gates. Turning around she shot back, 'I have lost an ancestral house but have gained a father, and that is something you will never have, Natiya.'

'Dafa ho! Get lost!' came the frustrated reply. Just then Natiya saw Munna Mia limping out of the grounds too.

'And where do you think you are going, pimp?'

'Pimp indeed I was, but not anymore.'

'And what will you do you, cripple?'

'Anything but this.'

'Uh, you make me sick Munna Mia. Dafa ho! Get lost!'

As they made their way to the guest house, dawn was about to break. Pigeons fluttered around the minarets and the three marble domes of the Jama Masjid. The deep, masculine yet soothing voice of the muezzin reverberated with the Azaan call for Fajr prayers.

'Abbajaan, you know its basant – spring,' said Sana looking below at her father leading the horse.

'I know my Noor-e-Chashm.'

'A new beginning, my darling,' Catalina said in Spanish, almost intuitively knowing what to say and caressing Sana's dark brown hair. Sana didn't understand the language but understood the feeling of genuine love coming from Catalina and she leaned her head back against Catalina's chest. 'Think of me as your mother now,' she said. When they reached the guest house Munna Mia kissed Sana's forehead.

'I have brought you up as my daughter and protected you as best I could. Now you have a new life to look forward to.'

Sana embraced him.

'Where will you go Munna Mia?' Qaraar asked, with one arm around Sana and the other around Catalina.

Looking at the minarets of the Jama Masjid he said, 'I too will begin a new life. Delhi bears heavy on my heart,' he sighed. 'I will head to Lucknow where people don't know me as a pimp. Khuda Hafiz.' He placed his right palm on his chest and limped off, disappearing down a lane.

For the next fortnight Qaraar, Catalina and Sana did not leave the Musafir Khana. The impact of that one night was such that the three needed days to understand it all, make peace with life's ways and destiny, and also enjoy each other. For the first few days, Sana wept for her mother at nights, and Catalina would creep into her bed and hold her tight. But as days passed, Sana's deep nature inherited from her father made her search for serenity and calm in knowledge. She read books that she had brought with her, particularly Khusrau's *Diwan*. She was also drawn to understand her father's eclectic mix of friends and their varied cultures. Sana's charm was such that all of Qaraar's friends soon came to develop a fondness for her.

She spoke with an etiquette that reflected her parent's refined backgrounds, although she had been brought up by Munna Mia. It was Munna Mia who had told her about her paternal and maternal lineages, brought her a regular supply of books and got her educated at Basalat-Gah by bringing in local teachers and ustads, some of whom he paid, and some, who on realising who Sana was out of respect for the martyred brave Shahbaz Khan, the murdered master artisan Faiz Ali, and Qaraar himself, all having reputations that still lingered in Delhi's air, taught her for free.

Meanwhile the friends enjoyed Delhi's landmarks. Aalf particularly loved the cockfights that took place every morning near the Jama Masjid. They visited the Red Fort, the shrine of the Armenian mystic poet Sarmad, which Hova had insisted on seeing, the shrine of Hazrat Nizamuddin Auliya and Humayun's Tomb. They told Qaraar that everywhere they went people still spoke of him as the great hero – the Qaatil-e-Salaar. Qaraar listened to them but didn't feel the need to go out and declare who he was, instead preferring to be confined to his room.

One night, Qaraar woke in the middle of the night shivering, having broken into a cold sweat. He got out of bed, wrapped himself in a shawl and rushed down the stone stairs of the guest house. Flinging the door open, he sat on the steps that opened onto the street, breathing heavily. An ominous feeling of being sinful descended on him. He thought of his relationship with Catalina, which in reality wasn't formally within the confines of a marriage and about Sana, his love child with Abeerah. He felt an acute sense of conflict within. His love for both Catalina and Sana was deep and sparkled with truth, but yet the voice of sin gnawed at his conscience. He whispered questions to the Divine; at times begging forgiveness and yet also thanking the Divine for making him the benefactor of true love. His face was buried in his shawl, his lips murmuring those questions when he heard the approach of soft footsteps and a voice.

'What sin are you talking about? Look at me.'

'Hova?'

'Yes Hova, who was once a prostitute. Do you want to talk to me about sin?' Hova also hadn't been able to sleep and when she heard Qaraar rushing down the steps, she had followed him.

Then she continued. 'Fate has its ways – you and I are only its slaves. I didn't choose to be sold as a prostitute.'

Qaraar nodded, as he felt a lightness listening to Hova.

'We sit not far from Sarmad's shrine.' Hova pointed in its direction.

'Yes, I know.' A slight smile broke on Qaraar's lips.

'Think of his verses – and hold them close to your heart when you feel burdened by the thought of sin.'

She recited some, sitting next to him.

No doubt that greater than my sins is… Your mercy:
Always everywhere, I've all of my sins added up, totally,
Though from head to foot I am filled with sins,
Inspite of this … they do not exceed your mercy, obviously….[127]

Hova's recital of Sarmad's verses calmed Qaraar's restless state, and after watching the sunrise the two went back to their rooms.

Izzet had looked frantically for his father Holar Pasha but with no success. Speaking to shopkeepers in broken Urdu he got vague answers. Some said he had left for another land, others said they hadn't seen him, a few thought hard and told him that he had been killed in the massacre, yet others just shrugged their shoulders and nonchalantly walked away. It was apparent Holar Pasha wasn't important enough to be remembered. Exhausted, Izzet returned one evening confused with all that he had heard but having convinced himself that his father still lived in another land. Qaraar heard Izzet's confusion and thought it best to leave him with his belief. After two weeks in Delhi Qaraar expressed a desire to leave; he had even packed his belongings.

'I'd like to leave tonight.'

'Tonight?' said a surprised Aalf.

'I came for the one I love,' he said looking at Catalina, and then looking at Sana, '…and I return with more love. I have nothing more to give or take from this city.'

'Uh okay. I'll tell Hova to pack.'

By sunset they had loaded up the horses and made their way out. But Gul and Izzet were missing. Aalf told Qaraar that they were at the steps of the Jama Masjid, and had asked to be met there. As they rode up to the Jama Masjid steps, the scene became familiar to Qaraar – the sunset poetry session was about to begin. Qaraar covered his head with his black shawl not wanting to be recognised. Straight ahead down the Ballimaran lane was Hunar-

Abaad, and he looked down the lane nostalgically, but something within him held back Haider, turning him away and entering a tiny passageway instead. From there he watched the poets approach. Dard was there and so was Sauda and even Mir. But Qaraar didn't want to draw attention to himself and so he stayed back. As Sauda went up to recite he paused and looked towards Haider. A slight smile and nod came Sauda's way from the mounted rider who then slipped away followed by Aalf and Hova. Sauda didn't follow. Just then Gul ran up behind them and finally caught up.

Panting and looking up at Qaraar, Gul spoke. 'We got married just now, and – we will stay.'

Qaraar had an expression of disbelief.

'Izzet and I have found jobs at the most prestigious school here. They've even given us a part of a haveli to stay in.'

'Go on,' Qaraar had a smile. 'You never fail to surprise me, Gul!'

'I will be teaching everything,' she laughed. 'From Persian, Turkish, Spanish, Geography, History...'

'Mashallah.'

'...and Izzet will teach physical education.'

Qaraar dismounted and so did the others. Gul embraced each one holding back her tears, then she looked at Qaraar and hugged him tight and smiled.

'What a life I have, thanks to you – such an adventure.'

Just then Izzet came running holding the reins of a horse. Gul took the reins from his hands.

'Here, this horse is for you Sana – ride away to your new life,' she said with excitement. Gul had bought the horse from her advanced salary that she had insisted on.

Sana kissed Gul's hand, placed it on her eyes and then mounted the robust steed. 'Khuda Hafiz.' As Qaraar passed Gul, he placed his palm gently on her head.

'Look after those hens, Aalf! Maybe the butcher's taken them all while you've been away!' Gul laughed, and waved along with Izzet as they watched their friends make their way out of Shahjahanabad.

'Abbajaan, see how fast Omar is!' shouted Sana in Spanish as she stormed past the orange orchard, the earth shuddering under galloping hooves. Sana had named her horse after Omar Khayyam.

'Steady now, Jaan.'

'Come on, Abbajaan!' She turned and looked at her father, her hair flying everywhere.

'We'll see you there,' responded her father, raising his hand.

Within minutes Qaraar saw a dust cloud climbing at meteoric speed up the Andalusian mountain. Qaraar and Catalina mounted Haider and made their way up at a gentler pace that suited their horse's age. Under the gazebo's magnificent geometric-patterned roof, most of the villagers of Zahara de la Sierra had gathered to celebrate Sana's eighteenth birthday. It had been four years since Sana had arrived in Spain. Since dawn Catalina and Hova had been busy in their kitchens cooking up dinner. Under the carved roof, candle flames seemed to dance in joy as a beaming Sana, who was by now fluent in Spanish, talked with everyone.

'Sana, my daughter has a question for you,' said the butcher, leading in Maria. 'Go on,' he nudged her.

'Will you teach me your language?' Maria asked shyly.

'Of course, my dear.... Come to the barn after school and we'll get started.' They walked to a corner of the gazebo and sat under one of the pillars looking at the party in full flow swaying to Rodrigo's guitar tunes. Maria sat on a small stool with her back against Sana, who held her in an embrace from behind.

'What's your language called?' Maria asked.

'It's called Urdu and it's a beautiful and special language,' Sana said stroking Maria's hair.

'Why is it special?'

'Urdu is like a rainbow.'

'Rainbow!' Maria turned and looked at Sana with eyes sparkling in amazement.

'Yes. A rainbow has many vibrant colours, but when you see it as one, its beauty is striking – and so is Urdu. It has Persian, Arabic and Hindi words woven into it, and when they all come together, spoken as one language it sparkles. It's the language of Sufis and poets.'

Maria had a look of wonder in her eyes.

Then looking at the roof Sana said, 'Look up – what do you see?'

This was the first time Maria had visited the gazebo. Her eyes widened in astonishment.

'Stars, triangles, hexagons, pentagons – and stars again,' she pointed.

'Exactly. Urdu is like the roof pattern – different words coming together, merging into one another, its beauty infinite and never-ending.'

Maria strained her neck back further, struck by the fantastic roof pattern. Just then Sana saw Qaraar approaching.

'Come now Maria, we start Urdu tomorrow, but now I must go.'

'Why? Where are you going?'

'My university walks towards me – and for him I must stand and go to him.'

Maria watched as Sana rose and walked towards her father. She bowed slightly, lifted her right palm that curved like a crescent and brought it up to her forehead without touching it. 'Aadaab Abbajaan,' she said with her eyes lowered.

'Jeetay Raho.'

Maria closely watched this exotic custom playing out.

'Here my Jaanam, I have your birthday gift.' Qaraar held out a heap of books in both hands.

Sana excitedly took them, placed them on the ground and went through them. They were the works of Ibn Rushd, including his commentaries on Aristotle and Plato, and also Ibn Rushd's stand-alone philosophical writings titled *On the Intellect, On Conjunction with the Active Intellect* and *On Time*. Sana leapt to her feet and wrapped her arms around her father. 'Thank you, Abbajaan!'

As the night progressed people finally made their way back down the mountain and towards Zahara de la Sierra. Sana stayed back until the last guest was seen off. Then she kissed her father and Catalina and rode back to the barn behind Aalf and Hova. Both Qaraar and Catalina prepared for the night, sweeping the gazebo floor, laying out their bedding and lighting two candles one on each side. Then both lay under the roof looking at the pattern above them and listening to the night's silence. Placing her head on his shoulder, Catalina played with his muslin tunic. Qaraar kissed her gently, blew out the candle on his side and shut his eyes. For a few moments Catalina continued to feel the muslin, then just as she was about to blow out the flame on her side, she noticed the tiniest and most delicate shape right next to the central star in the roof. It was a sunflower.

5 March 1788
Zahara de la Sierra
Andalusia
Spain

I am Qaraar Ali. The craftsman of Delhi, the slave of Samarkand, the tile-restorer of Bursa and the geometry teacher of Zahara de la Sierra. I write in my diary from my orange orchard, sitting next to a mound that is the tomb of the fastest and most faithful horse I rode – Haider. Now in my 72nd year, my hair, my students tell me, resembles the silvery leaves of the olive tree in summer when they catch the rays of the Spanish sun. It has been several years since I have heard from Gul and Izzet. From Hikmet and Saad too there has been nothing but silence. A few years ago, we, the humble people of Zahara de la Sierra, learnt of a successful voyage undertaken by one Captain Cook of England. His expedition found an enormous landmass beyond Indonesia as an easterner would see it, although they say he took a different route. With new exploration, though, comes great responsibility. Indigenous cultures must not be destroyed. If the West is able to blend and merge with the local culture of that land, then what a wonderful mosaic it would be. After all, that is what the Sufis did. They blended in with the existing societal tapestry and added new dimensions to it.

My daughter Sana teaches philosophy at the University of Paris, specialising in the commentaries on Aristotle by Ibn Rushd. Like the father of Hamda bint Ziyad, who too was a teacher and had just one child, a daughter, I too – like that father – gave Sana the best possible education I could. Recently, Sana visited us with a writing of Leonardo da Vinci. This genius – who was an illegitimate child and had married science and art in the West, had written: "The infinite works of nature are woven together in a unity filled with marvellous patterns" – Sounds familiar? From

Istanbul to Delhi nothing new, philosophically or scientifically has emerged.

I must leave you now as I see Catalina, Aalf and Hova gesturing to me out of the corner of my eye; it is Abeerah's death anniversary today and we mark it with a little prayer under an orange tree and an old Spanish love ballad that Rodrigo will string on his guitar. But I will leave you with a question – Will mankind follow the Sufi way?

Time will tell.

NOTES

1. Saiyid Athar Abbas Rizvi, *A History of Sufism in India*, Vol.1, (Munshiram Manoharlal Publishers Pvt Ltd, New Delhi, 1978), p. 18.
2. Andrew Wheatcroft, *The Enemy at the Gate: Habsburgs, Ottomans and the Battle for Europe* (Pimlico, London, 2009), pp. 182–7.
3. Evliya Chelebi, *The Ottoman Traveller*, translations and commentary by Robert Dankoff and Soo Yong Kim (Eland, London, 2010), p. 18; Chelebi who was a contemporary of Sultan Mehmed IV mentions that with a spyglass Bursa could be seen from Istanbul.
4. Brad Gooch, *Rumi's Secret: The Life of the Sufi Poet of Love* (Harper Collins, New York, 2017). Rumi's verse translated by R.A. Nicholson, p. 2.
5. Halil Inalcik, *The Ottoman Empire: The Classic Age 1300–1600* (Phoenix Press, London, 2003), p. 197.
6. Ibid., p. 190.
7. Frederick Starr, *Lost Enlightenment* (Harper Collins, Noida, Uttar Pradesh, 2014), p. 170.
8. Ibid., pp. xxv, 170, 399, 400, 408, 409, 427, 431, 434.
9. Ibid., pp. 408, 409.
10. Ibid., p. 427.
11. Peter Washington (ed.), *Persian Poems*, translated by R.A. Nicholson (Alfred A. Knopf, New York, 2006), p. 177.
12. Starr 2013 and 2014, pp. 172, 173, 399.
13. Washington 2006, pp. 41, 42.

14. Ernest Bloch 2019, *Avicenna and the Aristotelian Left* (Columbia University Press, New York, 2019), p. 1.
15. Peter Adamson, *Philosophy in the Islamic World* (Oxford University Press, Oxford, 2016), p. 122; A.M. Goichon, *La Distinction de l'essence d'aprés Ibn Sina pais 1937* (Desclée de Brouwer, Paris, 1937); F. Rahman, 'Essence and Existence', in Avicenna, *Medieval and Renaissance Studies*, 4 , 1958, pp. 127, 128
16. Adamson 2016, p. 127, 128.
17. Bloch 2019, pp. 16, 17.
18. Ibid. pp, 16, 17.
19. Ibid., p. 2.
20. Ibid., pp. 10, 11, 12.
21. Ibid., pp. 10, 11, 12.
22. Ibid., pp. 10, 11, 12.
23. Ibid., pp. 10, 11,12.
24. Ibid., pp. 10, 11, 12.
25. Ibid, p. 2.
26. Michael Axworthy, *The Sword of Persia: Nader Shah, from Tribal Warrior to Conquering Tyrant* (I.B. Taurus, London, 2009), pp. 161–64.
27. Paul Smith, *The Book of Dara Shikoh, Life, Poems & Prose* (New Humanity Books, Victoria, Australia, 2015), pp. 155, 156, 162.
28. Ibid., pp. 155, 156, 162.
29. Ibid., pp. 10, 162.
30. Ibid., p. 165.
31. Saiyid Athar Abbas Rizvi, *A History of Sufism in India*, Vol. 2, (Munshiram Manoharlal Publishers Pvt. Ltd, New Delhi, 1978), p. 366.
32. Smith 2015, pp. 212, 213.
33. Ibid., p. 98.
34. Ibid., p. 156.
35. Katherine Butler Brown, *Hindustani Music Thirteenth to Twentieth Centuries*, eds. Joep Bor, Francoise Nalini Delvoye, Emmie Tenijenhuis (Manohar, New Delhi, 2010), pp. 160, 161.

36. William Dalrymple and Anita Anand, *Kohinoor* (Juggernaut, New Delhi, 2016), p. 43.
37. A.J. Arberry, *Fifty Poems of Hafiz,* particular verse translated by J. Richardson (Cambridge University Press, digital version, 2008), p. 88.
38. Ibn Arabi, *Bewildered: Love Poems from Translation of Desires,* translated by Michael A. Sells, (The Post Apollo Press, 2018), pp. 11, 19, 20.
39. Mir K. Kutbuddin *The Path of Peace,* p. 8.
40. Rizvi 1978, p. 109.
41. Translation by S.A.H. Abidi.
42. K.C. Kanda, *Master couplets of Urdu Poetry* (Sterling Publishers Pvt Ltd, Delhi, 2001), p. 121.
43. Ibid., p. 121.
44. Saif Mahmood, *Beloved Delhi* (Speaking Tiger, Delhi, 2018), p. 75.
45. Kanda 2001, pp. 231, 239.
46. Ibid., p. 127
47. A. Mayar, *Transliteration from Bedil's book of Hemistiches,* pp. 18, 19.
48. Starr 2014, pp. 10, 398, 400.
49. Ibid., p. 272.
50. Rizvi 1978, p. 342.
51. Paul Smith, *Bedil* (New Humanity Books, Victoria, Australia, 2012), p. 10.
52. Arberry 2008, p. 124.
53. William Dalrymple and Anita Anand, *Kohinoor,* p. 51.
54. Michael Axworthy, *The Sword of Persia: Nader Shah, from Tribal Warrior to Conquering Tyrant* (I.B. Taurus, London, 2009), p. 6.
55. Ibid., p. 6.
56. Ibid., p. 7.
57. Ibid., p. 7.
58. Ibid., p. 8.
59. Rizvi 1978, pp. 34, 35, 36.
60. Ibid., pp. 38, 39.
61. Peter Washington (ed.), *Persian Poems,* translated by A.J. Arberry, (Alfred A. Knopf, New York, NY, 2000), pp. 144, 146.

62. Peter Frankopan, *The Silk Roads* (Bloomsbury, London, 2015), pp. 114-17).
63. Starr 2014, p. 430.
64. Edward Fitzgerald, *Rubaiyat of Omar Khayyam,* ed. Y. Jamshidipur, (Tehran, 1963), p. 37.
65. Rizvi 1978, p. 375.
66. Ibid., p. 170.
67. Arberry 2008, p. 103.
68. Smith 2015, p. 22.
69. Kanda 2001, p. 349.
70. Brad Gooch, *Rumi's Secret: The Life of the Sufi Poet of Love* (Harper Collins, New York, 2017), pp. 277, 278.
71. Idries Shah, *The Sufis* (Anchor Books, New York, 1971), p. 70.
72. Ibid., p. 66.
73. Rizvi 1978, p. 60.
74. Ibid., p. 60.
75. Ibid., p. 60.
76. John Freely, *Storm on Horseback* (I.B. Taurus, London, 2008), p. 60.
77. Gooch 2017, p. 300.
78. Freely 2008, p. 96.
79. Ibid., p. 49.
80. Evilya Chelebi, *The Ottoman Traveller*, translations and commentary by Robert Dankoff and Soo Yong Kim (Eland, London, 2010), p. 20.
81. A.J Arberry, *Fifty Poems of Hafiz*, verses translated by A.J. Arberry and J.H. Hindley (Cambridge University Press, digital version, 2008), pp. 89, 93.
82. Richard Fletcher, *Moorish Spain* (Phoenix, London, 1994), p. 169.
83. Edward Fitzgerald, *Rubaiyat of Omar Khayyam*, ed. Y. Jamshidipur, (Tehran 1963), p. 102.
84. Ibn Arabi, *Bewildered: Love Poems from Translation of Desires*, translated by Michael A. Sells, (The Post Apollo Press, 2018), p. 34.
85. A.J Arberry, *Fifty Poems of Hafiz*, verses translated by Elizabeth Daryush (Cambridge University Press, digital version, 2008), p. 84.

86. Peter Washington (ed.), *Persian Poems,* verse translated by Coleman Barks, (Alfred A. Knopf, New York, NY, 2000), p. 91.
87. Frankopan 2015, pp. 140, 141.
88. Stanley Lane-Poole, *Muslims in Spain* (Goodword Books, New Delhi, 2008), p. 37.
89. Ibid., p. vii.
90. Ibid., p. vii.
91. Ibid., p. v.
92. Ibid., p. v.
93. Ibid., p. vi.
94. Ibid., p. 38.
95. Ibid., p. 40.
96. Ibid., p. 40.
97. Ibid., p. v.
98. Richard Fletcher, *Moorish Spain* (Phoenix, London, 2001), p. 89.
99. Ibid., p. 90.
100. Ibid., p. 90.
101. Peter Adamson, *Philosophy in the Islamic World* (Oxford University Press, Oxford, 2016), p. 181.
102. Ibid., p. 184.
103. Arberry 2008, p. 83.
104. Ibid., p. 84.
105. Washington 2000, pp. 142-144.
106. Peter Washington (ed.), *Persian Poems,* verse translated by R.A. Nicholson (Alfred A. Knopf, New York, NY, 2000), p. 139.
107. Adamson 2016, p. 205.
108. Ibid., p. 206.
109. Washington 2000, p. 102.
110. Arberry 2008, p. 119.
111. Hugh Thomas, *Rivers of Gold: The Rise of the Spanish Empire* (Penguin, London, 2010), p. 8.
112. Matthew Carr, *Blood and Faith* (Hurst, London, 2017), p. 13.
113. Carr 2017, p. 67, and cited in L.P. Harvey, *Islamic Spain* (University of Chicago Press, Chicago, 1992), p. 316.

114. Ibid., p. 16.
115. Elizabeth Drayson, *The Moors Last Stand* (Profile Books Ltd, London, 2018), p. 117.
116. Thomas 2010, p. 85.
117. Ibid., p. 85.
118. Ibid., pp. 125, 126.
119. Ibid., p. 337 and Vicente Cadenas, *Carlos I de Castilla, Senor de las Indias* (Madrid 1988), p. 123.
120. Carr 2017, pp. 74, 75, 106, 107.
121. Ibid., p. 125 and cited in Henry Kamen, *Spanish Inquisition* (Yale University Press, 2014), p. 223.
122. Carr 2017, p. 285.
123. Ibid., p. 1.
124. Ibid., p. 342.
125. Brad Gooch, *Rumi's Secret: The Life of the Sufi Poet of Love* (Harper Collins, New York, 2017), pp. 169, 183.
126. Arberry 2008, pp. 131-134.
127. Smith 2015, p. 20.

GLOSSARY

Aadaab: A hand gesture used in the Indian subcontinent for greeting
Adaa: Style and grace of a woman
Agha: A term of respect used when addressing someone older in Mughal India, Persia, Afghanistan and Turkey
Angarkha: A garment that is tied to the right or left shoulder. The term angarkha is derived from Sanskrit, which means protection of the body. The angarkha was worn in various parts of the Indian subcontinent, but while the basic cut remained the same, the style and length varied from region to region
Ashrafees: Any of various gold coins formerly used in Persia (now Iran) and India, specifically one originally equivalent to the mohur
Azaan: The call to ritual prayer made by a muezzin from the minaret of a mosque
Baingan: Aubergine
Basant: Spring (season)
Begum Sahib: Respected term for a lady from a noble family
Bhishti: These were poor men who were hired to water stone floors and roads that got very hot during the summer months in Delhi and northern India. They carried leather bags filled with water and sprinkled them as and when requested. Bhishti is derived from the Persian word Behisht which means paradise
Chapatti: A thin pancake of unleavened wholemeal bread cooked on a griddle
Chapka: Jewellery for hair

Charpoy: A bedstead of woven webbing or hemp stretched on a wooden frame on four legs

Chugirmas: Traditional Uzbek fur hat

Chula: A small earthen or brick stove

Dastar-khwan: A big, ceremonial dining spread which is laid out on the floor

Degh: A large outdoor cooking pot

Dupatta: A long scarf worn around the neck or over the head and across the shoulders, chiefly by women in South Asia. An essential part of salwar-kameez

Fakir: A Muslim (or, loosely, a Hindu) religious ascetic who lives solely on alms

Fatiha: The short first sura of the *Quran*, used by Muslims as an essential element of ritual prayer

Fez cap: A felt headdress in the shape of a short cylindrical peakless hat, usually red, and sometimes with a tassel attached to the top

Gajar: Carrot

Gardan surahi: Slender, curving wine flask

Gharara: A pair of loose trousers with pleats below the knee, worn by women from South Asia, typically with a kameez

Girih: In Persian it means knot. The interlocking geometric tile designs also carried this name

Halwa: A sweet dish/dessert consisting of carrots or semolina boiled with milk, almonds, sugar, butter and cardamom

Howdah: A seat for riding on the back of an elephant or camel, typically with a canopy and accommodating two or more people

Huzoor: A term of respect used in Mughal India, Persia, Afghanistan, Central Asia and Turkey

Jashn: Celebration

Kabrastan: Graveyard

Khadims: The men who are caretakers of Sufi shrines

Khanqaahs: Sufi retreats where study, meditation and devotion to God was practised

Khyal: Imagination
Korma: A mildly spiced Indian curry dish of meat or fish marinated in yogurt or curds
Kotwal: A police officer
Mahout: A person who works with rides, and tends an elephant
Meher: Settlement money that a Muslim husband gives his wife if they were to separate
Mohalla: An area of a town or village; a community
Murgh Mussallam: A rich chicken curry
Murshid: A Sufi guide or master
Mutteqa: The staff Sufis carried with them
Naan: A type of leavened bread, traditionally cooked in a clay oven
Naqqara: A drum that is beaten either to announce the arrival of a King or the arrival or departure of the army
Nikaah: Muslim wedding ceremony
Paan: Betel leaves prepared and used as a stimulant
Paandan: A small box, usually of decorated metal/wood, used to hold paan or the ingredients for making paan
Pasanda: A rich Mughal meat dish made with lamb, gentle spices and yoghurt
Pasha: Noblemen in the Ottoman court
Pukhraj: Yellow sapphire
Qahwah: An exotic mix of Kashmiri green tea leaves, whole spices, nuts and saffron, traditionally prepared in a brass kettle known as samovar
Qalamdan: A safe box
Qawwali: A style of Muslim devotional music now associated particularly with Sufis
Qawwals: Qawwali singers
Qazi/Qadi: Religious Judge who also had powers to legitimize marriages
Rukhsati: Ceremony when the bride leaves her home for her husband's
Sama khana: Music rooms in Sufi Khanqaahs
Sehri: The morning or pre-dawn meal eaten by Muslims during Ramadan
Shamiana: A ceremonial tent, shelter or awning, commonly used for outdoor parties, weddings, feasts etc. Its side walls are removable

Sherbet: A drink made of sweetened fruit juices diluted in water and served cold. Could also be made from milk

Shervani: A knee-length coat buttoning to the neck, worn by men from South Asia

Suji: Semolina

Supari: A betel nut

Tassawuf: Deep contemplation through which Sufis reach spiritual ideals and closeness to the Divine

Teeka: A piece of jewellery that rests on the forehead and is worn by women in the centre parting of hair

Zamburak: A mounted swivel gun

Zenana: Women's quarters in forts/palaces